MRS. PLANSKY'S REVENGE

SPENCER QUINN

TOR PUBLISHING GROUP
New York

This is a work of fiction. All of the characters, organizations,
and events portrayed in this novel are either products of the author's imagination
or are used fictitiously.

MRS. PLANSKY'S REVENGE

Copyright © 2023 by Pas de Deux

A Forge Book
Published by Tom Doherty Associates / Tor Publishing Group
120 Broadway
New York, NY 10271

www.tor-forge.com

Forge® is a registered trademark of Macmillan Publishing Group, LLC.

Library of Congress Cataloging-in-Publication Data

Names: Quinn, Spencer, author.
Title: Mrs. Plansky's revenge / Spencer Quinn.
Description: First edition. | New York : Forge, Tor Publishing Group, 2023.
Identifiers: LCCN 2023007718 (print) | LCCN 2023007719 (ebook) |
ISBN 9781250843333 (hardcover) | ISBN 9781250843340 (ebook)
Subjects: LCSH: Swindlers and swindling—Fiction. | LCGFT: Novels.
Classification: LCC PS3617.U584 M77 2023 (print) |
LCC PS3617.U584 (ebook) | DDC 813'.6—dc23/eng/20230228
LC record available at https://lccn.loc.gov/2023007718
LC ebook record available at https://lccn.loc.gov/2023007719

Our books may be purchased in bulk for promotional, educational, or
business use. Please contact your local bookseller or the Macmillan Corporate and
Premium Sales Department at 1-800-221-7945, extension 5442, or by email at
MacmillanSpecialMarkets@macmillan.com.

First Edition: 2023

Printed in the United States of America

0 9 8 7 6 5 4 3 2 1

MRS.
PLANSKY'S
REVENGE

OTHER BOOKS BY PETER ABRAHAMS
WRITING AS SPENCER QUINN

The Chet and Bernie Series

Dog on It

Thereby Hangs a Tail

To Fetch a Thief

The Dog Who Knew Too Much

A Fistful of Collars

The Sound and the Furry

Paw and Order

Scents and Sensibility

Heart of Barkness

Of Mutts and Men

Tender Is the Bite

It's a Wonderful Woof

Bark to the Future

The Bowser and Birdie series
(for younger readers)

The Queenie and Arthur series
(for younger readers)

The Right Side

OTHER PETER ABRAHAMS NOVELS

The Fury of Rachel Monette

Tongues of Fire

Red Message

Hard Rain

Pressure Drop

Revolution #9

Lights Out

The Fan

A Perfect Crime

Crying Wolf

Last of the Dixie Heroes

The Tutor

Their Wildest Dreams

Oblivion

End of Story

Nerve Damage

Delusion

Reality Check (young adult)

Bullet Point (young adult)

The Echo Falls trilogy
(for younger readers)

Down the Rabbit Hole

Behind the Curtain

Into the Dark

For Ben, Cassie, George, and Owen

MRS. PLANSKY'S REVENGE

ONE

"Hello, it is I, your grandson, insert name here," said Dinu.

"Correct," said Professor Bogdan, language teacher at Liceu Teoretic. He leaned back in his chair and lit up a Chesterfield. "But too correct, you know?"

Too correct? Dinu did not know. In addition, he was asthmatic and the mere presence of a cigarette aroused a twitchy feeling in his lungs. No smoking in school, of course, but these private lessons, paid for by Uncle Dragomir, weren't about school.

Professor Bogdan blew out a thin, dense stream of smoke, one little streamlet branching off and heading in Dinu's direction. "There is English, Dinu, and then there is English as she is spoken." He smiled an encouraging smile. His teeth were yellow, shading into brown at the gumline.

"English is she?" Dinu said.

"For God's sake, it's a joke," said Professor Bogdan. "Is there gender in English?"

"I don't think such."

"So. You don't think so. Come, Dinu. You've studied three years of English. Loosen up."

"Loosen up?"

"That's how the young in America talk. Loosen up, chill out, later." He tapped a cylinder of ash into a paper cup on his desk. "Which is in fact what you need to know if I'm not mistaken, the argot of youth." He glanced at Dinu. Their eyes met. Professor

Bogdan looked away. "My point," he went on, "is that no American says 'it is I.' They say 'it's me.' The grammar is wrong but that's how they say it. You must learn the right wrong grammar. That's the secret of sounding American."

"How will I learn?"

"There are ways. For one you could go to YouTube and type in 'Country Music.' Now begin again."

"Hello, it's me, your grandson, insert name here," Dinu said.

"Much better," said Professor Bogdan. "You might even say, 'Yo, it's me.'"

"Yo?"

"On my last trip I heard a lot of yo. Even my brother says it."

"Your brother in New Hampshire?"

"No *P* sound. And 'sher,' not 'shire.' But yes, my brother."

"The brother who is owning a business?"

"Who owns a business. Bogdan Plumbing and Heating." Professor Bogdan opened a drawer, took out a T-shirt, and tossed it to Dinu.

Dinu shook it out, held it up, took a look. On the front was a cartoon-type picture of a skier with tiny icicles in his bushy black mustache, brandishing a toilet plunger over his head. On the back it said: Bogdan Plumbing and Heating, Number 1 in the Granite State.

Dinu made a motion to hand it back.

"Keep it," said Professor Bogdan.

"Thank you."

"You're welcome. New Hampshire is the Granite State. All the states have nicknames."

"What is nicknames?"

"Like pet names. For example, what does your mother call you?"

"Dinu."

Professor Bogdan blinked a couple of times. Like the skier, he had a bushy mustache, except his was mostly white. "Texas is the

Lone Star State, Florida is the Sunshine State, Georgia is the Peach State."

"Georgia?"

"They have a Georgia of their own. They have everything, Dinu, although . . ." He leaned across the desk and pointed at Dinu with his nicotine-stained finger. "Although most of them don't realize it and complain all the time just like us."

"Does your brother complain?" Dinu said.

Professor Bogdan's eyebrows, not quite as bushy as his mustache, rose in surprise. "No, Dinu. He does not complain. My brother grew up here. But his children—do you know what they drive? Teslas! Teslas almost fully paid off! But they complain."

Those state nicknames sounded great to Dinu, even magical in the case of the lone star. He knew one thing for sure: if he ever got to America, Tesla or no Tesla, he would never complain. Just to get out of the flat where he lived with his mother, much better than the one-room walk-up they'd occupied before Uncle Dragomir started helping out, but still a flat too cold in winter, too hot in summer, with strange smells coming up from the sink drain and—

The door opened and Uncle Dragomir, not the knocking type, walked in. Professor Bogdan's office got smaller right away. Bogdan half rose from his chair.

"How's he doing?" Uncle Dragomir said in their native tongue, indicating Dinu with a little chin motion. He had a large, square chin, a nose that matched, large square hands, and a large square body, everything about him large and square, other than his eyes. His eyes were small, round, glinting.

"Oh, fine," said Professor Bogdan. "Coming along nicely. Good. Very well."

"In time," said Uncle Dragomir.

"In time?"

"How much longer. Days? Weeks? Months?"

Professor Bogdan turned to Dinu and switched to English. "Weeks we can do, don't you think?"

"I don't know," Dinu said.

Professor Bogdan turned to Uncle Dragomir, switched back to their language, and smiling as brightly as he could with teeth like his, said, "Weeks, Dragomir."

Uncle Dragomir fastened his glinting gaze on Professor Bogdan. "In my career I've dealt with types who like to stretch out the job. I know you're not like them."

Professor Bogdan put his hand to his chest. "The furthest thing from it. Not many weeks, Dragomir, not many at all."

"*Hmmf,*" said Uncle Dragomir. He took out his money roll, separated some bills without counting, leaned across the desk, and stuffed them in the chest pocket of Professor Bogdan's shirt. Then he turned, possibly on his way out, but that was when he noticed the T-shirt, lying in Dinu's lap. "What's that?"

Professor Bogdan explained—his brother, the Granite State, plumbing and heating.

"Let's see it on," said Uncle Dragomir.

"It's my size," Dinu said.

"Let's see."

Dinu considered putting on the T-shirt over his satin-lined leather jacket. Not real satin or leather although very close. But the T-shirt would probably not fit over the jacket. It was a stupid idea. The problem was that he wore nothing under the jacket, all his shirts dirty, the washer broken and his mother once again dealing with the swollen hands issue. He took off the jacket.

Professor Bogdan's gaze went right to the big bruise over his ribs on the right side, not a fresh bruise—purple and yellow now, kind of like summer sunsets if the wind was coming out of the mountains and blowing the pollution away—but impossible to miss. Uncle Dragomir didn't give it the slightest glance. Instead he helped himself to a Chesterfield from Professor Bogdan's pack, lying on the desk.

Dinu put on the T-shirt.

"The plunger is funny," said Uncle Dragomir, lighting up.

Desfundator was their word for plunger. *Plunger* was better. The smoke from Uncle Dragomir's cigarette reached him. He began to cough. That made his chest hurt, under the bruise.

TWO

Something amazing happened on Court #2 of the New Sunshine Golf and Tennis Club just before lunchtime on the day after New Year's, although it was amazing to only one person, namely Loretta Plansky, a seventy-one-year-old widow of solid build and the only female player in the whole club with a one-handed backhand. She and her partner, a new member Mrs. Plansky had met just before stepping on the court that morning and whose name she had failed to retain even though she'd repeated it several times to herself as they shook hands, were playing in the weekly match between the New Sunshiners and the team from Old Sunshine Country Club, the hoity-toitier of the two, dating all the way back to 1989. Mrs. Plansky had been something of a tomboy as a kid, actually playing Little League baseball and Peewee hockey on boys' teams, but she hadn't taken up tennis until she'd married Norm, so although her strokes were effective they weren't much to look at. Now, up 5-6 in a third set tiebreak, Mrs. Plansky and her partner receiving, the better of the opponents, a tall, blond woman perhaps fifteen years younger than the others, lofted a pretty lob over Mrs. Plansky, a lob with a touch of topspin that was going to land inside the baseline for a clean winner. Mrs. Plansky wheeled around, chased after the ball, and with her back half-turned to the net flicked a backhand down the unguarded alley. Game, set, match. A nice shot, mostly luck, and not the amazing part. The amazing part was that Mrs. Plansky had wheeled around without giving it the slightest thought. She'd simply

made a quick thoughtless instinctive move—quick for her, at least—
for the first time since her hip replacement, nine months before. Mrs.
Plansky wanted badly to tell Norm all about it. He'd say something
about how she'd found the fountain of youth, and she'd say let's call
it a trickle, and he'd laugh and give her a quick kiss. She could just
about feel it now, on her cheek.

"What a get!" said her partner, patting Mrs. Plansky's shoulder.

The partner's name came to her at last, literally late in the game.
That bit of mental fun liberated a little burst of happiness inside
her. Those little bursts, based on tiny private nothings, had been a
feature of her life since childhood. Mrs. Plansky was well aware that
she was one lucky woman. "Thanks, Melanie," she said.

They hustled up to the net, touched rackets, then collected their
tennis bags and headed to the clubhouse patio for lunch. Mrs. Plansky's phone beeped just as she was pulling out her chair. She dug
it out of her bag, checked the number, and stepped away from the
table, off the patio, and onto the edge of the putting green.

"Nina?" she said.

"Hi, Mom," said Nina. "How're things? Wait, I'll answer—no
complaints, right?"

Mrs. Plansky laughed. "Maybe I should be less predictable."

"Whoa! An out-there version of Loretta Plansky! You'd rule the
world."

"Then forget it for sure," said Mrs. Plansky. "How are the kids?"

"Great," Nina said. "Emma's still on winter break—right now
she's out in Scottsdale with Zach and Anya." Emma, a junior at UC
Santa Barbara, being Nina's daughter from her first marriage, to
Zach, and Anya being Zach's second wife, whom Mrs. Plansky had
met just once, at Norm's funeral, and very briefly. But in that brief
time, she'd said something quite touching. What was it?

"Mom?" said Nina. "You still there?"

"Yes."

"Thought I'd lost you for a second."

"Must . . . must be a bad connection. I'm at the club. The service is iffy." Mrs. Plansky moved to a different spot on the putting green, even though she knew there was nothing wrong with . . . well, never mind.

"The tennis club?" Nina said. "How are you hitting 'em?"

"No one would pay to watch," said Mrs. Plansky. "And Will?"

"Will?"

"Yes. How is he?"

Will being Nina's other child, fathered by Ted, Nina's second husband. There'd been a third husband—called Teddy, kind of confusing—now also by the wayside, which was how Mrs. Plansky pictured all Nina's husbands, Zach, Ted, Teddy, left behind by a fast and shiny car, the hair of the three men—none bald, all in fact with full heads of hair—blowing in Nina's backdraft. Was that—a full head of hair—a criterion of hers when it came to husbands? Were there in fact any other criteria? Why had she never considered this question before? And now came one of those many moments when she wished that Norm was around. Yes, he'd say, it's her only criterion. Or, no, there's one other, and he'd name something that was funny, amazing, and true, something she'd never have imagined. And then: "Now can I go back to being dead?"

Whoa. Mrs. Plansky heard Norm's voice, not in her head—although of course it was—but somehow outside, like he'd come down from heaven—in which Mrs. Plansky did not believe—and onto the putting green at the New Sunshine Golf and Tennis Club. She actually cast a furtive glance around. An errant ball came bouncing over from the ninth fairway.

"Fine as far as I know," said Nina.

"Sorry, what?" Mrs. Plansky, moving away from the still-rolling ball, suddenly felt a little faint.

Nina raised her voice as though speaking to someone hard of hearing, which Mrs. Plansky was not. All systems go, said Dr. Ming at her annual physical. Just keep doing what you're doing.

"Will," Nina went on. "He's fine, far as I know."

Mrs. Plansky gave her head a tiny shake, putting everything right inside. "Is he back in school?"

Over at the table, Melanie caught her eye. The waiter was pour-ing wine and Melanie pointed to the empty glass at Mrs. Plansky's place, seeing if she wanted some. Mrs. Plansky didn't drink wine at lunch. She nodded yes.

"Not exactly," said Nina. "Will's missed so much time already and it's late in the year. He's planning on staying in Crested Butte."

"Teaching skiing."

"There's been a glitch with that. It looks like he'll be working the lifts."

Working the lifts? She and Norm had done some skiing in Ver-mont in the early days of Plansky and Company, the southernmost ski hills in the state close enough to their home in Rhode Island for Sunday visits, full weekends impossible because of work. The homeward drive at twilight with the kids, Nina and Jack in the back, Norm in the passenger seat, Mrs. Plansky at the wheel—they did it the other way around on the trip up, Norm's night vision never very good—and everyone exhilarated, exhausted, relaxed to the core: that was Plansky family life at its best. But working the lifts was all about getting through to your day off and hoping it would be powdery, in other words a spinning your wheels type of job, which ski instructor was not. When had she last spoken to him? Probably on his birthday, back in July, although she had sent him a check for Christmas. But to what address? She made a mental note to check on that, and a second mental note to call him soon. The fact that he hadn't thanked her yet for the check didn't mean he hadn't gotten it. For whatever reason, he'd missed out on a thing or two in his upbringing. Mrs. Plansky didn't get judgmental about that sort of thing. Will and a buddy had stayed for a night the week after her hip replacement, on their way to spring vacation at the buddy's par-ents' house in Lauderdale. She hadn't been able to find her bottle of OxyContin—always at the far right of the top medicine cabinet shelf—after they left. Mrs. Plansky was inclined to be more judg-mental about things like that.

"But the reason I called, Mom, is I've got exciting news," Nina said.

"Let's hear it!" What a terrible person she was, making her voice so bright and cheery when she was steeling herself inside. But she knew Nina.

"I've met someone fabulous," Nina said. "His name's Matty but I call him Matthew. It's more serious." Mrs. Plansky felt the fast and shiny car speeding up. "You're going to love him, Mom. Guess how tall he is?"

Mrs. Plansky glanced around, a feeble physical facsimile of getting her mental bearings. What she saw was the pretty side of Florida on a bright and sunny winter day. How lucky to be able to afford retirement in a place like this, and while she'd have preferred Arizona she'd kept that fact to herself, mostly on account of the look on Norm's face when the real estate agent drove them up to the big but not too big house at 3 Pelican Way, the style New England as envisioned by someone who'd never been there, and the inland waterway right out the back door. Norm had been thrilled, and the fact that he totally missed the faux part—in fact was incapable of catching it even if prompted—only made her adore him all the more.

"Tallish, would be my guess," said Mrs. Plansky. Norm had been five foot seven on their wedding day, losing an inch or two over the course of forty years. And his body had gone through many other changes as well. But somehow he'd been physical perfection the whole time. At least until those last months. She couldn't fool herself about that.

"Six foot four, Mom!" Nina said. "And three-quarters."

"Oh, my," said Mrs. Plansky. "Tell me a little more about him."

Nina laughed. Right from childhood she'd had this rippling musical laugh—like a song, as Norm had told her, perhaps too often in retrospect, but only due to the love in his heart. Was there something studied now about that musicality? Maybe she was imagining it. Over at the table the waiter seemed to have finished taking the orders and was looking her way.

"Salad," mouthed Mrs. Plansky. The waiter gave her a thumbs-up.

"I don't even know where to start," Nina was saying. "But guess what? You can see for yourself tomorrow."

"Oh?" said Mrs. Plansky.

"We're flying down for a quick weekend with some friends in Boca and thought we'd stop by on the way tomorrow night and take you out to dinner."

"Wonderful," said Mrs. Plansky. "But I'll make dinner. You can see the new place."

"Are you all settled in?"

"Oh, yes."

"Then that'll be great. Bye, Mom. Love you."

"Love you," said Mrs. Plansky, but Nina had already hung up. She walked over to the patio, sat at the table, took a sip of her wine, and then another. Surprisingly soon her glass was empty. The waiter appeared with the bottle. "No, thank you," said Mrs. Plansky, covering the glass with her hand to make sure.

There were two routes home from the tennis club, home meaning Mrs. Plansky's new residence, a condo on Little Pine Lake. One, the shorter, cut straight through the woods to the lake. The longer route followed the inland waterway for two miles, therefore passing right by 3 Pelican Way. The last time Mrs. Plansky had taken that route was the day before she moved out. Now, after lunch on the club patio, her mind on other things, she found herself taking it again, although the realization didn't strike her until Norm's flamboyant tree came into view. He'd decided that if they were going to live out their days in Florida they were going to do it right, and doing it right meant a flamboyant tree in the front yard, and not just a flamboyant tree but the mother of all flamboyant trees, which he would plant from a cutting—definitely not a seedling!—and nurture like no flamboyant tree had ever been nurtured. No nursery in the entire state had been up to the task when it came to supplying a cutting of the quality he'd demanded, the cutting eventually coming from Madagascar, ancestral home of flamboyant trees. The soil in the front yard had also proved less than first rate—not loamy enough and lacking in organic matter—so Norm had replaced most of it and added organic matter he'd come across at a woodlot deep in a Georgia forest, organic matter that had led to trouble with the HOA. But the result—Big Mama—oh, the result: a flamboyant that not only bloomed in May, like everyone else's flamboyant, but also at Christmas, most of the flowers the brightest red on earth, but also some bursts of the much rarer yellow flowers, both on the same tree! Norm invited a Rollins biology prof to take a look. "Unheard of," he'd said. "This is publishable."

They'd had sex twice that night, a double dip, as Mrs. Plansky had called it—she could be a bit bawdy when it was just the two of them—a feat, if it could be so called, that hadn't happened in at least twenty years. For some time after that she would say "Any new arboreal ideas?" at unexpected moments.

Retiring right also meant getting a metal detector and taking it for long beach walks, Norm wearing headphones and sweeping the detector back and forth with an intent look on his face and Mrs. Plansky taking a peek or two at that intent look. She could see little kid Norm at those moments and in an irrational way enjoy the false feeling of having known him all her life. They'd actually met for the first time on graduation day at college. The point about the metal detector was that after a big storm Norm had found an old Spanish silver coin with it, a four reales piece with a shield on one side and two strange pillars in the other. Mrs. Plansky bought a plaque for displaying the coin in the front hall.

"Which side out?" she asked.

"The pillars, of course."

She slowed the car. Big Mama was in her glory—golden suns shining in a red fire. "When you sell the house," Norm said, pausing to get more air inside him from the nasal tube, "you could always take a cutting."

"Why would I sell the house?"

Pause. Pause. "You know."

"I do not."

Norm reached his hand across the bedcover. He lay on the special invalid bed they'd ended up renting. "Normally I always say buy," Norm had said, "but maybe not in this case." And the hand—so withered and also purplish from getting stuck with IV needles so often. She'd laid her own—so indecently healthy in contrast—on top.

Pause. Pause. "For moving on."

An overwhelming urge to weep, to cry, to sob, rose up in her. Mrs. Plansky mastered it. "I'm not moving on."

Norm gazed at her, his eyes now deep in his skull and getting deeper, but she could still see him way down in there, her Norm. He began to sing "My Funny Valentine." Norm was a terrible singer— although he did a lot of singing during the course of an average day— scratchy, out of tune, unstable in pitch—but this one time, two days from death, as it turned out, and until he'd run out of oxygen, he'd sung like an angel, or, to be more specific, Tony Bennett.

Now, beyond Big Mama, a gardener was at work, planting something in the yard. At first she couldn't make out what it was, and then there seemed to be some mental refusal to accept the optical fact. But the something being planted was one of those plastic jockeys, outfitted in painted racing silks. Mrs. Plansky moved on.

THREE

Norm's smell lingered in corners here and there at 3 Pelican Way for a few months after he died. Not the smells of death and dying—those vanished almost at once—but the smell of healthy, living Norm, a smell she loved. Then one morning it, too, was gone. Three Pelican Way was on the market by lunchtime. Remaining there would have meant living life half dead. Pick one or the other, Norm would have said.

The condos at Little Pine Lake were very nice. For one thing they stood at the top of a rise, rises being hard to come by in the county. Then there was the lake itself, almost a perfect circle, and the water wonderfully refreshing, fed by a spring down below. There were only a dozen condos, all at ground level, backing onto the water and taking advantage of the slope. Mrs. Plansky had number twelve, one of the end units, with a private little patio where she liked to sit and watch the sunsets seeming to set the lake on fire. It wasn't cheap, but she'd paid cash and still had almost $400,000 left over from the sale of 3 Pelican Way.

Mrs. Plansky didn't have to worry about money but she hadn't grown up rich so at least she knew what worrying about money was like. She and Norm had started with nothing—actually less than nothing if you factor in the $10,000 loan from her dad at prime plus four and a half, paid back the very first day they could afford it. The ten thousand and all they could save from their paychecks—Norm working for a small engineering firm in Providence at the time, and

Mrs. Plansky a paralegal at a small law firm in Newport—was sunk into the effort to bring Norm's idea to life.

Actually Mrs. Plansky's idea, but it was such a random out of the blue sort of thought, more or less just passing through her, that she never could see taking credit for it, although Norm disagreed strongly and made sure that everyone knew. He himself had had several ideas before hers came along, none of them viable for one reason or another, from the realization that there wouldn't be sufficient demand to the deflating discovery that the invention he'd had in mind was already out there and doing killer business. Then, in the tent on what turned out to be a rainy weekend camping trip in the Berkshires, Mrs. Plansky—pregnant with Nina, and Jack standing but not quite walking—had been slicing a loaf of rye bread for sandwiches, when she'd suddenly said, "Wouldn't it be nice if the knife could toast the bread while you sliced?"

Norm, still dozing in the two-person sleeping bag, sat right up. "What did you say?"

Mrs. Plansky said it again.

Three years later, they sold their first Plansky Toaster Knife, actually fifty of them, to a start-up kitchen store in Oslo. The name of the product was also Mrs. Plansky's idea—Norm had pushed for Lasers by Loretta—as was the choice of the first client. Mrs. Plansky had met the owners at a trade show in Atlanta, a young, hip, sophisticated couple, very unlike her and Norm, except for the young part, and decided they were a good bet. Their next order, for five thousand knives, came from a chain based in Barcelona, after the CEO stopped by the Oslo kitchen store. And after that, the deluge.

"We're going to make billions!" Norm had said.

"That would be a headache," said Mrs. Plansky.

"How about hundreds of millions?"

"The feeling you get when you know a headache is on the way."

In the end—Norm running manufacturing and distribution, Mrs. Plansky sales and marketing—they'd made a nice amount of millions, some—but not too much to be harmful, they hoped—

given to Jack and Nina along the way, and maybe half, almost five million, to various charities when they sold the company and moved down to Florida, envisioning a nice and long last act. Well. When it turned out to be so short, a line of Shakespeare's had kept popping up uninvited in her mind over and over: *As flies to wanton boys are we to the gods; They kill us for their sport.* Mrs. Plansky hated that line and didn't buy it for one second. Finally it went silent, or went away, possibly to some other grieving mind. She didn't like that thought, either.

Mrs. Plansky, unlocking the door to her condo from an app on her phone—she'd refused to grow fossilized regarding things like that—at least not completely, an inventor's wife, after all—went inside. Yesterday had been the day Maria came to clean so everything was spotless, although it was always spotless, never more so than right before Maria's arrival. But now Mrs. Plansky didn't remember whether Nina had said she was spending the night with . . . with whoever it was, the new paramour. Just in case, she went upstairs to the guest bedroom in the loft and made the bed. Then she checked the guest bathroom, made a quick inspection, switched out the flamingo towels—bought on a post-Christmas sale at All Things Bathroom—for plain white. After that, she brewed herself tea in the kitchen and drank it at the island. There were shortbread cookies in the pantry and she wanted one, but hadn't she just had lunch? Loretta! Get a grip! She finished her tea, washed the cup, put it in the rack, gazed out the window at the lake.

Her phone pinged, meaning a text had come in. Mrs. Plansky found she was standing in the pantry for some reason. She went back to the island, checked her phone. A message from Jack: **You there?**

Mrs. Plansky's index finger hovered over the screen. Yes, Jack, I'm here. Good to hear from you. Too wordy? How about, Hi, Jack, present and accounted for. Good grief. Perhaps a simple Yes. Probably the right call, but wasn't it a bit uncivilized? Was there something uncivilized about machines which forced you yourself into being uncivilized if you wanted them to play nice? Oh, how she wished she could be pouring Norm a small glass of that bourbon he liked—there was still some left—and hearing what he'd say about that, or any other—

The phone—such a busy little device and only half smart, the bad half of smartness—rang, snapping her out of her little reverie or whatever it was. On the screen scrolled the name of the caller: Arcadia Gardens.

"Hello," she said. "Loretta Plansky speaking."

"Hi, Loretta. It's Jeanine. Any way you can swing by here, maybe settle things down?"

"What's the problem?"

"Something about football."

The plaque with the four reales piece now hung in the front hall of the condo. Back at 3 Pelican Way, headed out for Norm's first brain scan, Mrs. Plansky had glanced back and spotted him touching the coin for luck. She hadn't let on. Now, on her way out the condo door, Mrs. Plansky touched the old Spanish coin. Her hand pretty much did it on its own.

Arcadia Gardens, a forty-five minute drive south of Little Pine Lake, had beautiful landscaping—weedless flower beds lined with conch shells, big shady trees, mostly cabbage palm but also some ancient bald cypress—and looked like a well-preserved hotel from prewar Florida days, even though it was not yet ten years old. Jeanine, a trim woman of forty or so wearing a tan business suit, was waiting in the lobby.

"Thanks for coming," she said.

"Of course." They stepped into an elevator and rode to the top floor. "A football problem?" Mrs. Plansky said.

"There was an argument about a penalty call," Jeanine said. "Offensive pass interference, maybe? Is that even a thing?"

"Yes," Mrs. Plansky said. Jack had played in high school. She knew football.

They walked down the hall on the top floor, a sunny hall with nicely framed prints of clipper ships on the walls. The last door was closed.

"He's got something wedged against the doorknob," Jeanine said. "We can't get in."

Mrs. Plansky knocked lightly. "Dad?"

Silence from the other side of the door, and then: "Go away. And I'm not paying a goddamn cent. Don't you, neither." Then came more silence, followed by "Disloyal bitch," spoken in the low, confidential tone some people reserve for talking to themselves.

Mrs. Plansky turned to Jeanine. "Paying for what?"

"The TV in the lounge," Jeanine said, "but I don't know where he got the idea there'd be a charge. No one would have told him that. It's covered by our insurance."

"He broke the TV?"

Jeanine nodded. "With a beer bottle."

"He threw it that hard?"

Jeanine shook her head. "He wheeled right up to the screen and used the bottle like a club. Have you met Mr. Blucher?"

"I don't think so."

"He's new. That's who the argument was with. Naturally a staff member was on scene, serving refreshments and such, but it all happened very quick."

"Dad's ninety-eight. How could it have been quick?"

"I should have said surprisingly quick. Unfortunately Mr. Blucher was struck by a shard of glass and needed a stitch or two."

"My God. Struck where?"

"The arm. We dodged one there."

Mrs. Plansky turned to the door and knocked harder this time. "Dad. Open up."

His voice came from closer, like he was right on the other side. "Why should I?"

"Dad! What kind of question is that?"

More silence. And finally: "A head-scratcher."

Mrs. Plansky and Jeanine exchanged a look. Jeanine called through the door. "Your daughter drove all this way to see you, Mr. Banning. Please open the door."

"It's only thirty-two miles," her dad said. "And I'm not moving. This is my room and that's final. Finito. End of story. Full stop."

Mrs. Plansky plucked Jeanine's sleeve, drew her a step or two down the hall. "What's he talking about?"

"Well," said Jeanine, "it's not just this incident but there have been a few other things, too. We're recommending a move down to the third floor. The room will be just as nice but we can give him more assistance there."

"You think he needs more assistance?"

"Not just me, the whole team," Jeanine said. "Including Dr. Albert."

"If more assistance is necessary, why can't he stay here and have it?"

"Procedure. The third floor is where we provide the next level of assistance." Jeanine touched Mrs. Plansky's hand. "Our concern is self-harm."

"Self-harm?"

"Not intentional. But with the temperamental side of him maybe getting the upper hand a little more often these days . . ." Her voice trailed off.

Mrs. Plansky went back to the door, and this time didn't knock. "Why are you making this so hard?"

"This is all about the shekels, that's why."

"What are you talking about?"

"The so-called move. The third floor's another ten grand a month." Mrs. Plansky could feel a tiny breeze as Jeanine shook her head. "Any notion what this place costs?" he said.

Since she'd been footing the bill, Mrs. Plansky had a precise notion. What would happen if she voiced that thought aloud? Mrs. Plansky wasn't sure, but she'd shut down any such experiments on her father long ago. She took a deep breath and played her last card, the only one in the deck with any chance of working.

"Nina's coming for dinner," she said. "Do you want to join us?"

"At that condo of yours?"

"It's where I live, Dad."

"I like the old place better. With the tree. Why the hell did you move?"

"We've been through this."

"Not your best decision. Also not your worst."

That last part was code for marrying Norm. He knew and she knew but anyone else would have had trouble believing it for so many reasons, such as after all this time, and how long and happy the marriage was, and most of all the fact of the specialness of Norm. He'd never been good enough for her, but not in the ancient no one could be good enough for my daughter way. That, Mrs. Plansky understood—suddenly and parenthetically—was more like the way he thought about Nina. No, in her case there was another reason. *Shekels* was the clue. She came close to saying forget it. Damn it, yes. The words were on the way. But before they got out in the world, her father spoke again.

"All right, all right, the itty-bitty condo it is," he said. "I better poop first." Scraping and bumping went on behind the door and then it opened. There he was—slumped sideways, but somehow aggressively, in his wheelchair, her dad, once a good-looking man in a *Mad Men* sort of way, and now much reduced, even a bit orc-like. He raised his voice. "Julio! Julio!"

"Who's Julio?" Mrs. Plansky said.

"The attendant who helps him with his sanitary needs," said Jeanine.

"The other guy was better," Mrs. Plansky's dad said.

"Marcus is no longer here," Jeanine said, and Mrs. Plansky knew at once how come.

FOUR

Julio wheeled Mrs. Plansky's dad across the Arcadia Gardens parking lot. Mrs. Plansky opened the passenger door. Julio helped her dad to his feet.

"I can get there myself," her dad said, batting Julio's hands away in a movement that was meant to be forceful. And it was true that on their last outing a month before—ostensibly for milkshakes although they'd detoured into a bar he liked the look of, where he'd been a big hit, downing two shots of bourbon and entertaining the barflies with his age, saving the puking part for the ride back—he'd managed to get into the car by himself. But not this time. He took one step, stopped, and teetered. Julio gathered him up smoothly and got him sitting comfortably on the front seat.

"Give him a tip, Loretta."

"You know there's no tipping, sir," Julio said.

"Yeah? How about at Christmas?"

"That's different," Julio told him.

"I win," said her dad.

Mrs. Plansky drove out of the parking lot to the main road and headed north.

"Some music, Dad?"

"Nosireebob."

A few miles passed in silence and then they hit the section with all the strip malls, auto body shops, and car washes, including the one where you could have your car washed by sudsy young and not so young women in bikinis. Her dad turned his head to watch, then sat back, folded his gnarled and veiny hands, and said, "Seeing anybody?"

Mrs. Plansky glanced over at him. He was gazing straight ahead.

"Lots of people," she said. She came close to itemizing them for him but in a deus ex machina way her phone, sitting in the cup holder, pinged the incoming text, saving her from a really bad move. Mrs. Plansky, whose vision after cataract surgery two years before— "I've found the best guy for this," Norm had said. "No random bozo gets to mess with those eyes"—was very good, had no need to bring the phone closer. The text was from Jack and it was just this: ? She realized she hadn't gotten back to him. Mrs. Plansky did not send texts while driving and even if she did she wouldn't have now.

"Did I hear something?" her dad said. "Like one of those pings?"

"No," said Mrs. Plansky.

"You know what I meant."

"Excuse me?"

"Seeing anyone like a man. An XY to squeeze into your XX."

"For God's sake!"

"After all, you're still reasonably attractive."

"Thanks."

"Matter of fact I have a candidate, if you don't mind the type with lots of chins. I'm talking about Ernie Oberst's kid brother. Bruno, I think it was. Came to visit a while back. His girlfriend walked out on him."

Mrs. Plansky made no comment.

"Meaning he's available," her dad explained. "Based in Tampa. Lives in one of those developments with lots of swingers."

She wanted to throw up, or at the very least turn around and deposit him back at Arcadia Gardens. But she did neither of those things, just drove on in silence. That side of her, the sexual side— but for certain not swinging, physically, mentally, or spiritually, and how could swinging be in any way spiritual? Surely it was the total absence of. But not the point, which was about the sexual side: now gone. And if not gone, then in a coma of some sort. She knew comas up close. The last time she'd held Norm he'd been in one. Her eyes welled up and a tear or two got free and slid down her cheek. She glanced over to see if her dad was watching. He was asleep. She could let those tears flow to her heart's discontent. But she did not.

Six foot four and three-quarters could look like an NBA player but it didn't have to, and Matthew DeVore, Nina's new beau, was the proof. Narrow-shouldered, knock-kneed, splayfooted, chinless: Mrs. Plansky silenced that judgmental part of her mind and gave him a friendly smile as they shook hands. She'd left out wet-palmed, and also paunchy. But he did have a full head of hair, the rusty-colored kind you see on men too old not to be graying, and that was another issue, although in disguise: he was a lot older than Nina. She would soon turn forty-six and this gentleman had certainly crossed the sixty barrier, making him closer in age to the mom, meaning her. Mrs. Plansky re-silenced the judgmental part of her mind.

"Nina's told me so much about you," he said during the slightly damp handshake. "And call me Matty."

Ah. Didn't Nina prefer Matthew? More serious, wasn't it? Mrs. Plansky didn't quite remember, but she pushed past that little roadblock and said, "And I'm Loretta."

"Yeah?" said Matty. "I had a Loretta."

"Excuse me?" said Mrs. Plansky. She glanced at Nina, still smiling her introduction smile, seemingly unaware, although of exactly what Mrs. Plansky was not sure. Maybe the fault was hers, imagining nonexistent shortcomings. It hit her at that moment that some part of her mind might benefit from the brain equivalent of a hip replacement.

"My first high school girlfriend was Loretta," Matty explained.

"Perhaps a more common name back in the old days," said Mrs. Plansky. Maybe postreplacement she would have gone with something nicer.

Matty's own smile seemed to stiffen a bit. Nina took him by the hand and led him toward her grandfather, sitting in his wheelchair by the little bar in one corner of the living room, drumming his fingers on the armrest.

"Hi, Pops," she said, leaning down to kiss his forehead. He reached up, did his best to wrap his arms around her.

"Hello, beautiful." He clung to her. She patted his shoulder, kissed his forehead again, and straightened.

"Pops, I want you to meet Matthew. Matthew, this is Pops, a legend in the family."

They shook hands. Mrs. Plansky caught a change of expression on her dad's face, which had to have been when he grew aware of the dampness of the handshake.

"Nice to meet you, Pops," Matty said. "And call me Matty."

"Or Matthew," said Nina.

"Which is it?" said Mrs. Plansky's dad.

"You pick, Pops," said Matty.

"Am I your grandfather?"

"No, sir. What would you like me to—"

"What do you call your own grandfather?"

"Well, they're both passed."

"There you go."

"But what would you like me to call you?"

Mrs. Plansky's dad opened his mouth but no words came out. Instead he licked his dry lips with his dry tongue and closed his mouth. Nina and Matty gazed down at him, Nina worried, Matty confused and somewhat put off. Mrs. Plansky came over.

"How about calling him Chandler?" she said. "That's his given name."

Her dad nodded and returned from wherever he'd been. "Chandler Wills Banning," he said. "Princeton, '46."

"Chandler it is," said Matty.

"Where'd you go to school?" her dad said.

"You're lookin' at a Fightin' Blue Hen."

"Huh?"

"University of Delaware."

"Who wants a drink?" said Mrs. Plansky.

Nina, Matty, and Mrs. Plansky's dad had drinks at the bar—white wine for Nina, JD on the rocks for Matty, the smallest scotch Mrs. Plansky thought she could get away with for her dad. She turned on the Golf Channel, her dad's favorite and which had his full attention at once. Nina and Matty sat on the barstools. She leaned against him. Mrs. Plansky went into the kitchen to make sure she caught the crab soufflé at the exact right moment.

She was a bit nervous about the crab soufflé. Mrs. Plansky liked to cook and the crab soufflé was one of her specialties, but she hadn't done any cooking in quite some time, her diet now consisting of toast and fruit for breakfast, a salad—often at the club—for lunch, and whatever happened to be in the pantry, tuna, for example, or even sardines, for dinner, unless she was going out with friends, of which they—she—didn't have many in Florida, and none of them close. She'd never felt the need for a lot of friends, at least not since her wedding day. When Norm was alive she'd cooked up a storm, a storm that had weakened with his loss of appetite and died with him.

So in the kitchen she kept squatting down and gazing through the oven window. Why wasn't the darn thing rising? She was checking her watch when Nina came in.

"Here's some wine, Mom."

"Thanks." Mrs. Plansky rose, one of her knees grinding in pain—in an uncomfortable manner—which she hoped was inaudible.

"Oh my God," Nina said. "Are you going to need a knee replacement, too?"

"Of course not." She took her glass. "And if I do it's not a big deal."

Nina thought about that. Mrs. Plansky read the thought, all about Norm and what a big deal actually was, medically. The inward look on Nina's face at that moment, deep and dark: it had never been in evidence when she'd had Nina under her roof, appearing for the first time around the time she'd left Zach, and showing up more often early in her marriage to Ted the first, a marriage that took her to L.A. for ten years or so, Mrs. Plansky losing track of Nina's inner journey during that time. But what a beauty she'd always been and still was, with fine features and shining hazel eyes, both coming from Norm. Her body was more like her mom's, shapely in a sturdy way, Mrs. Plansky's shapeliness no longer what it was, although she seemed to be hanging on to the sturdiness.

"I like the place, Mom. Is it expensive?"

"I'd call it affordable," said Mrs. Plansky.

Nina laughed her musical laugh. "Otherwise you wouldn't be here. I know my mom." She gave Mrs. Plansky a hug. Mrs. Plansky hugged her back. She hadn't hugged Nina—or Jack—in months, and didn't want to let go. At the same time, she felt tension inside her daughter, and plenty of it. They stepped away from each other, sipped their wine.

"I'll set the table," Nina said.

"Done," said Mrs. Plansky. "But you could make that vinaigrette of yours."

"Sure thing."

Nina got busy with oil, vinegar, Dijon mustard, a touch of maple syrup. Mrs. Plansky took another peek in the oven. Still no action.

"So what do you think of him?" Nina said. "Matthew, I mean."

"He seems very nice, but I've only just met him."

"And now you want a thumbnail."

Mrs. Plansky laughed. "Shoot."

Some people were capable of telling stories in an organized way, but not Nina.

"Wow, I don't even know where to start."

"Where he's from, for example."

"Originally? West Hartford. His father had a small law practice that Matthew joined and eventually took over. He retired early and we met on one of those sunset cruises. After, he came down to Hilton Head. For retirement, if you're following this."

Which Mrs. Plansky was. "You went on a sunset cruise?" she said. When Nina married Ted the second, she left L.A. and moved into his house on Hilton Head, a house she ended up with when that marriage fell apart, although that was all she got. The point was she was a Hilton Head resident and Mrs. Plansky had never heard of locals going on sunset cruises in their own harbors.

"I know," Nina said. "Total impulse. I was out power walking, saw the boat, and hopped on board, if you can believe it."

Mrs. Plansky could.

"And now," said Nina, "we're remodeling."

"Your place or his?"

"Oh, mine. Matthew's renting at the moment. Way too soon to be telling you this, but we're contemplating marriage."

"Ah."

"I know, I know. Numero quatro. But—call me conservative if you like—I've come around to thinking these arrangements should be formalized."

What arrangements exactly? Were they in love? Those were the questions Mrs. Plansky kept to herself. Instead she said, "Does he have any formalized arrangements in his past?"

"Ha-ha. The iron fist in the velvet glove!"

"Really?"

"No, of course not. Sorry, Mom. And yes, he was married once and had a relationship after that. What else? There's a son in the Bay Area but they're not close. And yes, he's a little older, if that's what's coming next. But he's super energetic and witty in a quiet way, and aren't you as old as you feel?"

The answer to that was no, and so far Matthew's quiet wit was pitched at a decibel level beneath her hearing range. She was about to say something about how nice it was that Matthew felt energetic

when the soufflé rose, rose quite abruptly, almost popping up like . . .
well, you know. Would a bolder mom have now said, "And how is
he in the sack?" Mrs. Plansky was not that mom. She donned oven
mitts and pulled this tumescent wonder—certainly the best-looking
soufflé she'd ever made—out of the oven.

"Wow!" said Nina. "You go, Mom!"

Mrs. Plansky set the soufflé on the counter. The scent of the
shore spread through the kitchen.

"By the way," Nina said, "I'm shutting down the gallery."

"Oh?"

Nina had owned a few art galleries in her life, this latest one on
Hilton Head specializing in landscape and seascape photography.
She had a wonderful eye, in the opinion of Mrs. Plansky, who'd
gone with Norm to opening night and bought a strange close-up of
a moray eel caught in a moment that seemed to be contemplative,
which had hung in Norm's study back at 3 Pelican Way and had not
yet been unpacked.

"Business has been slow with the economy and all," Nina said,
"but it's not just that. Matthew and I have this fabulous idea. In
fact, we'd like to talk to you about it."

"I'm listening," said Mrs. Plansky.

"How about at dinner?" Nina said. "When we're all together."

FIVE

The Americans had a Georgia of their own. Their Georgia was a state. There turned out to be fifty of them. So many, and they all had nicknames. Dinu—his back to the radiator in his seven square meters' bedroom, with part of that space taken by an old, jutting-out, unusable, coal fireplace, the radiator working sometimes although not today—had his laptop on his lap and was supposed to be solving ten trigonometry problems for class tomorrow at 9 a.m. Dinu gazed at the first problem. *If the shadow of a building increases by 10 meters when the angle of elevation of the sun rays decreases from 70 degrees to 60 degrees, what is the height of the building?* The first answer that came into his mind was this: the builder cheated and the building fell down, therefore zero height. There were ways of working this out, of course, probably beginning with a diagram. A notepad and pencil were visible under his bed, partly concealed by the socks he'd worn yesterday and maybe for a few days before, just about in reach if he leaned forward as far as he could. But Dinu decided to put that off for the moment, and instead check out those state nicknames.

Dinu found a list almost at once and opened a second window on the screen showing a map of the whole country. He had super-good Wi-Fi in his bedroom—far faster than at school—thanks to Romeo, a computer genius actually slightly younger than Dinu, who had piggybacked Dinu's Wi-Fi, as he'd put it, using one of those cool American expressions their own language lacked, off the Wi-Fi from the private clinic two blocks away. Alaska was a state? Way up there with this other country—so that was Canada!—in between? Did that make Alaska something like Transnistria? He checked out a few photos of Alaska and decided the answer had to be no. But if the whole continent was like some sort of animal, then Alaska was the head and Florida was the tail. He glanced at the nicknames of both. Alaska: the Last Frontier. Florida: the Sunshine State. Ah, yes, sunshine. Frontiers, as he had good reason to know, meant problems. Dinu spent some very pleasant time viewing photos and videos of the Sunshine State. He found a rather long account of its history and read it carefully from beginning to end. Dinu had a very good memory if he switched it on, which he did now. Seminoles! The Fountain of Youth! Key Largo! He had it all in his mind forever, and was researching luxury car dealerships in Miami Beach when Aunt Ilinca laughed her harsh, smoky, boozy laugh in the kitchen, just on the other side of the wall with the radiator. A thin, uninsulated wall—there was no insulation in the whole apartment block—and Aunt Ilinca's laugh seemed to be originating a few centimeters from his ear. Aunt Ilinca lived in the apartment block across the street and came visiting once a week or so, always with a bottle of Stalinskaya vodka, his mama contributing little squares of dark bread spread with the cottage cheese they called zamatise to these get-togethers.

"All men are useless," Aunt Ilinca was saying, "but why do I end up always with the most useless?"

"Is he really so bad?" Mama said.

"I could tell you some of his habits but we're eating."

"Habits?" said Mama.

Dinu did not want to know about the habits of Aunt Ilinca's new boyfriend, or maybe an old boyfriend recycled. And luckily at that moment a text came in from Romeo: We need you.

Dinu got his socks from under the bed—cheap thin socks patterned with little circles featuring the face of Megan Thee Stallion—pulled on a hoodie, stuffed his phone in his jeans pocket, grabbed Professor Bogdan's script, and went into the kitchen. They were sitting at the table, Mama in her old woolen housecoat, Aunt Ilinca in an unzipped puffy coat with what might have been a nightie underneath, drinking from dainty little cups, hardly bigger than thimbles.

"There he is," said Aunt Ilinca.

"Salut, Auntie."

She gave him a look, quick but rather close, from head to feet and back again. "My, my, could this one still be growing?"

"You think so?" said Mama. There was brightness in her pale green eyes—the same color as Dinu's—meaning she and Aunt Ilinca were just getting started with the dainty little cups.

"Oh, yes," said Aunt Ilinca. "He will grow to be a strapping fellow like—"

She left it right there, although perhaps not soon enough, Mama's eyes dimming a bit. Dinu went to the door, slid his feet into his sneakers, put on his almost-leather jacket.

"Going somewhere?" Mama said.

"Work."

Mama opened her mouth to say something, closed it, then decided to go ahead with whatever it was. "Maybe this is a good time to discuss a raise?"

Dinu didn't answer. He slid the bolt to the side and opened the door.

"Or how about a commission?" said Aunt Ilinca, blowing smoke through her nostrils like some sort of dragon. "In business there are commissions."

Dinu went out and closed the door, maybe a little harder than necessary.

Dinu's workplace was the Club Presto in the nicer part of the nightlife section of the old town. He went inside.

"Hey, kid," said Marius the bouncer, in English.

"Hey," said Dinu. Marius was a huge guy who spoke a lot of English. Well, not quite true. He spoke a little bit of English often, for example, "Hey, kid." Or "Even my muscles have muscles," a phrase that came up whenever pretty girls were around, which was often. One of the pretty girls was Tassa, a classmate of Dinu's who worked behind the bar a few nights a week. Too young for that, strictly speaking, but strictly speaking did not apply at Club Presto. They'd been in the same class for many years, which was how the system worked, but he was just noticing her lately.

"Yo," he said as he went by.

"Yo?" said Tassa.

"That's hello in Miami Beach," Dinu told her.

Tassa spread her arms like she was an airplane and waggled them.

He stopped in front of her. Tassa had very beautiful ears. She must have had them all this time—not the ears, of course, but their beauty—the endless hours they'd sat at their desks in those cold, drab rooms. Why had he never noticed? In fact, all of her was beautiful. Not just the ears, but the face and surely the breasts, partly visible in her tank top, and . . . and . . . was this a good time for a fist bump? He made a fist and sort of poked it at her.

"What are you doing?"

"Fist bump. Also Miami Beach."

Tassa nodded like . . . like that made sense! Then she raised her hand like she was about to give him a fist bump but just then a guy down the bar rapped his glass with the thick bejeweled ring he wore on his finger and she went off to serve him.

At the back of Club Presto, up and down some stairs and along a narrow corridor lit with a few red bulbs, stood a steel door with a sign saying CAMBIO, meaning foreign exchange, and below it a pasted-on cartoon of the Ceauşecus standing on a balcony addressing an unseen crowd. They were both wearing furry Russian ushankas and nothing else. Elena, in the word balloon above her head, was saying to Nicolae, "Talk to them." It was a famous scene and true, except for the nudity part. They would soon be shot.

Dinu raised his hand to knock but the door was already open-ing. Thanks to Romeo, surveillance at Club Presto was world-class. Dinu entered the room that Romeo called mission control, after the place where the Americans had run their flights to the moon, although it was nothing like that, very small, smoky, and the key-boards stained by oily fingers, like in a mechanic's garage.

"Hey," Dinu said.

"Hey," said Romeo.

There were three people in the room: Romeo, who'd opened the door; Timbo, the other bouncer, cigarette in his mouth, head-phones on, eyes closed, foot tapping; and Uncle Dragomir, sitting in front of one of the screens, a cigar in one hand and a glass of whiskey on the desk.

"Hello, Uncle," Dinu said.

"Ready to go?" said Uncle Dragomir, not turning from the screen.

"I hope so," said Dinu.

Now Uncle Dragomir looked at him. "Hope?"

Timbo took off his headphones and opened his eyes. He was a wiry little guy with a very full handlebar mustache and a quiet voice, not at all like Marius, although while the occasional drunk or group of drunks might try something with Marius—never with a good result—everyone behaved like a gentleman around Timbo.

"I meant yes," Dinu said. "I am ready."

"Do the briefing," Uncle Dragomir told Romeo.

Dinu and Romeo went to a table at the back of the room. Timbo put his headphones back on, Uncle Dragomir sipped his whiskey and returned to the screen. He was watching footage shot at a firing range. Sometimes, although not tonight, Uncle Dragomir moni-tored these events through a one-way mirror in a tiny room on the floor above. Both methods made Dinu uncomfortable, but in dif-ferent ways.

Romeo opened a bottle of Miranda orange drink and filled two paper cups.

"Salut."

"Salut."

Romeo was a chubby kid with acne and wild hair and certainly not good-looking in any way Dinu could see, and also he came from a poor family rumored to be part Jewish but some girls—and not just a few—were interested in him. He was already making lots of money—he wore a gold chain around his neck and had two real leather jackets, one black and one red—but it wasn't just that. Romeo was a genius—the whole invisible structure behind computers, the internet, all that, was transparent to him, out in the open.

"Teach me, Romeo." Dinu had heard more than one girl say that, even an older girl from the university. Girls liked geniuses. It made sense, but of course Dinu had known for a long time that he himself would have to find another way.

Romeo unfolded a printout of his research, but before he could get going, Dinu said, "Do you know about survival of the fittest?"

"Sure. That's what we do."

"What do you mean?"

He waved the printout. "They're soft. We're hard."

"Who is they?"

"The Americans. Brits, French, all of them."

"The Russians?"

"Very funny. They're hard but clumsy. We are subtle."

"Oh?"

"Romance languages make you subtle. But none of the others are hard, just us. There are huge forces at play. It's a dynamic situation, Dinu."

"I don't get you."

"A dynamic situation is a chance for the poor to get rich and the rich to get poor. But it doesn't happen automatically. You have to work. So let's work." They bent over the printouts. "This is the grandpa, eighty-six, widower, lives alone in Texas."

"The Lone Star State," said Dinu.

Romeo looked puzzled for a moment and then continued. "And

this is the grandson—Tucker. Almost three thousand kilometers to the northeast of Texas—a university student at Penn State."

"The Keystone State," Dinu said.

"What are you talking about?"

"All the states have nicknames. Also flowers and songs."

Romeo sat back. "The states have songs?"

"Like 'You Are My Sunshine' for Louisiana."

"How does that one go?"

Dinu had looked up several of the state songs on YouTube, including "You Are My Sunshine." He opened his mouth to sing the beginning, at the same time noticing that Timbo was watching. No singing happened. Dinu and Romeo got busy with Romeo's research, Romeo pointing out details from time to time and Dinu filling in the blanks in his script.

"Hi, Grandpa, it's me, Tucker."

"Huh?"

Grandpa's voice, whispery and wavery and all the way from Texas, came in very clear, but Dinu knew Grandpa was hearing what sounded like a bad connection, all due to a special box with lots of switches and dials that Romeo had made, a box Dinu's headset was plugged into. Also plugged into the box were all their headphones, the kind for just listening—Romeo's, Timbo's, Uncle Dragomir's. They all sat close together, listening with an intensity Dinu could feel. He could also smell them: Romeo smelled like he needed a shower; Timbo smelled of cologne; Uncle Dragomir smelled of garlic, whiskey, cigars.

"It is I, Grandpa. Me. Tucker. Yo." Dinu, who'd already been a bit nervous, got more so. His hands were so sweaty they were dampening the script. "I am in—I'm in a bad situation, Grandpa. I need your help."

"My grandson Tommy?"

"No, Grandpa. Tucker. Your grandson Tucker. I am in—I'm in a bad situation."

"What kind of bad situation?"

Dinu squinted at the script, now smeared in places. "A dwee, Grandpa."

"Huh?"

Romeo kicked him under the table. "I beg pardon, a DUI. I am sorry, Grandpa. I'm sorry. But the police have seized my car and for getting it back and for bail I need nine thousand seven hundred and twenty-six dollars and eighteen cents."

"You need nine thousand dollars?"

"Plus seven hundred and twenty-six dollars and eighteen cents."

There was a long pause. Then Grandpa said, "How am I supposed to get you that?"

"It's easy, Grandpa. Have you got a pen?"

"Hang on."

Silence. It went on for some time. Dinu exchanged looks with the others. Romeo's eyes were excited, Timbo's thoughtful, Uncle Dragomir's unreadable. Finally, a voice came back on the line. At first Dinu thought that Grandpa had somehow gotten stronger during the break, had maybe downed a quick drink.

"Hey, who the hell is this?"

No, not Grandpa, but a much younger man. Dinu shot a quick glance at Romeo, Timbo, Uncle Dragomir. No help was forthcoming.

"BJ? Is that you? It's not very funny."

"Oh, no, not BJ," Dinu said. "It is I, Tucker."

"I'm Tucker, you stupid son of a bitch."

Click.

Romeo rose, put his hands to his face. "Oh my God!" If there was any fault, it was probably his, although it was maybe just one of those things and no one could be called at fault. But certainly not Dinu, who had only been following the script prepared by others. In fact, hadn't he improvised pretty well in a tricky situation? Still, Romeo was not replaceable and Dinu was, which was why Dinu got backhanded across the face twice, first by Uncle Dragomir, which didn't really hurt a lot, no more than that punch to the ribs awhile back, and second by Timbo. He'd never been struck by Timbo be-fore and Timbo didn't seem to put much effort into it, did not even look at him, but the blow hurt him very much. A tooth flew from his mouth and clattered softly on the floor. Dinu did not pick it up. Neither did he raise the issue of commissions or discuss a raise.

At home, a rat—or a weirdly huge mouse—was on the kitchen table, busy with the remains of the little dark bread squares spread with zamaste. His mother lay sleeping on the couch, Stalinskaya on her breath, her housecoat in disarray. Dinu covered her with a blanket, hurled a dishcloth at the rat or mouse, and went to bed.

Six

When Mrs. Plansky went into the bar to summon her father and prospective new son-in-law to dinner, she found they'd moved outside to the patio, leaving the slider open. They were gazing at the lake and smoking cigars. Mrs. Plansky had never seen her dad smoke a cigar, not once in her life. Was he taking it up now, at ninety-eight? What harm could it do? Still the sight made her pause before calling out, "Dinner is served." And in that pause, she heard them talking.

"Met the kid yet?" her dad said, tapping a cylinder of ash onto one of the wheelchair arms.

"You mean Emma?" Matthew said.

Her dad turned to him. "Matty, is it?"

"Yes."

"Or Matthew? What the hell's going on?"

"Nina prefers Matthew."

"Why?"

"Good question." Matthew tossed back the rest of his JD on the rocks, or possibly a second one, which Mrs. Plansky deduced from the fact the whiskey level in her dad's glass was above that of her original pour. "We all have our quirks."

"Tell me about it. There's some that are nothing but quirks. Head to toe. Name any one of my girlfriends."

"You have girlfriends, Chandler?"

"Had a boatload. This was after Alice died. Breast cancer and so goddamn young." He wagged his finger at Matthew. "Trust doctors and you deserve everything you get."

"Alice being Loretta's mom?" Matthew said.

"Old news," said her dad. "You haven't answered my question."

"About Emma?"

"Why would I be asking about her? Got no problems with Emma. She calls me on the first Sunday of every month, like clockwork. I'm talking about her brother."

"Will?"

"Is there another brother?"

Matthew laughed. "Were you a lawyer, Chandler?"

"Never practiced."

Which was true as far as it went. Going a little further would have meant reaching the full truth: no, I was not a lawyer. Her dad had been first a reckless waster of his inheritance, followed by various jobs in the finance industry, the family living higher and higher above its means, like an untethered balloon. Mrs. Plansky's mother's last words to her—before they put her on the ventilator for what turned out to be the final time—were "I just don't understand." Mrs. Plansky had assumed her mother had been referring to the cancer and dying so young, forty-nine to be exact, but she'd come to realize it was actually about Chandler. Her husband had ended up bewildering her.

"But," Mrs. Plansky's dad went on, "are you ducking my question?"

"About Will?" Matthew said. "I've met him."

"And?"

"He seems like a nice kid."

Her dad turned to Matthew, meaning that instead of the back of his head, Mrs. Plansky now saw him in profile. His visible eye was glaring. "You didn't sell that very well, Matty."

Matthew turned so that he, too, was now in profile, and also glaring. "All right," he said. "The kid's a selfish pothead, a leech, and a born loser. But Nina can't see it."

"I like the way you think," said her dad.

"Dinner," Mrs. Plansky said, and walked away.

"Three Michelin stars," said Matthew, dabbing the corners of his mouth with one of Mrs. Plansky's seagull-patterned napkins, her favorite, but missing a tiny lump of crab on his upper lip. "I knew you were an astute businesswoman but I had no idea you were a fabulous cook as well."

"Well, thanks," Mrs. Plansky said.

"Astute businesswoman?" her dad said.

Before dinner, he'd guided his wheelchair swiftly to what he'd probably assumed was the head of the table because of its proximity to the wine bottle. Mrs. Plansky sat at the other end, and Nina and Matthew were on opposite sides, Nina shifting the candelabra slightly so she could see him better.

"Plansky and Company," Matthew said. "Nina's told me the whole wonderful story. It should be a book, one of those case studies on how to get filthy—how to build a successful business from nothing."

"From nothing?" said Mrs. Plansky's dad. "Did Miss Nina mention the part about me lending ten grand?"

"I—I don't recall. Did you, Nina?"

"I honestly don't remember. But of course it was very good of you, Pops." Nina gave him a big smile.

It was not returned. "And also"—he slapped his hand on the table, a dessert fork taking flight—"besides quote, very good, doesn't that make me pretty goddamn astute as well?"

He looked from one to another. For a few moments it looked like the bait would go untaken—Mrs. Plansky's preference—but then Matthew took a gulp of wine and said, "I suppose, strictly speaking, it depends on your return."

"My return? My return on what?"

"Your investment." Matthew started to say more but then caught a look Nina was sending his way, and stopped himself. Mrs. Plansky also caught the look but couldn't interpret it. All she knew was that she felt like she was watching a tennis match featuring no players she wanted to root for. Not a very nice thought, and she sent it packing at once.

"What investment?" said her dad, batting the ball back at Matthew.

In tennis, most players were attackers to the best of their ability, but there was an unpopular subgroup of pushers, content to merely pitty-pat the ball back until the opponent made a mistake, and almost in contradiction, some were very aggressive about it. That was her dad: an aggressive pusher. After all these years—decades!—she had, at last, the scouting report on him.

"It was a loan, my young friend," her dad said.

"Oh," said Matthew.

There was a silence. With pushers you could try to outpush them, leading to a long and miserable dead zone in your day that ended with making you want to hang up your racket for good, or you decided you'd had enough and you went after them with a deep drive to one corner which you followed to the net, taking the angle and putting away whatever pushy-wushy bullshit came back. Excuse the language, Mrs. Plansky said to herself. To her dad she said, "Which was so nice of you, Dad. Remind me of the interest rate."

His mouth opened but no sound came out. The look on his face was the look of a pusher who realizes that pushy-wushy will no longer get it done. By this time, Mrs. Plansky was at the net. She glanced Matthew's way. "I'm sure the number will come to him. He has a wonderful memory."

Oh, dear. Too much. Mrs. Plansky wanted that one back in the silo. The silo was where, in Norm's blueprint for making a Loretta—his image, not hers—she kept her heavy artillery, which she hardly ever rolled out and remained a secret from almost everyone they knew, with the exception of the occasional enemy. You couldn't be in any sort of business for long without making enemies, a fact that would have undone Norm if he was on his own, which he very much was not. Meanwhile all eyes were on her dad.

"Prime plus four and a half," her dad said, his tone sharp, all in on showing off his memory.

"More wine, anyone?" said Mrs. Plansky, trying to move onto something else.

But no use. Matthew—and now they were leaving tennis and entering pro wrestling territory—stepped in, two against one. "And what was prime back then, Chandler?" he said.

"We could switch to red," Mrs. Plansky said. "There's a nice Pinot."

"I don't recall," her dad said. He wagged his arthritic finger at Matthew. "But something low. Prime, right? Low by definition."

Matthew didn't respond, not directly. Instead he slipped his phone from the inner pocket of his powder-blue blazer and said, "What year are we talking about specifically?"

Her dad wrinkled up his already deeply lined forehead. He actually had artillery of his own, but not heavy, just loud. If Nina had heavy artillery, Mrs. Plansky had never seen it. Perhaps, in the privacy of a bedroom, some men had. Mrs. Plansky had no desire to pursue that idea one inch further. But she was pretty sure Matthew had heavy artillery. Just because you were unsuccessful—although what right did she have to assume that about him?—didn't mean your silo was empty. She smiled at Matthew and looked him right in the eye, using mental telepathy to plant the next utterance in his mind: the Pinot sounds great.

Instead he looked her right in the eye, smiled back, and said, "I'd bet anything you know not just the year but the exact date."

Nina gave him an adoring look, meaning she was pleased that Matthew was flattering her mother. Why, Mrs. Plansky wondered, would that be? In fact, she was pretty close to knowing already, lacking only the details of the ask. She told Matthew the year, the least cumbersome of any responses she could think of.

Matthew tapped at his phone and looked up. "The prime rate in that twelve month period fluctuated between ten and ten point five. So plus four point five would be . . ." He left that sentence unfinished, sliding the phone back inside the powder-blue blazer.

"Usury!" Mrs. Plansky had told Norm, bringing him the news. He'd laughed, hugged her, and said, "It won't even be a blip in the long run." That was Norm. Meanwhile, her dad had now gone pale and looked his age and more. Mrs. Plansky rose. "I hope everyone left room for dessert."

For dessert Mrs. Plansky had thawed one of the pecan pies she'd baked around Thanksgiving, using a recipe she'd learned in Miss Terrance's ninth grade home economics class. "Now don't you girls be cloying," she'd said, brandishing a spatula. Miss Terrance had looked ancient at the time but had probably been around Nina's present age. "Not with people and not with this pie. Less sugar! More pecans! And if your parents are okay with it, two ounces of bourbon. But we won't be doing that part this morning."

"Wow," said Matthew. He had two slices, Mrs. Plansky one, her dad just a sliver and then another sliver, and Nina a bite or two. After that, Mrs. Plansky poured coffee. Matthew took a sip, sat back in his chair, shot Nina a look.

"So, Mom," Nina said, "ready to hear our idea?"

"What about me?" said her dad. "Do I get to hear it?"

"Of course, Pops," Nina said. "I'd appreciate your input."

Mrs. Plansky's dad beamed at his granddaughter. He was smitten by her and always had been. Anything she asked for he would have given. The problem was he had nothing to give—or rather nothing of what Mrs. Plansky was pretty sure Nina was looking for. But she could be wrong, and hoped she was.

"Matthew?" Nina said.

"Oh, no, you go, hon," said Matthew. "I'll jump in as needed."

Nina rubbed her hands together. She wore a ring on each, the lovely little emerald in a platinum setting from Zach and the bloated ruby in a twisted golden rope setting from Ted the first. There'd been a largish diamond from Ted the second but when Nina had taken it to Tiffany's for a sizing adjustment they'd discovered an authenticity issue. That had opened the door to other authenticity issues with Ted the second—of which Mrs. Plansky had no details—the marriage ending soon after, the divorce itself authentic and rock solid. But she was over-dwelling on the rings. What about the fact that Nina's fingernails were bitten to the quick? That was new.

"Well, Mom," Nina said, "you can fight for market share or you can make a brand-new market, right?"

"That seems . . . logical," said Mrs. Plansky.

"Great. So hold that thought. Meanwhile what's the most important human emotion there is?"

"Stupidity," said Mrs. Plansky's dad.

Matthew folded his arms across his chest and pursed his lips. Once, on the way to a meeting with a potential distributor, Norm had said, "There are always two conversations going on, the verbal and the bodily." "Oh, yeah?" Mrs. Plansky had replied, mussing his hair at the same time. The meeting was a disaster but a much bigger distributor had called out of the blue the very next day.

"Isn't stupidity more of a state of mind, Dad?" Mrs. Plansky said. "I think Nina means something else, like love, for example."

"Wow, Mom, exactly!" said Nina. "Love. That's our whole concept."

Matthew unfolded his arms, unpursed his lips, shook his head. "My, my," he said. "Astute, as advertised, and more so, Loretta, if I may call you that. Or would you prefer Mom?"

"Loretta," said Mrs. Plansky.

"Our concept," Matthew said, Mrs. Plansky realizing he was jumping in as needed, "was born in love and is also about love. That probably sounds touchy-feely but did anyone ever go broke selling touchy-feely? As for the nuts and bolts, both of us, me and Nina, feel so lucky to have found real love after one or two unsuccessful attempts."

"Or more!" said Nina.

"But," Matthew went on, "we know many others of the post-spring-chicken—" here he inserted air quotes—"generations who have given up. The existing social media structure has failed them. Yes, they can meet anyone from anywhere, but then what? It's all too unfocused. That's where our concept comes in. It's called 'Love and . . .' with three dots after the 'and.' Dot dot dot."

"Is this about the goddamn internet?" said Mrs. Plansky's dad.

"I hear you, Pops," Matthew told him. "But it's about the internet only in the way that . . ." Matthew paused. Searching for an idea? Or just trying to remember where he was in the pitch? Mrs. Plansky hadn't figured that out before Nina spoke up.

"Only in the way that Columbus was about the ships."

"Beautiful, sweetheart!" Matthew reached across the table to touch Nina's hand, a somewhat awkward gesture given the width of the table and the fact Matthew's arms were on the short side for a man of six foot four and three-quarters. "What comes after the 'and' can be just about anything, as long as it narrows the love pool down to genuine prospects. For example—" Matthew glanced around the table, his gaze falling, perhaps a little too dramatically, on the remains of the pecan pie. "Pecan pie," he went on. "Not something on our list, but why not? Love and Pecan Pie."

Nina whipped out her phone. "I'm adding it this second."

"So this is about pie?" said Mrs. Plansky's dad.

"Yes, in the sense of everyone getting their slice," said Matthew. "But broadly speaking it's about finding love in all the right places. The plan is to start with Love and the Caribbean, a place for lovers of the Caribbean who are looking for love."

"The Caribbean's one big slum when the sun don't shine," said Mrs. Plansky's dad.

Matthew blinked.

Nina said, "Pops! What a thing to say!"

Mrs. Plansky said, "Place meaning an internet site?"

"We have a dynamite developer all set to go, Mom," said Nina.

"Pending funding, of course," Matthew said.

"He says it's the best start-up concept he's ever seen," Nina said.

"Naturally he's very expensive," Matthew said. "We're looking for a supplemental two hundred and fifty K. Work starts the day we get it."

All eyes were now on Mrs. Plansky. A list of questions unspooled in her mind, none of them particularly astute to her way of thinking, but simply obvious. What kind of law had Matthew practiced? How successful had he been? How much of his own money was he putting into this? Why had he moved into Nina's house? Had he tried borrowing from a commercial lender? Was he already up to here in debt with nowhere else to go? And what about Nina? Mrs. Plansky had given her—well, no point going into the exact figure, which would have been graceless. But was it all gone? Where?

"If you're wondering about revenue," Matthew said, "it will be subscriber based with an initiation plus a monthly hit, with the prospect of advertising as well, from resorts, for example, in the case of Love and the Caribbean."

Mrs. Plansky had not been wondering about any of that, had assumed something of the kind. As for all her questions? Nah. She could afford it. And this was her daughter, a daughter with fingernails now bitten down to the quick. If you were being exploited knowingly were you actually being exploited? Mrs. Plansky did not feel exploited. She was stepping up. That was all.

"Am I an investor or a lender?" she said.

"Oh, Mom." Nina's eyes moistened.

Matthew's remained nice and dry. "A lender, if you don't mind."

"There'll be interest," Mrs. Plansky said.

"Wouldn't want it any other way," said Matthew, a grin spreading across his face. He appeared to be missing a tooth, lower right, toward the back. "You name it."

Mrs. Plansky fought off a mad impulse to say prime plus ninety-nine, and went with prime plus zero. Her dad looked shocked, but perhaps his mind was elsewhere at that moment, or he'd had a sudden inner pain.

"I love you, Mom." Nina hurried over and gave her a big kiss. Mrs. Plansky buried what she knew well: that the upcoming marriage would be the arranged kind, although not arranged by some old-world parents but by the participants themselves.

Nina was in love with love. Matthew was in love with himself. They were closing in on the last chance café. So why not together? That was the arrangement. Mrs. Plansky buried it a little deeper.

SEVEN

Nina and Matthew cleaned up, wouldn't hear of Mrs. Plansky lifting a finger. She and her dad watched the Golf Channel.

"Men hit the ball sixty percent farther than women," he said. "I bet you didn't know that."

"I did not," said Mrs. Plansky. "It seems a little high."

His voice rose. "You're not entitled to your own facts!"

Mrs. Plansky nodded. "That would be my opinion, too, Dad. All set for the ride home?"

"How about I stay here for the night? Maybe a couple of nights. Three or four. A week wouldn't be out of the question."

"That would be nice, but Nina has the guest bedroom tonight."

"And Matty?"

"Yes."

"Matty sleeps with her?"

"Come on, Dad. Do you have to use the bathroom before you go?"

"You never know."

He rolled into the bathroom, insisted on managing by himself, stayed for not very long, then came rolling out and said, "Nope."

Mrs. Plansky told Nina and Matthew not to wait up. She got her dad in the car and drove south toward Arcadia Gardens. Mrs. Plansky expected he'd fall asleep, like a baby out for a ride at that hour, but his eyes were wide open, greenish in the light from the dashboard. He was silent until the point where the road took an easterly curve and they caught a distant view of the ocean, with a cruise ship all lit up and steaming south.

"Everything's different at night," he said.

"Yes," said Mrs. Plansky.

"I tried Viagra a few times."

Mrs. Plansky made no response.

"This was after your mother passed, of course, when I started with the girlfriends. I never cheated on your mother, not one single time."

Mrs. Plansky nodded.

"Well, if you're going to get all huffy there was actually this one time. Never repeated and it wasn't my fault. A secret I'm taking to my grave."

Mrs. Plansky sped up. The road swung inland, the ocean and the cruise ship disappearing from sight. Her dad was silent all the way to the front door of Arcadia Gardens.

"I want in on the deal."

Mrs. Plansky stopped the car and turned to him. "What deal?"

"What deal? Hells bells! The Caribbean sex deal or whatever it is. The whole thing they were going on and on about."

The door to Acadia Gardens opened and an attendant came out to get him.

"Why not sleep on it?" Mrs. Plansky said. "There's no rush."

"No rush? I'm ninety-eight goddamn years old. I want in."

The attendant opened the car door. "We'll get you right in, sir."

For a moment Mrs. Plansky thought her father would explode, but he slowly deflated instead.

On the way home was an upscale-looking bar called the Green Turtle Club, set in a little clearing off the road and backing onto a canal. Mrs. Plansky had never been inside and couldn't remember the last time she'd walked into any bar alone, but now for a few moments she slowed down. Would she have actually stopped and gone inside? She never found out, because at that moment her phone made that irritating buzz she'd been meaning to change. It was Jack. She still hadn't gotten back to him? Good grief.

"Hey, Mom. Are you hard to reach or what?"

"Sorry, Jack. It's been busy. Nina's here and—" She cut off any further excuses. "But it's good to hear your voice." And that was true. The lights of the Green Turtle Club faded in the rearview mirror. "How's everything?"

"Not too bad. How's Nina?"

"Seems good. I met her new . . . fella."

"Fella, Mom? What century are we in?"

Mrs. Plansky laughed. One thing about her son, through all the ups and downs—he could make her laugh. "His name's Matthew. Or sometimes Matty. He seems very nice."

"That bad, huh?"

"Now now," said Mrs. Plansky. "I see you've been having lovely weather."

"Blue skies and seventy, day after day."

"There must be lots of action at the club."

Then came a silence, and in that silence Mrs. Plansky inferred that there was not lots of action at the club, meaning the Red Desert Tennis Center in Scottsdale, one of the biggest tennis facilities in Arizona, where Jack was director and head pro. He was an excellent tennis player—his gift obvious the very first time she'd had him on a court at the age of three—although not in the sense that Roger Federer was excellent, or any touring pro, for that matter, the top of the tennis pyramid being very steep and narrow. But Jack had been good enough to play number one singles at a D-3 program—in fact, tennis had probably gotten him into Bowdoin, an unlikely result if he'd been relying on academics alone—and it had taken him all over the world as a teaching pro, a tennis journey that had reached, in Mrs. Plansky's understanding, a happy destination where he could finally settle down and . . . and do whatever he wanted, possibly finding some woman with fewer problems than the usual women who appeared in his life and . . . and even raising his own darn family! There! She'd said it. If only to herself. But why was her mind wandering like this? She reined it in. And then all at once couldn't remember . . . couldn't remember . . . And then it came to her: blue skies! Blue skies and seventy, height of the Arizona tourist season, and a lack of action at the club? What was going on? There. She was back on track.

"Well, Mom, life's funny, you know?" Jack said.

Yes and no. Mrs. Plansky saw a safe spot to pull off the road and did so, parking beside a palm tree, its leaves very still although a breeze was blowing in from the ocean.

"I've actually resigned," Jack said. "Effective last Friday."

"Ah."

"It's not that I hated the job or anything. I've always liked working with people, Mom. You know that. But I want more. Do you see what I'm getting at?"

"Not really."

In tennis, having a temper could be good, and a number of champions have been able to channel their tempers and feed off the inner anger in the crucial moments, but most players of the temperamental type ended up letting their tempers get the best of them and falling apart. Jack had always had a temper of the unchannelable type. Mrs. Plansky could feel it awakening now, all the way from the Valley of the Sun.

"What I'm getting at is ownership," he said, speaking perhaps a little too much on the deliberate, extra-clear side. But perhaps that was just the connection. "Like you and Dad had," Jack explained. Nope, not the connection. "And an opportunity's come up. Really exciting, actually. Not tennis related at all, which is kind of refreshing, I admit it. What do you know about the cold chain?"

"Gold chain?" said Mrs. Plansky.

"Cold. Not gold. Cold chain, Mom."

"I've never heard of it."

"Think of the cold chain as a subsection of the supply chain," Jack told her.

"Okay."

"The point is that the failure of just one link on the cold chain means big trouble. And right now the weak link is freezing storage. There just isn't enough capacity. Low supply, high demand—what happens to price?"

"I think I remember," Mrs. Plansky said.

Jack laughed. "Freezing warehouses, Mom. We're going to build a thousand of them every year for the next ten years."

"Who's we?"

"My partners, Ray and Rudy, developers based in Tempe. Two very sharp dudes. You'd love them. I'm one lucky bastard just from the fact they're letting me in."

"In what?"

"This company we're forming, Mom—RJR Inc.—to build freezing warehouses. Sorry if I'm not being clear."

"To build and sell them?" said Mrs. Plansky. "Or own and operate?"

There was a pause. Was it possible the question hadn't occurred to Ray, Rudy, or Jack? Impossible, surely. "That's a real good question, Mom. We've been going back and forth about that and we'll be ironing it out going forward. Um. Speaking of going forward, this is sort of a heads-up."

"What is?"

"This call, Mom."

Another pause, this one longer than the first, which gave her mind time to drift back to a Labor Day weekend in Wellfleet, Nina seven and Jack five, when the two of them had gotten caught in a rip and begun screaming. Norm had frozen—well, not frozen, just hadn't reacted as quickly as she had: dropping the skewer of shrimp and onion rings on the sand and sprinting to the water shouting, "Don't fight it! Ride it out!" Which Nina had done, the rip dissipating about twenty yards out and leaving her bobbing in the swell, but Jack had fought the rip and gone under. Mrs. Plansky had plunged in, grabbed him, yanked him to the surface, and swum him to safety, swimming on her back with Jack facing up on her chest, and one of her hands on his chest. How his little heart had beat! So quick, like a hummingbird's. Her hand could feel it now.

"The thing is," Jack was saying.

Uh-oh. Had she missed something? Mrs. Plansky pressed the phone to her ear.

"I may have . . . what's that British expression? Put my foot wrong. I was trying to line up the ducks, that's all. But I may have done things in the wrong order. If so, my bad."

"I don't understand," Mrs. Plansky said.

"Well, the thing is, I . . . have you heard from Connie Malhouf?"

"Not recently. Why?"

Connie Malhouf, practicing in Rhode Island, was Mrs. Plansky's lawyer.

"Hmm. I kind of thought she might get in touch with you. The thing is, Mom, I got the feeling Connie was a bit pissed at me."

Mrs. Plansky was lost. "I wasn't aware you knew her."

"We met at Fenway Park."

"Fenway—But that was so long ago. Weren't you in high school?"

"College actually. I snagged that foul ball and gave it to Jordan."

"Jordan?"

"Connie's son, Mom. He was about ten."

"I know who Jord—" Mrs. Plansky cut herself off. The point was Jack remembered his name after all these years. He was good with people, no doubt about it. Other than that, there was no surety to be had at the moment.

"Apparently Jordan's in Singapore now, doing something with container ships," Jack said. "Connie mentioned that before our conversation went a bit south, or let's say southerly." He laughed, a little self-congratulatory heh-heh that was new. Oh, how Mrs. Plansky hated to put it in those terms. The phone really was a dangerous invention. We were meant to see the people we were talking to. What if there wasn't a trace of anything self-congratulatory on Jack's face at the moment? She told herself to rein in the judgmental side and pronto. But it balked.

"A bit south?" Mrs. Plansky said.

"Although . . . maybe since she hasn't called you, I—I might be overthinking this."

"Jack? Out with it, if you don't mind."

Then came a big intake of breath. "The rationale being it was a sort of homework call."

"Homework for what assignment?"

"Ah, Christ, Mom. Do you have to be so smart?"

"That won't work," said Mrs. Plansky.

"Oh, do I know that."

"I'm listening."

"Okay, okay. Concerning prospective financing—of the creative type—for RJR Inc., I wanted to sound you out about certain things. In retrospect I take Connie's point. I should have gone directly to you. And never listened to Rudy."

"Rudy?"

"The first *R,* Mom. Some guys have all these subtle moves— Ray's like that—and some have just one, but it's killer. That's Rudy."

Mrs. Plansky took a deep breath of her own. "And what was Rudy's advice?"

"To find out all I could before talking to you."

"About what?"

"Your will, Mom."

Now Mrs. Plansky's heart was the one beating way too fast— maybe not like a hummingbird but enough to remind her of something she actually never thought about, namely her age.

"Ray knows a guy—a lender, a reputable lender—who has a service for borrowing against an eventual inheritance. Uh, well, I know of course what you said after Dad passed, that everything would go equally to your descendants, which is so nice of you. But

Ray pointed out I was operating under this assumption that the descendants were me and Nina, when in fact there's also Emma and Will. Which was how come I wanted to—"

Mrs. Plansky—or rather her voice, operating on its own—interrupted. "I get it."

She was not an interrupter. Neither of them spoke for what might have been a full minute. A car sped by and out an open window came spinning an empty nip, sparkling for a moment in someone's headlights.

"I'm sorry, Mom. Connie wouldn't discuss it anyway. A big mistake on my part. It won't happen again. I mean nothing like it will ever . . ."

What Mrs. Plansky wanted to do now was to sit down at the kitchen table—not the kitchen table in the condo, or even the one at 3 Pelican Way, but the old original one back in Rhode Island—and hash this out with Norm.

"How much money are we talking about?" she said.

Jack's voice brightened right away. "Seven hundred and fifty K would be nice but even half a mil would do."

From out in the swamp—Mrs. Plansky had assumed the open country beyond the palm tree she'd parked under was a golf course, but now realized what it actually was—came a harsh animal cry.

"Why don't you fly out here?" she said. "This isn't a phone conversation."

"Sure, Mom. Thanks." For a not-so-good second or two she thought he was about to ask for the fare. Instead he said, "Love you."

Jack was her son. She could afford what he was asking. But Ray and Rudy were not her sons. Thank God, by the way. And wasn't Jack's call to Connie a sneaky sort of move? She didn't want to put that label on it but she somehow felt Norm nodding yes, sneaky for sure, like he was following along in her thoughts. Therefore, a bit of a conundrum.

"Love you, too," Mrs. Plansky said. Which she did, so much so that just saying the words diminished all her doubts.

Twenty minutes later she was back at her condo. It was quiet, Nina and Matthew upstairs in the guest bedroom. Mrs. Plansky thought about getting a goldfish, even considered a name or two, such as Goldie and Flash. Meanwhile she was on the move from room to room, switching off the lights. At the bar she found herself standing in front of the drink shelf. Why? Because that might be a good home for Goldie's bowl? Plausible enough. She reached for the bottle of Norm's bourbon, untouched since their last evening drink together. Mrs. Plansky opened it, sniffed, and then—not bothering with a glass!—took a way too big swig right from the bottle, like some sorority girl on a night that would not end well.

She went to bed.

EIGHT

Mrs. Plansky had lain in her bed for some time, trying various positions—back, side, front, other side—when it hit her that she hadn't brushed her teeth. Going to bed with teeth unbrushed? When had that last happened, if ever? She entertained herself with a silly thought—the idea of calling out, "Julio! Julio! Teeth brushing assistance!"—but still, this was bad. The proper course of action was obvious. Get up, two minutes of Sonicare, back in the sack with a clear conscience, but her body refused to cooperate, or had simply turned to lead. She lay there, the taste of Norm's favorite bourbon on her tongue. Gradually the bourbon taste began to change, slowly becoming the taste of Norm himself. Night differed from day, all right. Hadn't someone mentioned that, maybe even recently? Mrs. Plansky tried to think who but the answer wouldn't come. Instead she shut down all cogitation and luxuriated in the taste of Norm.

She heard footsteps from upstairs, heavier than Nina's. Then came the sound of the upstairs toilet flushing, followed by return footsteps and silence, all that adding up to one of those night time journeys men of a certain age went on. But why go on about Matthew? Was there something creepy about older men marrying much younger women? There was plenty of it—Aristotle Onassis, Hugh Hefner, Larry King, Clint Eastwood—and no one seemed to mind. But it seemed creepy to Mrs. Plansky, although not in the case of Clint Eastwood.

Annette Franco's husband, Bob—they lived in the condo two over from her—had died six months ago and she was already dating a guy Mrs. Plansky knew vaguely from the tennis club. His service motion was like some Rube Goldberg device. Was he Rube Goldbergy in more intimate activities? Oh, for God's sake! Enough! And as for the six months—so what? The clock was ticking, that was all. Maybe sex made more sense than marriage—or even dating—in old age. Wasn't courtship for the young? Certainly true in nature, with ducks, for example. Mrs. Plansky tried to feel what it would be like to be pregnant, right now, in this present body, and couldn't do it. She went back to the taste of Norm on her tongue. He was gone. Mrs. Plansky turned over, got into the most comfortable position she knew—a sort of twisted *K*—and fell into a sleep that was stormy at first and then quieted down.

Her phone was ringing, and a dream took shape around the sound, a dream in which she was at the club, playing Annette Franco's boyfriend, and beating the crap out of him. Then her conscious mind woke to the fact that her actual unimaginary phone was doing the ringing. Mrs. Plansky reached for it on the bedside table, fumbling and almost knocking it off. The room was very dark, the screen on her phone kind of blurry, or possibly that was the fault of her eyes. She rubbed them with the back of her free hand and now could make out the ID scrolling across the screen: Will.

Will. In the middle of the night.

"Hello?" she said.

"Yo."

A bad connection, static and muffled at the same time. It sounded like he'd said yo, but it might have been the end of hello. Mrs. Plansky pictured one of those Colorado blizzards. It was earlier out there, of course, maybe still party time for the lift line guys and other staff on the mountain. She was pretty good at guessing what might be coming next: he was finally thanking her for the Christmas check.

"Hello?" she said again.

"Yo. It's me, Grandma, Will. Your grandson, Will."

Right away she knew he didn't sound good, his voice higher than normal, maybe nervous about something, although since they hadn't spoken in some time she couldn't be sure.

"I'm aware of the relationship," she said, with a little laugh, hoping to settle the kid down a bit. Maybe this wasn't about Christmas at all, but perhaps some problem. A problem with Nina, for example, with Matthew as the root cause? Ah-ha.

A pause, and then Will said, "Oh, yes, the relationship. Grandparent and grandchild."

This was new: a kind of dry, offbeat, humor. But the connection was still bad. "Will? Try moving a bit."

"Moving? You wish—want me to move?"

"The connection's bad. Maybe stand somewhere else."

"The connection? Right, right. Very good. I will step over here like this. How is—how's the connection now, Grandma?"

"Maybe a little better."

Will lowered his voice. The connection was so bad he hardly sounded like himself. "The truth is, Grandma, I can't move far right now in this situation."

"What situation?"

"A . . . problem. A dw—a DUI. I am in a DUI situation."

Mrs. Plansky sat up. "Are you all right? Are you hurt?"

"Hurt? Oh, no, not hurt, not at all hurt."

"Maybe I should let you speak to your mom. She's here."

"My . . . what?"

"Your mom. She came for dinner and they're staying overnight. She and Matthew. I'll go wake her. Hang on."

"No! I mean no, please. No."

"You don't . . ."

"No, please don't. I—I wish, want to speak to you, Grandma."

Pretty clear what was going on. The mention of Matthew had done it. Will had to know where he stood with the new beau.

"I'm so sorry for this, Grandma, but I have no one else for help. To . . . to turn to. The police have seized my car and for getting it back and for bail I need nine thousand seven hundred and twenty-six dollars and eighteen cents. It's only temporary, Grandma. The money comes right back when I go to the court next month."

Mrs. Plansky found that she was on her feet, her heart beating way too fast. Her mind was in turmoil. She didn't know what to say or do. She didn't feel like her real self.

"I'm sorry, Grandma." Will lowered his voice even more. "There are bad people in this cell. I'm afraid."

"Let me speak to whoever's in charge," Mrs. Plansky said.

"In charge?"

"A policeman, a deputy, someone like that."

"But . . . but they do not know about the phone. They will seize it also. Too. They will seize it, too!"

The poor kid was terrified—although not at all drunk, Colorado possibly having one of those extra-low blood alcohol limits—could barely string a few words together. Some problems were objectively terrifying and maybe not solvable. This was not that kind. It was solvable with money, and not really a lot, most of it even coming back when Will appeared in court, minus a fine and some inevitable surcharges.

"It's going to be all right, Will. Try to stay calm. What was that figure again?"

"Figure?"

"The amount—the car, bail, all that."

"Ah. Yes. For sure. The figure is nine thousand seven hundred and twenty-six dollars and eighteen cents."

At one time—and not so long ago—Mrs. Plansky could hear a number like that—and much more complicated ones—and see them clear in her mind, as though chalked on a blackboard. Those days seemed to be over. "We'll round it off," she said.

"Round it off?"

"To ten thousand. We can sort out the details later. How do I get it to the jail?"

"The jail?"

"Or the police station. How do I get it to you?"

"Oh, not the police station, Grandma. I do not trust these people. It should come to me."

"How?"

"The best system is to send to my Safemo account."

"What's Safemo?"

"Like Venmo or PayPal but better."

Mrs. Plansky had heard those names but knew nothing about them. "Better how?"

"Much. Much better."

"But in what way, Will? That's what I'm asking."

"Oh, I see," said Will. "Safer. Faster. Both of them. Safer and faster. The whole transaction is encrypted and disappears immediately."

"I don't understand."

"Like Snapchat, Grandma. Or WhatsApp, all of them. Totally private for a few seconds and then gone forever."

Mrs. Plansky felt a bit dizzy. She sat on the edge of the bed.

"Grandma?"

"I'm here."

There was a pause and then Will said, "I forgot to mention! Safemo gives one percent of profits to saving the whales!"

Mrs. Plansky's mind—like a dog scenting something it liked—wanted to pull her away to memories of the whale watch she and Norm had gone on, the one where—But she didn't let it, and getting herself back on firmer ground, said, "How do they make a profit?"

"Advertising, Grandma. They take nothing from the . . . the transaction."

Advertising. She should have known. Mrs. Plansky knew all

about it from the other side, having run Plansky and Company's advertising all by herself in the early years. "All right," she said. "What are the details?"

"Details?"

"For sending you the funds."

"Funds?"

"Money, Will."

"Oh, thank you, Grandma, thank you. All you need to do is give me the bank routing number and account number."

Mrs. Plansky rose, felt for her purse on the bedside table, groped inside for her checkbook, took it into the bathroom.

"Grandma?" Will's voice was even quieter now, and sounded shaky.

"It's all right. Hang on." She switched on the overhead light, blinked a few times until her eyes adjusted. Then she said, "Palm Coast Bank and Trust," and read him the numbers. "Are you writing this down?"

"Oh, yes, Grandma. On my phone."

"On your phone?"

"Into my Safemo account. And now it just asks for the password."

"What password?"

"For the account, Grandma. It will encrypt and vanish right away, immediately, tout de suite."

Tout de suite? Yes, he was developing a sense of humor, and somehow, even out of school, getting at least a bit of an education: his French accent sounded pretty darn good. She gave him the password, the same one she used for most things: !NorManConQuest!

"And presto, Grandma. Already vanished forever. Thank you, Grandma!"

"That's it?"

"Finito!"

"Will? Call me as soon as you're out."

"Out?"

"Of jail."

"Oh, yes. The moment I am free. Here . . . here is com . . . here comes the cop."

"Okay, I'll let you go. Love you, Will."

"I . . . I love you, Grandma."

Click.

Looking up, Mrs. Plansky caught her reflection in the mirror. She looked a mess, ancient and distraught. But ten minutes later—Mrs. Plansky back in bed and wide awake—her phone buzzed.

"I am free, Grandma, out on the street, like a bird."

The connection was clearer this time. He really was growing up to be quite funny. Mrs. Plansky felt better at once. "Good news. Stay in touch."

"Yes, for sure."

"And you'd better get a lawyer."

"Oh?"

"To represent you in court."

"Excellent idea, Grandma. Good night."

"Good night."

Mrs. Plansky tossed and turned for a while, then got into the twisted K and fell asleep. When she awoke and drew the curtains midmorning—or even later!—daylight came streaming in. She checked the time: eleven fifteen. Eleven fifteen? When had she last slept in until eleven fifteen, or even past six thirty? Mrs. Plansky showered, dressed, made herself presentable, tried not to look sheepish, opened her bedroom door, and emerged.

But Nina and Matthew were already gone. A note was propped up beside the coffeepot.

Mom, thanks for everything. It was so lovely to see you. You're such a rock for the whole family—like Gibraltar, Matthew says! (We'll be in touch re the loan thingy, no rush.) Lots and lots of love, Nina.

And, in another hand: *and Matty.*

NINE

Uncle Dragomir's pats on the back were more like slaps or even blows, although Dinu did not know what normal back pats felt like, having never before gotten any in his life. All he did know was that these heavy-handed back pats felt great. He felt great in general, couldn't recall ever feeling like this. They sat in the private VIP lounge on the topmost level of Club Presto, where Dinu had never been before: Dinu, Uncle Dragomir, Uncle Dragomir's Polish girlfriend and also his Moldovan girlfriend—but not his wife, Aunt Simone, who often traveled in the West—Romeo, Timbo the bouncer, a Russian businessman who seemed to know Uncle Dragomir quite well, the Russian businessman's bodyguard, and the Russian businessman's date for the evening, a beautiful young woman whose name Dinu didn't know, although he was pretty sure he'd seen her face on the billboard opposite the train station, advertising one of the local brands of toothpaste.

Tassa entered with more champagne on a tray, delicious Carpathian champagne that made Dinu's body tingle. She looked right into his eyes as she filled his glass.

"Have you done your homework?" he said, an inane remark and also making no sense, since they were on vacation. But Tassa seemed to find it very funny.

"Fist bump," she said, raising her free hand. They fist bumped. Was it possible Tassa had made the touching part of the fist bump linger somehow, or was it just his imagination? Even if it was, how nice to have the imagination imagining good things. Until now, Dinu's imagination had mostly worked the other way.

"You see?" Uncle Dragomir said to the Russian businessman. "The little prick has a way with women, young, old, makes no difference."

The Russian businessman said something in Russian. Dinu knew no Russian, and that was fine with him. English—American English—was the only language that interested him, not excepting his own. He did wish that Uncle Dragomir hadn't called him a little prick. Uncle Dragomir had meant no harm. It was just his way, but still. Dinu took a gulp of champagne and forgot all about it.

Marius, the other bouncer, entered the VIP lounge, bringing Professor Bogdan.

"Hello there, Professor," said Uncle Dragomir. "Thanks for joining us. Is this your first time in the VIP lounge?" He snapped his fingers. Tassa hurried over with champagne for the professor.

Professor Bogdan glanced around—spilling a bit of champagne on the lapel of his tweed jacket, a baggy jacket frayed at the cuffs—his gaze pausing over the women in their tight party dresses and then moving quickly on. No one smiled or waved. The professor, Dinu realized, didn't have a way with women, or possibly with men, either.

"First time in your club, period," Professor Bogdan said.

"But not the last!" said Uncle Dragomir. "Timbo, a gift card for the professor."

"Ten euros or twenty?" said Timbo.

"Fifty! The professor is a first-class teacher of English and we are a first-class business."

Timbo gave Bogdan a gift card. The professor put on his eyeglasses and studied it. Everyone laughed. The professor's cheeks turned pink.

Uncle Dragomir rose. "And now, Professor, we put you to work, yes?"

"That's why I'm here," Bogdan said.

Uncle Dragomir did not like that remark. His nostrils widened momentarily, like a horse. Dinu knew that sign and several others, but as for exactly what had displeased him he had no clue.

Behind a curtain of gold streamers at the back of the VIP lounge was a small alcove where Uncle Dragomir, Romeo, the professor, and Dinu squeezed together at a round table, all of them wearing earbuds. Romeo did something with his phone and the sound of another phone, a phone with a noisy connection, came through the earbuds.

"Hello?" said an American woman.

And then came Dinu's own voice: "Yo."

Professor Bogdan's eyebrows rose, like he was surprised and maybe even impressed. They all listened for a while. Then Uncle Dragomir, who had very little English, took out his earbuds, sat back, and sipped champagne, his heavy-lidded eyes half closed like he was deep in thought. For some reason, Dinu, too, wanted to remove his earbuds, to stop listening. That happened first around the point in the conversation where Grandma said, "Are you all right? Are you hurt?" and then a few more times. But Dinu kept his earbuds in. Wasn't this an assignment, another part of the job?

Okay, I'll let you go. Love you, Will.

I . . . I love you, Grandma.

That was the end of the recording. The second call—the brief one when he'd reassured Grandma that he was back out on the street— was not in the script and hadn't been recorded. He'd made it on a burner phone Romeo had given him when the two of them were alone in the office. Why? Romeo had asked that very question. Dinu actually hadn't known, but he'd replied, Because I'm not finished being Will. To which Romeo had nodded like that made sense and said, Cool, in English, so maybe that was in fact the reason.

Dinu, Romeo, and Professor Bogdan removed their earbuds. Bogdan gazed at Dinu. Everyone else's eyes were on the professor.

"Well?" Uncle Dragomir said.

Bogdan licked his lips. "I—I would say fascinating. I've never heard anything quite like it."

Uncle Dragomir waved that away with his meaty hand. "I'm not asking for some pussy . . ." He turned to Romeo. "What's the word I'm looking for?"

"Critique," said Romeo.

"I don't want your pussy critique," Uncle Dragomir went on. "I'm asking how he did."

"Dinu?"

"Who else?"

"Dinu, then. In what sense are you asking?"

"In the sense of his English, moron. Why else do I pay you?"

The professor's cheeks pinkened again. "His English was good. Remarkably good." Bogdan looked at Dinu, perhaps not quite in the eye. "You've improved a lot," he said in English.

"Cool," said Dinu.

"What was that?" said Uncle Dragomir. "What did you tell him?"

"Just that he improved."

Uncle Dragomir grunted. He got out a pack of cigarettes, took one for himself, and offered one to Bogdan. Bogdan took it. Uncle Dragomir leaned forward with a light. For a moment their faces were very close. In Dinu's eyes at that moment they were almost like two different species of men.

"Any mistakes?" Uncle Dragomir said, sitting back.

Bogdan took a deep drag, let it out slowly, and seemed to relax a bit. "Sure, but Americans make little mistakes in grammar all the time. They have the Latinate underpinnings like us, but mixed in is a whole other stream of Anglo-Saxon, which is what you hear in everyday—"

"Did I ask for a lecture?" Uncle Dragomir said. "Was he believable?"

"Certainly, just judging from the results alone."

Uncle Dragomir's nostrils widened. Bogdan shrank back. "The

results—of which you know nothing—are not your concern. Understood?"

"Oh, yes."

"Completely understood in all possibilities?"

"One hundred percent."

"Then we have no problems and nothing but smooth roads
ahead. Do they have smooth roads in America, Professor?"

"The smoothest, and so many. President Eisenhower built a
whole interstate system that . . ." This time he stopped himself. "As
for Dinu, he was not only believable but . . ." He glanced at Dinu,
again not quite meeting his gaze. "Talented," he went on.

"Talented? The kid has talent?"

"A talent for improvising."

"Explain."

"For quick reactions. For thinking on his feet. There were moments in the conversation, regarded strictly as a narrative without any moral—regarded strictly as a narrative, where the process
threatened to take a turn that might have frustrated your—that you
might not have liked, but Dinu managed to steer things right. The
part about saving the whales? You could almost say brilliant."

Uncle Dragomir gave Dinu a long look. "That is all, Professor."

Bogdan rose. Uncle Dragomir handed him an envelope.

"Thank you," said the professor.

"You will be pleased," said Uncle Dragomir.

"Thank you, thank you."

Bogdan went out through the golden streamers.

"That will be all for you as well, Romeo," Uncle Dragomir said.

"Do I get an envelope?" Romeo said.

Uncle Dragomir laughed a huge happy laugh with no trace of
meanness in it. "You get a kick in the ass."

Romeo laughed, too, although his laughter ended abruptly the
second he passed through the golden streamers.

Uncle Dragomir took out his cigarettes, held the pack for Dinu
to take one.

"No, thanks."

"You don't smoke?"

"No, Uncle."

"What about cannabis? I have some."

"No, thanks."

"Everyone your age smokes cannabis."

"I have asthma."

"Pussy. Drink your champagne."

Dinu sipped his champagne. His asthma hadn't bothered him for a long time, like it had gone to sleep, but all at once he felt it stirring.

"Your father would have been proud," Uncle Dragomir said.

"You think so?"

They'd never discussed Dinu's father, Uncle Dragomir's younger brother who'd died when Dinu was very young.

"Sure," said Uncle Dragomir. "Every father wants a son with talent. He was no different." Uncle Dragomir waved his cigarette at Dinu. "A very strong guy, your dad. A bull. Maybe you'll have a growth spurt." Uncle Dragomir picked up his champagne glass, found it empty, drank from the bottle instead. He wiped his mouth with the back of his hand. "Rule number one in this country, Dinu—don't get involved in politics."

"What about other countries?"

"Same thing. We're all human. There is only one thing to do with politicians. Can you guess what that is?"

Supply them with women. That was Dinu's only idea, based on seeing several politicians ushered into the Playroom, an off-limits part of Club Presto.

"No," he said.

Uncle Dragomir leaned forward. "We pay them to leave us alone. That's it. Finito." He took out an envelope. "Keep this up and there will be more, lots more."

"Lots more . . . ah, um?"

"Money, Mr. Talent. What else is this about? First perform. Then money. Save the whales, you little shit."

Dinu took the envelope.

"And I've set you up with Dr. Vizi. Go see him."

"Who's Dr. Vizi?"

"The dentist. You lost a tooth. Did you forget?"

Dr. Vizi's office turned out to be in the private clinic two blocks from Dinu's flat. They even had their own ambulance with the name of the clinic on it, parked out front. Dinu had never been in a private clinic before, private clinics reserved for rich people and foreigners, but as he rode up in the elevator—a spotless, silent elevator with mirrored walls and a mirrored ceiling, an elevator unlike any he'd ever been in, his mind paused on the fact that, thanks to Romeo, he was secretly sharing their Wi-Fi. Once in English class Professor Bogdan had said, "All the world's a stage," maybe demonstrating something about contractions, and some wiseass student had said, "Then who is directing the play?" To which the professor had answered, "What if no one is?" A remark that had aroused no interest, so he'd returned to the grammar lesson. But now, his mind on the Wi-Fi situation, Dinu thought: *me, I am directing.* At least on this little stage of the Wi-Fi play. But what about on the big stages of life? Were there secret directors? Like Uncle Dragomir, for example?

The elevator door opened and Dinu stepped out, not into a corridor, as he'd expected, but directly into Dr. Vizi's waiting room, large and softly lit, more like a living room in an American movie. There was only one other patient, a man with longish dark hair and a closely trimmed white beard, leafing through a magazine. He glanced up at Dinu, his eyes a very pale blue, and went back to reading. Dinu approached the receptionist, sitting not behind some glass wall, but at a tidy desk in the open.

"Dinu Tiriac," he said.

The woman checked her screen. "Referred by Mr. Dragomir Tiriac?"

"Yes," said Dinu. From the corner of his eye he saw the other patient look up again, this time not so casually, those pale blue eyes intelligent, unreadable.

The woman pressed a button on her desk. A door on the far wall slid open. "Second left," she said.

Dinu went through the doorway. The door closed behind him but somehow he still felt that pale blue gaze on his back.

When he left two hours later with a brand-new state-of-the-art tooth in place—the exact same shade as his other teeth, in the top 10 percent on the whiteness scale, according to Dr. Vizi, and all of this for free!—the man with the closely trimmed white beard was gone. Dr. Vizi had also given him a bottle of pills to take away the pain. Dinu had no pain, but in the elevator going down he swallowed one dry anyway, to enjoy the buzz on his walk home. On the way he noticed a red leather belt in the window of a women's clothing shop. He bought it as a present for his mother—expensive, yes, yet now affordable—but she was asleep on the couch, her breath alcoholic. Dinu flushed Dr. Vizi's pills down the toilet.

TEN

Mrs. Plansky, eating breakfast—toast, hard-boiled egg, coffee—glanced at Nina's note—*like Gibraltar, Matthew says!* She and Norm had actually visited Gibraltar once, on a day trip from Malaga. They'd had lunch at a pub called the Sir Winston. "How many beers do you have to drink before this feels like the real thing?" Norm had asked. "One, we could run an experiment," Mrs. Plansky had said. "Or two, we could zip on back to Spain." They'd flipped a coin. Running an experiment had won. They'd downed a couple of pints each, found the Sir Winston growing more unreal, an unexpected result. Also unexpected was Norm's idea to rent a room right away—at the Admiral Nelson Inn, across the square—just for the afternoon. Mrs. Plansky was drifting into something of a reverie concerning the events of that afternoon at the Admiral Nelson when she got a phone call.

"Loretta? It's Melanie, from the club."

Mrs. Plansky didn't quite let go of the admiral immediately.

"We played the other day," Melanie said.

"Of course. Just . . . just a bit of distraction."

"Is this a bad time?"

"Not at all."

"Sorry for the late notice. Pindar—that's my boyfriend—and I are supposed to be playing mixed at one with Kev Dinardo—do you know Kev?"

"No."

"He's another new member, like me, has a nice game. Anyway, his cousin from Ponte Vedra was supposed to be the fourth but she can't make it and I was wondering—"

"Sure," said Mrs. Plansky, checking the time. It was what she needed.

Kev Dinardo—about her own age, medium size, in decent shape, still pretty light on his feet—turned out to be one of those players who enjoyed his every minute on the court and did his best to make it enjoyable for everyone else, handing out compliments—

"That one-handed backhand of yours, Loretta! Best I've seen since Steffi Graf."

"Right," said Mrs. Plansky.

—and deprecatory of his own game, but not in the fishing for reassurance way. On top of that he, like Norm, was a lefty, and Mrs. Plansky liked having a lefty partner. Plus he was a fine player, with a reliable slice serve he seemed to be able to place wherever he wanted, and put-away volleys. And although almost always in mixed the man takes the ad court, he insisted it was Mrs. Plansky's—"your crosscourt backhand will set me up real nice, I'll hardly have to move." In short, they were what you wanted in doubles, a team better than the sum of its parts. They won 6–4, 6–2, even with easing up toward the end.

"The most fun drubbing of my life," said Melanie, although Pindar, even younger than she was, with a big serve and a big forehand, didn't look as happy about it. "Let's do it again."

Kev turned to Mrs. Plansky, an expectant look on his face, a rather nice face, although not so easy to put your finger on why. Maybe she would give some thought to it.

"Sounds good," she said.

"Okay with you if we exchange phone numbers?" he said. "In the interest of logistics?"

"Sure," Mrs. Plansky said.

He took out his phone.

"Mine's . . ." she began, but the darn number, her own darn number, wouldn't come to her.

"Tell me about it," Kev said. "Happens to me all the time. It's because no one has to memorize anything anymore. Not only can't I remember my passwords, I can't even remember where I've written them down."

Mrs. Plansky, rummaging through her tennis bag, laughed. She had no need to write down passwords, having pretty much just the one— !NorManConQuest!—surely unforgettable for the rest of her life. Meanwhile, no phone in her tennis bag. "Must have left it in the car."

He handed her a card. "You can call me and then my phone will do the memorizing and I won't have to lift a mental finger."

"Okay," she said, and headed toward the parking lot. Her number came to her as she opened her car door, but the phone itself was not there. All at once her memory switched on to full power—its former full power—and she pictured it on her bedside table, where she'd put it after talking to Will. She realized it was wrong to keep this secret from Nina. First, she'd have to let Will know. That was the right course of action. But what about the turmoil this was going to cause, even raising the possibility of Nina getting boxed into the position of having to choose between her son and her fiancé or whatever the hell he was. Could the wrong way sometimes be the right way in some grander scheme of things? She considered sleeping on the problem but it wasn't even noon. Mrs. Plansky started the car, only then glancing at the card in her hand.

KEV DINARDO, it read. No photo of him, just a sketch, with only a few lines, suggesting a sailboat. There was also his phone number and this: RETIRED FROM PAYING WORK, BUT NOTHING ELSE. She just sat there in the idling car for a moment, feeling a bit strange, as though in her own house but coming upon a door not previously there.

Mrs. Plansky entered her bedroom, and there on the bedside table lay her phone, just as she'd thought. At that moment she had a realization about Norm. He'd been a lefty not just physically, but in every other way—mentally, emotionally, spiritually. So, despite the fact that he was gone, he seemed to be capable of new self-presentations, the dead taking on a life of their own.

She picked up the phone and saw that Will had left a message: *"Hey, Grandma, it's Will. I've been meaning to say thanks for the Christmas present. So generous of you! And, um, hope you're well. Take care. Bye."*

Mrs. Plansky smiled and shook her head. No mention of last night's drama. How nice to be young—at least young of a certain type—and carefree, and also so quick to revert to the carefree reset position. He sounded so much better than he had less than what—twelve hours ago?—his voice deeper, all tension gone. But listening to the message resurrected the problem of Nina and whether to keep her in the dark. The fact that Will sounded so good seemed to support closing the book and moving on. Except in a big picture way—

The phone buzzed and the caller's name scrolled across the screen: Palm Coast Bank and Trust.

"Loretta Plansky speaking."

"Hi, Mrs. Plansky. Allison Suarez calling. Assistant manager at the bank."

"Yes, of course. Hi, Allison."

"I was just wondering if you wanted me to close out your account. Are you moving or something like that? I hope it's not something about our service."

"No, I'm not moving. Or closing the account. Why would you think I'd want to do that?"

"Sorry if I've gotten ahead of myself. It's just that you drew the account down to zero last night, so I just wondered, you being such an excellent customer and—"

"I what?"

"Drew down the account. To zero, from a balance of . . . let me see . . . um, sixty-eight thousand, three hundred dollars and twenty-one cents."

"Oh, my goodness, no," Mrs. Plansky said. "There's been a mistake—I only withdrew ten thousand. Ten thousand even. Please check again."

Allison Suarez was silent but Mrs. Plansky could hear her fingers tapping on a keyboard. "I don't see anything relating to the figure you mention, ten thousand."

"But that was the amount. I sent it to my grandson and he assured me he'd received it. Ten thousand, even."

"Sent it how?" said Allison.

For a moment the name wouldn't come to her. Why now, of all times? But then something in her mind—call it her old self—rose to the occasion. "Safemo," she said. "We used Safemo."

"Safemo?"

"He said it was the best."

Another silence. "Mrs. Plansky? Can I get back to you on this?"

"Yes, please. I'll be right here."

Throughout her career, Mrs. Plansky—unlike Norm—had been good at waiting, meaning she'd endured the common periods of suspense in business—waiting to hear if you snagged the bank loan, won the big order, avoided a lawsuit from a rival—without getting too wound up inside. But now, pacing back and forth, feeling a bit light-headed, her heart beating too fast, she was wound up, almost the way she'd been while waiting for some of Norm's test results. There'd been no pacing then, or course, no outward sign at all—how would that have helped him? But now there was no one to help. Withdrew the account to zero? That was crazy. How on earth—

"Enough," Mrs. Plansky said aloud. Enough with the passivity. She grabbed the phone and called Will.

"Hey, Grandma."

"Will, I—"

"Did you get my message?"

"Message? Yes, yes, I did. Thanks. I mean you're welcome. But what I actually want to talk about is last night."

"Last night?"

"That whole incident."

"Incident?"

"Will? Did I wake you? Please stop answering questions with questions. Did you receive the money?"

His voice got gentle. "Grandma? Are you all right?" He laughed a very small laugh. "More questions, sorry. But yes, I got the check. That's why I left the message. I'm very grateful. I should have been more timely. Sorry."

"Check?" said Mrs. Plansky. "There was no check."

"Sure there was, Grandma. The Christmas check—five hundred dollars, so generous. And how you wrote 'merry, merry' on the memo line. That was very—"

"Will! This isn't about the Christmas check. I'm talking about the DUI, the arrest, the bail money, the ten thousand dollars, Safemo, all the rest of it."

"Huh?" said Will.

Mrs. Plansky repeated the whole thing, slowly and carefully.

There was a slight pause and then: "Grandma? Are you okay?"

"Stop asking me that. Please, Will. Just, just tell me you received the ten-thousand-dollar transfer last night. And if it somehow turned out to be more than that—much more—that's all right. Although why you wouldn't have—but it's all right. It can all be fixed, easily fixed. I just need to know so I can start the ball rolling."

"Jeez, I don't understand. I don't understand what you're saying. It doesn't make any sense. I apologize but it just doesn't."

"Look, Will, are you in some sort of trouble you didn't tell me about last night? Bigger than the DUI? Or . . . or maybe you can't speak freely right now. Ah. Is that it? If that's the case, and you can't speak freely," she lowered her voice, "give some sign—like clearing your throat, for example."

Mrs. Plansky listened, listened hard, for the sound of Will clearing his throat. She heard nothing.

Finally he spoke. "Grandma? Have you talked to Mom recently?"

"Of course. She was here last night when you called. I asked if you wanted to speak to her and you said no."

"Oh, boy," he said. "Oh, boy."

"Will?"

"I didn't call you last night, Grandma."

"But . . . but you most certainly did." Mrs. Plansky sat down on the edge of the bed, sat down hard, her normally sturdy legs failing her.

"No," Will said. "I called this morning to thank you for the check. I left a message. We didn't talk, not then and not last night. This is the first time we've talked in I don't know how long."

Mrs. Plansky's mind was operating at a furious speed but moving in the same circle, over and over.

"Grandma? Is Mom still there? Can I speak to her?"

"Mom?"

"My mom. Nina."

"Nina? No. They left before I got up. I never sleep in but . . ." Mrs. Plansky caught herself rambling. This was ridiculous. There had to be some explanation, like . . . like Will had taken some sort of drug last night. Hadn't she been reading just recently about a new drug, popular with teenagers, that led to a pleasant delirium of some sort but interfered with short-term memory? She didn't want to accuse him, but was there some decent way of approaching the subject? "I'm getting a little worried about you, Will."

"You're worried about me?"

"Are you feeling all right? Your usual normal self?"

"I'm fine. Except for now I'm worried about you."

"I'm fine, too, darn it!" Then, in a calmer tone, Mrs. Plansky added, "Except for this. I don't get what you're up to. I don't get it at all."

"Grandma! I'm not up to anything. I don't know what to tell you. Has, um, have any of your medications changed?"

Medications? She wasn't on any stupid medications. Well, not strictly true, but she definitely wasn't on any medications that would affect her mental—And then she got what he was suggesting, that she was imagining or fantasizing or hallucinating the whole thing—phone call, DUI, money transfer.

"Will? Are you listening?"

"Yes."

"I'm not making this up. I'm telling you exactly what happened. So whatever the slipup is it's happening on your . . ." At that moment the implication of Will asking to speak to Nina just now began to unfold in her mind. How could he do that without revealing the whole story of his arrest, the very thing he'd wanted so badly to keep from her, badly enough to wake his grandmother in the middle of the night? Therefore the very fact that a conversation with Nina was fine with him now meant . . . oh, God. Another furious circle got going in her mind, but just then she saw a way out, a path forward. "What about your friends? Your friends on the mountain?"

"What about them?"

"Is it possible one of them was playing a trick on you? One of those pranks that gets out of hand?"

Will's voice went—not cold, but a little cooler. "My friends aren't like that. And they don't even know about you, Grandma. Maybe you should, I don't know, like talk to somebody."

"I'm talking to you."

"Someone who can help."

"And who would that—" Another call came in, Allison Suarez Palm Coast Bank and Trust scrolling across her screen. "Hold on, Will. I just need to—" Mrs. Plansky tapped at the phone, tapped again—"Hello? Hello?"—and heard nothing but dial tone. She'd somehow lost both calls.

Mrs. Plansky pressed the little round indented button, the name escaping her, and started over, first calling Allison Suarez.

"This is Allison Suarez at Palm Coast Bank and Trust. Please leave a message and I'll get back to you as soon as I can."

"Allison?" Mrs. Plansky took a breath, went on in a lower register. "I seem to have missed your call. I'd appreciate—"

Another call came in, Nina now, and this time Mrs. Plansky didn't lose the connection.

"Mom? Are you all right? I just had a disturbing call from Will."

"What did he tell you?"

"Well, all about what the two of you were discussing."

"Did he mention . . ." Mrs. Plansky hesitated, then charged ahead. ". . . the DUI situation?"

"Mom? There was no DUI situation. Will wasn't arrested or any-thing like that."

"Well, he didn't want you to know. That's the whole point."

There was a long silence. Then Nina, her voice extra-gentle and annoying at the same time, said, "Are you okay? Are you feeling all right?"

"I'm fine except for this," said Mrs. Plansky. "And I don't need to hear that question again."

"Fair enough," Nina said. "But Will didn't call you last night, and certainly not from a jailhouse. He wasn't even in Crested Butte. He was on the red-eye from JFK to Denver, coming back from a weekend with his dad."

"But . . . but . . . Ted doesn't live in New York. He's on Hilton Head." That little outburst got free before Mrs. Plansky realized how woeful it was.

Actually, she hadn't realized quite how woeful until Nina said, "That's Teddy, Mom. Ted's in Brooklyn."

Mrs. Plansky moved to sit down on the bed and discovered she was already there. She sat and just breathed. Where was her self-control? Her sense of dignity? Her inner strength? "The bank must have made a mistake, Nina." Did that sound better? Maybe a little flat and affectless, but surely better? "I'll get to the bottom of it and call you back."

"Are you sure? Do you want me to come up there?"

"I'll be fine," said Mrs. Plansky.

"You're sure?"

"Positive. Don't worry about me."

"Okay. Love you, Mom."

"Love you. Bye."

Another call came in right away, the caller ID reading: Newport Asset Management. Newport Asset Management was a midsize financial services firm where the Planskys had all their investments, formerly in several accounts but after the sale of the company and Norm's death they'd all been merged into one—the LP account—for tax and estate planning purposes.

Mrs. Plansky held the phone to her ear. "Loretta Plansky speaking."

ELEVEN

"Hi, Loretta. Jerry Levin here."

"Hi, Jerry." Jerry was a friend of Norm's going all the way back to high school in Providence, had later gone to Wharton, and had been their financial advisor from the beginning of Plansky and Company. Back then Jerry was on his own, but his talent was obvious and he'd climbed high on several corporate ladders, the Planskys staying with him. He was now the number-two person at Newport Asset Management, in charge of big-picture things and running only a few of his oldest clients' accounts.

"How's everything—kids, grandkids?"

"Fine. And yours?"

"Same. The reason I'm calling—always good to hear your voice, of course—is something's come up and I'm hoping you can enlighten me."

Norm, not Mrs. Plansky, had always been the mental leaper, at least in her understanding of their marriage and their partnership, with her more as the mental ballast, but now she made a mental leap of her own, knew what was coming. The money—not just the ten thousand but all of it, the exact number or even an approximation momentarily unavailable—had ended up in the LP account at Newport Asset Management. How? She had no idea. But Jerry was a real smart guy. They'd figure it out.

"Summing up, Loretta, I've known you a long time and I'm having trouble believing you'd suddenly close your account without talking to me. In fact, I don't believe it."

"But I didn't close the account. I haven't even looked at it in weeks."

"Then where's the money?"

"The money?"

"The balance. You drew it down to zero last night."

Mrs. Plansky needed to get out of the bedroom. There was no air in it, all silently sucked out in an instant. She hurried across the floor, stubbing her toe on something but not falling, threw open the slider, stepped onto the patio, and sucked in a deep deep breath.

"Loretta? Still there?"

"Yes, yes. Go on."

"Go on?" Jerry said. "I'm waiting to hear something from you."

"But . . . but Jerry!" She took another breath, tried to get a grip. "I don't understand what's happening. Any of it. And I didn't close the account. Or draw it down. Or . . . anything. I didn't touch it."

"Did you authorize anyone else to have access to the account?"

"No."

"Have you shared the password with anyone?"

"No."

"I hear a little hesitation in that no," Jerry said.

Mrs. Plansky hadn't been aware of that, but it was true that last night she'd shared her Palm Coast Bank and Trust password—!NorManConQuest!—with Will. But . . . but not Will. It was looking very much like it hadn't been Will. And then came a revelation of a very bad kind. She used the same password for pretty much everything, including the LP account at Newport Asset Management. But why not? It got a green check mark, meaning highly secure, every time, and it was unforgettable, at least to her.

"Loretta?"

"You sure?" she said. "Sure the account is empty?"

"I checked and double-checked. And so did my assistant."

"But . . . but where did it go?"

"Damn it, Loretta. I was hoping you'd tell me."

"But I don't know, Jerry. I don't—" Another call came in, Allison Suarez from the bank, getting back to her. "The thing is the same problem seems to be happening at my bank. In fact, the assistant manager's calling right now."

"Can I talk to her?"

"Yes. I'm just not sure how to—"

"Press the accept button."

She pressed it.

"Hello?" said Allison.

"Hello," said Mrs. Plansky. "I've got Jerry Levin on the other line. He . . ." Suddenly she was breathless again, almost like this normal sort of business introduction was too much for her.

"With whom am I speaking?" Jerry said.

"Allison Suarez, Palm Coast Bank and Trust."

"Nice meeting you. Jerry Levin, Newport Asset Management. I'm Mrs. Plansky's longtime financial advisor and also a friend. I gather there's been some irregular activity in her account with you."

"It was emptied last night," Allison said. "Apparently without Loretta's knowledge. I'm calling now to ask her—to ask you, Loretta—if you've ever shared your password with anyone."

"No," she said. "Not, that is, till last night."

"Last night?" said Jerry and Allison together, in a sort of frightening harmony. Mrs. Plansky still didn't really understand but at that moment she knew the worst. Not that she believed it. She just knew.

"I gave it to my grandson over the phone. Norman Conquest with two—" She stopped herself. "But . . . but it wasn't him. I get that now. Almost certainly not him."

Silence. Then Jerry said, "Do you use the same password with us?"

"Yes," said Mrs. Plansky, her voice sounding very small, like a four-year-old caught red-handed.

"May I speak to your grandson?" Jerry said. "Will, isn't it?"

"Yes," said Mrs. Plansky, "but don't tell him . . ." She searched for the best way to put it. "Anything," she explained. "Don't tell Will anything." She gave Jerry the number.

Another silence. When Jerry spoke again his voice was gentle. "You don't want the family to know? Or you prefer to tell them yourself?"

What she wanted was for this—whatever it was—not to be true. "Both," she said.

"I suppose I don't really need to talk to him at all," Jerry said. "Water under . . ." He left that part of it unfinished.

"Mr. Levin?" Allison said. "Has Loretta mentioned Safemo yet?"

"What's that?"

"Safemo." Allison spelled it for him. A discussion started up, a technical and very important discussion with Jerry and Allison doing the talking and Mrs. Plansky listening. At first. But then her attention was drawn to some movement in the greenery across the lake, and an alligator appeared, not particularly big—although hard to be sure from this distance—and the first one she'd seen since moving to the condo. The alligator, in no hurry, moved to the shoreline and slipped into the water, disappearing without a ripple.

Although there was a ripple, an icy one, down her spine.

Jerry caught a flight that afternoon, arriving in time for a six thirty meeting in a conference room at Palm Coast Bank and Trust, twenty minutes from Mrs. Plansky's condo. She'd spent the afternoon in a kind of trance, first indoors, an indoors that now suddenly seemed insubstantial to her, like a stage set made of cardboard, and then outdoors, standing by the lake, eyes on the water. After some time—possibly an hour or more, a pair of flamingos—unusually far north—flew down and stood in the shallows, not far from her. In *Casablanca*—a movie she and Norm had watched a dozen times, maybe two dozen—Rick tells Ilsa that the problems of three little people don't amount to a hill of beans in this crazy world, and every time that line rolled around Norm would shake his head no. Thinking of the alligator lurking down there somewhere, Mrs. Plansky clapped her hands and called, "Shoo, shoo." The flamingos paid no attention and were still standing there doing nothing, each on one leg, when she left for the bank. Other than that, all she remembered of the afternoon was a call from Nina and several texts, all of which she ignored. Will must have talked to Nina—how had she not foreseen that?—and it was possible that other family members knew. But what? Only that she was caught up in some sort of misunderstanding involving the loss or failure to locate $10,000, possibly somewhat more, but not . . . everything. And wasn't there still a chance that was the bottom line? A misunderstanding, some sort of computer mix-up? Didn't they happen all the time? Just last week, for example, when they'd had to abort a space flight on account of a software glitch? One of the bartenders at the club had taken his kids out of school to go down and watch. So there was still hope, reasonable hope. In the bank parking lot, Mrs. Plansky leaned in toward the rearview mirror to put on her eyeliner, but her hand wasn't steady enough.

Jerry, Allison, and a woman she didn't know were already at the conference table when she walked in. Jerry came right over and gave her a hug. She wasn't important enough as a client for him to have come all this way and at once. This was about friendship, his and hers, but even more than that, his and Norm's. She hugged him back, an imitation of a friendly hug—the realization shamed her—to keep herself from an anxious clinging. Nonsense like that had to be avoided.

"Good to see you, Jerry," she said in a totally normal voice. "And thanks so much for coming."

"Of course," Jerry said. "And I want you to meet Senior Special Agent Rains from the FBI. She flew down with me."

Senior Special Agent Rains, who'd been sitting at the table and going through a folder, rose and shook hands. She was a tall woman, early forties, in a dark pantsuit and with her hair in a tight bun.

"Nice to meet you," said Agent Rains. "Sorry you're going through this."

"Thanks," Mrs. Plansky said, when she wanted to say was, *Does the very fact you're here rule out the computer glitch escape clause?*

"Agent Rains is with the cyber division," Jerry said. "We've worked together before."

"Call me Sheila," Agent Rains said. "And before we get started I'm a big fan of your toaster knives."

"Oh, well, we no longer . . . thanks," said Mrs. Plansky.

They sat at the table. Agent Rains opened her folder, took out a pen. "First I need to confirm something. According to Allison, the mode of transfer was something called Safemo. Is that correct?"

"Yes," Mrs. Plansky said.

Agent Rains made a check mark. "Okay, run me through it—everything you remember from the call."

For a moment Mrs. Plansky couldn't recall one single thing about it. Well, except for Safemo. Like a huge neon sign it flashed in her head: SAFEMO! SAFEMO! SAFEMO! Then she became aware of the gazes, all on her, and all of them smart. And with this in common as well: they were waiting for this elderly person to catch up. Even Jerry, who was the same age, a third-grade classmate of Norm's. Then it hit her that whatever was going on, whatever had been done, done to her, had been done to Norm as well. That realization was sickening but it kicked her brain into gear. She owed him her best.

"It was the middle of the night and I was asleep," she said. "A phone call came in from my grandson, Will, in Colorado." She gave them all an angry look. "It said so right on the screen. He told me he'd been arrested on a DUI charge and needed money for bail and getting his car back." And from there, Mrs. Plansky sailed right through it, even maybe dramatizing a little—as though telling a made-up story for entertainment purposes—when she reached the password part: "'And presto, Grandma. Already vanished forever. Thank you, Grandma!'" Mrs. Plansky looked at them one by one—Agent Rains, Allison, Jerry—in a challenging way, half-aware that the heavy artillery was warming up in the silo, for the first time in ages. Challenging—as though the three of them were somehow responsible! Good grief. She amped herself down and came quietly to the end, at which point she realized she'd lowered her head. Mrs. Plansky raised it back up.

The three of them looked from one to the other. Agent Rains spoke first. "What was the phone connection like?"

"Not so clear," said Mrs. Plansky. "But I could hear perfectly well." She stopped herself from adding, *My hearing's good! My eyesight's good! Even my sense of smell!*

Agent Rains nodded. "Prior to this call, when was the last time you spoke to Will?"

"I've been trying to remember," Mrs. Plansky said. Oh, how she wanted that one back! She saw the looks in their eyes, subtle, hidden, but confirmation looks, for sure. Wait—hadn't she actually remembered it already, somewhere along the way? Ah-ha! "And it was—it must have been on his birthday in July."

"July the what?" said Agent Rains.

Every grandmother in America knew the birthdates of all her grandchildren. That was Grammy 101. But all she knew for sure was that it couldn't be the fourth. That would have been impossible to forget. "It's written down at home," she said. "I could get back to you."

"It's not important," Agent Rains said. "Call it eight months, tops. Did it occur to you at any time that it might not be Will on the other end?"

"Of course not! Why would I have . . ." At that point—rather late in the game—Mrs. Plansky's mind flagged a moment from her conversation with—what to call him? The Will impersonator? The moment and suddenly very clear in her mind, like a ray of sunshine had suddenly poked through a thick fog: "Yo. It's me, Grandma, Will. Your grandson Will." That greeting followed by her silent reaction: *Right away she knew he didn't sound good, his voice higher than normal, maybe nervous about something, although since they hadn't spoken in some time she couldn't be sure.* My God. From the very top she'd been suspicious, but she'd rationalized it away. And even more, she'd tried to settle him down a bit, making a little joke: "I'm aware of the relationship." How shameful! Mrs. Plansky felt herself flushing, a sort of bodily heat wave starting at neck level and rising up.

Meanwhile Agent Rains was waiting for an answer. Mrs. Plansky was good at looking people in the eye. It came naturally to her. But now, despite giving it everything she had, Mrs. Plansky couldn't quite do it. At that point Allison—whom Mrs. Plansky didn't know well, ignorant of basic facts like whether she was married or had kids—although today she wore no wedding band and looked tired, so possibly a single mom—spoke up.

"Whatever's going on I think it's important we all acknowledge Loretta is blameless."

"Totally," said Jerry.

Agent Rains nodded the smallest perceptible yes.

Mrs. Plansky's gaze rose the last millimeter or two and met hers. "In retrospect, it might have occurred to me, but not at the time."

Agent Rains made a note. "Let's circle back to Safemo. Had you ever heard of it?"

"No."

"How did he explain it?"

"That it was one of those PayPal things."

"So why not PayPal itself?"

"Safemo was better."

"In what way?"

"The vanishing, as I already mentioned." And something else, something about . . . "Encryption. Before the vanishing the whole thing was encrypted. Plus—plus some percent of their profits went to saving—went to a charity for whales."

Agent Rains' pen, which had been writing busily away, came to a stop. She was looking down, so Mrs. Plansky couldn't be sure she'd caught a flash of amusement in her eyes or imagined it.

"God almighty," Jerry said. "Diabolical."

"Exactly," said Allison.

"So you're saying that's not true?" Mrs. Plansky said. "The whale part?"

Agent Rains looked up, her eyes expressionless. "The whale part? Unlikely but possible, and anything else you can recall about Safemo will be valuable."

"I can't think of anything else," Mrs. Plansky said. "But—" She was struck by an obvious thought she should have had hours ago. "But shouldn't we get in touch with them? Right away?"

Agent Rains seemed a bit surprised. Jerry and Allison exchanged a look that defied Mrs. Plansky's interpretation, but showed no signs of enthusiasm for her idea.

"Get in touch with Safemo?" said Agent Rains.

"Sure," said Mrs. Plansky. "In case the money's still on their books. Or—" She made what she thought was a little joke. "Or do the books vanish, too?"

No one laughed. No one seemed to get it at all. They did that looking at one another routine again, a routine of which Mrs. Plansky had had more than enough.

"I'm afraid it's probably the second one, Loretta," Jerry said.

"What second one?" Mrs. Plansky said.

"The books vanish, too," said Agent Rains.

Ah. She should have known, but so much of the digital world was a mystery to her. There was plenty she could do no problem—linking, attaching, downloading—but whenever she strayed off a known path, usually by accident, it was time to call in IT. Of course in retirement there was no IT. The good news was that the fact of the books vanishing was at least an indication that Safemo was real. A hideous thought to the contrary had been snaking around in her mind.

"Still," she said, "wouldn't it be worthwhile to get in touch with them?"

"With who, again?" said Agent Rains.

"Safemo," Mrs. Plansky said, unable to keep her impatience bottled up. "If this in fact is all a—" She made herself utter the word.

"Scam. If it is all a scam, then shouldn't we—or you, Agent Rains, the FBI, after all—be asking them, or pressuring them, whatever it takes, to tell us who was on the other end? And—and wait! Jerry! Oh my God, Jerry! Are you saying my Newport account got rolled up into the same transaction?"

There was a bit of a silence. Then Jerry said, "I thought you understood."

"But how could that happen?"

"There are a number of ways," Agent Rains said. "A number of known ways, plus unknown ones as well. But the simplest way would be the password. Jerry tells me you used the same password for the Newport account and the Palm Coast account. True?"

Mrs. Plansky nodded, a defeated little motion she thought of repeating more forcefully. But at the moment she lacked the strength. She made herself do it anyway.

"That would be it, then," Agent Rains said. "They got lucky. It happens, actually a lot. Have we come up with a total? For the record?"

"Ours is sixty-eight thousand, three hundred dollars and twenty-one cents," Allison said. Somehow the fact that she didn't need to check any notes, just reeled it right off from memory, made it—made the whole thing—incontrovertible, undeniable, final.

"As for us." Jerry took a sheet of paper from an inside suit jacket pocket and donned reading glasses. "Three million, six hundred and ninety-nine thousand, and . . ." He bit his lip and put the paper away. "And change. The portfolio was approximately sixty-five percent equity, twenty-five bonds, five cash, five miscellaneous."

"Making three million eight, give or take," said Agent Rains. She turned to Mrs. Plansky. "Thinking back, did anything in the call suggest where it was coming from? Did the caller have an accent, for example?"

Mrs. Plansky thought about that. In retrospect, in oh so clever retrospect, he'd sounded like Conrad Veidt or Arnold Schwarzenegger or Maurice Chevalier or . . . She let go of all that, and thought again. "Maybe not an accent, so much. More like he was a bit stilted at times. But I interpreted it as Will growing up, developing a sort of detached, ironic sense of humor. If you see what I mean." One quick glance and she knew they did not.

"Not my area," said Allison, "but re the stocks and bonds, is it possible—"

Agent Rains interrupted. "Same as cash in terms of ease of unloading. I'm sure that's taken place already, through an offshore broker, online broker, crypto broker, dark web broker, or some combo. But it's a nice thought."

Allison made a motion like she was going to reach over and touch Mrs. Plansky's hand. Mrs. Plansky put her hands in her lap, out of sight.

"Where do we go from here?" Jerry said.

"First," Agent Rains said, "I'm of course opening a file on this matter and the bureau will devote its full resources to finding out who did this, bringing them to justice, and recovering what was stolen. But as you know, Jerry, and as I'm sure Allison knows, this particular type of case is very difficult and our record of success at hitting any of the three targets I mentioned is not good."

"What three targets?" said Mrs. Plansky.

There was a silence, and in that silence Mrs. Plansky's flush, which had receded, came flowing back. Quietly, Jerry said, "Finding, punishing, recovering."

"Especially two and three," said Agent Rains. "Most especially three."

Mrs. Plansky got the feeling that Agent Rains was wrapping things up, or had even wrapped them up already, and was about to leave. Agent Rains didn't seem warm or charming but she was strong and tough. Mrs. Plansky didn't want her to go, didn't want to be alone. Her mind thrashed around desperately and came up with something.

"But—" Mrs. Plansky lowered her voice, restarted. "Aren't you forgetting Safemo? Isn't that a . . . a clue at least?"

Agent Rains nodded. "It's all we've got to work with, if it still exists."

"I don't understand."

"Safemo might have been a onetime thing created for this specific purpose and"—Agent Rains made quotation marks with her fingers—"vanishing at completion. But that's where I'll start."

She rose, turning out to be smaller than Mrs. Plansky had first thought, shook hands with everyone, and gave Mrs. Plansky her card. "I'll be in touch. And if you think of anything, or if there's more contact, call right away."

"More contact from the same people?" Mrs. Plansky said. She heard the fear in her voice but could do nothing about it.

"Highly unlikely, unless they're very stupid."

What would that make me? thought Mrs. Plansky.

Jerry walked her to her car. It was a nice evening, a gentle breeze carrying the smell of the sea. Mrs. Plansky again recalled the time she'd overcome the rip tide and pulled Jack to safety. Really? That was the same person as her now?

"Thanks for coming," Mrs. Plansky said. "And for setting all this up so well."

"Please," said Jerry. "And Loretta? I have to ask. How are your finances, other than this? If nothing is recovered, is what I mean. Do you have other holdings of some kind? Other investments? Accounts somewhere else? I won't be offended." He smiled a quick smile. Jerry was a lovely man.

Mrs. Plansky hardened herself—inside, invisibly. "Not to worry," she said.

TWELVE

"It's not a tragedy," Mrs. Plansky said to herself out loud on the drive home from Palm Coast Bank and Trust. No one died. No one even got sick. She owned her condo outright, also her car, the mileage still pretty low. Actually, Mrs. Plansky had no idea what the mileage was. She checked the dashboard display—so very complicated now that she eyed it carefully for the first time—and couldn't find it right away. Ah, that had to be it: 17,842. The car itself was three years old, making annual mileage six thousand, give or take, and with cars these days lasting so long it was conceivable she might never need another. How nice when the numbers were working for you! She and Norm had had many moments like that, for example for a full month after the *Wall Street Journal* included the Plansky Toaster Knife in a feature on kitchen gadgets in its weekend On Duty section.

The Green Turtle Club went by on her left, its sign a neon turtle upright on its hind legs, and raising a glass. She hit the turn signal, pulled off the highway and into the Green Turtle parking lot. "I'm going to go in," she said, again talking to herself aloud, which wasn't her at all. Or was it? Had she been talking to herself lately and simply not noticed? "Never mind. I'll sit down, order a drink, be a normal person being normal." Drinks, of course, cost money. She pictured herself ordering a drink in one of those Belle Epoque spaces on the *Titanic,* after the collision but before the realization. Whoa. She was making herself grandiose and ridiculous. Lucky for her there were no witnesses. But now the numbers that weren't working for her, just discussed in the conference room, came flooding back, and Mrs. Plansky did not go into the Green Turtle Club for a drink, instead merging carefully back onto the highway and heading home.

Mrs. Plansky sat at her kitchen table, a single row of ceiling can lights switched on and the rest of the condo in darkness. She had a pen, a calculator, a sheet of paper, a glass of water. A glass of water at first, and then a very small glass of brandy, as well. She made three columns: *Assets, Liabilities, Income.* Her mind was humming. This was work, and she hadn't worked in some time, possibly too long. Make that obviously too long. Life without work could be so vague. There were vagaries in work, too, but also specifics. She would cling to specifics. Under income she wrote: *Social Security.* And then paused. Mrs. Plansky did not know the amount of her monthly payment, could not even make a rough guess. Didn't that say so much about then, now, and the future? She put her hands to her face. There was a shift in her emotional bedrock and an eruption of tears threatened to get loose. She steeled her inner self, sat up straight, and under Social Security wrote: *TK.*

What else? When she and Norm sold out, the only sticking point in the negotiations was the patent issue, not the patent for the knife itself, which had to be included in any sensible deal, but other patents in Norm's name based on his technology but for other potential devices. Norm had wanted to hang on to them.

"But why?" she'd said. "Are we retiring or not?"

"Maybe someone down the line will be interested."

"What line?"

"Our genetic line."

Which at that time, as now, had consisted of Nina, Jack, Emma, and Will.

"Such as who?"

"TBD."

In the end, the buyer had kicked in a couple hundred thousand or so—the exact figure not coming to her—and Norm had given up the patents. Too bad. Otherwise TBD could have been her, starting tomorrow. She sat back. What would that be like, doing it all over again, and with Norm, now sort of hovering above? Mrs. Plansky felt a slight twinge in her new hip, the first in months. Her phone rang. It was Nina. She let it ring. Tomorrow would be a good time for explaining. Tonight was for figuring out the explanation, a partial explanation, as non-alarming as possible, but wasn't keeping it partial justified by the fact that whatever had happened was not resolved? The FBI was working on it, had just started. There were people, flesh and blood people, who had done this. Safemo was not just ones and zeros in chains of code. It was people. People occupied physical space, somewhere on the globe. They could be found.

Mrs. Plansky picked up her pen and took a long look at the heading marked *Assets*. Beneath it she wrote: *Condo. Car. Jewelry.* She took a sip of brandy, found the glass was empty. She moved onto *Liabilities. Utilities, gas, food*—none of which she had exact figures for. *Condo Fees $1,000/mo. Club membership—$1,200, due in June. Club dining monthly minimum—$300. Gifts, tips, etc.* Mrs. Plansky had no idea what her customary figure would be for that. If you could afford material giving you did lots of it, and not just to family members. What else was the point?

She made a subheading under *Liabilities: Family*. Not that family could ever be a liability—she was using the word strictly in the accounting sense. She stressed that to herself and only then added a sub-sub heading: *Promises:* She began with Nina and the loan thingy: *$250K, matchmaking start-up.* Then came *Jack: $750K*, not exactly promised, but since he's coming all this way to send him back with nothing at all would be . . .

Mrs. Plansky left the Jack entry just like that and moved on to: *Dad.* Oh, boy. She rose, went to her bedroom, opened the desk drawer containing all the files, took out the folder labeled *Dad*, and returned to the kitchen table. Dad's folder included some smaller subfolders, all labeled in Mrs. Plansky's distinctive handwriting. She hadn't known it was distinctive until Norm pointed it out. "No one forms the letters like that. Totally clear but so plump and sexy." Her handwriting was sexy to him. Who had it luckier than her? Mrs. Plansky fell into a brief reverie, or possibly dead zone. She snapped out of it and opened the Arcadia Gardens subfolder. Dad was now receiving tier-two care at $7,500 a month, not including extras like his bar tab, snack tab, excursion tab, and several other tabs unnamed and simply grouped under Tabs—Misc. There'd also been a nonrefundable entrance fee of $100,000. And now there was this talk of moving him down to the third floor where the cost was $10,000 a month more. Surely that couldn't be right. He must have meant the cost was $10,000, not $10,000 more, meaning it was actually only $2,500 more—that "only" applying only in a former time, like yesterday. Mrs. Plansky took another sip of brandy, found the glass still empty. She returned to the bedroom, removed her jewelry box from the safe, brought it into the kitchen, and then just stood there. Did she really want to go through the jewelry box right now in this dark, silent condo? She pictured herself doing that, an old lady bent over a little pile of bright things, speculating.

Mrs. Plansky left the jewelry box unopened, stripped off her clothes, and went to bed. Her body was inert, exhausted. Her mind went round and round, unstoppable, trying out various do-overs. After who knew how long, she realized she hadn't put on her nightie. She always wore a nightie to bed. Right away, she knew that if she didn't wear a nightie tonight she was closing the door—in some cosmic way—to things, specifically this thing, ever being right again. Through sheer mental effort she forced her inert form to rise, don the nightie, and while she was at it brush her teeth, floss, the whole dental shebang, also never neglected before bed. She did all that in the darkness, no way risking the sight of herself in the mirror.

But back in bed, sleep would not come, not even with her in the twisted K position. After what might have been hours she hit rock bottom. Rock bottom was the abrupt realization that in her stupidity, her sloppiness, her vulnerability—and worse, because of her unacknowledged but now so obvious love of the power that came with being the giver—she'd failed Norm. What a pathetically easy mark she'd been! Safemo must have been laughing his or her head off. And now everything she and Norm had built, not just the money but way more important, his trust in her, was—poof. The tears came then. Mrs. Plansky couldn't stop them, didn't even try.

You might think that after a cry like that at least sleep would come at last, but it did not. Instead she just lay there, mind now as inert as body. But not quite. One little idea popped up in her mind, like a creature in a moonscape: the OxyContin, namely the OxyContin left over from the hip replacement. She actually hadn't taken any during her recovery, not even on night one, but wasn't now the time for an Oxy, or two, max, to get her to sleep? Mrs. Plansky was on the point of making herself get up again when she remembered the story of that little bottle, namely how it had disappeared following the spring break night she'd hosted Will and that buddy of his, on their way to the buddy's folks's place in Lauderdale.

The sketchy buddy. Mrs. Plansky couldn't recall his name but somehow she could retrieve a clear image of his face: scruffy beard, weak chin, evasive eyes. And a mumbler. What was more she could picture him texting, his soft, childlike fingers just flying over the screen. A computer adept? He was the type, for sure. Smart enough to come up with Safemo and execute the plan? That remained to be seen, but the moral question was settled. The buddy was already a proven thief.

Mrs. Plansky drifted off.

Someone was knocking on the door. Mrs. Plansky opened her eyes. Her bedroom was full of light. She hadn't closed the curtains before going to bed? That was strange. How could she have neglected to—

And then it all came back to her. She got light-headed and came close to sinking to the floor.

Meanwhile the knocking.

"Coming. Just a minute. Coming."

She hurried out of the bedroom, down the hall, into the kitchen, took in the sight of the kitchen table and everything on it—papers, folders, jewelry box.

Knock knock. "Mom? Are you there? It's me."

Nina. Nina? Wasn't she supposed to be in Boca? Mrs. Plansky took a hesitant step or two toward the front door, then spun around, half-running to the bathroom. Nina was not going to see her like this. Mrs. Plansky raced through the regime of making herself presentable—ending up in a tennis outfit only because it was on the nearest hanger, and at some point dabbing on lipstick in a muted shade, although no other makeup—then tore her quilt off the bed, threw it over all the stuff on the kitchen table, and opened the front door, remembering almost too late to put a smile on her face.

And there was Nina, Nina with a worried look on her face. But not alone. Standing with her was Jack, also with a worried look. Mrs. Plansky had to put a stop to the worry at once. The mere sight of Jack helped with that. She hadn't seen him in months and months—such a handsome man, still young or youngish, and he'd been lovely to look at from birth. Also funny, from a very early age. During toilet training he'd started giving his poops names, depending on their size—Babar, Stuart Little, etcetera. Mrs. Plansky felt her smile turning somewhat real. She opened her arms and hugged Jack tight.

"What a nice surprise!" she said, drawing them both inside. "To what do I owe it?"

"Hey!" Jack said. "Aren't you still my mom?"

"What a question!" said Mrs. Plansky. "Of course you don't need a reason. Come on in. Coffee, anybody?"

"But we do have a bit of a reason," Nina said glancing around as they moved toward the kitchen. "Are you on your way to the club?"

"Not right away," said Mrs. Plansky.

"Oh, good. Because Jack and I are a bit concerned about this situation that came up with Will."

"No need for concern," Mrs. Plansky said. "We're in the midst of sorting it all out now." She got busy with the coffeemaker.

"Sorting what all, exactly?" Jack said.

"That's part of the concern," said Nina. "We're a bit mystified."

"It's just a banking snafu," Mrs. Plansky said. Where was the coffeepot? Had she left it in the dining room, after the dinner with Dad, Nina, and Matthew? She went looking for it, calling over her shoulder, "These things take time."

The coffeepot stood on the sideboard, still partly full. How careless of her to have forgotten it in the cleanup. She picked it up, took it back to the kitchen.

Nina and Jack were standing at the table, now uncovered. Jack was holding the quilt and gazing at her paperwork, folders, jewelry box. Nina had a sheet of paper and was reading what was written on it—in plump, sexy letters—her eyes going back and forth, back and forth, very fast. She looked up.

"Mom? What's all this?"

"Nothing. Nothing important." She made a move to take the quilt from Jack and re-cover everything on the table, but stopped herself in time. "Just some paperwork, that's all."

Nina put down the sheet of paper, opened the jewelry box. "Mom? What's going on?"

"I already explained! Please can we talk about something else?"

Nina and Jack were watching her in a way they never had and that she didn't like one little bit. She got a bit angry at her own children.

"You could help, you know." Oh, God, had those words really come out of her mouth?

They looked stunned.

"Of course," Nina said.

"How?" said Jack.

"How?" And now she was out of control and couldn't stop. "How about giving me the name of Will's friend for starters?"

"What friend?" Nina said.

"The one who stayed here on spring break."

"Luke Easterbrook? But why? Did you want to send a card or something?"

"What are you talking about?"

"His accident."

"What's this?" Jack said.

"A friend of Will's from Hilton Head. He was in a terrible wreck last month. He's still in the hospital—they had to wire his jaw shut, among many other things."

"They wired his jaw shut?" Mrs. Plansky said.

"Just for now until his face heals. It's not that unusual, Mom. And they say he's going to be all right in the end."

But Safemo. Some god above kept that remark unspoken.

"I don't get it, Mom," Jack said. "What sort of help did you want with him?"

"I—" Mrs. Plansky began, but before some new stupidity got loose, there was another knock on the door, as though a stage farce was gathering speed. She answered it.

Another female/male duo stood on the front step. The woman she knew: Agent Sheila Rains. The man was new.

"Hi, Loretta," Agent Rains said. "This is Agent Gatling, one of our technicians. He'd like to examine your phone—the one the call came in on."

Nina and Jack approached from behind.

"Mom?"

Mrs. Plansky stepped aside. Soon Agent Gatling was plugging her phone into some device he'd brought with him and Agent Rains was telling the kids the whole story. Mrs. Plansky sat at the table in her tennis outfit, feeling heavy and dim, and hardly spoke a word.

THIRTEEN

"Do you know what Steve Jobs said?" Uncle Dragomir asked.

They were in the Cambio office at Club Presto, Dinu and Romeo called in early by Uncle Dragomir, Timbo pouring coffee. Neither Romeo nor Dinu offered up an answer. Romeo, so brilliant, may have known and simply opted for caution. As for Dinu, the name Steve Jobs was new to him.

"Look at them, Timbo," Uncle Dragomir said. "Bleg and bleg," *bleg* being their word for *dolt*. "Tell them what Steve Jobs said."

"*A* bosses hire A workers," Timbo said, adding extra cream to Uncle Dragomir's mug. "B bosses hire C workers."

"Exactly," said Uncle Dragomir. "Timbo here is an A worker, a master of his craft." All on its own, Dinu's tongue curled around in his mouth and felt the new tooth. "Am I an A boss?"

"Yes," said Dinu.

"A plus," said Romeo.

"You're an asshole, Romeo. You're both assholes. The moment you slide down from A, the moment I even sniff the first stink of you sliding down, you're out on the street. But not before Timbo and Marius tune you up a little bit. Timbo knows how to tune up. He's a gypsy, don't forget."

"Partly," said Timbo. "One grandmother."

"More than enough to have tuning up in the blood. You getting all this, gentlemen?"

Dinu and Romeo nodded yes.

"Pen," Uncle Dragomir said.

Timbo handed him a gold pen. Uncle Dragomir scratched off a quick note on a pad, tore off the top sheet, handed it to Romeo. "Go see this guy. He's knows you're coming."

"Who's the guy?" Dinu said when they were outside.

"It just says Mircea." Romeo showed the Dinu the note. *Mircea 96 Ion Ghica Road.* Ion Ghica Road was in the industrial part of town, across the river, about two kilometers away. They walked. A cold day but sunny, the river less brown than usual and a swan out in the middle, going with the flow.

"You should ask Tassa on a date," Romeo said.

"Yeah?"

"She likes you."

"How do you know?"

"She told me."

"She said that? 'I like Dinu'?"

"Not in those words."

"What were the words?"

"'He's not so bad.'"

Dinu gave Romeo a push.

"Whoa. I can't swim."

"No?" Dinu was a good swimmer. His father had taught him when Dinu was three. It was just about the only memory of his father he had. "Paddle like a doggie, little guy. Paddle like a doggie!"

"Although from this height," Romeo was saying, "I'd probably be dead as soon as I hit the water."

"You think?"

"Sure. From here the density differential between solid and liquid is immaterial."

Dinu took a sidelong glance at Romeo. He was picking a pimple on his chin, one of those whiteheads. Romeo had an A-plus-type mind, no question about that.

Ninety-six Ion Ghica Road turned out to be a garage, just a few steps past the cement works and not far from the sprawl of the old soot-stained Communist factories. The bay door was open and a car was up on the lift, a man working underneath, his head in shadows, his arms thick and oil-stained. The whole inside of the bay was oil-stained, the walls smoke-blackened, cigarette butts and food wrappers on the floor, but the car on the lift was a Mercedes 500, shiny and new.

The man moved out from under the lift, a stocky guy with short bristly hair on his head and face, and a bristly expression in his gaze.

"We're looking for Mircea," Romeo said.

"Feast your eyes. You Dragomir's boys?"

"Well, uh," Romeo said.

"He sent us," said Dinu, showing off this new improvising skill of his.

"Then you're his boys," Mircea said. "Come."

He led them to the back of the bay, where a tarp lay over something with two big bumps underneath. "Voilà," said Mircea in what sounded to Dinu like good French, not unusual in this part of the country. He whisked away the tarp, revealing two shiny although perhaps not new motorcycles.

"What's this?" Romeo said.

"You blind?" said Mircea. "Yamaha XT660Z, times two. Four stroke, four valve, fuel-injected, rebuilt with these two hands, so better than the original." Mircea held up his hands, gigantic for a man his size. "And brand-new tires, almost." He gave the nearest tire a soft kick. "So who's got seniority?"

"What's that?" Dinu said.

"I do," said Romeo. "I've got seniority."

"Then pick one out," Mircea said. "Red or black?"

"Are they the same price?" Romeo said.

"Huh?"

"The two? Same price for each or is one more than the other?"

Mircea squinted at him. "You making fun of me?"

"No, sir." Romeo put his hand to his chest.

"Then you're slow." Mircea turned to Dinu. "You, pretty boy. Are you also slow?"

"They're gifts?" Dinu said.

"Presto!" said Mircea. "Get it? Presto!"

Dinu and Romeo both got it but they didn't laugh quite as hard as Mircea.

"So?" he said to Romeo. "What'll it be? Red or black?"

"But I don't know how."

"To choose?"

"To ride."

"You don't know how to ride a bike?"

"Not a motorbike."

"What the hell? How old are you?"

"Sixteen."

"Then your buddy here can show you."

"I don't know how, either," Dinu said.

"What the hell?" Mircea said. "What happens when the Russians come?"

"The Russians?" Romeo said.

"What are pussies like you going to do about it?"

"They won't come," said Romeo.

"We'll fight them," Dinu said.

Mircea nodded. "Pick one out, Dinu."

Dinu picked red. Mircea sold them each a used helmet, cheap, and gave them a quick riding lesson. Romeo, on the black 660Z, was very wobbly but Dinu had a feel for it right away, like he'd been born in the saddle. They rode off, across the bridge and back to the new part of the old town—*new* meaning it dated only from the defeat of the Ottomans—Romeo in joy mixed with terror and Dinu in pure joy. As they took the ramp off the bridge and onto the boulevard, a guy with longish dark hair and a close-cropped white beard turned to watch. Dinu thought he'd seen him before but couldn't think where or when.

On Saturday, Dinu took Tassa for a ride on the bike. The word *date* did not come up. It was just a ride. Dinu picked Tassa up on the street outside her apartment block, a Soviet-style apartment block just like his. She was so beautiful standing against the background of the shabby building that he could hardly look at her. Tassa had always been nice-looking, but now this? What was going on?

"I've never been on a motorcycle before," she said.

"Just hop up behind me. First put this on." He gave her Romeo's helmet, borrowed for the day. Romeo hadn't ridden again after the first time. Dinu rode every chance he got.

Tassa donned the helmet and hopped up. "With this helmet on, my head will be fine when the rest of me's destroyed."

Dinu laughed and revved the engine. "Nothing's going to happen."

"Where do I put my hands?"

"Do that raising-the-roof motion."

Tassa laughed and put her hands around his waist. They roared out of town, headed for Tassa's older sister's place, a farm in the foothills, about forty kilometers away. There was hardly any talking, just Tassa saying "turn here," or "second right," the route going from wide two-lane pavement with lots of traffic to narrow two-lane pavement with less, to gravel and dirt with hardly anyone on it except for an occasional tractor, horse-drawn carts, and barking dogs who chased after them. At first, Tassa's hands felt awkward to him, but she changed the position a bit, maybe simply relaxing, and after that things felt right, like the three of them—Dinu, Tassa, the 660Z—were one. She hummed to herself.

"What's that song?" Dinu said, raising his voice.

"It's American," Tassa said, practically in his ear. "'Eight Miles High.'"

Tassa's sister and her husband lived in a small, drafty farmhouse and grew grapes to sell to the winemakers. There wasn't much to do at this time of year so they were taking their two small boys to a movie that afternoon. First they had a nice lunch—black bread sandwiches with sausage and cabbage, plus a red wine made from grapes grown on vines they could see through the window, just one small pour each for Dinu and Tassa. Then Dinu took each of the boys for a ride on the bike, their dad holding them.

"You and Tassa are in the same class?" the dad said.

"Only she's at the top and I'm at the bottom."

"Really? The bottom?"

"The middle."

"Any idea what you want to do when you graduate?"

"Not really. Maybe something with English."

"You speak English?"

"A little," Dinu said in English. "But it's starting to come to me."

"Nice bike," said the dad after a little silence.

After the family left for the cinema, Dinu and Tassa took a walk through the silent vineyard, the vines all bare and the ground hard. They came to the guest cottage, a very old, very small structure with a thatched roof and a view across a valley toward the mountains, the most distant ones snow covered, a view that could be easily seen from the lumpy but clean couch by the window. After a while things began to happen on that couch, but fairly far down that road Tassa put a stop to them.

"What?" Dinu said.

"That's enough for now."

"What do you mean?"

"We have time."

"But we have time right now."

"You know that's not what I mean," Tassa said.

"Then what do you mean?"

"What's hard has more value. That's what I mean."

"So then this has value!"

Tassa laughed. "Something to look forward to." She bent her middle finger, pressed the nail against her thumb and then released, a surprisingly forceful and perfectly aimed flick that changed the conversation.

FOURTEEN

"Loretta! So good to see you!" Sylvie Benoit hurried out from behind her desk in her beautiful office, a wonder of contemporary design that had the effect of having been assembled from light alone. She gave Mrs. Plansky a kiss on both cheeks. "You look just great!"

Mrs. Plansky, who'd checked herself in the rearview mirror on the drive down to Fort Lauderdale, knew that wasn't true. "Well," she said, "you sure do."

They sat on a couch by a bay window, Middle River and all the boat traffic far below, the couch insubstantial-looking but perfectly adapted to the human body, at least Mrs. Plansky's. An assistant poured tea, also offering a plate of a kind of French pastries Mrs. Plansky liked, but she found she couldn't remember the name and just said, "They look great but no thanks."

"Oh, try one," Sylvie said, helping herself. "You won't be disappointed. They're from Joel LeMaire—do you know him?"

"No." In fact, Mrs. Plansky had never heard of him.

"Joel's the brains behind Delice Moderne."

Mrs. Plansky knew Delice Moderne, a chain of high-end pastry shops, one of them not far from Arcadia Gardens. She'd taken her dad once. He'd voiced—not in a shy way—his incredulity at the prices, and downed cutting-edge versions of a napoleon, a Florentine, and a mocha éclair before huffily wheeling himself out the door. Now she tried one of the pastries. She somehow knew it was delicious even though she couldn't taste a thing, washing down what felt like a mouthful of dust with the tea.

"Delicious," she said.

Sylvie nodded. "Joel's the real deal, although come to think of it, maybe he started to make it big after you retired. He's a customer, of course. I supply him everything except the butter and the sugar." Sylvie's family owned a worldwide kitchen design business, had sold tens of thousands of units of the Plansky Toaster Knife.

Sylvie was looking at her closely. "I know what you're thinking. You haven't changed a bit! Still with that wicked internal sense of humor ticking away. You're thinking, 'Sylvie, you moron, butter and sugar are the whole bleeping product!'"

Mrs. Plansky hadn't been thinking that. She'd been trying to figure out how to steer the conversation toward what she wanted.

Sylvie gave her a big smile. "I'm so glad you called. I've been meaning to get in touch. When was the last time I saw you?"

"It must have been Norm's funeral," Mrs. Plansky said.

"That I'll never forget," said Sylvia. "Especially when you spoke from the podium. There wasn't a dry eye—except for yours. I don't know how you did it. But oh, what a wonderful man." Sylvie sighed. "So tell me—how are you doing? Still taking no prisoners on the tennis court?"

"Let's just say I'm still playing." Mrs. Plansky put down her teacup. "The fact is I'm thinking of getting back into the working world."

"Really?" said Sylvie. "I know retired folks who get bored, but none of them are resourceful like you."

"I'm not sure I'm—"

"Of course you are! You're still interested in the big wide world out there. Plus there's that rock star family of yours."

"Nevertheless," Mrs. Plansky said, "I miss . . ." What was it she missed about the working world? Actually, nothing. "I miss the problem-solving."

"Take up Sudoku," said Sylvie with a laugh.

Mrs. Plansky laughed, too, just a little. She saw the shadow of a thought pass across Sylvie's eyes. Sylvie was a shrewd operator. She, too, put down her teacup. That was the moment Mrs. Plansky considered making one or two more pleasantries and calling it a day. But she did not.

"Besides," Sylvie said. "What would you do?"

Mrs. Plansky plunged ahead. "Consulting."

"In what sort of business?"

"This sort." Mrs. Plansky made an encompassing gesture with her hands.

"Gee, Loretta, I can't think of any consultants at all in this business. Not successful ones."

"I was thinking more of an in-house setup."

"There are in-house strategizers, of course. I've got a planning committee. But they're department heads, not consultants. And, not to discourage you, but I'm pretty sure all my competitors are much the same."

Well, it was just a thought. That was what Mrs. Plansky should have said, and then made a graceful exit. Instead she went with this: "Are all your department heads, ah, firmly ensconced?"

"Oh, dear," Sylvie said, "you really do have the bug." Her lips turned up in another big smile, although this one wasn't real. Then her expression changed again, and became frank and open. "No reason you'd know this but we have a rule here, meant to encourage the development of young talent. The rule is sixty-five and out. We've stretched that in a few special cases to sixty-six or sixty-seven, but it's universal. I'll be gone in eight years and seven months."

"Oh," said Mrs. Plansky.

"So don't waste time on all this hurly-burly, Loretta. You been there, done that. Now go on and enjoy your life. You deserve it."

"The key fact, the underlying fact, got left out," Mrs. Plansky said to herself, although again out loud, as she merged onto 95 and headed north. She'd sat on other side of the desk for many job interviews, enough to know that the same key fact usually went unspoken. She had a clear memory of one time when it got into the open. This was early in her career and the applicant, a defeated-looking middle-aged woman with no relevant experience and euphemistic recommendations had suddenly blurted, "I'm at my wits end. I just need a job."

Thank God it got left out, Mrs. Plansky said to herself, making sure to keep silent this time. As for the desperate applicant, Mrs. Plansky, not quite so businesslike in the early days, had hired her, the result not good. She glanced in the rearview mirror, checking for signs of desperation and not seeing them. And why all this internal drama? Wasn't it possible that Agent Gatling would unearth something on her phone—about the names behind Safemo, for example—and set the feds in motion? The feds had an amazing history of bringing elusive criminals to justice: drug lords, for example, like that Noriega character, although he might not have been a drug lord. But still, the point was made. She was not alone, had the crime-fighting power of the most powerful nation on earth at her back. Mrs. Plansky was picturing a sunlit upland where this was all in the past, reduced to a surefire anecdote at cocktail parties, when her phone buzzed. She glanced at the screen: Jeanine at Arcadia Gardens. Mrs. Plansky took the next exit, pulled over on a wide, safe verge, and called her back.

"Oh, hi," said Jeanine, "thanks for getting back. I was just wondering if you had any questions about what we were discussing."

What had they been discussing? Mrs. Plansky searched her memory and found something. "The TV thing?" she said.

"I'm not sure I—ah, you mean when the screen got broken? Covered by insurance and not a problem. Sorry if I forgot to mention that. No, what I'm calling about is the underlying situation."

"Don't tell me there's been another incident."

"Well, yes, in fact, a couple, although no damage or injuries. But it's really motivated us to get going on the move ASAP. I just want to make sure you're on board with it and get the paperwork started."

"And this would be for . . . ?"

"The move. I'm afraid it involves a new contract. We're trying to simplify the process—and it will be simplified when the new software's up and running next year—but for now it's like starting over. Without all the financials, credit checks, of course, you already being a member of the Arcadia family."

No financials, no credit checks. That sounded good but where were we going with this? The move, that had to be it. Mrs. Plansky—the best part of her mind not on this but mired in other things despite having her mighty nation on her side—rolled the dice. "You're talking about the move to another floor?"

"Exactly. I should have been more clear. And it is kind of confusing. In terms of care level he moves up but within the building he moves down. Up to level two, down to floor three."

"Right," said Mrs. Plansky. "Gotcha. I think where we got stuck was on whether he couldn't just stay where he was and have level two care. He seems attached to that room."

"That he does. So rather than fight it, here's the plan. We'll have a third floor room of the same dimensions and configuration available five days before the end of the month. That gives us time to repaint and redecorate, make it the identical twin of his current room. At no charge, by the way."

"You do think of everything," Mrs. Plansky said.

"We try," said Jeanine. "So are there any questions?"

"My dad did mention the expense. I wasn't clear on whether he meant it was ten thousand a month or ten thousand more a month. On top of what I'm—what we're already paying."

Jeanine laughed. "He really is a character. The answer is none of the above. My goodness! Ten thousand more a month! What you're paying now is seventy-five hundred a month, although that's being adjusted to nine thousand next fiscal year, which is April for us. And we have a special promotion right now on level two, fifteen percent off for six months, bringing the monthly total down to . . .

let's see—sixteen thousand, even. So it's only seven thousand more, not ten."

Mrs. Plansky had had some business experience with people who could get tricky with numbers. She just hadn't identified Jeanine as the type, until now. But did it matter? All those numbers were impossible until—she corrected herself—unless and until the Safemo problem was sorted out.

"I think for now," she said, "I'll leave Dad where he is."

Silence. "Loretta? I don't seem to be communicating well today. At this stage of your father's case, our protocols, state-approved, mandate a move to level two care, which means a physical move to the third floor. I know he can be stubborn, but you have a way with him. I know you'll bring him around."

"I'll have to get back to you," said Mrs. Plansky, for the second time that morning leaving the underlying fact unspoken.

"Wonderful. And there is a bit of a time issue—his present room is already spoken for by a new client starting the first of the month."

Mrs. Plansky spent the rest of the day checking out—in person or over the phone—much cheaper and then somewhat cheaper, assisted-living places, and imagining introducing them to her dad and him to them. It was grim.

There was a small visitor parking lot at the Little Pine Lake condos that Mrs. Plansky had to pass on the way to her own driveway. As she went by, the driver's side doors of two identical-looking black sedans opened and both drivers got out, Agent Rains and Agent Gatling. Mrs. Plansky hit the brakes. Over the years she and Norm had developed a list of pithy truths—pissy truths, he always called them—that applied to their business. For example: good news travels fast, bad news travels slow. Mrs. Plansky got out of the car—not jumping or hopping out, but quickly for this seventy-one-year-old version of her.

They came toward her, their faces unreadable.

"Hi, there," said Agent Rains.

"Yes?" said Mrs. Plansky, forgetting her manners in her eagerness to hear the speedy news.

"We've developed some information, thanks mostly to Agent Gatling here. Agent Gatling?"

"Well, Mrs. Plansky, it looks like there's been some carelessness on the other end. Safemo has been used before, just the once, but I hadn't expected even that. I assumed it was a one-timer, set up for this little operation and then deep-sixed. Everybody makes mistakes, of course, the good, the bad, and the ugly."

Agent Rains frowned, a quick look that Gatling missed although Mrs. Plansky did not.

"The point being," Gatling went on, "that on the previous case, through a complicated series of events that aren't relevant to yours, the bureau was able to make a geographical hit."

"I don't understand," Mrs. Plansky said. She kept *Am I getting back my money or not* bottled up inside.

"Sorry," Gatling said. "A lot of these scammers are based in Eastern Europe. Also Russia, of course. We're sure—"

"Ninety percent sure," said Rains.

"That the Safemo folks operate out of Romania, specifically a town called—" He fished in his pocket.

"Alba Gemina," said Rains. "And the percentage on that part falls a bit, down to say seventy-five, eighty."

"So we're making progress," Mrs. Plansky said. "What happens next? I assume the first case got solved?"

"What you have to understand," Rains said, "and it's a hard lesson we all learn, is that different countries play by different rules. There's a lot of politics, a lot of quid pro quo, and—"

"But did the people in the first case get their money back?" Mrs. Plansky said.

Rains shook her head. "The embassy—meaning the cyber-crime liaison—was unable, at least so far, to determine the perpetrators."

"But they're whoever's behind Safemo!"

"Possibly. Possibly not."

"But even if not, Safemo will know who they are!"

"That, too, will have to be determined," Rains said. "We've forwarded the complete file to the cybercrime liaison at the embassy. The moment we have any news from them we'll be in touch."

"When will that be?"

"There's no telling."

"That's it?" said Mrs. Plansky.

"For now." Agent Rains stood a little straighter and she was already standing very straight. "The truth is these cases are very challenging, Mrs. Plansky. But don't give up hope."

Agent Rains and Agent Gatling said goodbye and returned to their cars. Mrs. Plansky watched them drive off, except that Gatling did not drive off. Instead he got out of his car and came toward her, loosening his tie.

"This is my last case," he said. "I'm retiring at the end of the week."

"So young for that," said Mrs. Plansky.

"Moving to the private sector, actually. So I feel free to let my hair down a bit. Hate to see folks living under a delusion. Seen too much of it, to be honest. The thing is, at the other end, aside from the obvious corruption, of course, goes without saying, there's also what you might call a demotivating factor."

"Which is?" said Mrs. Plansky. For some reason she was now finding Agent Gatling easy to understand.

"From our point of view the scammers are bad guys, end of story. But to the elite running the show over there the scammers are bad guys who also have a nice little industry going, bringing in the Yankee dollar and lots of 'em. And to the everyday Joe they're punching up, the kind of outlaw people have a soft spot for."

"Like Robin Hood."

"You got it."

They gazed at each other. The message was in his eyes. Mrs. Plansky voiced it.

"You're telling me to lose hope."

"Not in so many words."

FIFTEEN

Mrs. Plansky was up at dawn the next morning. Actually, she'd been awake all night. Dawn was when she got out of bed.

She had a plan, the execution of which was going to require inner steeliness. She could do that. To take one example, there was the time, close to the end of Norm's life, when he asked her what she thought about taking a swing at a new and drastic form of radiation, still in the testing phase and a real long shot according to the oncologist, but Mrs. Plansky could see in his eyes how much he wanted her to say yes. Also in his eyes she saw that he was mostly dead already. She hadn't voiced that, had just simply given her head one little shake.

First, she sat down at her laptop and completed the application to drive for a rideshare company, the same rideshare company one of the waitresses at the club drove for and spoke highly of, and if not highly then at least without loathing. Second, she took out the jewelry box again, dumping out the contents on her bed. Mrs. Plansky didn't have a lot of jewelry but what she had was nice, and some of it very nice. Like this emerald-cut diamond ring in platinum, with a total carat weight she couldn't remember but it was up there. The ring had belonged to her mother and Mrs. Plansky had intended to give it to Emma on her twenty-first birthday or her wedding day or just some ordinary day. Maybe something else instead? But weren't there futures mapped out for everything in the jewelry box? This was where the steeliness came in. She had some cash in her purse and maybe five or six hundred dollars in the safe and that was it.

Down the road she could sell the condo and rent somewhere cheap, eking things out for the rest of . . . She left that thought unfinished. That was later and now was now.

Mrs. Plansky showered, brushed her hair, did her face, dressed in khaki slacks with a royal blue belt, light blue silk shirt, royal blue pumps, put her mom's ring in her purse, and drove to Frischetti Fine Jewelers, in the town center not far from her old house at 3 Pelican Way, and where she was known, at least a little.

Mr. Frischetti was alone in the shop, a loupe over one eye and a bracelet in his hand.

"Ah, Mrs. Plansky. So nice to see you. I heard you moved some time back."

"Hello, Mr. Frischetti. Yes, but not far. I'm down at Little Pine Lake."

"Hidden gem," said Mr. Frischetti. "Hey! Kind of funny for a man in my profession."

Mrs. Plansky didn't get it.

"Anything I can help you with?" he said.

Mrs. Plansky showed him the ring. He loved it, examined it with care, loved it even more and wrote a check for $29,000. Back in her car, she realized she'd forgotten to ask him the carat weight. But now she did get the hidden gem joke. "Everything evens out in the end," she said aloud, quoting what she thought was a bit of common folk wisdom. Just not in a way that we can understand, she added silently. She drove straight to Palm Coast Bank and Trust and deposited the check in the drive-through machine.

On the way home, Mrs. Plansky swung by Arcadia Gardens, checked in, and got up to the fourth floor without running into Jeanine, a lucky break. She knocked on her dad's door.

"That better be dinner," he called from inside.

Mrs. Plansky checked her watch. Two fifteen, perhaps a little early for dinner. "It's me, Dad."

"You?"

She opened the door and went in. Her dad, shirtless, had wheeled himself in front of a full-length mirror and seemed to be flexing his biceps.

"What are you doing here?" he said, not taking his eyes off the mirror.

"Just thought I'd drop in," Mrs. Plansky said. "Do I need an invitation?"

"I guess not. This isn't really my place, is it now? Not my own God-given place."

"Interesting you should mention that. The fact is—"

"It's not interesting to me. What I'm interested in is HGH. Can you get me some? Like today, if it's all the same to you."

"What's HGH?"

"Seriously? Don't you know anything?"

His gaze was still fixed on his own image so he missed the quick reddening of Mrs. Plansky's face, a reddening at first furious and then the precursor to a flood of tears. But she'd entered the time of steeliness and kept them inside. She crossed her arms.

"One thing going forward, Dad. There'll be no more *shekels* references or anything similar."

He glanced at her. "What are you talking about?"

"Anti-Semitism. I don't want to hear it."

"Me? Anti-Semitic? I deny it. Also I don't get it. Unless you're saying I think the Jews control HGH, which I absolutely do not."

Mrs. Plansky leaned against the back of her dad's TV chair, her legs suddenly weary. "I give up. What's HGH?"

"My hope and savior," said her dad. "Human growth hormone."

"You want to take human growth hormone?"

"Starting this very minute."

"Why?"

He gestured at her with his bare arms. "Look what's happened to my guns."

"Guns? Your arms are your guns?"

"More like just biceps. Never heard that expression? And you, a jock?"

"I'm not a jock."

"Sure you are. The only—one of the things I always loved about you."

Those tears also, Mrs. Plansky kept within. She came forward. "How would you like to come live at my place?"

A huge smile spread across his wrinkled, mottled face. It had the strange effect of making him appear more orc-like, but a lovable orc. "Really?"

"Really."

He wheeled around and zoomed over to his clothes closet.

"Not today, Dad. At the end of the month."

"Why the wait?"

"It's a matter of days. And I need the time to get things ready for you. Plus you're paid up here until then."

"So what's a few shek—"

He clamped his mouth shut.

"I'll come help you pack in a few days. Until then stay out of trouble."

"You're the boss."

Her heart sank. She was at the opposite end of that continuum. Safemo was the boss of her.

"What?" he said. "Something wrong?"

"Nope."

"The HGH, right? Don't worry about it for now. I'll hold off until the big moveroo." He gave himself a sort of celebratory hip shake, not so easy in a wheelchair.

"You know what makes me feel better about this?" said Mrs. Plansky's mother, on her deathbed, although Mrs. Plansky, much less familiar with dying back then, refused to believe what the doctors were saying, less and less euphemistically as the hospital days went on and on.

"You're going to be all right, Mama. Everyone says this round of chemo takes time to kick in."

"I hope it doesn't kick in when I'm six feet under."

Mrs. Plansky had smiled more than once in later years at the memory of that remark but she'd been stunned at the time.

Her mom patted her hand. "Just listen. What makes me feel better is knowing that when I'm gone you'll be living the life I could have."

"Oh, Mama, I don't—"

"Just look at you. I got the job done."

Those were just about the last words of her mother's that Mrs. Plansky heard. Now, driving away from Arcadia Gardens—which she had no desire to see ever again—she wanted the ring back from Mr. Frischetti. In one careless night she'd thrown away the life her mother could have had, or, to put it another way, Safemo had taken a piece of not just her but of her family, past, present, future. She wanted it back. Mrs. Plansky pulled over the first chance she got, coming to a stop in a parking lot. She scrolled through her phone until she came to Connie Malhouf, her lawyer—hers and Norm's—going all the way back to the first incorporation papers.

"Ah, Loretta. I thought I might be hearing from you."

"Oh?" said Mrs. Plansky, confused from the start.

"About—if I'm not telling tales out of school—Jack."

Jack? What in God's name was she—? Then the pieces started coming, in little shards that needed some help to form a whole. Cold chain? Ray and Rudy? $750K? Her will? Yes, Jack's call to Connie about her will, not a real big deal to begin with, and now irrelevant. Events had moved on.

"Loretta?"

"Right, Jack. I spoke to him. No problem. At least that isn't the problem. It's peripheral at most."

"What's the problem?"

Mrs. Plansky took a deep breath. She could feel Connie concentrating on the other end. Connie was one of those fierce concentrators, missing nothing and impossible to fool, impregnable, for example, to the Safemos of this world.

"I got this call in the middle of the night," she began, and out came the whole hodgepodge, so disorganized, disjointed, and dumb in the telling that no one could doubt that the teller was the just the type to have fallen for it. She came to the end, the part about no hope.

"Jesus," said Connie. "The FBI guy said that?"

"Not in so many words—which he actually did say."

"Jesus," said Connie again. Then came an expression of sympathy, totally sincere, and maybe more meaningful in her case, Connie not at all the warm and fuzzy type. But that wasn't what she wanted from Connie, or from anybody.

"What do you think?" Mrs. Plansky said.

"Beyond what I just said, you mean?"

"Yes."

"Is there something you want me to do?" Connie said.

"Fix it."

Had that sounded gross? Connie was silent for a few seconds. Yes, it had sounded gross.

"Are you raising the possibility of going after Newport Asset Management and or Palm Coast Bank and Trust for the losses?" Connie said.

Mrs. Plansky was doing precisely that but shrank from doing it aloud. It was weasely, cowardly, disgraceful. She said nothing.

"If so," Connie went on, "let me say three things. First, I do some work for Newport, meaning I couldn't represent you. Second, you might be able to find some lawyer to take this on. Third, I'd have to refresh myself on the case law, but any lawyer who'd say you had a chance in hell would be lying."

"Thank you," Mrs. Plansky said. In a strange way that turned out to be the answer she wanted.

That upright green turtle with a raised glass in its flipper was hard to miss. This time Mrs. Plansky turned in, parked, and went inside. She took a seat by herself at the end of the bar.

"Welcome to happy hour," said the bartender.

"Happy hour?" said Mrs. Plansky.

"Two for the price of one, now till six. What'll it be?"

For a moment she couldn't think of a single drink name. "Maybe a beer," she said.

"What do you like?" He recited a list that went on and on. Mrs. Plansky realized that she'd be getting two of whatever she ordered. Two beers were a lot of volume.

"Instead I'll do bourbon," she said, conscious of sounding like it was her first time in a bar.

"Any special kind?"

He was losing interest, and fast. She remembered the name of Norm's favorite. They didn't carry it, but had something just as good. He poured her two bourbons on the rocks from a bottle with a prancing thoroughbred on the label.

Mrs. Plansky sipped drink one. The Green Turtle Club was bright and airy, darkest at her end of the bar, with a Bahamian theme and free conch fritters. She had a weakness for conch fritters but she wasn't at all hungry. A guitarist began to play on the other side of the room and things got busy. Mrs. Plansky was aware of that. She moved on to drink two. All the seats at the bar got taken except for the one next to hers.

Mrs. Plansky was putting an end to drink five when someone behind her spoke.

"Loretta?"

Mrs. Plansky turned. Standing before her, wearing tennis shorts and a warm-up jacket was . . . was Kev? Yes, Kev Dinardo, lefty, wicked slice serve, pleasant manner, pleasant—even handsome— face.

"Hi, Kev. I don't usually—" Whatever that was going to be never got said, because in twisting around to see him better, she overbalanced, tipping the stool and heading for a crash on the tile floor.

Kev Dinardo, his white tennis shoes splashed with bourbon, caught her on the fly and set her upright on her feet. A bit of a hubbub rose and fell around her and she was aware of blurry faces. Mrs. Plansky made some sort of reassuring gesture, but lacked the stability to pull it off and started to go down again. And again he caught her.

He got her safely home, driving her car, with a taxi following to take him back. Mrs. Plansky sat in the passenger seat, seeing two of some things but picturing only one image of herself, a drunk old woman unable to take care of herself.

Kev glanced over. "No worries," he said. "That's why they call it *tipsy*."

She was silent.

At the Little Pine Lake condos he walked her to her door, made sure she got it open and that lights were on inside.

"Thank you, Mr. Dinardo," she said, making a big effort not to be slurry.

"Let's keep it on a first-name basis," he said.

Mrs. Plansky passed out fully dressed on her bed. She awoke in darkness and drank water right from the faucet, lots and lots of water. A wave of anger—real, hot fury—swept over her, anger directed only partly at herself. She found her laptop and opened a map of Romania.

SIXTEEN

"Did you hurt yourself?" Professor Bogdan said.

"No," said Dinu, back in the professor's office at the Liceu Teoretic for another English lesson.

"I only ask because you're limping."

Dinu did not know "limping" but he figured it out from the context. "It's these new boots. I have to break them in."

Professor Bogdan half-rose from his chair, gazed over the desk, took in the sight of Dinu's boots—cowboy boots, real ones, ordered online from a store in Santa Fe. Not only did the Americans have their own Georgia, but also their own Mexico, newer, better. Besides his cowboy boots, Dinu was wearing his new leather jacket, real leather with a red satin lining, and new ripped Levi's 501s. Only his socks, the Megan Thee Stallion ones, were old. Socks didn't show and at home the washer still wasn't fixed.

"Break them in?" said Bogdan. "That's very good American English. But I didn't teach it to you. Where did you learn it?"

Dinu shrugged. He'd actually ended up talking to a woman at the shop—she had a lovely, slightly slow way of speaking, had called him "honey"—and he'd learned it from her.

"No matter," Bogdan said. "The fact that your vocabulary is growing unconsciously is a good sign. Do you understand 'unconsciously'?"

"Yes."

"Define, please."

"Happening on their own, without knowing."

Bogdan sat back and nodded. "Even your accent is improving, as though you've been talking to native speakers."

"What are native speakers?"

"In this case, born Americans."

Dinu caught an expression on Bogdan's face that he didn't like. The professor knew damn well that he talked to native speakers. That was the whole point. Was he making fun of him?

Bogdan took out a notepad. "Let's forget about grammar today and simply converse. What do you want to talk about?"

"I don't know."

"Sports?"

"Okay," Dinu said. Then came an idea. "Explain baseball."

Bogdan laughed. "That I cannot do. A complete mystery, and do you know I attended a real game? Yankee Stadium—my brother took me on my last visit. He tried to teach me but it was impossible. There are thirteen ways to balk. Can you imagine?"

"What is 'balk'?"

"I have no idea but it ends in a big argument and the referee throws the coach out of the game."

"He throws him?"

"Not physically. He forces him to depart. But let's talk about something else. How about movies? Americans usually say movies, not films."

"Okay, movies."

"Have you seen many American movies?"

"No."

"What kind of movies do you like?"

Dinu shrugged. He hadn't seen many movies from any country. His mother watched a lot of TV, but not movies, preferring cartoons and game shows. As for going to the cinema, that cost money.

"I'm predicting that you'll like crime movies," Bogdan said.

Dinu sat back in his chair.

"There are many fine American crime movies—*The Maltese Falcon*"—the professor began writing on the pad—"*Double Indemnity, The Sting,* but you would probably like the more violent kind, like *Pulp Fiction, Reservoir Dogs,* or—"

"Can you put that out?" Dinu said, gesturing with his chin to the Chesterfield smoking in the professor's ashtray.

Bogdan looked up. Dinu made the chin gesture again. He didn't repeat the request, didn't bother mentioning the asthma, which had in fact been much better lately, didn't say please. Bogdan put out the cigarette.

The lesson came to an end soon after. Bogdan handed Dinu the list of crime movies. "Let's make this the last lesson," the professor said in their own language. "I've taken you as far as I can."

When Dinu reported for work that night, he told Uncle Dragomir that the lessons were finished.

"Who says?" said Uncle Dragomir.

"The professor."

Marius the bouncer was standing nearby, cleaning his fingernails with the knife he always wore in an ankle sheath, out of sight.

"Are you catching this, Marius?" said Uncle Dragomir.

"Pretty funny," Marius said.

"Funny?"

"Not ha-ha—the other kind. Want me to get him on the phone?"

Uncle Dragomir shook his head. "In person is always best in doing business. Go see him and have a talk."

"Just a verbal talk?"

"For now. I'm sure he'll be reasonable."

"What if he wants more for the lessons?"

"Now that's the ha-ha kind of funny. Tell him verbally there's a sale on the lessons—twenty-five percent off until further notice."

"Hey, there, Grampy, it's me, Robby."

Grampy in this case, not Grandpa or any of the other choices. Romeo's research was getting better all the time.

"My grandson Robby?" came the reply, the voice the thinnest, wobbliest, and scratchiest they'd come upon yet.

"The one and only," Dinu said. He, too, was getting better all the time. "How are things in Big Sky Country?"

"Colder than a well-digger's ass."

Wow. What a fabulous expression! Dinu glanced around the Cambio room at Club Presto to see if anyone else appreciated it, but not one of them—Uncle Dragomir, Romeo, Timbo, or Tassa—had enough English for that. Tassa, by herself in the back corner, had asked if she could sit in, a bit of a surprise, but a nice one, and Uncle Dragomir had said yes, also a surprise. Dinu felt totally relaxed, like a pilot landing his plane for the thousandth time.

"Pretty warm down here, Grampy."

"Still at Arizona State? Haven't heard from you in a while."

"Go Sun Devils. And I've been studying hard, but sorry for not calling. And sorry for the reason I call—I'm calling now."

"Huh?"

Dinu got going on the whole discurs, as they would say in his language. The DUI, the aggressive police, the $9,726.18—by now a lucky number to him—self-destroying password, Securo, the new Safemo, set up by Romeo in that clever and cautious way he had, always a step ahead. When Dinu came to saving the whales—his favorite part, his brain wave, as the Americans said—he glanced over at Tassa. And then came another surprise. She was staring at him, frowning so deeply she almost looked ugly. Maybe her mind was on other things completely, like her home life, just as messed up as his. But no time to figure that out now. The climax—this was like a Shakespeare play, always with a climax, according to Professor Bogdan—came: bank account, password, money—in this case the $9,726.18 plus the remainder in the account, slightly less than twenty thousand, but Dinu, busy with the thankful and affectionate denouement, might not have caught the figure right as it flashed on Romeo's screen. Bottom line, as the Americans said: nothing else, no real riches to mine, Romeo finding no other accounts, in other words just an adequate job.

Still, Uncle Dragomir seemed pleased. There were some high fives and then Uncle Dragomir told Timbo to hand out gift cards to Salle Privé, the deluxe restaurant next door, also owned by him. Dinu, Romeo, and Tassa stayed behind while Romeo got busy at several keyboards, erasing digital tracks and turning the event into a nonevent for anyone who came looking, even themselves.

"I'm starving," Dinu said.

The three of them went outside. It was cold and snowy. Dinu tried to take Tassa's hand, but it slipped away.

"Something wrong?"

She didn't look at him. "I lost my appetite."

"Come anyway. Maybe you'll find it again."

Tassa shook her head. When they reached the door of Salle Privé she kept walking.

"Tassa! Where are you going?"

"Home."

"But why?"

"I told you."

"Then just come sit."

She shook her head and walked on.

"Wait. I'll take you on the bike."

"To hell with the bike."

"What do you mean?" he called after her.

Tassa didn't answer, just hurried to the end of the block, rounded the corner, and vanished from sight.

"What's with her?" Dinu said.

"Maybe it's her period," said Romeo. Then he laughed. "You hope and pray, right?"

Dinu punched him on the shoulder, not gently.

"Ow! What's wrong with you?"

Dinu took a deep breath, got a grip. "Sorry."

They went inside, were taken to a nice corner table, ordered steak frites with Cokes to drink.

"We're getting good at this," Romeo said, his mouth full of frites.

"Yeah."

Romeo leaned forward. "Ever ask yourself why we even need Dragomir?"

"No," said Dinu.

"Think about it."

For dessert they had chocolate cake with chocolate ice cream. Romeo checked his watch and left soon after, but Dinu found he was still hungry and ordered another dessert, this time chocolate cake with maple walnut ice cream, which he'd never had. Maple, he knew, was a syrup that came from the Green Mountain State. He fell in love with maple walnut ice cream, tasting America in every bite.

Dinu was still eating when an older woman who'd been sitting at the bar came over. Older but not old, maybe in her twenties. Estimating the ages of older people wasn't easy. He'd seen this woman before. She'd been a dealer at one of the fancy casinos in Bucharest and was working with Uncle Dragomir on some sort of casino plan for here in Alba Gemina.

"Dinu, isn't it?"

"Yes." The smell of her perfume reached him. He felt like maybe his mouth needed wiping but his napkin had fallen to the floor. The woman wore a tight red dress, high translucent heels, had thick, wavy platinum hair, and a rose and bloody thorn tattoo on her shoulder; in short, she looked like a movie star.

"I'm Annika."

"Right, Annika. I've seen you at, um, next door."

"Correct. I hear, Dinu, you've got a head on your shoulders."

"Well, ah, I don't know about . . ."

"What else have you got?"

At first Dinu had no clue. Then a thought came to him. "Boots," he said. "Cowboy boots from Santa Fe." He stuck them out where she could see. She saw. The problem with Tassa—whatever it was— got very small very fast.

SEVENTEEN

Mr. Santiago handled maintenance at the Little Pine Lake condos. Mrs. Plansky walked him through her place, explaining what her father could and could not do.

"Don't worry, Mrs. Plansky, I got this. Thirty years of maintenance in Florida—I've done every kind of these upgrades you can imagine."

"Good to hear. Any suggestions?"

"The time to install what you need for what's down the road is now. You'll save money in the long run."

"What's down the road, meaning further deterioration?"

"It never goes the other way in my experience. Who do you have coming in, don't mind my asking?"

"My father. I thought I'd—"

"Sorry. I meant coming in to help you out—a home health care aide, a professional."

"I'm pretty sure I can handle it, at least for now."

"I hear you," said Mr. Santiago. "If things change you might want to contact my sister-in-law Lucrecia. Experienced, reliable, hardworking, honest, and half the price of anyone you'd get from an agency."

"I'll keep her in mind," said Mrs. Plansky.

Mrs. Plansky's condo was a two-bedroom, master on the first floor and guest room upstairs. To avoid the stair problem, Mr. Santiago turned the little first-floor study into a bedroom. Her dad was delighted with it.

"This calls for champagne. I prefer Krug but I'm flexible."

"I don't have Krug. There may not be any champagne at all."

"That's gonna change. I'll buy some right now, on me. Where's your account?"

"What account?"

"Your liquor store account. I'll have them deliver."

"I don't have a liquor store account."

"Now I've heard everything."

A little later she found him in the pantry.

"No Fritos? Can't live without Fritos. Where's your account?"

Soon after that he got sleepy and Mrs. Plansky put him to bed. Over the next few days she observed that he did a lot of sleeping—morning nap, afternoon nap, and nighttime, which was really two long naps with a period of activity in between.

"I'll be quiet as a mouse," he promised about that active period. "You just get your beauty sleep. I won't wake you."

And he didn't wake her because Mrs. Plansky wasn't getting her beauty sleep or any other kind of sleep. Night after night she lay awake although her mind was dreaming, the same dream—in fact, a nightmare—over and over. This nightmare was like one of those noirish movies where everyone but the central character could see what was coming, a short little movie in this case that took place completely on the phone. Mrs. Plansky lay in bed, wide awake, sometimes soaked in sweat, sometimes shivering, never able to stop the movie. Over breakfast on day four or five—her dad had bacon and soft-boiled eggs every morning, stipulating three bacon strips and two eggs, although he never got past the first of either—he said, "No offense, but we're family, and all. You're not looking your best, Loretta."

When he went down for his morning nap, Mrs. Plansky called Mr. Santiago and got the number of Lucrecia, his sister-in-law.

*   *   *

"Dad, I want you to meet Lucrecia. She's Mr. Santiago's sister-in-law I was telling you about."

"In what context?" her dad said.

"Lucrecia will be staying here while I'm gone. Just a short business trip, as I explained."

"But you're retired."

"This is something new, remember?"

"No, but I'm listening."

"I'll have more details when I get back. For now please say hi to Lucrecia. Lucrecia Santiago, my dad Chandler Banning."

They shook hands. Lucrecia was in her fifties, looked something like Carmen Miranda, but a Carmen Miranda that never was, who eschewed makeup, fussing over her appearance, or glamor, bringing the inner strength of character into plain sight.

"Nice to meet you, Mr. Banning," she said.

He gazed up at her from his wheelchair. A sly look crossed his face. "Call me Chandler," he said.

"If that's your preference," Lucrecia said. "And please call me Lucrecia."

"That's my plan."

She smiled down at him. Her teeth were big and beautiful, gave her smile a lot of oomph, a complex sort of oomph that was only part-friendly. "Then we're off to a great start," she said. "It's like Ping-Pong."

"Ping-Pong?"

"Ping-Pong's my philosophy of life," Lucrecia said. "If you ping me that's what you get back, a ping. But if you pong me I pong you."

Mrs. Plansky's dad eyed her. Just as the silence was about to grow uncomfortable, he said, "I never used to like Ping-Pong."

That struck them all as very funny. They laughed and laughed. Mrs. Plansky put a lid on it when she felt tears on the way.

Mrs. Plansky no longer had much in the way of winter clothes. She went through what there was, folded neatly in a cedar chest at the back of the closet. She found shearling gloves, a knit hat featuring a logo with snowflakes forming the word ALTA, which had to date from their one ski trip to Utah, three decades ago, and a three-quarter length wool coat in navy blue that was warmer than it looked, as she recalled, and would have to do. Then, just as she was about to close the chest, she spotted a scarf tucked away in one corner.

Mrs. Plansky pulled it out. She herself had never gone for scarves but Norm had had many, only this one somehow surviving. It was a Scottish tartan, with autumnal hues laid out in a grid of little squares, one of his worst and frayed here and there. But when she tried it on and checked herself in the mirror, it looked right—or more accurately felt right—so it made the cut. Unlike Norm, when Mrs. Plansky traveled she traveled light, for this trip packing just the one suitcase, a hard-case roller type that could be jammed into the overhead bin. Shoes were always the problem. In the end she cut to the bone, taking only the pull-on low-heeled booties with the least tapered toes on the market, the warm, quilted indoor-outdoor mules in black, and her Italian ballet flats, which she just had to have.

Mrs. Plansky had her hair cut at Delia's on the Waterway, tipping more than usual on account of her booking the appointment so late. There had to be standards. Also she paid all the bills now due or that would become due for the next month, erring on the safe side, and withdrew $2,600 in cash—$1,600 covering two weeks' pay for Lucrecia and another $1,000 to give her for food and any other expenses—Mrs. Plansky shying away from checking the balance to see what remained. The other expenses seemed to already include a new Cuban place her dad had somehow heard of, although he always spoke disparagingly of ethnic food. There was no point wondering why on the suddenly Cuban part. The answer was the obvious one.

Mrs. Plansky booked a round-trip flight from Miami to Bucharest with a short stop in Zurich, leaving the return date open. On

Lucrecia's second day on the job—the first one having gone well, her dad taking over more of his self-care than he had in a long time, and also making the point that Mrs. Plansky needn't have stuck around—she rose before anyone was up, hoisted her suitcase into the trunk of the car, and drove down to Miami. She parked in an off-site lot, writing the space number in the notebook she'd bought special for the trip, took the shuttle to the terminal, and got to the gate with plenty of time to spare.

The man sitting next to her at the gate was on the phone, speaking an unfamiliar language. But Mrs. Plansky had taken both French and Latin in high school, and thought she was beginning to pick out some of the words. Frigorific, for example. That would be cold.

EIGHTEEN

Mrs. Plansky had a window seat in coach. Her phone pinged just as the plane was pulling away from the gate, and in came a text from Emma.

Grandma! Mom just told me the news! Is there anything I can do to help? I feel so bad for you. And also I'm furious! I want to hop on a plane to Bulgaria is it? Mom didn't seem sure. And shake those people down.

Mrs. Plansky texted back. Something to think about. Ha-ha. But I don't want you to worry about this for one second. How are things in your life?

She waited for a reply but none came before the airplane mode announcement. Mrs. Plansky put her phone away. Winter break had to be over now, meaning Emma was back in class at UCSB. What was her major? If Mrs. Plansky had ever known, she no longer did. But whatever Emma had chosen would have been the result of careful thought. Mrs. Plansky would never call her own daughter scatterbrained, but Emma was the opposite of what she wouldn't call her daughter, so Emma's mental discipline hadn't come from Nina. Nor had it come from Zach, Emma's dad, scatterbrained for sure, one example being that he'd forgotten on more than one occasion that husbands shouldn't sleep around, in his case leading to the Teds and now Matty and/or Matthew, who perhaps was better considered as two people, and with that thought came the certain premonition that the Matts, too, were temporary. Unless she somehow came through with the 250K! Maybe better to get off the plane this very minute and save Nina from the Matts!

Uh-oh. Had she spoken that last part aloud? It was just a joke. She had promises to keep. Mrs. Plansky glanced over at her seatmate, a gum-chewing boy of eight or nine, and quite literally a snot-nosed kid. He was watching her with what appeared to be mean little eyes. Mrs. Plansky gave him a vague smile. He turned away and got busy jabbing at the onboard screen, stopping when he came to the flight tracker. She was surprised to see they were already airborne, an inch or an inch and a half offshore. She looked out the window hoping for a sight of the Atlantic down below but they were above the clouds. "Why don't artists ever paint the clouds from above?" Norm had asked. She'd given him a nice print of Georgia O'Keeffe's above-the-clouds painting for his next birthday. Norm pretended to like it, but he could see she wasn't fooled. "It's a mathematical take," he explained. "That's what I do for a living." Mrs. Plansky gazed down at the cloud layer, like meadows of gold, and saw no math. If Norm had been seated next to her instead of the snot-nosed kid a very nice conversation might have been struck up now. Instead Mrs. Plansky took out her digital reader and opened a book on the history of Romania, downloaded yesterday.

There's losing yourself in a story and then there's getting lost in a story. Her experience with this history of Romania began with type one but after seventy or eighty pages descended into type two. Was it the writer's fault or did some countries just make better stories than others? The Romanian story, which she was in no position to judge a bloody mess, did seem to be both messy and bloody. The real Dracula, for example, often resorted to impaling. Mrs. Plansky looked up what impaling was, exactly, and put the reader aside for the moment.

She closed her eyes, resting them, in fact. Giving her eyes a little rest from time to time? That was new in her life. Her eyes had gone along for more than seven decades content to take their rest when the rest of her was resting—team players, the pair of them—but now they were making demands.

Rest when the rest of me rests, darn it! That was kind of funny. She thought of texting it to . . . to whom, exactly? Emma popped up first in her mind. Was it true that some traits skipped a generation? Mrs. Plansky had seen Emma far more in the early part of her life, then less, and now, in the past two years, hardly at all. You could say that's just the way things work nowadays. Or you could do something about it. She realized that she hadn't tried hard enough and decided there and then, skimming along over meadows of gold, to do something about it.

Emma's middle name was Loretta, one of the honors of Mrs. Plansky's life. Zach's mother's name was Emma. That part didn't bother Mrs. Plansky at all. The fact that Loretta was the middle name made it better—like a ring with a secret compartment.

At that moment, she thought of the emerald-cut diamond ring, intended for Emma, now in the hands of Mr. Frischetti. Her eyes decided they'd had enough rest. They snapped open and scanned the plane, saw everything in a new way, not how the eyes of a normal traveler for business or tourism would see, but more like the eyes of someone on a secret mission. And it was a secret mission in the sense that she'd told no one her destination. Mrs. Plansky never drank alcohol on planes, but when the drinks cart came around, she took one. She didn't order a martini, shaken not stirred, but she thought of it. She was going rogue.

When Mrs. Plansky awoke, needing to use the bathroom, the snot-nosed kid was gone, replaced by a sleeping and beefy middle-aged man in a tracksuit. He seemed to be the wide-stance type.

"Excuse me?" Mrs. Plansky said.

No reaction.

She raised her voice slightly and tried a few more times, also without success, then gave his shoulder a little nudge. His near eye opened slightly.

"Sorry to bother you." She made a little gesture toward the aisle. Sleeping next to the man was a beefy middle-aged woman, also in a tracksuit but with a narrower stance. He elbowed her. Ah, a couple. Soon they were both in the aisle. Mrs. Plansky got to her feet, with not close to her usual ease, and made her way to the back of the plane. On the way she glanced out the window for another sight of those golden meadows, but it was night.

"How much longer to the stop in Zurich?" she asked the flight attendant.

"Zurich?" said flight attendant with a marked German accent. "Zurich was an hour ago."

Mrs. Plansky resolved to be sharper, starting that very minute.

In Bucharest, she'd booked a room in a small hotel near the airport. It had Vila as part of a long name, which she presumed was like villa and therefore promising in her scheme of things, and also she'd liked the photo of the small breakfast room, with a few simple candlelit wooden tables and a buffet visible in the background. She was asleep five minutes after check-in, and didn't stir until daylight pinkened the insides of her eyelids.

When she awoke she saw she'd neglected to close the curtains. Outside was a very small patio with an alley beyond, partly obscured by a trellis with nothing growing on it. A rusty, tireless motorcycle leaned against the patio side wall. Snow was falling. The image— snow, motorcycle, trellis—somehow made her feel the foreignness of the place, deeply foreign, as though this visit was happening in the age before mass tourism. She closed the curtain, figured out the shower, got herself ready. Before Norm, back in college, she'd worked on a ranch in Montana one summer, the whole thing set up by her dad, the details now gone. There'd been a little fling with one of the wranglers—pretty much her sole venture into the flinging life—a wonderful rider although his passion was motorcycles. He'd taught her to ride his Harley Super Glide, an enormous howling beast that should have scared the bejeezus out of her, but did not. She'd been quite good at it.

The man at the desk called a taxi. It pulled up and Mrs. Plansky stepped outside, wrapping the Scottish scarf tighter around her neck. "Brr," she said as she got in the back seat. "Frigorific."

The driver glanced back in surprise. "You speak Romanian?"

"Only the one word."

He laughed, and then was quiet almost the whole way. Finally, slowing down, he said, "Here is another one. Noroc."

"What's that?"

"Good luck."

He pulled up in front of a large, low, gray building, actually more of a blocky compound, fenced and gated.

"U.S. Embassy," the driver said.

She paid him, tipping more than usual, encouraging noroc in a magical thinking way.

Mrs. Plansky presented herself at the reception desk.

"Hello," she said. "I'm Loretta Plansky from Punta D'Oro, Florida. I'd like to see whoever's in charge of cybercrime, please." She laid her passport on the desk.

The receptionist didn't touch it. "Do you have an appointment?" she said.

"No," said Mrs. Plansky. "But I'm happy to wait."

The receptionist nodded. "The problem is that in order to meet with anyone on staff, an appointment is required."

"Very well. I'd like to make an appointment with whoever's in charge of cybercrime as soon as possible. Preferably today."

The receptionist consulted her screen, the back of which was turned to Mrs. Plansky. The monitor hid the receptionist's face from below the eyes. The eyes, expressionless, were not moving. Time passed, perhaps the point of the whole exercise. Mrs. Plansky felt a twinge in her new hip.

"I'm an American citizen," she said.

"Yes," said the receptionist, glancing at the passport, still unopened. "I see that."

"Who has been," Mrs. Plansky went on, and then stopped herself. She didn't want to voice the word *victimized*, certainly not in front of this, well, child, a nasty designation she regretted. But still. "Who has been on the receiving end of a cybercrime. The FBI believes the crime originated in this country." Mrs. Plansky smiled in a way she hoped was encouraging. "Which is why I'm here."

"The FBI?" the receptionist said.

"Federal Bureau of Investigation," said Mrs. Plansky.

"That's not what I meant." The receptionist's tone, which had been right down the center began to veer toward the hostile lane. "Did the FBI send you?"

"Very much so," said Mrs. Plansky. "If indirectly."

The receptionist blinked. The reception desk was the circular kind. She rolled her chair to the other side and got on a landline phone, back turned and voice low. After a minute or two she hung up, wheeled to the front, handed Mrs. Plansky her passport, and said, "Please wait in the waiting area."

"Thank you."

Mrs. Plansky sat in the waiting area, her purse in her lap. A framed photo of the president hung on the wall. How confident he looked! Which was probably the point of presidential photos. On the other hand, picturing in her mind a photo of Lincoln, ol' Honest Abe hadn't been projecting much in the way of confidence and yet hadn't he inspired plenty of the real thing? Her mind was wandering along those lines when she realized she'd made a mistake. Her purse—brown leather, brass clasp—did not match the booties with the low heels and roomy toe boxes, which were black.

"Ms. Plansky?"

"Mrs.," she said, looking up.

A young man—although not as young as the receptionist—stood before her. He wore a subdued tie, gray flannels, and a blue blazer with a stars-and-stripes lapel pin. Some sort of gold badge was superimposed on the stripes, the writing on it too small for her to see.

"Mrs. Plansky, my apologies," he said. "My name's Jamal Perryman."

They shook hands. Mrs. Plansky rose. Still holding her hand, Jamal Perryman gave her a bit of a boost. She thought of resisting but her legs, which still seemed jet-lagged, took over the decision-making.

"Loretta Plansky," she added. "U.S. citizen."

"And currently residing here in Romania?"

"Oh, no. I live in Florida. Punta D'Oro. Are you in charge of cybercrime, Mr. Perryman?"

"Not in charge, but it's one of my duties."

"Are you with the FBI?"

"Secret Service." He tapped his lapel pin. Mrs. Plansky leaned forward. The words were right there.

"I thought you guarded the president."

"That, too. I gather you've been affected by cybercrime."

"Correct. I'd expected the file on my case would have already crossed your desk."

His eyebrows rose. "Are you telling me you flew over here especially for this?"

"That's right." She was a little confused. "Is it surprising?"

"Let's just say unprecedented, in my experience," said Mr. Perryman. "How about we go on upstairs and look into this?"

Mr. Perryman's small, tidy office was on the floor above. Through the window she could see a basketball half-court just inside the embassy perimeter. Two marines in full uniform were shooting hoops, a third one still clearing away the snow. On the shelves were what Mrs. Plansky took to be family photos—a smiling wife and two serious-looking little kids.

"Your children?" she said.

"Yes."

"Adorable. What are their names?"

"We don't divulge details like that."

"Ah. Sorry. I should have known."

"No reason why you should."

"Well, there is the secret part, after all. Right in the name."

He shot her a quick, less formal look. She'd gotten his attention. He pulled up a chair for her and sat at the desk.

"May I see your passport?"

She handed it over. He opened it, then turned to his laptop and got busy, typing and reading while Mrs. Plansky sat with her purse in her lap and clouds moved across the sky, darkening things a bit. Mr. Perryman had a handsome face, not closed off, not unfriendly, not uneasy, intelligent and maybe even predisposed to warmth. But that was the problem with human faces, and maybe also the reason they were so fascinating: you just never knew, beauty and truth maybe not being so congruent after all. Some famous movie stars turned out to be rather foul when the lights were off, if you could believe what you read. After Norm's death, in those many sleepless nights that had followed, she'd taken to reading Hollywood biographies, which she'd never done before or since. She was informed on the subject: that was the point.

Mr. Perryman looked up to find she was staring, perhaps staring hard, at his face.

"Whoa," he said. "Is something wrong?"

"No. Sorry. Well, yes. What happened to me was wrong."

He gestured toward the screen. "Yes, I see that. Can you walk me through the details of the contact?"

"You mean the phone call?"

"If you please."

"Certainly," said Mrs. Plansky. "But first—am I right in thinking you weren't aware of my case until I walked in?"

Mr. Perryman's face closed up the littlest bit. "I'm aware of it now," he said.

He looked her in the eyes. She did the same to him. After probably too much of that, Mrs. Plansky told herself to grow up, and started in on her story.

Some people are real good listeners, have an active way of doing it, as though a kind of ear magnetism is pulling the words right out of your mouth. Others are only listening for some sort of cue so they can jump in and take over the talking themselves. Mr. Perryman was the first kind, although his face remained totally formal the whole time. There was a slight shift of the eyes when she came to the part about saving the whales.

"Well?" she said.

"First," Mr. Perryman said, "I want to make sure I understand. There were actually two calls?"

"Yes, but the second one was very short."

"Can you go over that one again?"

"Sure, but I don't see how it's important. In terms of finding clues, I mean. Clues for solving the case, Mr. Perryman."

"Humor me," he said.

She couldn't help smiling. Mrs. Plansky decided they were beginning to hit it off. That had to be good.

"Start with how much time elapsed between the two calls," Mr. Perryman said.

"Five or ten minutes. The first thing he said was that he was free as a bird and out on the street."

"Did you hear any street sounds? Anything in the background?"

"Not that I remember. But the sound was better. I was happy, of course, thinking he was out of jail or the police station or whatever it was. I suggested he get a lawyer."

"What did he say to that?"

Mrs. Plansky thought back. "I can't remember. Maybe nothing.

Wait, no. At first he didn't seem to understand. I explained that he'd need a lawyer to represent him in court. When his case came up, you see. I thought he wasn't thinking things through. Like a typical teenager."

"Did he sound like a teenager?"

"Yes. And next he said it was a good idea and he said good night."

"In what way?"

"In what way did he say good night?"

"Straight up?" said Mr. Perryman. "Or—and bear with me—like he was amused inside?"

Mrs. Plansky felt stirring in the silo where the heavy artillery was stored. She knew at that moment she was done with crying. "Straight up, Mr. Perryman. You seem to think this second call was important. Mind filling me in on why?"

He tapped on his keyboard and a printer on a shelf behind him started up. "It's unusual," he said. "Maybe unique, and I see a lot of these cases. An awful lot. The point is we're always on the lookout for fingerprints. Not that the second call is a fingerprint for sure. But it's a candidate. Why make that second call? The game was over." He reached behind him for the printout, laid it on his desk, tapped it. "Off the top, I'm happy to say that your case has already been looked at here by one of my associates. She mentions the second call but doesn't seem to have flagged it as anything special."

"Shouldn't she be in this meeting?" Mrs. Plansky said.

"Ideally, yes, but she was posted back stateside two days ago. That probably explains the second call situation—she ran out of time." Mr. Perryman took out a red pen, and circled something on the page.

"So who's in charge of my case now?" Mrs. Plansky said.

"Good question. Let's see what I can do about that. Please wait here. I'll be right back." He rose and walked out of the room, leaving the door open.

Mrs. Plansky sat with her purse in her lap and waited. She remembered a recent appointment where she'd sat just like this, only at the DMV. She rose and went to the window. The marines were still shooting hoops. They were laughing and trash talking—she could tell that part from the body language—and having fun far from home but not far from boyhood. Mrs. Plansky took a closer look at Mr. Perryman's anonymous family and then wandered over toward the desk and sat back down. She gazed at the printout, the writing upside down from her vantage point, the font too small to be read from this distance anyway. But that was academic, the point being that you didn't read the paperwork on the desks of others. That would be snooping.

And snooping was wrong, end of story. Here, in this office of the Secret Service, Mrs. Plansky suddenly saw the irony. Snooping was wrong, yes, but this office was on a different planet, where snooping was the whole point! Therefore did refusing to join in make you impolite, a boor, brought up in a barn? Well, a stretch, maybe, but why take the slightest risk of being a boor if by merely rising and taking three or four little steps around the desk you kept your membership in polite society, at least polite society as it functioned on Planet Snoopy? Mrs. Plansky gazed down at the printout and was just starting to read when she heard footsteps approaching in the hall.

Something amazing happened at that moment, reminiscent of the tennis match not so long ago when she'd spun around and run down that lob without a thought to her new hip, which by the way seemed to be making its presence known since that late-night call. Mrs. Plansky didn't make the connection between that tennis match and what took place now until later, but the connection was absence of thought, the triumph of pure instinct—in the case of the tennis spinning around and running, in the case of the here and now whipping her phone out of her purse and snapping a quick photo of the top printout page.

She was back at the window, phone in purse, purse in hand, when Mr. Perryman walked into the room.

"The jarheads still shooting hoops?" he said.

Mrs. Plansky turned. "They're having so much fun."

Undercover ops? Was that the expression? She'd been born for this.

NINETEEN

"My wife swears by your toaster knife," Mr. Perryman said when they were back in their places at his desk.

"How nice," said Mrs. Plansky. "Although we sold the company some years ago," she added, updating the research he'd just been doing.

"You and your husband?"

"My late husband."

"Sorry."

"Thank you."

Mr. Perryman glanced down at the printout. Mrs. Plansky suddenly wondered whether his office was equipped with security cameras. It almost seemed like a no-brainer, given his profession. She forced herself not to scan the room.

"I'm going to be taking over this case myself," Mr. Perryman said.

Because of his wife and the toaster knife? Whatever the reason, this was good news. Nothing beat face-to-face relationships in business. Why wouldn't undercover ops be the same?

He checked his watch. "I'll be reporting to you either by voice, text, or email as soon as I have any news, and I'll also be checking in once a week whether there's news or not."

"Great," said Mrs. Plansky. "Any chance you're free this afternoon?"

Mr. Perryman's handsome face wasn't formed for expressing

confusion. It came close to making him appear ugly. "Not following you."

"I was thinking we'd drive up to Alba Gemina. It looks to be about three hours away on the map."

Mr. Perryman folded his hands on the desk. "Why Alba Gemina?"

"Why, because of the Safemo connection." She gestured toward the printout with her chin. "Isn't that in there?"

Mr. Perryman didn't answer that question. Instead he said, "What do you know about Safemo?"

"Just what the FBI told me. Safemo's like Paymo or Venpal—a way to transfer money, except it was set up by the scammers, probably just for onetime use, they said." She saw in his eyes that she'd gone wrong somewhere. "They being the FBI, not the scammers," she explained. "But they—the scammers—made a mistake. It turned out that Safemo had in fact been used before. The FBI didn't tell me the details of that case, but in working on it they'd zeroed in on Alba Gemina. As the place where the scam originated from, is the point."

Mr. Perryman said nothing, just gazed at her.

"Oh, dear," she said. "Did I say Paymo? And Venpal?"

He nodded a slight nod.

"I meant the reverse, of course. Not reverse, but . . ." She let that trail off.

His gaze was on her but his eyes had an inward look. He gave his head a little shake. "I don't want to speak ill of a brother agency."

"Oh, go ahead," said Mrs. Plansky. "I won't tell."

Mr. Perryman's eyebrows rose slightly. Was a laugh on the way? It didn't come. Instead he said, "I'll have to ask you to forget about that initial Safemo hit, Mrs. Plansky, which should not have been mentioned. It resulted from another investigation, a classified investigation having nothing to do with cyberfraud."

"That's not what I was told."

Mr. Perryman had no comment.

"And I don't want to forget about it," she went on.

"Excuse me?"

"It's an important clue. How do you forget something like that?"

He sat back. He rubbed his hands together. His desk phone buzzed. He ignored it. "You're clearly an intelligent woman," he began.

"That won't work," Mrs. Plansky said.

Oh, dear. Had she spoken that aloud? She wasn't quite sure until she saw the hardening in his face, or more like a revelation of his inner self. Mr. Perryman was a tough guy—and why not in a job like his?—but also very smooth. He might have been around the same age as Jack, but he wasn't Jack, not close. She didn't even try to imagine Jack in a job like Mr. Perryman's.

"Okay," he said. "Let's skip on down to the bottom line. What happened to you has happened and will happen to huge numbers of people. I've seen the data. The perpetrators are all over the place, but especially in Eastern Europe, including this country, where Alba Gemina is a particular locus point. All you have to do is drive through it and see all the luxury car dealerships—like Brentwood, on a per capita basis, but there are no Brentwood-type jobs. The skill level is an important variable ranging from the crudest—just throwing out any sort of bait hoping to hook something—to sophisticated. Your case is on the sophisticated end. There are many indicators—the fact that they knew your grandson's name, to take one."

"How did they know that?"

"It just takes a little work—almost none if they've bought or designed an algorithm to crawl through social media twenty-four seven, three sixty-five."

Technology was good enough in, say 1959, thought Mrs. Plansky, a thought she held firmly to herself.

His phone buzzed again, and again he ignored it. "Any questions?"

Any questions? Didn't question time come at the end? Mrs. Plansky wasn't ready for the end of this meeting. She didn't want to be rude but there were still plenty of questions. She boiled them down. "What happens next?"

"On our end, we—meaning USSS and the FBI—will loop in our Romanian colleagues, specifically the Cybercrime Directorate, and open a joint file on the case. The actual boots on the ground are theirs. Our role is to provide technical and intel support. Plus encouragement, if necessary."

"Why would encouragement be necessary?"

"We're not at home, Mrs. Plansky. It's a different culture. We make mistakes if we make assumptions, even basic ones of right and wrong."

Mrs. Plansky was happy that such an intelligent and supple-minded man was carrying the standard of her nation overseas. On the other hand, she was unhappy with where he seemed to be headed.

"Is there any culture where stealing is okay?" she said.

Could a smile be somehow impatient? That was the expression she thought she saw crossing Mr. Perryman's face. "Not that I know of. I'm just trying to give you a heads-up on what might lie ahead."

"Go on."

"My goal is the same as yours—find the perpetrators, bring them to justice, recover what can be recovered. The goal of our Romanian colleagues is also the same but the context is different."

"How so?"

"The reasons for that are beyond my pay grade. That's what other people in this building, on the diplomatic side, work on for a living. Namely understanding another culture well enough to make their future actions predictable. What I'm trying to get across is the need for patience."

"You want me to be patient."

"A big ask, I know. But maybe now that you understand the situation it'll be a little easier."

Mrs. Plansky felt no easier, but had no idea what to say next. So she said what Norm would have said. "Finding the perpetrators, bringing them to justice, recovering what's recoverable."

"You've got it."

"Please estimate their probability, if you don't mind," she said. "In percentages, for example."

Mr. Perryman laughed, laughed—or at least she thought so—like the real Mr. Perryman inside, husband to the beautiful wife and serious kids on the shelf at his back. "I'm not going to do that," he said.

"I won't hold you to it," said Mrs. Plansky.

He just shook his head. "Now, as for you, I first want to say how much I admire you coming all this way, for being so proactive. It's really been a big help, and as I said I'll be in touch every week, at the minimum. I've booked you on a flight home at five this afternoon, first-class to Miami with that stop in Zurich, no nonstops, I'm sorry to say. Marine Corporal Avery will drive you to your hotel, wait while you pack and get ready, and take you to the airport." Mr. Perryman rose. "Here's your boarding pass."

"Is this the bum's rush?" she said.

"You're no bum, Mrs. Plansky. This has been a real pleasure. You've done your job, above and beyond. Now let us do ours. If it was any other season I'd say maybe stick around for a day or two, take in the sights. But winter's not the right time for Bucharest."

Mrs. Plansky rose. "Thank you." She took the boarding pass. They shook hands. "Noroc," she said.

"Sorry?"

"Uh, Romanian for good luck."

"Don't tell me you speak Romanian."

"Just a couple words."

"Same," he said.

Something in her chest seemed to make a sudden descent, like a too-fast elevator. Or her confidence in Mr. Perryman. He led her to the door. Marine Corporal Avery—no longer in uniform but she recognized him from the basketball half-court outside—was waiting in the hall. She hadn't realized how tall he was. Mr. Perryman introduced them.

"At your service, ma'am."

Corporal Avery walked her down the hall. His physical strength radiated a force field Mrs. Plansky could sense. She felt small. Counteracting that in some way was the knowledge that she had purloined and undoubtedly secret—if at a low level, far from the top, your eyes only—goods in her purse.

Back in her room—Corporal Avery waiting in the lobby—Mrs. Plansky took out her phone, went to photos, examined the picture she'd taken of the top page of Mr. Perryman's printout. She read it from beginning to end, a bureaucratic summary of her case prepared by a colleague of Mr. Perryman's with the initials FR in the appropriate box, now posted back stateside. Mrs. Plansky went over it a few more times, coming to the conclusion she was learning nothing new. Only the angle of incidence, as Norm would say, was different. Except for one little thing, a handwritten notation in the margin, with a handwritten FR at the bottom. This notation was what Mr. Perryman had circled in red.

Suggestion: Loop in Max Leonte in Alba Gemina? Then in parenthesis came a string of digits she took to be a phone number.

Mrs. Plansky took a deep breath and started entering in that number. But. But. There were so many buts circling around this little move. If she was going to take a shot—almost surely a one-shot sort of shot—shouldn't she maximize her chances? But how, exactly? There, one more but, just what she didn't need. Mrs. Plansky put away her phone and started packing. She'd emptied out her suitcase the night before, of course, hanging the hangables in the closet, with her mules and her ballet flats on the shoes shelf on the bottom and her foldables on the shelves above.

Mrs. Plansky went to the desk, found that Uncle Sam had taken care of her bill.

"This all?" said Corporal Avery, lifting her suitcase even though it had wheels.

"Yes, but you don't have to—"

"My pleasure, ma'am. My mom travels just like this, too, real light."

"She sounds like a very smart woman, Corporal."

"That's for sure, ma'am. No one messes with my mom."

Corporal Avery dropped her at the international doors at the terminal. Not quite dropping: in fact he carried the suitcase, walked her to the door, extended the suitcase handle, held the door.

"Safe travels, ma'am."

"Thank you, Corporal. Thanks for everything." Did her voice catch a bit, there at the end? She began to think this particular day was a strange one indeed.

Mrs. Plansky checked the board, saw that she had plenty of time, which was how she handled air travel. She got out her passport, stuck the boarding pass inside, entered the security line.

It turned out to be one of those slow-moving lines, through a not very big yet endless maze. But it was for this very type of situation that Mrs. Plansky allowed herself extra time! The line shuffled forward, halted, shuffled forward, halted. At the halts, she took to reading the purloined document, not technically purloined since she'd merely photographed it, but still. Then came a halt where she pocketed the phone, said, "Excuse me," and stepped out of line.

Mrs. Plansky reversed course and made her way out of security. A few minutes later she was at the counter of a rental car company she couldn't pronounce the name of. No one messes with Corporal Avery's mom. That was her guiding—if somewhat crazy—thought.

TWENTY

Almost all the available cars were stick shift. Automatic cost much more. Mrs. Plansky could drive stick, no problem, a bit of a surprise to the clerk. Way back in high school, the old guy who ran driver's ed insisted on all the kids learning to drive stick. "With automatic you're just sittin' thumb up your butt doin' nothin' and that's when the trouble starts." Even then the kids sensed he was a holdover from a previous age.

The clerk helped her program the route to Alba Gemina on her phone. "On your way to the mountains?" he said. "There's not much to see in Alba Gemina itself."

"The mountains sound beautiful," Mrs. Plansky said.

"The most beautiful drives in Europe, according to several polls. But there are many road closures in winter. Use caution."

"That's me," she said.

He laughed. "Bonne route, madame! The hard part is getting out of town."

That proved to be true. At least it was one of the hard parts. Also hard was just getting out of the airport. Then there were the road signs, the distance in kilometers, which meant multiplying by point six something or other, a task always done by Norm on their five or six European trips. She drove. He sat in the passenger seat and mused aloud, a driving trip always bringing that out of him. It was bliss. Sometimes they sang. He had a terrible voice, except for that Tony Bennett moment at the very end, but Mrs. Plansky could sing.

She'd been in various glee clubs and vocal groups straight through high school and college, could read music, carry different harmony parts, play a bit of piano and guitar and also harmonica, the only instrument she was actually any good at. All that in the distant past, except for the duets with Norm, in the more recent past.

Another problem with the road signs was the writing on them. Whenever a road sign appeared, she chanced a quick peek at her phone in its little holder on the dash to see if things were matching up, but the things, the words themselves, refused to make sense. The alphabet was the one she knew but while that was also true in Italy or France, the Romanian take was much more difficult. Mrs. Plansky decided to ignore the many diacritics and silently pronounce all words exactly how they'd be in English.

That worked. She kept to the speed limit on a fairly well-paved two-laner, at first dead straight through flat farm country lightly covered in snow, then getting curvier in some low hills. Traffic was heavy but then thinned out all at once, for no reason she could see. Mrs. Plansky even tried a bit of passing, overtaking an ancient truck with black smoke pouring from the tailpipe, and a horse-drawn cart with an old woman in black holding the reins, a not warmly-enough dressed little boy beside her, the breath of all three—woman, boy, horse—making tiny clouds in the bright sunshine.

The road began to climb in broad sweeping curves into what were probably the foothills of snowcapped mountains in the distance. Every so often a village went by, none looking prosperous, the houses and shops lining the road with very few buildings farther back, and always a church in the Orthodox style, the domes unpainted except for a single gold dome in one village. Mrs. Plansky drove carefully around a dog lying in the road and began to sing "I'm in the Mood for Love," one of her favorites. There were many versions but in a dopey kind of way the one she preferred wasn't Nat King Cole's or Jo Stafford's or even Billie Eilish's, but the doo-wop version by the Chimes, which she'd tried and utterly failed to teach Norm. Now she sang and sang, unaware at first that she'd driven up into fog, or that it had drifted down to her. She slowed way down. The fog grew thicker, and to her surprise she realized she was on a dirt road, quite narrow. That had to be wrong. Up ahead she could just make out what seemed to be a lookout off the side of the road. She pulled in and stopped the car.

Mrs. Plansky checked her phone, trying to figure out where she'd gone wrong. Was this a split she'd passed maybe ten kilometers back? Had she gone left instead of right? And what was this? Another split, this one a three-way, even farther back? And there she'd been, crooning away without a care in the world.

"Darn," she said. She didn't have the margin to do anything but devote full attention to what needed doing, full stop.

Mrs. Plansky got out of the car and headed toward what she assumed was the edge of the lookout, hoping to get her bearings. She thought she could make out a trash barrel, and headed for that. The fog thickened and thickened even though the wind was rising, a chilly wind. She tightened the Scottish scarf, feeling far from home. The silence was complete, like she'd been balled in cotton batting. Then from somewhere ahead came voices. She moved toward the sound.

Yes, she saw, a trash barrel for sure. Beside it she could make out the form of a man, leaning on something. And nearby another man, also leaning on something. She took a few more steps and the shapes of those two somethings resolved into bicycles. No, not bicycles. Motorcycles. What was hello, again? She'd memorized it on the flight, or meant to. But it wasn't there.

"Hello?" she said in English, wondering a little late if the Hell's Angels had overseas chapters.

The forms of the two men changed position, came forward through the fog. Small forms for Angels, and not men, but teenagers, one with a can of soda in his hand, the other munching on an end piece of dark bread spread with something garlicky she could smell. They were dressed similarly in jeans and leather jackets, the difference being in footwear, one wearing gold high-top sneakers, the other in cowboy boots. They gazed at her, mouths open.

"Hello," she said again. "Sorry I don't speak Romanian. Do either of you speak English?"

The one in the high-tops—plump, pimply, sixteen or seventeen—pointed to the other one—slight, fine-featured, with a James Dean–type forelock half over his eyes.

"Yes," said the slight one, hardly more than a boy from his appearance, "I speak English. Are you American?"

"I am," said Mrs. Plansky.

"From where in America?" said the slight one.

"Florida."

"Ah. The Sunshine State."

"That's right. Have you been there?"

"Only in my dreams."

The pimply one said something that sounded like "ᶜchay." The slight one spoke to him in Romanian. Mrs. Plansky was starting to get a feel for the sound, a mix of Italian, French, and some other more elusive element, but the only word she could identify was "Florida."

The slight one turned to her. "Is it sunny every day?"

"Not every day, but lots."

The wind rose a little more, not dissipating the fog at all but blowing scraps of newspaper and Styrofoam toward the edge of the lookout. The slight one seemed to be thinking. The pimply one downed the rest of his soda and tossed the empty can over his shoulder into the void.

"Have you been to the spring break?" the slight one said.

"Once," said Mrs. Plansky, "but a long time ago."

"You didn't like it?"

"No, I did, but spring break is for young people."

"Chay?" said the pimply one again, which she guessed was spelled C-E and probably meant *what?*

Again the slight one spoke to him in Romanian. A back-and-forth ensued, the pimply one growing more animated at what Mrs. Plansky assumed was a description of the goings-on at spring break. He turned to her and smiled, tapping his chest.

"Romeo," he said.

Uh-oh. No, it couldn't be. Some sort of wildly mistaken come-on based on a cartoonish image of female America, specifically the Florida spring break variety, combined with an adolescent inability to see what was in front of his face, namely a seventy-one-year-old woman, going on seventy-two? Just then, when she was about to try "You're not lookin' at Juliet, buddy boy," or something like that, he pointed to the slight one and said, "Dinu."

Ah. "Those are your names, Romeo and Dinu?"

They nodded.

"I'm Loretta," she said. "Nice to meet you."

They shook hands, Romeo and Dinu first removing their gloves—a polite gesture not lost on Mrs. Plansky—well-worn gloves with tears on some of the fingertips. Even though she hadn't been wearing her gloves, their hands felt cold in hers, meaning hers was warmer.

"Loretta?" Dinu said. There was something nice about how he spoke her name. Maybe it was just that he had one of those likable voices. "Like Loretta Lynn?"

"You know about Loretta Lynn?"

"Daughter of a coal miner. Excuse me—coal miner's daughter."

"Right, but how do you know about her?"

"Country music," said Dinu.

"You like country music?"

"Some. But the reason is for learning the right way of speaking English wrong, you know? For sounding like an American."

Mrs. Plansky laughed. "You're going to be very successful."

"I am?"

"Because that's a brilliant idea. I'll bet someone will monetize it, if they haven't already."

"What is monetize?"

"Turn into money."

"Ce?" said Romeo.

Dinu started in on an explanation of what Mrs. Plansky took to be country music, American language, and monetization. None of that appeared to interest Romeo much, certainly not to the level of spring break.

When that came to an end, Mrs. Plansky said, "Are you guys from around here? The truth is I'm a bit lost. I'm trying to get to Alba Gemina but I think I took a wrong turn."

"You were driving from Bucharest?" Dinu said.

"Yes."

"Then you took a wrong turn for sure but . . ." He paused, thought for a moment, and went on. "No biggie. In fact, you found the shortcut."

"Ce?" said Romeo.

This time Dinu didn't bother explaining. "We are from Alba Gemina. We will guide you there. Follow, please."

"That's so nice," Mrs. Plansky said. "But I don't want to interrupt your day."

"We have to go to work anyway," said Dinu.

"What is it you do, if you don't mind my asking?"

Dinu glanced at Romeo. Their eyes met. "Students," he said. "We're students. Where in Alba Gemina do you want to go?"

"I actually haven't made a reservation yet. Any recommendations?"

"For a hotel?"

"Or a B and B."

"What is B and B?"

"Well, it's . . . yes, a hotel. A hotel will be fine."

"There's the Duce," Dinu said. "It's very nice. All renovated. My uncle owns it." Mrs. Plansky hesitated. Dinu noticed that. "But the Royale is nicer. Also more expensive."

"Royale?" Romeo said.

He and Dinu got into a long discussion. Mrs. Plansky caught four or five hotel-type names but nothing else. The wind blew much harder and colder, opening a gap in the fog, and revealing a rather dramatic drop-off quite nearby, a matter of a few steps.

"How about this idea, Loretta?" Dinu said. "We can take you to the Duce. If you don't like it, the Royale is right across the square."

"Sounds like a plan," said Mrs. Plansky.

"Sounds like a plan. I love that one."

"Ce?" said Romeo.

Dinu launched into what must have been a translation of *sounds like a plan.*

Understanding spread across Romeo's face, followed by delight.

"Sound like plan!" he said in English. The two of them high-fived, then did it again, this time including Mrs. Plansky.

Mrs. Plansky followed them up through some switchbacks, the road still hard-packed dirt with gravel stretches, almost out of the fog, and into a golden haze. The boys—well, not boys, call them young men—led on their bikes, Romeo on the black one, Dinu on the red. From time to time the haze swallowed them up and she was alone, her wheels touching down on Georgia O'Keeffe's golden meadows. For a few moments Mrs. Plansky gave herself up to silly, grandiose thoughts, like "this is what travel is all about!" Then she rolled down her window—her car, the make of which was new to her and at the moment forgotten, equipped with the old-fashioned-type handles for the windows—so she could hear the motorcycles and not lose contact with these very nice young men. Mrs. Plansky felt good about her chances. The tide had turned, she'd turned the corner, was turning things around—all those turning clichés. The point was she was doing, not being done to.

The rest of the drive into Alba Gemina took place back in deep fog, unpenetrated by golden rays. Mrs. Plansky, trying to keep Dinu and Romeo in sight, could form only vague impressions of winding descent, flattening landscape, human structures, first rural, then urban. Toward the end they crossed a bridge, joined bumper-to-bumper traffic, turned into a quiet, cobblestone square with an equestrian statue in the center, and came to a three-story, slate-roofed, yellow building with blue drainpipes. Over the door—old, dark wood, brass studs—hung a gold-painted sign: DUCE. Romeo, waving goodbye, kept going with a slight wobble, across the square and down a side street, but Dinu stopped, put a foot down, and motioned for Mrs. Plansky to come alongside.

She drove up. Dinu's face was red from the cold. He pointed to the sign. "Hotel Duce," he said.

"Thank you, Dinu."

"And there," he went on, pointing to a bigger slate-roofed building on the other side of the square, this one blue with yellow drainpipes and also three heavy yellow columns, "Hotel Royale, ten stars."

"Ten?" said Mrs. Plansky.

"Whatever is the most," said Dinu. He laughed, maybe at himself in an ironic way. An unusual kid, thought Mrs. Plansky, laughing with him.

He revved the bike. "Happy traveling, Loretta!"

"Same you to. But—but wait a minute." She fumbled through her purse. She had no Romanian money yet, didn't even know if they had their own or used euros, but she found a twenty-dollar bill and held it out. "For you and Romeo."

"Oh, no, please," Dinu said, making a little gesture of dismissal, a gesture that struck her as aristocratic. He drove away, popping a wheelie. Maybe much more of a street urchin than an aristocrat, but an odd combo for sure. Mrs. Plansky eased forward between the lines of a marked space, getting herself properly parked, hauled her suitcase out of the trunk, locked the car, checked to make sure it was locked, and entered Hotel Duce.

TWENTY-ONE

The Hotel Duce lobby was small, with whitewashed stone walls, dark ceiling beams, a dark wooden floor, old and worn but highly polished. A few paintings hung on the walls, gleaming paintings all with the same subject, namely racing cars. Also there was a poster of Bela Lugosi, not in costume. Mrs. Plansky didn't recognize him at first. She liked this hotel already.

She went up to the desk. A very pretty young woman sat there, typing away on a laptop. She wore a tank top and jeans, an outfit that seemed a little scanty for the time of year. Pinned to the tank top was a name tag: ANNIKA. She looked up and said something in Romanian.

"Sorry," said Mrs. Plansky. "Do you speak English?"

"A little."

"I'm looking for a room for two or three nights, possibly more."

"No problem at all. Is winter." She handed Mrs. Plansky a brochure. "Available is the president suite."

"Oh, I don't need anything that fancy." Mrs. Plansky found pictures of the different classes of rooms. The presidential suite looked suitable for a very undemanding president. But simple and nice. All the rooms were that way, although the prices seemed rather high.

"Price is in lei," Annika said. "You are American?"

"Yes."

"Divide by five."

"Ah."

"And you can have president for regular deluxe rate. Off-season discount."

Mrs. Plansky did a quick calculation. They were talking around forty-five dollars a night. "That'll be fine," she said.

"Includes breakfast, Wi-Fi, and twenty-dollar gift card to Club Presto."

"What's that?" said Mrs. Plansky.

Annika gave her a close look. "Instead we do gift card to Salle Privé. Is nice restaurant."

Mrs. Plansky got out her passport and credit card. Annika was just finishing checking her in when a huge man entered through an inner door. Once she and Norm had signed on with an ad agency that had a relationship with a very popular former NFL lineman who starred in a TV barbecue show, and they'd ended up spending a lot of money hiring him to do a commercial. He'd turned out to match his image in terms of being relaxed and funny, and Mrs. Plansky had stood right next to him backstage, showing him how to use the knife. She'd felt like a member of some different species. This man—wearing a tight T-shirt that revealed enormous shoulder muscles rising up and sort of taking possession of his neck—had the same body type and size.

"Oh, Marius," Annika began, making what sounded like some sort of request.

"Ce?" said Marius.

Annika handed her the room key and the gift card. "Marius will take you to your room."

He came over, not in an enthusiastic way. "Hey, there," he said.

"Hi," said Mrs. Plansky. "You speak English?"

"Then and now," said Marius. He reached for her suitcase, plucked it up with just his thumb and index finger on the handle and led Mrs. Plansky across the lobby and up a flight of stairs covered in a threadbare oriental runner, stairs that creaked under Marius's massiveness. The pant legs of his jeans rode up slightly with his movements, revealing an ankle sheath with a knife in it, practically in her face. How interesting, she thought, two giants—the NFL lineman and Marius—had made a brief appearance in her life, with knives as—what would you call them?—props? Knives as props in both cases.

At the top of the stairs he turned down a hall, passing another poster of Bela Lugosi, this time in his famous role. They came to a door with a framed photo of a smiling Richard Nixon on the wall above. A planned juxtaposition by whoever had done the decor? Or just random? The fun she and Norm would have had with that!

"President suite," Marius said. He made a little motion with his fingers. She handed him the key. He opened up.

"Did he stay here?" she said. "Nixon?"

"Here no," said Marius. "Romania, yes. Was big moment in our history."

"He had lots of big moments in ours," Mrs. Plansky said.

Just a little joke, but wasted, Marius's face without expression. He rolled the suitcase inside but didn't enter, just gave her the key.

"Enjoy visit, lady."

"Thank you." She reached in her purse.

Marius made a windshield wiper gesture with his index finger.

"My goodness," Mrs. Plansky said. "Is there no tipping in Romania?"

"No tipping in Romania?" Marius laughed, a surprisingly high-pitched sound coming from him. "Very excellent joke. I tell the guys."

The presidential suite at the Hotel Duce turned out not to be a suite, but it did have a little seating nook.

The bed, a double, was a mahogany hulk from a past age with fluted posts and a canopy. Also, the presidential suite was very cold, one of the windows, a casement-style leaded window, being fully open. Mrs. Plansky cranked it shut, at the same time taking in a nice view of the square and the bronze equestrian statue, the horse and man both larger than life, the bronze old and oxidized, making for a deep glowing patina. The rider, in armor except for his *Doctor Zhivago*–style fur hat, was brandishing a wide-bladed sword. She locked the window.

After that she unpacked, hanging the hangables, folding the foldables, shelving her toiletries in the bathroom, which she'd expected to be tiny but was in fact as big as the bedroom, although it lacked a tub and was mostly empty space. Perhaps it had been its own room at a previous time. There was a door in the wall right next to the shower stall, an old, heavy wooden door with no knob or keyhole. Mrs. Plansky gave it a push. It didn't budge.

There was nothing more to unpack. She'd done all this careful unpacking because that was how she did things, but also as a way to postpone a tricky moment. Mrs. Plansky was well aware that she'd had plenty of time on the drive up from Bucharest to think about what was coming, but—and how lazy of her!—she'd waited for inspiration instead.

"And how did that work out, girl?" Out loud? No. She was almost sure.

Mrs. Plansky went into the sitting nook, sat at the desk—"back straight, feet together on the floor," as Miss Terrance had taught—and arranged the hotel notepad and pen in front of her. Then she took out her phone and looked over the purloined document once more. What had seemed like a great idea at the time no longer did. But it was her gut idea, and hadn't she always ended up going with her gut at the big moments? The truth was she really couldn't say. How was it possible to be this ancient and still not know thyself?

Suggestion: Loop in Max Leonte in Alba Gemina? And then in parenthesis what she took to be a phone number. But what if it wasn't?

"Why don't you just turn tail and go on home?" she said, out loud for sure, and angry, angry at herself. In her anger, Mrs. Plansky entered the number on her phone, stabbing out each and every digit. Except for the last one. Right then she had what seemed like a clever idea, just in case—well, just in case. Leave it at that. The clever idea was to change things up on her phone so her name would not appear to the receiver of the call. She was pretty sure it could be done, but how, exactly? Settings! Wasn't there some obscure region of the phone that dealt with settings?

Sometime later, not too long, her phone was set to go, now in a craftier mode. Mrs. Plansky dialed the number. It rang on the other end, wherever that might have been. Was there any reason to think this man, Max Leonte, was even in Alba Gemina right now? He could be anywhere, Washington, D.C., for example, which suddenly seemed more likely. Also phones no longer rang. Instead they made some sort of digital sound engineered and product-tested, no doubt, to induce a state of mind that—

"Da?"

Mrs. Plansky rose to her feet. Her hand, gripping the phone, had suddenly gone all sweaty.

"Da?"

A male voice, baritone, not exactly unpleasant, but certainly impatient.

"Da?"

Mrs. Plansky took a deep breath. "Hello? Do you speak English? I'm looking for Max Leonte."

"Who is this?" said the man, his English accented slightly but very good.

"Are you Mr. Leonte?"

"Who is this?" he repeated.

It was just a feeling but Mrs. Plansky didn't want to offer her name, at least not right now, and over the phone. This was a problem she hadn't foreseen, and foreseeing in general wasn't her strength these days. Maybe the foreseeing part of her brain had been wiped out in one of those silent strokes you heard about. She was only half-joking with herself about that, and during this little pause a sideways move occurred to her.

"My name wouldn't mean anything to you," she said.

"I am now ending the call," said the man.

"Wait! Don't do that. My name's Loretta."

"Just the one name? Like Beyoncé?"

"Not like Beyoncé," Mrs. Plansky said.

He didn't respond right away. Then he said, "What is it you want?"

"Well, first to know if you're Max Leonte."

"And then?"

"Maybe we could meet and talk."

"About what?"

"Cybercrime."

Mrs. Plansky expected some question about her interest in cybercrime or her relationship to it, but that was not what came. "Where are you?" he said.

"In Alba Gemina," she said. "Are you here, too? I'm talking about Alba Gemina in Romania."

"I know of no other," he said. "Where in Alba Gemina? A hotel?"

"I'd prefer to meet in some neutral place."

"Name it."

"I actually don't know of any yet. Maybe a coffeehouse?"

"There are many," he said. "In what part of town?"

She gazed through the window. "The old part. Is there a coffeehouse near the square?"

"What square?"

"With the equestrian bronze."

"*Michael the Brave*?"

Mrs. Plansky recalled the name from her reading on the flight, but the details, beyond many confusing and bloody battles, perhaps against the Ottomans, were gone.

"Possibly," she said. "Is there more than one equestrian statue in Alba Gemina?"

"Oh, yes," he said. "Is the rider brandishing his sword like a homicidal maniac?"

"Brandishing, yes."

"*Michael the Brave*," he said. "Meet me at Café des Artistes, eighteen hundred."

"Is that the address?"

He blew out an irritated-sounding breath. "Six," he said. "Six o'clock this evening. Your hotel—the Royale, I assume—can give you directions."

"How will I know you?"

"I'll wear a billboard with a question mark."

Click.

Mrs. Plansky checked the time. She had two hours. In one of the desk drawers she found a map of the old town and quickly located Café des Artistes—down a street that led off the square, left at the second corner, halfway along the block on the right. She took the map over to the couch—more of a love seat, actually—and sat. Her legs were grateful for the move. Her whole body was grateful. She studied the map of the old town. There was nothing grid-like about it. Sun Tzu had written that understanding terrain was vital, as Mrs. Plansky had learned years ago while helping Jack with an essay for his college apps, in the end researching and writing it herself, more or less. More. But that wasn't the point, which was not to get lost.

Mrs. Plansky opened her eyes. It was dark, very dark for the bay window alcove across from the bar where she liked to sit on her chintz and maple love seat and gaze at the pond, even at night when, yes, she sometimes nodded off, although this deep darkness was unusual, the lights from the windows of the other condos reflected in the water and—

Mrs. Plansky sat up straight, a shock passing through her body, like she'd been paddled by one of those EMT crews. Surely not as bad as that, but . . . but what time was it? She rose, took a hurried step in the direction of the desk in this little hotel sitting nook. Where she was, of course, not back home at all! What was wrong with her? She took another hurried step, bumped into something, twisted around in a way that her new hip did not like in the least, and fell on the floor pretty hard. But—she took stock of herself—but somehow she'd got-ten a hand, maybe both, out in front of her, breaking her fall with-out breaking her wrists, which, even with her mind in turmoil, she realized was the best way to fall, if she had indeed now reached the random falling-down stage.

Mrs. Plansky got to her feet—not so easily—her eyes now tun-ing in the weak light coming through the window overlooking the square. She switched on a lamp, saw that she'd tripped over a footstool, a footstool where she must have laid her phone and now there it was, on the floor. She snatched it up and checked the time. Twenty twenty-two? What sort of time was that? Then she realized her phone, much savvier than she, had already adopted Eu-ropean ways. Twenty twenty-two was 8:22 p.m. She was two hours and twenty-two minutes late. Had he called or texted? No. All she found were some unread texts that had come in from Emma.

Mrs. Plansky grabbed the map of the old town, threw on her coat, headed for the door, then stopped when she realized she was wearing the quilted mules. She kicked them off, put on the low-heeled booties, hurried out of the presidential suite, through the lobby, and into the square.

A cold wind was blowing. From the west? Didn't the European continental wind blow from the west in winter? Mrs. Plansky checked the map under her phone light as she walked, not as quickly as she wanted, the cobbles feeling tricky under her feet—and found no helpful indicators. Not important, but she always liked to know her compass direction. She reached the street leading off the square, checked its name on a plaque, but for some reason saw only the diacritics and none of the letters. The cobblestones came to an end and pavement began. Mrs. Plansky picked up speed.

Second left, and there it was on the right, Café des Artistes, the scripted letters of the sign followed by the image of a pen and two ink blotches, as though the sign painter had just finished work. A yellow glow leaked from the window and onto the street, otherwise dark. Mrs. Plansky had a strange feeling, like she was a time traveler on her way back. Was she losing her silly mind? She wrenched the door open with more force than necessary.

She had not gone back in time. For one thing, no one was smoking. The room, not big, was about half full. Mrs. Plansky sat at a side table, picked up a menu—a deceptive move of the type that would surely be in an undercover op's bag of tricks—and glanced around, then backtracked and glanced around again, less furtively this time.

The first thing she discovered was that she was the oldest person in the Café des Artistes, not even a close call. How old would the man on phone—maybe Max Leonte, maybe not—have been? Not a youngster, for sure, which eliminated most of the customers, who looked to be college age or the age of professors just starting out. Then there was a couple in their fifties, both wearing berets, two women maybe slightly older than that with shopping bags at their feet, and two bald men who seemed to be having a quiet argument. In short, not her guy, who surely would have been alone.

A waitress with a number of piercings on her face came over and said something in Romanian. Before Mrs. Plansky—who still wasn't able to take facial piercings in stride—could reply, the waitress switched to English for the undercover operator, who ordered coffee, the house blend with cream, although not extra cream, her usual coffee order. Those who missed meetings because they'd nodded off had to discipline themselves somehow or other.

The coffee was good. Two or three sips and she felt a change inside, like some rusted parts were getting oil. She checked those messages from Emma. The first one must have been sent during the flight: **Everything's good! I got accepted for a semester at Oxford! But sure you're ok?**

The second: **You ok?**

The third: **Mom says Pops says you're on a business trip? Everything all right?**

Mrs. Plansky typed her reply: **Short biz trip. Congrats on Oxford. Everything fine!!!**

That was the first time she'd ever tripled up on exclamation points, or even doubled up. But she had to find the right breezy tone, somehow stop any worrying—actually any interference—on the home front before it got going. This was hard enough without all those people. Yes, the people she loved with all her heart, but each one lacking a certain capability or two, a fact she was now voicing to herself for the first time. The reasons for the capability gap, which might prove unsettling—especially if they had something to do with this new and troubling concept of the power of the giver—she would deal with some other time.

Mrs. Plansky caught the waitress's eye. The Oxford reference had triggered a little something in her mind. The waitress came over.

"Is there something I can get you?"

"Not just now. Wonderful coffee. I can't help noticing how good your English is."

"Thank you. I lived for two years in London."

"Ah." Mrs. Plansky glanced around. "I was supposed to meet someone here but I'm a little late."

The waitress didn't seem to find anything interesting in that. She gazed over Mrs. Plansky's shoulder at the next table.

"Maybe he was here and couldn't wait," Mrs. Plansky said. "He would have been sitting alone."

"We had several men sitting alone," said the waitress. "What does he look like?"

"Well," said Mrs. Plansky, her only idea being something about a blind date, a ridiculous response given her age.

The waitress caught a signal from another table. "Excuse me."

Not long after that, Mrs. Plansky was back out on the street. The night was colder and the wind stronger, a few hard, stinging little snowflakes in the air. She wrapped her scarf more tightly and headed back to the hotel.

TWENTY-TWO

Mrs. Plansky walked quickly, partly on account of the cold, but also because speed seemed to be making her new hip feel better, perhaps warming up all that titanium. How lucky she was! She knew other tennis players, men and women, who had replaced hips, knees, shoulders, even an ankle or two in the hope of getting back on the court. But often it didn't work out that way and yet there she was, playing the way she'd played ten or fifteen years ago! Naturally she'd need to check video to confirm that judgment, video that luckily did not exist. Mrs. Plansky was occupying herself along those lines when she got the feeling that maybe she should have reached the square by now. She checked her surroundings and recognized nothing.

It was a dim street, with old-fashioned lampposts here and there, most not working. A car went by, lighting up a few shops, all closed, and some two-and three-story structures that she took to be apartment buildings, but old ones from a middle-European past. She walked toward the nearest corner, hoping for a street sign, and wasn't quite there when she thought she heard footsteps behind her. Mrs. Plansky turned and saw no one, just a lot of shadows, some in humanlike form. But that was the way the imagination worked, often overcooking things. She reached the corner, looked for street signs, and found none. But around the corner a blue neon sign hung over a doorway: POLITIA.

Mrs. Plansky walked up to the door. Through a small window, she saw a uniformed woman behind a counter listening to a man standing on the other side, making emphatic gestures while he talked. A police station, for sure. She could go in and get directions, or . . . or do something more than that. A crime had been committed against her, a crime originating in this town. What did you do in a situation like that? You reported it to the police. Mrs. Plansky, feeling like whoever it was who'd sliced through the Gordian knot, opened the door and strode inside.

She was in a small lobby with a few plastic chairs, framed wall photos of half a dozen unsmiling men in uniforms with lots of braiding, and no one else except the gesticulating man and the female cop. The man was very annoyed about something but Mrs. Plansky couldn't pick out a single word. The cop was very patient or perhaps bored. She had her hair drawn back very tightly in a complicated bun, distorting her face a little and making her facial expressions hard to read.

Mrs. Plansky sat on a plastic chair, feet together, purse on her knees. It was nice and warm in the police station. She loosened her scarf and began organizing her little speech. Her mind didn't want to do that, instead wanted to think about distortion. For example, being in a foreign land was distorting. Wasn't that really the main attraction of travel? Yet people often came back saying, "When you get to know them they're just like us." So when they were distorted the foreigners were actually like us but we didn't know yet? Did we end up discovering our own distortion? Mrs. Plansky found she was confusing herself, perhaps proving the point.

A door opened on Mrs. Plansky's side of the counter but across the room. Inside was an office where a man who looked like he could have been in one of the framed photos—even down to the braiding on his uniform jacket—was sitting at his desk, glass in hand. An empty glass sat on the desk beside a whiskey bottle. A second man was at the door, on his way out, when the uniformed man said something that made him laugh. The second man replied. Whatever he said the uniformed man found very funny. He laughed and laughed and downed the rest of his drink. The second man closed the door and turned, taking in the scene at the counter. He caught her attention, maybe because of how imposing he was, how capable he seemed, with his large, square chin, nose that matched, large square hands, and a large square body, everything about him large and square, other than his eyes. His eyes were small, round, glinting, and not pleased with the goings on at the counter.

"Hei!" he said, his voice forceful but a little higher than she would have thought. For a moment she'd been wondering without any rational basis if this man might be Max Leonte, or more precisely the man on the phone, but their voices were very different—and not just in pitch but in sensibility, Mrs. Plansky allowing herself another unjustifiable mental leap.

The gesticulating man whirled around at the sound of that "Hei!" with something very aggressive on the way. At the sight of Mr. Squareman that aggression faded fast. He turned to the female cop, made a what-the-hell motion with his hand, said, "Ach," and walked quickly out of the building.

Mr. Squareman tied the belt on his black leather coat and pulled on black leather gloves lined in sheepskin. He headed for the door, then seemed to sense Mrs. Plansky's presence. He glanced her way. Those glinting eyes seemed to make a quick study of her with no attempt to pretend they were not, like some sort of scanning machine. He turned and walked out the door, not one of those big guys who was surprisingly light on his feet. She felt his strides through the soles of her booties.

The female cop looked over at her and said something in Romanian. Mrs. Plansky rose.

"Hello, Officer," she said. "Do you speak English?"

"No English," said the cop.

"I want to report a cybercrime," Mrs. Plansky said, speaking very slowly and distinctly, a caricature of an unsavvy tourist abroad for the first time.

The cop made an Italianate sort of elaborate shrug, most of her body involved.

Mrs. Plansky, a friendly smile on her face, approached the counter. "Does anyone here speak English?"

That got her a blank look from the cop.

"English?" said Mrs. Plansky, attempting a gesture meant to take in the whole building.

"Da," said the cop. "Capitan Romulu." She pointed to the office that Mr. Squareman had just left.

"Can I talk to him, please?"

No reaction.

Mrs. Plansky tried French. "Discuter?"

"Ah, discutu." The cop raised her fist, went *knock knock* in the air.

"Thank you."

Mrs. Plansky moved toward Captain Romulu's office. The sound of ice cubes dropping into a glass came through the closed door. She raised her fist to knock, now hearing the gurgle of pouring liquid. Her fist froze, all set to knock but not knocking. She thought of Agent Gatling, on his last day on the job and possibly speaking more openly than normal. *"But to the elite running the show over there the scammers are bad guys who also have a nice little industry going, bringing in the Yankee dollar and lots of 'em."*

Mrs. Plansky backed away from the captain's door. The tinkling of the ice cubes as the captain drank sounded impossibly loud. So was her heartbeat. She felt way too hot and a bit dizzy. Mrs. Plansky realized she'd entered a zone of extreme distortion. She walked quickly and somewhat unsteadily to the front door and out to the street. From inside came the voice of the female cop: "Hei!"

Mrs. Plansky hurried away, forcing herself not to run. As though she were guilty of something! That was how distorted this was. It seemed to be affecting all her senses. For example, she got a strange feeling between her shoulder blades, like she was being watched, but when she looked around she found herself all alone.

Mrs. Plansky retraced her steps, which didn't make sense since she'd already been lost when she'd taken them, but she kept going just because walking felt good. She was no longer hot or dizzy, and the distortion field, still present, was much weaker. What she needed now was a carefully thought-out plan. What she did not need were sudden impulsive moves made while lost on the dark streets of a town she didn't know. But where to begin?

"Think," she said, and at that moment turned a corner and strolled directly into the cobblestone square, her hotel on one side, the Royale on the other, like she knew what she was doing. Right away she felt more like herself, as though a dissonant soundtrack accompanying her had finally gone silent. The night was still cold but the wind had died down, and gaps were opening among the clouds. The moon came out, a half moon and very clear: she thought she could make out the missing half. Mrs. Plansky walked up to the equestrian statue and had a good look.

Michael the Brave gazed down at her. So did the horse. Their bronze eyes were sightless of course but the moonlight was playing tricks with that. *Michael the Brave* looked fierce and medieval, although not a particularly good listener. That didn't stop her from speaking to him. "I could use someone like you, Mikey."

No answer from Mikey. Mrs. Plansky began to think she preferred the horse, also fierce and medieval, but somehow more approachable. She moved closer and reached up. The horse seemed to have been caught in a cantering pose, hooves up high, but she could just touch a rear one, icy cold.

From behind came the voice of a man. "Going for a ride?"

And now Mrs. Plansky came through for herself. Although all the usual clichés applied to her state of mind—she jumped a foot off the ground, almost had a heart attack, was scared to death—

none of them showed. In fact, she turned quite slowly, in a measured way.

Standing before her was a somewhat younger man. He had dark hair, quite long but at least somewhat kempt, in a style she associated with European intellectuals, although she'd never met one. While there might have been only a hint or two of gray in his hair, his closely trimmed beard was pure white. He was sturdy of build and his eyes appeared to be the color of the moon.

"You're American?" he said.

Maybe because of the fright she'd kept inside, Mrs. Plansky forgot her manners and made a rude gesture, backhanding his question away. "I recognize your voice," she told him.

He didn't seem offended, but neither did he answer, but just watched her closely.

"Are you Max Leonte?"

He kept silent.

She raised her voice, simply couldn't help herself. "Yes or no?"

He smiled, his teeth also moon-colored. "Yes or no—it doesn't get more American than that. No need to see your passport."

"You haven't answered the question."

"First please explain where you got that name."

That was a tough one. The true answer, very complicated but climaxing with the purloining of a document, wouldn't do. "It . . . it came up in the course of an investigation."

"Who is conducting this investigation?"

"Well, me." The truth of that hit her as she spoke, the tongue somehow barging in front of the mind. But it was good to hear. Somewhat intimidating, certainly, but she had taken charge. And whose life was it, after all?

Meanwhile her remark seemed to have had an effect on this man as well. "Don't tell me," he said, putting his hand to his chest. "A member of the tribe?"

What tribe was that? Did he think she was of Romanian heritage? That was her only thought. "Tribe?" she said.

"Metaphorically," he said. Other than slight differences in how he spoke the vowel sounds, shortening some and lengthening others, his English seemed as good as hers, or better. "But I should have said fraternity. That's more accurate and expresses the spirit of the thing."

"What thing are you talking about?" Mrs. Plansky said.

"The journalism thing," he said. "But I can see you're not a journalist. It wouldn't be your style." He held up his hand before she could react to that. The moonlight turned it silver, like another sculpture in the square, this one airborne. "Not that I'm criticizing your style, not in the least." He lowered his hand, held it out. "Max Leonte, at your service."

In the shadow of *Michael the Brave* his hand was no longer metallic, so clearly flesh and blood. Mrs. Plansky took it in her own. They shook. Their breath clouds rose and merged in the air.

TWENTY-THREE

"Loretta Plansky," said Mrs. Plansky, letting go of his hand. Did he show any reaction to the name? None that she could see. "You've been following me."

"Oh, yes," Max Leonte said. "A circuitous course that tired me out. From the Café des Artistes to the old town precinct house, and now to here. I was a little concerned you'd skipped our meeting and gone instead to perhaps see Captain Romulu, who works late but not hard. In fact, I'm still concerned."

"Why?"

"That depends on what you're investigating."

"You're a journalist?"

"Correct."

"Who do you work for?"

"At one time several print and television outlets, here and in other parts of Europe. Now—freelance."

"Meaning you're self-employed?"

"Correct again. I'm working on a book."

"What's it about?"

"Corruption. Specifically in Romania and other countries with close connections to Russia, historically, culturally, geographically— only one of which is necessary in my formulation. but they share the fact that the closeness was in all cases involuntary. My hypothesis, not set in stone, is that the closer those ties the greater the corruption."

Mrs. Plansky was out of her depth. She wasn't the type to ever think herself the smartest person in the room—or even think in those terms at all—but she'd always felt she could hold her own with most people. But not this one. He was one of those European intellectuals, for sure. Still, she plunged ahead.

"Does corruption include cybercrime?" she said.

"Very much it does," said Max Leonte. "Why do you ask?"

Mrs. Plansky had a little internal debate with herself before answering. On one hand, the appearance of Max Leonte's name on Mr. Perryman's document now had some context. On the other, it was a dark, cold night in a strange town far from home. But hadn't she just been asking *Michael the Brave* for help? If not this guy—probably not as violent as Mikey but almost certainly smarter—then who? There was just one thing to be nailed down.

"I'm assuming you're against cybercrime," she said.

He laughed. "Is there any reason we couldn't continue this conversation somewhere warmer?"

"I'm staying at the Duce. I think there's a bar."

Some thought seemed to pass just beneath the surface of his eyes. "Let's try the Royale. Their bar is nicer."

The bar at the Royale had a nineteenth-century hunting lodge decor, with lots of dark wood paneling, thick, smoke-blackened wooden beams, period photos of unsmiling hunters posed over their kills, and weapons—from spears and bows and arrows to shotguns with gleaming barrels—hung on the walls, interspersed with the mounted heads of brown bears, boars, wolves, and something sheep-like with enormous curving horns and contemptuous eyes. Although that part about the eyes might have been just an unusual reflection from the light of the fire in the stone fireplace—an enormous fireplace although the fire itself was rather small.

They sat close to it, Mrs. Plansky in a soft leather chair, the arms studded with the brass caps of shotgun shells, and Max Leonte on the stone hearth itself, with no one else in the room except the waiter, scrolling on his phone.

"Have you tasted tuica yet?" Max Leonte said.

"What is it?"

"Plum brandy. Our national drink. You could try it now and maybe never again, but at least check the box."

He ordered two plum brandies. They came in crystal mugs with a twist of lemon and a drop or two of honey. Mrs. Plansky took a sip and started to warm up, from the inside out. Their eyes met. His turned out not to be the color of the moon, but more like the pale blue of the sky in winter.

"What should I call you?" she said.

"Max. And may I call you Loretta?"

Mrs. Plansky nodded. "What I'm investigating, Max," she said, "is a cybercrime. It involves myself, the victim." How she wished there was another term. And just when needed, it arrived: potential victim, since she wasn't done yet. But would it sound ridiculous? She kept it unsaid.

Max nodded. "Go on."

Mrs. Plansky took another sip of her tuica, actually much more than a sip. Once they'd gone to a talk by a famous writer, she and Norm. After it was over, she'd seen the famous writer in the cloak-room, picking up one of the bookstore clerks with hardly a word, a woman of college age, or even high school, decades younger than the writer. That was disappointing, but now she remembered something he'd said in the talk: "When telling a story leave out most of it."

She started in on her story. She left out Norm. She left out her entire family, except for Will. She left out the toaster knife, her financial obligations, the promises—implicit and explicit—she had to keep, and her deep feeling of humiliation. All the rest she included, meaning the details of the crime as seen from her end, the amount that was stolen—because how could you discuss a theft and omit the amount?—Safemo, her conversations with the FBI agents, Rains and

Gatling, her visit to the embassy in Bucharest, her talk with Mr. Perryman. Well, she left out some of that, namely the important parts, like the purloined document and the fact that Mr. Perryman probably thought she was safely back home by now, and also the very name Mr. Perryman.

"That's pretty much it," she said, taking another big drink. The drink or something else began to ease her burden a little, and even if that was just momentary she gave herself to the feeling.

Max hadn't made a sound the whole time, or even moved at all, although she knew there was movement going on in his mind. His eyes told her that. Wintry blue, large yet not obtrusively so, symmetrical, but none of that was especially meaningful. If the eyes really were the window to the soul, then he was soulful. That was the important part. Journalists could be soulful? That had never occurred to her. Did learning go on right to the last breath? Mrs. Plansky didn't know but she wanted to depart that way herself. She had plenty of time for these irrelevant thoughts because Max was in no hurry to speak.

Finally he set his crystal mug down on the hearth and said, "Tell me about yourself."

Mrs. Plansky hadn't been expecting that. "There isn't much to tell," she said. His question seemed at odds with the famous writer's storytelling advice.

Max smiled. His teeth looked white and cared for, but one of the incisors was very crooked. That fit nicely with the European intellectual part.

"I'll tell you why that can't be true," he said. "I've looked into dozens of cyber scamming cases, am familiar with the details of hundreds more, and know enough about the tens of thousands, the hundreds of thousands originating in central and Eastern Europe to be almost certain that you're the first victim to come looking. That makes you special, so there must be something about yourself to tell after all."

She was the only one? How strange! That couldn't be. "I can't think of anything," Mrs. Plansky said. "I'm just an ordinary American woman." That didn't feel quite right. She made a slight edit. "Ordinary older American woman."

Max picked up his mug and took a drink, watching her over the rim. The fire, reflected at many angles through the crystal facets, lit his face in a devilish way. "I guess I never met one before," he said, lowering the mug. "Since I'm starting from zero, please tell me what you hope to accomplish."

She'd come for her dignity, of course. Did that sound melodramatic? Ridiculous? Unhinged?

"I'd like the money back," Mrs. Plansky said.

Was he about to smile, like she'd amused him in some way? That was her first thought, but it was wrong. Instead he simply said, "It's a lot of money."

"Yes," said Mrs. Plansky.

"Is it a lot of money to you?"

"I don't understand."

"The three point whatever is the exact digit million. What percentage of your wealth is it?"

Mrs. Plansky made allowances for her jewelry and this and that. "Do you want me to include the value of my home?"

"No," he said.

"Then it's about ninety-seven," said Mrs. Plansky.

Max seemed to think that over, and while he thought it over she began to get angry, a very rare event in her life. "But even if it was only one darn percent what does it matter? We earned that money, my husband and I."

He raised both hands, palms up. "Oh, certainly, certainly. I was only thinking from the angle of risk and reward."

"Okay, then." Her anger melted away.

"If I may ask, why didn't your husband come with you?"

"He's dead."

"Ah. I'm sorry."

"Thank you."

"Similarly, I lost my wife. Not to death, but to another man."

Mrs. Plansky had no idea what to say to that.

"But very different, of course. I apologize for being . . . what is the word?"

"Self-dramatizing?"

He looked shocked, then hurt, then amused, the changes coming so fast she almost couldn't keep up. "I was searching for flippant, but yours is better."

"I didn't mean—"

"No, no, I'm glad."

And he looked like he was having fun. One thing about being in Max's company, so far: she was wide awake.

A loud popping sound came from the fire and an ember flew out and landed on the floor. Max squished it out under his shoe. "What's your plan for getting the money back?" he said.

Mrs. Plansky faced facts. "There is no plan."

"Because you don't have enough information yet?"

She grabbed at that. "Yes, that's it."

"So you've come to find out what goes on in the enemy camp."

"Exactly," she said. He was making her sound very shrewd. Inside she felt the opposite, like a fake.

"Is that why you went to the police tonight?" Max said. "To find out what's happening on the ground?"

"Well, yes. But only after failing to meet you at the café."

"There was no other reason?"

"Like what?"

"I was at the café. I sat for forty-five minutes. Then I went outside and waited nearby."

"And you followed me to the police station?"

He nodded.

"How did you know it was me?" she said.

"Let's just say you look the way you sound. I mean that as a compliment. But that won't stop me from making sure your visit to the police station had no ulterior motive."

"I don't understand."

He gave her a careful look, making no effort to hide the fact that he was examining her. An odd feeling came over her. She let herself be examined.

"I have—I don't want to say enemies, but certainly not friends, among the police in this town. Captain Romulu, who I happen to know was the duty officer tonight and would have been the only English speaker there at this time of year, is the least friendly. Naturally I'm interested in what you told him."

"Nothing," said Mrs. Plansky.

"You didn't speak to him?"

"No."

"You spoke to someone else?"

"Just the lady at the desk, to find an English speaker. She pointed toward his office. But I left instead."

"Why?"

"This may sound harebrained," she began.

He interrupted. "That's one expression I've never understood."

"H-A-R-E," said Mrs. Plansky. "Like bunny rabbit."

Max smacked his forehead, so loudly that the scrolling waiter turned to look from across the room. "What an idiot!" he said, and started to laugh, a low sort of rumble deeper than his speaking voice, and surprisingly pleasant, as though the bassoon was taking the lead for an unexpected bar or two. Tears came to his eyes. He wiped them away. "Go on, Loretta. It can't be too harebrained—H-A-R-E!—for me."

"It's just that I'd already seen Captain Romulu through the doorway," Mrs. Plansky explained. "I didn't like the look of him."

"Very wise," Max said. "Captain Romulu would not be the contact you want to make."

"Who would be?"

"Good question," Max said. "I'll have to do some digging. We need to know as many of the answers as possible before we start with the questions. That probably makes no sense at all to someone like you."

"I've met a few people who operate that way," Mrs. Plansky said, omitting the fact that she'd never liked them.

"I don't like them, either," said Max.

Oh, no. Had she said the second part out loud after all? If not, he'd surprised her in a big way, so big she was almost missing something that had to be important: he was speaking of "we."

Was this a moment to be coy, shy, a wallflower? Absolutely not. "So," she said, "are you going to help me?"

"Obviously," said Max Leonte.

"Sorry to be so slow," Mrs. Plansky said. She felt a tremendous relief inside.

"Well, Loretta, I would have expected you'd know the first rule of journalism, the kind of journalism that gets read—put a face to the story."

"I'm the face of your story?"

"With your permission."

Mrs. Plansky nodded. She leaned forward. "In that case you should know a couple of things. First, I assume you're acquainted with Mr. Perryman at the embassy."

"We've spoken a few times but never met."

"He thinks I've gone home."

"Ah," said Max. "And I assume you got my name from him?"

"Not directly," said Mrs. Plansky. "Which brings us to the second thing." She told him her purloining story.

A smile spread across his face as he listened. That crooked tooth of his seemed to draw her gaze like something magnetic. "Therefore I won't be contacting Mr. Perryman," he said when she was done.

"Not about me," Mrs. Plansky said. "What do we do next?"

"Next you go back to your hotel, have a good sleep, and tomorrow perhaps take in the Museum of Carpathian History. There are a number of potential suspects but I'll try to narrow it down, based on what you've told me, and call you by four at the latest. Here is my card. I will add the home address." He patted his pockets, found nothing to write with. Mrs. Plansky opened her purse and handed him a pen. Max wrote on the card and gave it to her.

"Keep the pen," she said.

He read the writing on it aloud, as though intoning a mystical spell. "New Sunshine Golf and Tennis Club." He tucked the pen in his pocket. "Is there anything else you can remember about that second call?"

That second call again. Mr. Perryman had flagged it, too. "There's not much to remember. It was very short. Is it important?"

"Important? I don't see how. But interesting, yes, for the reason that it was unnecessary to the business at hand. So the question is—why?"

"You tell me."

"I have no idea." He laid his hand on his chest, right over the heart. "But I think Roma, romance, romantic, Romanian."

"You lost me."

"It's about our ancient legacy. Some ancestral relic in our minds, a deep feeling that always seems to rise up at the wrong time." He picked up his mug. "But enough of rambling. What shall we say? To justice?"

"Maybe something less highfalutin," said Mrs. Plansky. "How about noroc?"

His eyebrows rose, dark eyebrows, like his hair. "You're full of surprises."

"That's the lone one."

They clinked their mugs and downed the rest of their tuicas.

"Oh, and one more thing." He got out his phone and took her picture. "The face of the story."

"I wasn't smiling," said Mrs. Plansky.

TWENTY-FOUR

Dinu was high as a kite. They had the same expression in his language and Dinu liked it better, preferring the sound of zmeu to kite. He'd been high as a zmeu for two days, although he hadn't messed with any drugs or alcohol. It was all on account of Annika, the croupier from Bucharest who'd come to help Uncle Dragomir with his casino idea, and was also taking a shift or two at the Duce. Dinu had run into her on the street on a rainy morning, he coming out of the pharmacy—sent by his mother and Aunt Ilinca for aspirin, both of them suffering from splitting headaches, no mystery why—and Annika struggling with her umbrella, blown inside out by the wind. Without a word he'd taken the umbrella, gotten it straightened out, and handed it to her.

"Well, well, Dinu," she said. "What an efficient young man. Which of course I already knew. Here, you're getting wet. I'll save you." And she'd pulled him in close, under the umbrella, one hand on the umbrella grip, the other around Dinu's waist.

"That's all right, I'm—"

The hand around his waist gave a little squeeze. Looking back, that was the instant when the kite began to rise. It was like Annika's hand was a master communicator, sending a message from an earthly heaven he hadn't even known existed.

"Where are your cowboy boots?" she said.

"I don't wear them in the rain," said Dinu.

"So smart! What a good husband you'll make!" She drew him

out of the rain, under an awning, but kept the umbrella up as well, making for a strange feeling of privacy even though they were in the middle of town—as though they were tenting at a remote campsite. "How is that pretty girlfriend of yours?"

"I haven't seen her in a while."

"No? But she's such a peach. Don't you like peaches, Dinu?"

Annika looked up at him. He was a little bit taller. She was so beautiful, her skin so alive, her eyes impossible to look away from.

"Well, peaches, I haven't really—"

"Maybe you're not handling the situation well," she said. "Peaches like to be squeezed and kissed. Are you a good kisser? It's very important. Yet they don't teach it in school. What does that tell you?"

Dinu had no idea. He didn't know what to say or do, but also was in no hurry for this little camping trip to end.

"Here is Annika's lesson number one in the art of kissing," Annika said. "Your little peach can thank me later."

Her free hand slid upward, rounded itself over the back of his head, not gently, and kissed him, a deep kiss involving tongues and force and some sort of exchange of intimate knowledge he didn't understand, and that wasn't all he didn't understand. Then with a bright little laugh she was gone, leaving him under the awning, fully clothed, of course, although not ready for a public appearance. A minute or two passed before he descended into that state, although inside, the zmeu was almost in orbit.

"You don't think Annika's involved with my uncle, do you?"

"Involved?" said Romeo.

"You know."

"Well, there's his wife, Simone, plus the Polish girlfriend and the Moldovan girlfriend, so just from the time management angle I'd say no."

They were in their new and private office under the apartment block where Romeo lived with his older brother and his wife and kids, an apartment block even shabbier than Dinu's, but down in the subbasement was a storage room, long walled off, where Romeo had cut out a hidden back entrance. Now, sitting opposite each other at a card table cluttered with Romeo's equipment, they were all set for their very first operation, just the two of them.

"What about Annika?" Dinu said. "Do you think she has a boy-friend? Or—or maybe even a husband?"

"I don't know," Romeo said, switching on an array of monitors. "What difference does it make?" He glanced over at Dinu. "Hey, are you crazy? She's thirty years old."

"She is? How do you know that?"

"I took a look at the payroll. She's there because of helping out at the Duce."

"You took a look?"

"Hacked," Romeo said. "I hacked into the payroll." He slipped on his headphones. "Now can we get started?"

Dinu reached across the table. They bumped fists.

"Like those two guys who started Apple in their garage," Dinu said.

"Hewlett Packard," said Romeo. "But yes, like that."

Dinu checked his script. He wasn't nervous in the least. His English was getting better all the time, but it wasn't just that. He was good at this, had a knack. Had he shown a knack for anything else in his whole life? Well, maybe riding motorcycles. The two knacks went together in a way. He felt very strong at that moment, standing tall on his own two legs.

A phone rang, far away in the Cornhusker State.

"Hello?" said some little old lady.

"Hi, Granny. It's me, Eric."

"Eric?"

"Your grandson Eric. My goodness! Have you forgotten me, Granny?"

"Oh, no. I think of you so often, Eric. But it's been some time since I heard from you, that's all I meant. I hardly recognized your voice."

"I'm so sorry about that, Granny. I promise to do better. And the connection from here is pretty bad."

"Where are you?"

"That's the problem, Granny. And after so long I hate to be calling you about this, but there is nowhere else—but I have nowhere else to turn."

Dinu explained. Twenty-two minutes and seven seconds later—Romeo had decided to time all the calls and keep a record as part of their business plan—$38,492.17 had been deposited in an account he'd set up in Qatar, which Dinu now knew how to pronounce and find on a map.

"Hewlett," said Romeo, raising a hand.

"Packard," Dinu replied. They high-fived.

Dinu rode his bike to Bijoux Parisien in the old town, next door to the Porsche dealership. He'd been to the dealership a number of times, just to stare through the display window, but now he didn't even take a glance. Inside Bijoux Parisien he asked to see something nice. The woman gave him a friendly smile, then checked out his cowboy boots, the smile fading a bit.

"For your mother or girlfriend?"

"Oh, girlfriend."

"Were you thinking of rings? Bracelets? Necklaces? Brooches?"

Dinu hadn't gotten that far.

"How much did you want to spend?"

"I don't know. Three thousand, maybe?"

"Lei?"

"Dollars."

The friendly smile returned at full strength. Not much later he walked out with a sapphire necklace on an eighteen-carat gold chain—the first sapphire he'd ever seen!—beautifully gift-wrapped in a velvet lined box. Just the one single sapphire hanging on the chain, but a very nice one as the woman had explained and Dinu could see with his own eyes. For a few hundred dollars more, $3,600 in all, he could have had the same sapphire with a platinum chain, but Dinu rejected the idea, not because of the added cost but because platinum looked just like silver and everyone knew gold was better than silver. Platinum was a scam. The idea of him falling for platinum was pretty funny.

Uncle Dragomir's casino was going to be in the old Hotel Metropole, which had gone out of business and which he now owned and was renovating. It stood on a rise overlooking the river, not far from the bridge, and Dinu rode by at the end of that day, when work would be wrapping up. And well, well, well. There was Annika, walking away from the site, a roll of blueprints under her arm. He pulled up from behind.

"Hey, Annika."

She whirled around, annoyed, like he was some sort of pickup creep.

"Oh, Dinu, it's you."

"Yes. Hi. Can I take you somewhere?"

"On that?"

"You don't like the bike?"

"Riding around on the back of some guy's motorcycle? Do I look like the type?"

Didn't all girls like riding on the backs of motorcycles? Then he remembered she was thirty. So by thirty they were past that? Dinu filed the fact away.

"I guess not," he said. "Can I buy you a coffee?"

Annika checked her watch. "Sure, if we make it quick. Very nice of you. And please take off that ridiculous helmet."

He whipped it off.

A coffee place was just a few steps away on the other side of the street, with a patio, glassed in for the winter, by the river. They took the table with the best view, ordered coffee, Dinu also asking if they still had prajitura piersici, the little peach-shaped Christmas cookies, and being told no.

"Too bad about the cookies," he said, as they sipped their coffee.

"You have a sweet tooth?" said Annika.

"Well, no." He shrugged. "But peaches, that's different."

She showed no reaction, just added a little cream to her coffee, a faraway look in her amazing eyes. Faraway looks like that could happen when someone's mind was on something else, but Dinu would have bet anything that she was thinking of peaches, specifically the . . . the peachy moment they'd shared! That made this the perfect moment. He reached in his pocket.

"I have something for you."

"Oh?"

Dinu handed her the little gift-wrapped box, the paper thick and creamy, the bow deep purple. Annika took it. He noticed that one of her fingernails was dirty.

"What is this?"

"Only one way to find out," he said, and in English. Yes, he had a knack for sure.

"What does that mean?"

"Open it."

Annika untied the bow, removed the creamy paper, gazed at the gold lettering on the box: Bijoux Parisien.

"Dinu?"

He said nothing, just smiled the mysterious smile of an in-charge type who knew what was coming.

Annika took the top off the box. She stared at what was inside.

"To a peach," he said, a remark designed to be offhand and cool but his voice broke in the middle.

Annika looked up. "This is for me?"

"Uh-huh," he said. She was bowled over. That was plain to see.

"From you?"

Dinu tried to think of another cool, offhand remark but none came to mind so he just nodded.

"You shouldn't have," she said.

He shrugged, a cool, offhand shrug. That was more like it.

Their eyes met. Her eyes: so amazing, and now so full of emotion, including, he saw to his surprise, something like fear. Dinu made an astonishing mental leap: thirty-year-old women, especially of the beautiful and yes, sexy kind, like Annika, could have feelings so strong it scared them.

"Put it on," he said, taking control, like he was the thirty-year-old and she was the kid.

Annika glanced around, maybe not wanting their privacy disturbed at such a moment, but they had the glassed-in patio to themselves. She took out the necklace, gave it a close look, her eyes now revealing nothing, and put it on, fastening the clasp behind her neck with one simple twist of her fingers. Annika had taken off her coat, now hanging on the back of her chair. She wore a tight-fitting sweater of some soft material, maybe cashmere—a somewhat low-cut sweater. The sapphire nestled between her breasts. Dinu knew this was a sight he would never forget.

"Do you like it, Annika?"

"Oh, it's beautiful all right. You've chosen very well. But too generous."

"My pleasure," said Dinu.

"I mean it, Dinu. Too generous."

He spread his hands in an openhanded gesture that meant, Hey, what can I do? Hitting peak offhand cool without speaking a word. He felt, for the first time in his life, like a man.

Now she was looking at him again, again with a complicated expression in her eyes.

"What?" he said.

She leaned across the table and kissed him. Not a kiss of the peachy kind, actually more like one of his mother's pecks on the cheek. But he knew there was peachiness to come, lots and lots of peachiness.

"It looks great on you."

"It would look great on anybody."

"Well, thanks."

"No. Thank you."

"My pleasure," he said again, unable to top it with something else. "So what do you want to do?" he said.

"Excuse me?"

"Now," he said. "Well, not now, but after here, when we're done. We could go for a walk." He realized as he said it that the rain was coming down hard, beating against the glass walls. "Or maybe you're hungry? What restaurants do you like? Or—" He stopped himself, on the verge of inviting her back to the flat. What a terrible idea! A gem like her in a place like that.

Meanwhile she was reaching for her coat. "Now, in fact, I have a meeting with the builder."

"And, um, after?"

"A very long and involved meeting, followed by a good sleep, please, God. I have another meeting at seven in the morning. But of course you'll be at school in any case."

"Well, not so much these days."

"Naughty boy."

She rose, removed the necklace, placed it carefully in the box, tucked the box in her coat pocket. He tried to help her with her coat, but too late.

They went outside. Annika opened the umbrella but did not pull him under. He stood in the rain, getting soaked but not feeling it.

"I'll call you?" he said.

"All right."

"I don't have your number."

"Call the desk at the Duce. Leave a message if I'm not there."

"Okay, good. Um, don't get wet."

"Goodbye, Dinu."

Annika crossed the street, headed back to the Metropole. She hadn't taken the creamy wrapping paper and the ribbon, left behind on the table. Didn't girls like to hang on to stuff like that? Maybe not by the time they were thirty. Dinu put on his helmet and rode home on his bike.

Dinu knew he was dreaming but it was delicious nonetheless. In this dream he and Annika were on the bike on a mountain road high above the valley where Tassa's sister and brother-in-law had their farm. He could see the roof of the farmhouse from where they were—a kite was flying above it—but otherwise it didn't figure in the dream, just one of those strange things that happened in dreaming. The important part was how much fun he and Annika were having, she clinging to him, and him sometimes driving no hands. They weren't wearing their helmets, in fact weren't wearing anything at all. Except for the sapphire necklace, which kept getting bounced against her breasts and his bare back, a rather exciting back-and-forth that could only lead to something very good.

But before it did, a commotion started up.

"What are you doing?" his mother said. "You have no right."

His mother was in the dream? That wasn't possible. Not enough room on the bike, for one thing, and this was no time for mother to be in the picture. A door banged open. There were no doors in the dream. He smelled cologne.

Dinu sat up in bed. The door to his room was open, with two back-lit silhouettes in the doorway. One was Mama. The other was the silhouette of a man, bigger than Mama but not terribly big, although he had a way of standing like something powerful was coiled inside. His mama was tugging on the man's shoulder.

"You must leave here this minute," his mother said. "Or I'll call Dragomir."

The man laughed. Dinu already knew who he was, of course,

just from the cologne and the stance, but he knew the laugh as well, kind of soft, gentle. By now Mama lay on the floor in the hall, nightie askew, nose bleeding.

Dinu jumped out of bed. The bedroom light went on. There was Timbo in the doorway, an unlit cigarette dangling from his lips, his handlebar mustache, maybe freshly waxed, seeming to glow in the light. In the background Dinu could see the front door, hanging on its hinges.

Dinu yelled something—he didn't know what—and charged at Timbo, fists raised. Timbo made no move to defend himself. Dinu punched him in the mouth, or at least aimed a punch that way. It never landed. Instead Dinu felt a sudden and very sharp pain in his other hand, not the punching one, and the next thing he knew he lay on the floor, the baby finger on his non-punching hand sticking out sideways.

Timbo lit his cigarette, took a deep drag, shook out the match flame, and dropped the match on the floor. "You are not a type-A employee after all. Get dressed."

TWENTY-FIVE

Uncle Dragomir owned eight or nine cars. Dinu didn't know exactly how many. One was a black F-350 pickup, far too unwieldy for the many narrow twisted streets they had in Alba Gemina. Timbo drove. Dinu sat in the passenger seat.

"What's going on?" he said. "I don't understand."

"Seat belt," Timbo said.

Dinu fastened his seat belt, taking extra care that nothing touched that horribly bent pinkie finger on his left hand. The whole hand was throbbing, and in the midst of that came shooting pains all the way up his arm.

Timbo said nothing more. He turned out to be a poor and anxious driver, squeezing the wheel tightly, braking and speeding up at all the wrong times. He didn't look Dinu's way even once. Dinu considered unbuckling, flinging open the door, leaping out, running home to his bike, parked in the basement garage of the apartment block, racing off to where? Hungary? Serbia? He went on considering, but did nothing except try to control the pain. He was no longer high as a kite, had trouble believing he'd ever felt that way.

Timbo pulled into an unlit alley and drove a few hundred meters until he came to the back of Club Presto. No lights shone inside, meaning it was very late. The loading bay door rolled up and Timbo drove inside. The door rolled back down. Timbo cut the lights. That brought total darkness to the loading bay.

"Get out," Timbo said.

"I can't see."

"Don't be a baby," Timbo said. He opened his own door and the cabin lights went on. Timbo lit a cigarette and looked at him. His eyes could have been those of a stranger. "Or be a baby. It doesn't matter now."

Dinu got out of the car. It went totally dark again, except for the glow of Timbo's cigarette. Dinu followed that glow to a door that led inside the club at the basement level and the Cambio office. The name was a funny joke. Dinu had missed that all this time. Meanwhile Timbo was unlocking the door, his back turned. Dinu considered cracking him over the head with something, a hammer, say, or a brick, neither of which he had, of course. Timbo opened the door. They went in. A low light burned partway down the hall that led to the Cambio room, but Timbo didn't go that way. Instead he went down a rough, unfinished staircase that Dinu had never taken, lit by a naked hanging bulb. Dinu followed him down to a sublevel with an earthen floor to another door. Timbo held it open. Dinu went in. Timbo closed the door behind him, leaving Dinu by himself.

Dinu was in a small room lit by a floor lamp with a yellowed shade, the room itself like something out of a peasant's hut from long ago—earthen floor, two crude wooden chairs, a crude wooden table. He walked around. No windows to climb out of, not down underground like this, but there was another door. Dinu tried the handle. Locked. He sat in one of the chairs, holding his left wrist in his right hand. He considered trying to wrench the finger back into place. That would hurt, but he was already hurting. What if afterward, instead of better it was worse? And was there some trick, some right way of doing it? For the first time in a long while, he thought of the father he really hadn't known, except for a memory or two, and missed him.

The door to the hallway opened and Uncle Dragomir walked in. He was wearing the sapphire necklace.

"How do I look?" he said.

Dinu rose. "I . . . I don't understand."

"No? How do I look? It's a simple question. You're supposed to be smart. So let's hear a smart answer. How do I—your uncle and the brother of your father—look?"

Dinu got the idea the right answer could save him, like in some fairy tale. "You . . . you look angry, Uncle Dragomir."

"Really?" said Uncle Dragomir. "That surprises me. I don't feel angry, not the least bit. Do you know what I feel?"

"No."

"Think. How would you feel in my place?"

Dinu realized he had no idea how Uncle Dragomir felt at this or any other time, not a clue. "I'm sorry. I just don't know."

Uncle Dragomir pulled up a chair and sat down facing Dinu, an arm's length away. "What am I?" he said.

Dinu knew the answer to that one. "The boss," he said.

"Sure, the boss. But to you, pusti?" *Pusti* being like *kiddo* in their language.

"To me?" Dinu said. "You're my uncle."

"Now we are talking." Uncle Dragomir reached out and touched Dinu's knee very lightly. The sapphire swung freely out from its little nesting place in his chest hair—Uncle Dragomir wearing his shirt with the top buttons unfastened—and hung between them. "We are flesh and blood. Look at me."

Dinu looked at him.

"Am I the kind who could ever harm his own flesh and blood?"

Dinu knew the correct answer was no, you are not that kind. But it wasn't the right answer. How could it be, considering the time, quite recently, when Uncle Dragomir had punched him in the ribs? Dinu couldn't remember why. Something about showing up late for work? All he knew for sure was that the ribs still ached a bit. Then there was the tooth that got knocked out, and now this matter of the finger, both Timbo's work, but acting under orders, for sure. All that added up to the correct answer and not the right answer being the one to go with, beyond any doubt.

"No, you are not that kind."

Uncle Dragomir withdrew his hand. "Very good. Now we are on the same track, you and me, and I can freely tell you how I feel." He tucked the sapphire back inside his shirt. "I am disappointed, pusti."

From somewhere through the walls came what sounded like a groan.

Uncle Dragomir smiled. "Do you know why?"

Dinu shook his head.

"I'll tell you a story. Some people understand better from stories." Uncle Dragomir took a cigar from his pocket, cut it with a gold cigar cutter, lit it with a gold lighter. He blew a stream of smoke in Dinu's direction, but maybe not deliberately. Dinu started having trouble with his breathing right away. "But stop me if you've heard this. What do you know about how your old man died?"

"It was in Hungary," Dinu said. "He died trying to save some people in a fire."

Uncle Dragomir smiled. "And who told you that?"

"My mother."

"Did you know she wasn't always a drunk?"

Dinu didn't like that question. As for a response, he could think of none, except for violence. It wasn't exactly that he was afraid of violence. But he was afraid of Uncle Dragomir. Plus there was practical matter of his finger, the pain worsening.

"It's true," Uncle Dragomir said. "Before she was a drunk she was a slut."

Dinu rose from his chair, balling his right fist. The punch he had in mind never got thrown, because without getting up, Uncle Dragomir leaned forward a bit and gave Dinu's finger a wristy backhand flick. Dinu thought he might faint. He subsided on the chair, accepting the fact that he wasn't much of a puncher. He refused to cry out.

Uncle Dragomir tapped a little cigar ash cylinder onto the floor. "The Hungary part is false. It was Moldova. But there was a fire, although not part of the plan. Your old man—what a character he could be!—knew some gamblers over there. This was when we were just starting out, didn't really have a plan. It was like our high school years in this business." He took a drag off his cigar, sent more smoke Dinu's way. "Now I have my doctorate." Uncle Dragomir nodded to himself, pleased with this thought. "But back to your old man and his idea. These gamblers held a big poker game on Saturday nights, fixed, of course, but it attracted rich guys from all over—Odessa, Varna even. Rich guys who thought they were smart because they were rich. Those are the chickens the gamblers feed on, but we didn't care about any of that. We went in late at night, wearing masks—my idea—and throwing smoke bombs— his idea. This kind of operation you want to go fast fast fast. Not like you were thinking with Annika, huh? I've had some of that one. Not that good, believe me. Anyway, fast fast fast. Which was how it happened. At first. We scooped up all the cash in sight, thousands of euros, real money for us back then. But just as we were headed out the window—this was on an upper floor, with a fire escape—your old man spotted a safe on the wall and turned back. To find someone among all these panicking card players who could open the safe, you see. Meanwhile something had caught fire. I yelled forget it let's go. But—and this is the point of the story—he was greedy. My last sight of him he had a knife to the throat of some girl, maybe the girlfriend of one of the guys who ran the place. He could be persuasive, your old man. Then comes this tremendous boom. I was lucky to get away with my life. So, the moral of the story—don't be greedy." Uncle Dragomir tapped off another cylinder of ash, this time on Dinu's knee. "You are greedy, just like him."

Dinu did not believe the story. In his mind he changed it up a bit, making Uncle Dragomir the one with the knife, but he couldn't make it come out right like that.

"You shouldn't have gotten greedy," Uncle Dragomir said. "Your future was bright."

Dinu shook his head. "I just don't know what this is about."

Uncle Dragomir held out the sapphire. "Where did you get the money for this?"

"I—I've been saving."

"That's your answer?"

Dinu looked Uncle Dragomir in the eye. "Yes."

"You see, I was hoping you had sold your motorcycle and raised the money that way. But I am told the motorcycle has not changed hands. So one more time. Where did the money come from?"

"Savings. I've been saving all my life."

"You have talent, no question." Uncle Dragomir rose. "Come, please."

Dinu followed him to the door, not the door to the hall, but the other one, locked. Uncle Dragomir knocked. The door opened right away. Marius stood on the other side. This room was just like the other one—earthen floor, lamp, crude wooden table and chairs. Romeo sat in one of them. It was bad, what they'd done to him.

"Hello, Marius," Uncle Dragomir said. "Could you ask Romeo to kindly look up?"

"Hey, look up," said Marius.

Uncle Dragomir corrected him. "Kindly look up."

"Hey, kindly look up."

Romeo raised his head. One of his eyes was swollen shut, but the other found Dinu.

"Here's your friend Dinu," Uncle Dragomir said. "We have a little mystery happening now. Let's call it the mystery of the necklace bought from Bijoux Parisien right here in beautiful Alba Gemina for three thousand one hundred ninety-five American dollars. Maybe you can kindly help us solve our little mystery. Will you do that for us, Romeo?"

Romeo nodded, a very slight nod, but enough to start his nose bleeding.

"Thank you, Romeo." Uncle Dragomir came forward, removed the necklace. "Take it."

Romeo reached out, his hand shaking, and took the necklace. A drop of blood from his nose landed square on the sapphire.

"It's nice, isn't it?" Uncle Dragomir said. "Do you know the name of that stone?"

Romeo shook his head.

"Tell him, Marius."

"Jade," said Marius.

Now, for the first time since this horrible episode began, Uncle Dragomir did look angry. "What is wrong with you, Marius? It's a sapphire."

"Sorry, boss."

Uncle Dragomir turned to Dinu. "See how hard it is to find good help? That's what makes this all so upsetting." He turned back to Romeo. "Here's the question, Romeo. Your friend—or should I say business partner?—claims he bought this necklace for—do you remember the amount I told you?"

"Three thousand one hundred ninety-five U.S.," said Romeo, so quiet Dinu could hardly hear.

"Notice, Marius, how Romeo recalls the exact amount, just from hearing it once."

"He's a smart son of a bitch," said Marius.

"They both are," said Uncle Dragomir. "That's what's killing me." He sighed. "So, Romeo, Dinu claims that amount you just mentioned came from his savings over the years. Do you think that's possible?"

Romeo gazed with his one good eye at the necklace in his hand and said nothing.

"Or is it possible that it came from the profits of a little side business? Wasn't Romeo telling us about that business earlier tonight, Marius?"

"For sure," Marius said, stepping forward. "Do you want me to get him to tell it again?"

"Stop," Dinu said.

"You have something to say?" said Uncle Dragomir.

"That's where I got the money. And the side business was my idea."

Uncle Dragomir patted Dinu on the back. "That's the boy. So now let us all go up to the Cambio office where Romeo will transfer the total of the funds from your little side business into an account of mine, and we will be all square."

"As long as you keep the . . . the jewel, too," said Marius.

"Now you're thinking." Uncle Dragomir took the necklace from Romeo's hand. "Oh, and one more small matter. It's about your business partner's poor finger. Have you seen what happened to it, Romeo? Show him, Dinu."

Dinu raised his hand slightly.

"Your partner and your friend, Romeo. Before we go upstairs, let's take a moment to fix it."

No one moved.

"Meaning you, Romeo. I want you to fix it."

"I don't know how," Romeo said.

"It's easy," said Marius, holding up his own hand and sticking out his baby finger. "You just give it a pull at the same time you slide it back. Use some force, sure, but that's the trick, the pull. A real sharp pull."

Romeo lowered his head and shook it, blood dripping to the floor.

"That's disappointing," Uncle Dragomir said. "I'm afraid Romeo needs some persuading, Marius."

Dinu walked up to Romeo and held out his hand. "Just do it."

TWENTY-SIX

Breakfast at the Duce was served buffet style in a room with several tall potted plants on the floor—none of them doing well—and Django Reinhardt doing very well on the sound system. As Mrs. Plansky, the only customer, helped herself to coffee and a slice of black bread with plum jam, forgoing the only other offering, a dish that looked vaguely eggy, she remembered a movie she'd seen where a character playing Django had made an appearance. But that was all she remembered, the rest of the movie gone. If she saw it again would it all come back to her after the first minute or two? Or would the whole thing be brand-new? In that case, she'd reached a stage where just one movie would do. In death there were no movies, so the progression made sense: many movies, one movie, none. Death simplified things, no question. Mrs. Plansky understood something as she sat at a window table that was partly screened off from the rest of the room by one of the potted plants: she didn't particularly care about simplifying life. Complication was fine with her, and if more complications meant longer life, then bring them on! Meanwhile her foot was tapping to the music. She realized she was having one of those little happiness bursts that popped up inside her from time to time. But now? In her present situation? She must be mad. Mrs. Plansky bit into her toast. She'd been a sliced-white-only gal before Norm, like living in a bread desert. He would have loved this Romanian black bread. She spread on some more plum jam—anything plum appearing to be the way to go in this town—and laid her phone on the table, waiting for Max's call.

Annika, the pretty woman from the front desk, entered, poured herself a cup of coffee, and sat at a corner table away from the window side, partly screened from Mrs. Plansky's view by the potted plant. Even so, Mrs. Plansky could tell Annika wasn't happy today. Did all humans speak the same body language? She didn't know, but Annika had one of those faces where unhappiness made everything turn down, giving a preview of how she'd look after two or three more decades of gravity had done their work. Mrs. Plansky checked the reflection of her own face in the bread knife and saw what gravity could do when it got its hands on a real serious chunk of time. Then she focused on just the eyes, and everything was all right.

A man in a long black leather coat entered, helped himself to coffee, and sat down opposite Annika at her table. Mrs. Plansky, allowing her imagination to run free, said to herself that if they were romantically involved all those downturns on her face would now flip the other way. They did not, although there was a change, perhaps from unhappiness to caution. Did the man seem familiar? Mrs. Plansky peered between the dried-up, dusty, dying leaves of the potted plant, peered unobtrusively, undercover ops' style. Although not even turned toward her, his face with its big features, none remotely recessive, seemed to radiate power, and not simply brute power. But plenty of that, too. It was Mr. Squareman, from the police station last night, a drinking buddy of Captain Romulu, who was not to be trusted, according to Max. Mrs. Plansky sipped her coffee, watching over the rim of the cup. She knew, of course, that despite the leaves and the cup, if she could see them then they could see her. But they weren't looking.

Mr. Squareman and Annika talked in low voices, Mrs. Plansky catching just enough to know they were speaking Romanian, so they might as well have been shouting at the tops of their lungs. He seemed to be telling her a story of some kind, an involved kind

of a story with a this-happened-and-then-this rhythm, a story that
Annika seemed to like less and less as it went on. At one point Mr.
Squareman attempted a sort of pantomime, taking the pinkie finger
of one hand and bending it way down, as though trying to snap it
off or something. The only interpretation Mrs. Plansky could come
up with involved breaking a wishbone, meaning Mr. Squareman's
story probably had to do with some dinner, perhaps at Christmas,
and assuming that Romanians had the same ritual. But how to explain Annika's reaction, putting her hands to her face in horror and
disbelief?

That took Mr. Squareman by surprise. He'd clearly been expecting something different, maybe laughter, the little pantomime being the punch line to a shaggy dog joke.

"Annika!" he said, raising his voice, followed by something with
the tone of *oh for God's sake, lighten up.*

Annika did not lighten up. Instead, she pushed back from the
table.

"Okay, okay," he said in English, then raised both palms in a
pacifying gesture.

"Okay?" she said. "Is not okay."

Mr. Squareman frowned, a muscle bunching on his forehead,
above the bridge of his nose, bridge of the nose being very apt in
this case since his nose was like the prow of a ship. Then he said
something with a *will-this-change-your-tune* tone, reached into his
pocket, and took out a piece of jewelry, a necklace, maybe or . . .
yes, a necklace, the chain gold, the jewel some blue stone. He held it
out for Annika to take it. She shook her head, pushed farther back
from the table.

Mr. Squareman got angry. He said something that sounded
mean, possibly even disgusting, and smacked his huge hand on the
table. Annika's cup bounced in its saucer, like from an earth tremor,
and she shrank back. Just a little—she was a strong woman, but
afraid of Mr. Squareman. He jumped up and marched toward the
doorway, Mrs. Plansky losing sight of him behind the potted plant.

Then, through the leaves, she spotted something flying through the air, something blue and gold, the necklace, of course, but there was a little beat before Mrs. Plansky realized that.

In the little beat, Mr. Squareman stalked out of the breakfast room and the necklace landed on Annika's table with a soft thunk. The stone separated from the chain and came bouncing crazily across the floor, between two potted plants and coming to rest right at Mrs. Plansky's feet. She was wearing her ballet flats at the time.

Mrs. Plansky bent down, her skeleton picking this moment to make a creaking sound or two, and picked up the blue stone. Ah, a sapphire, and a nice one although not very big. One of the ladies at the club had a huge sapphire ring that she wore while playing. Sometimes it refracted the sunlight—an unfair advantage, Mrs. Plansky had said one day, a joke that made the other players laugh, although not the ring wearer, who perhaps transferred to the Old Sunshine Country Club soon after.

Meanwhile Annika was coming her way. She dangled the gold chain between finger and thumb, away from her body, like it had a bad smell.

"Here," said Mrs. Plansky, extending the sapphire. "This, um, fell on the floor."

"Ha," Annika said. "Sure. A fall for sure."

She made no move to take the sapphire, in fact looked a little pale. Mrs. Plansky didn't say anything, just pulled out a chair. Annika sat down. Mrs. Plansky went to the buffet table, poured a cup of tea, set it before Annika.

Annika reached for it, but the chain had gotten entangled in her hand and for some reason she couldn't get rid of it. Mrs. Plansky did it for her. Her fine motor had always been pretty good. She was deft at sewing on buttons, for example, or getting twisted-up shoelaces untied—how often she'd done that for Jack when he was a kid!

Annika took a sip of her tea, a tiny wave slopping out of the cup. She looked up, her eyes clearing, maybe really taking Mrs. Plansky in for the first time.

"You're the American lady?"

"An American lady, yes. My name's Loretta."

"In the presidential suite?"

"Right. It's very nice."

"Of course, of course. I apologize for being so . . . so malorganized."

"No apology necessary." Mrs. Plansky laid the sapphire on the table. "Drink some more tea."

Annika sipped her tea, this time spilling none. "I have met only a few American men. They are nicer."

"Nicer than . . . ?"

"Our men." Annika gestured toward the table on the other side of the room. "I don't know what you saw."

"Oh, not much. Nothing really. Not worth thinking about."

"I wish for that. That it would be not worth thinking about." She pointed to her name tag. "Annika."

They shook hands. Mrs. Plansky broke off some black bread, spread it with plum jam, gave it to Annika. Annika bit into it.

"Oh my God, so hungry," she said. "Sometimes you find that out when . . ." She finished the sentence by holding up the bread.

"You haven't been eating?" Mrs. Plansky suddenly realized she was sounding like a Jewish mother, in fact like Norm's mother. Fifty years late, give or take: if she'd pulled this one out of the bag back then maybe she and Norm's mom would have gotten off on the right foot.

"So much work to do, is the problem," Annika said.

"Is it busy here?"

"Oh, not the hotel, not in winter. But that is just my gig side."

Gig side. Mrs. Plansky liked that, and was also liking Annika. "And your main gig?"

"Main gig is the big job?"

"Yes. Your English is very good. I'm sorry I don't speak Romanian. I only know two words—noroc and frigorific."

Annika smiled. "With those you will do well here."

Mrs. Plansky pushed the sapphire a little closer to Annika. "This is very nice. I've always liked sapphires. They make me think of summer."

"Then you should keep it."

Mrs. Plansky laughed, a laugh she cut off as soon as she noticed the expression on Annika's face, the expression of someone thinking she'd stumbled on a good idea. Or was it possible this was one of those cultures where if you admired some object the owner was obligated by tradition to fork it over?

"Even if you meant that, I could never accept," she said.

"Why not? Is from Bijoux Parisien, a very nice store and not just for this town. The cost was three thousand one hundred ninety-five—and not lei but dollars."

"All the more reason, then, it being so valuable," Mrs. Plansky said. "And there are others. Supposing the gentleman in question and you patch things up? Or maybe he's your husband—so you're patched whether you like it or not! And then he discovers that some tourist is now wearing the thing. What an interesting situation that would be!"

Annika sat back. "I don't know to laugh or to cry," she said. "Patched whether you like or not! I will never forget that. But the gentleman, as you are putting it, is not my husband. Or even boyfriend." Some sort of cloud passed beneath the surface of her eyes. "Except on one—I don't know the word."

Mrs. Plansky could think of several that might apply. She went with the blandest. "Occasion."

Annika nodded. "Occasion, yes. And there will be no repetition. But we are patched in business so I have to build walls. Not real walls. Walls inside my head. You understand this meaning?"

"I do," said Mrs. Plansky. "What sort of business, if you don't mind my asking?"

"Casino business," Annika said. "We are building a casino here in Alba Gemina, in the old Metropole. I am partner—minor partner and employee for now." She made a gesture encompassing the hotel. "And why I am here. But my knowledge is casinos, from the Palace in Bucharest and WinBoss in Odessa."

"Ah," Mrs. Plansky said, understanding the business part but no further ahead when it came to the sapphire necklace. Was Mr. Squareman hoping for another occasion with Annika? And on an unrelated subject, had his meeting with Captain Romulu been about the casino? She'd been to a casino once but hadn't enjoyed the experience, and not because of the way Norm's foolproof black-jack method—which he'd worked on for days before their Las Vegas trip—played out. He'd lost his entire stake—$270—in eleven minutes. That part she'd actually enjoyed. Not that he'd lost, of course, but the look on his face after, so sweetly crestfallen. He was superb. But the feeling inside the place, like being trapped in a hellish spaceship stalled in the void—that she hadn't liked. None of that was relevant now and she hoped all this thinking was happening in a flash. The point was that all she knew of the actual business part of the casino world behind the scenes she'd learned from *The Godfather*. Hadn't there been a shady police captain somewhere in part one, or maybe part two? She was considering some question about Captain Romulu when Annika picked up the sapphire and the chain and stuck them in her pocket.

"Ah," said Mrs. Plansky again.

Annika shook her head. "Not for keeping. But returning to the owner."

"Even though—" Mrs. Plansky stopped herself. It was none of her beeswax. Of all things, late in life, was she turning into a nosy parker? On the other hand, wasn't that in the undercover ops hand-book, perhaps the most important chapter: Be a Nosy Parker!

"Even though," she went on, "that didn't go so well the first time?"

Annika looked confused.

"Returning the necklace to the owner," Mrs. Plansky explained. And then she got it. "Oh, I see, you mean the jeweler, Boutique, um . . ."

"Bijoux Parisien," Annika said. "And no, not there. But also not to Dragomir."

"Dragomir is the man in the leather coat?"

Annika nodded. "Dragomir Tiriac, my partner, businessman in town, owner for example of this hotel."

So Dragomir Tiriac was the actual name of Mr. Squareman, but somehow not the owner of the necklace? One puzzle solved, another rising up in its place. Mrs. Plansky was wondering what the undercover ops handbook might have to say to that, when a recent fact popped up in her mind, unfortunately not related to the necklace but kind of interesting on its own. One of the motorcycle boys—the good-looking one—had told her that his uncle owned this place, owned the Hotel Duce, possibly the reason he'd recommended it. What was the boy's name again? Mrs. Plansky remembered the name of the other boy, the pimply one, no problem. Romeo—who could forget? Now if she could just for God's sake come up with the name of the good-looking boy she could say to Annika, Hey, do you know *X*? But the name seemed to be gone, at least for now.

Meanwhile Annika was dabbing at the corner of her cheeks with a napkin and pushing back her chair.

"I must go, Loretta. I have much enjoyed our talk. Thank you. It is a help to me."

"Very nice getting to know you a bit."

"And if there is anything you need while here," Annika went on, "anything at all, here is card with personal number."

Mrs. Plansky took the card. "Thank you, Annika. And good luck."

Annika walked away. She'd reached the arched entry way leading to the lobby, when the name came to Mrs. Plansky: Dinu!

Hey, Annika, do you know Dinu? He's Dragomir's nephew. But Mrs. Plansky didn't say it. Why not? Was it in some way the sight of the back of Annika's bared neck, quite lovely but also vulnerable? Or the fact that Dragomir and Captain Romulu appeared to be pals, even drinking buddies, and Max had warned her about the captain? Or was it the memory of that bloody horse's head in *The Godfather*? For whatever reason, Mrs. Plansky kept silent. She thought of lending Annika her Scottish scarf.

TWENTY-SEVEN

Einstein said—well, Norm said Einstein said, not a caveat in Mrs. Plansky's mind but absolute proof—that if you went real fast—real real fast—then time would slow down. Now, back in her room after breakfast, time had pretty much come to a standstill. That should have meant Mrs. Plansky was currently speeding along, but she was not. She sat perfectly motionless, gazing out the window at the statue of *Michael the Brave,* also motionless. But at least he had plans, all about cutting off someone's head with that wide-bladed saber or whatever it was. She herself had no plans, other than waiting for Max's call. What would Einstein do in her place? He was probably in a league of his own when it came to mathematical problems, and hers was at least partly a mathematical problem, take the Safemo angle, for instance, algorithms and all that. On the other hand wasn't it also a people problem? She half-recalled something about Einstein: math wiz, yes; people wiz, especially female-type people, no. At that moment something clicked into place. That second call! Mrs. Plansky sat a little straighter. The second call, flagged by both Perryman and Max as being unnecessary, was a people thing. That was what made it so interesting, or anomalous, or important. Or all three. Drilling down, as they said in the consultancy world—she and Norm had once hired a consultant, very briefly—it was a thing about one particular person, namely the Will masquerader. Therefore even if Einstein had been around and hanging out in this very room, he couldn't have helped.

Mrs. Plansky decided to go for a walk. It looked cold and windy outside, but dry. She made a second decision, choosing the warm, quilted indoor-outdoor mules over the booties.

Yes, cold and windy. Mrs. Plansky turned right out of the Duce's entrance so she could have the wind at her back, discovering when she checked her map a few blocks later that the Museum of Carpathian History, ostensible object of the excursion, lay in the opposite direction. She kept going, the wind giving extra zip to her pace, like she was decades younger, or at least a year or two. Then, all at once, she found she was passing Bijoux Parisien. She stopped to look in the window.

The first thing Mrs. Plansky saw was her reflection. Oh, dear. She patted her hair into shape, or at least a shape of sorts. Then, changing the angle of view slightly, she got rid of the sight of herself, now replaced by the window display. She saw a string of pearls she liked—big, fat, excessive pearls—and a gold ring set with little rubies that looked like a throwback to the time when the Ottomans were in charge around these parts, although in fact she knew nothing about the Ottomans or—

Mrs. Plansky became aware that someone in the store was trying to get her attention. She peered beyond the display case. A woman—neatly dressed and very presentable, as Miss Terrance used to say—with a big, friendly smile was waving her in. Mrs. Plansky had no intention of—or means for!—buying anything, but did an undercover op remain aloof from the people or . . . or come in from the cold! Mrs. Plansky entered Bijoux Parisien.

"Welcome, madame," the woman said in French, a language Mrs. Plansky understood pretty well. "Better to look and be warm at the same time, no?"

"It certainly is," said Mrs. Plansky in English. She could have said the equivalent in French, but speaking it was laborious and the sound of her accent always made her feel like a female Pepé Le Pew.

"You're American?" the woman said, switching to English.

"Yes."

"Probably the only American in Alba Gemina today. Were you looking for anything in particular?" The woman's expert eye scanned her for jewelry. There was nothing to see but a plain little emerald ring and Norm's wedding ring, which she wore on a chain around her neck. Her own wedding ring she'd buried with Norm.

"What nice earrings, by the way," the woman said.

Oops. Mrs. Plansky had forgotten the earrings, also plain little emeralds—hardly even visible—and matching the ring, although she'd bought them much later.

"Thank you," Mrs. Plansky said. "You have a very nice store."

"Merci, madame. Please look around."

Mrs. Plansky pretended to look around, all the while working hard on a move that was taking shape in her mind, but not quickly.

"Recently, but I can't remember where," she began, and oh how pitiful, right from the start, "I saw a necklace I liked. A gold chain with a sapphire, I think it was oblong cut."

The woman's eyebrows, works of art deco type art all by themselves, rose. "Was it here in Alba Gemina where you saw it?"

"I—I really can't say," said Mrs. Plansky.

"Because just the other day I sold a piece very like what you are describing."

"Really."

"Yes. Unfortunately it was one of a kind. I do have a very pretty brooch with three sapphires, square cut in Italian style."

"That sounds nice, but I've just never worn brooches." Mrs. Plansky laughed gaily. The falsity of that sound: at that moment she was neck and neck with Judas. "Maybe you could put me onto whoever bought the necklace!"

"Pardon?" said the woman, back in French. *Pardon* in French cut to a depth *excuse me* never could.

"Just a thought," Mrs. Plansky said.

"A thought to contact my customer?"

"More as an after-market type of thing."

"After market? I do not understand."

"Well," said Mrs. Plansky, plunging ahead, "it's about the sapphire necklace. If I knew the buyer I . . . I could make him an offer he couldn't refuse!" The reaction she was hoping for did not appear on the woman's face. "Or her," Mrs. Plansky added, on the slim chance that was where she'd gone wrong. But it wasn't that, either. She was considering an explanation involving *The Godfather* when she caught a lucky break. A new customer entered the store and the woman went off—hurried off—to attend to her. Moments later Mrs. Plansky was out on the street.

The wind was blowing harder now. She took her phone out of her pocket to check the time but fumbled a bit, came close to dropping it. That could have led to all sorts of things, none good. Mrs. Plansky hurried across the street to a recessed doorway and tried again. Time: 14:11. Text and voice mail messages: zero. And there she was, reflected in another window, a lady with messy, windblown hair, not looking her best, in fact appearing a little lost, confused, apprehensive, even afraid. What did she have to be afraid of? Nothing. At least nothing concrete.

"Pull yourself together." Had she said that aloud? Just in case she hadn't she did it again, making sure this time. "Pull yourself together!" Then, in the midst of this—what should she call it? collapse?—she caught another lucky break. The etched sign on the window glass read: SALON DE COAFURA. *Coafura:* so close to the French *coiffure.* Not a sign on a window but a sign from above! Still she hesitated. Hadn't she had her hair done just the other day at Delia's on the Waterway? Could she afford this indulgence? Absolutely not. But Delia's on the Waterway was another world, and taking a closer look she spotted a price list card on the window shelf. If those numbers were in lei then this place was a bargain, if in dollars it was like Beverly Hills. Alba Gemina was not Beverly Hills. So far, Mrs. Plansky thought as she went inside, she was preferring Alba Gemina.

Twenty minutes later, hair washed, blown, and dried for a cost of twelve U.S. dollars including tip, unless she was messing up the math, she was back out on the street, feeling much better and looking, in her estimation, slightly European. And not only that, but the mysterious type of European woman, like, for example, Catherine Deneuve. Mrs. Plansky was well aware that she and Catherine Deneuve were on different planets when it came to beauty, and she had never felt in the least mysterious inside, but now, by God, she did! And what if Catherine Deneuve actually didn't feel that she was mysterious inside, and often thought, Oh, Catherine, what a bore you are! Unlikely, yes, but things had a way of evening out, as everyone said. Mrs. Plansky checked her phone again. Time closing in on 16:00, still nothing from Max. She was setting off at a nice pace, a spring in her step, when she noticed a woman walking quickly in the same direction, only on the other side of the street. It was Annika, wearing jeans, sneakers, and white jacket with red sleeves and a fur-trimmed hood.

Could you tell something about a person from how they were walking? That question had never arisen before in Mrs. Plansky's mind. Annika's head was down. Her arms weren't swinging, but held close to her sides. Yet she was moving fast. Mrs. Plansky deduced that she was on her way to do something she didn't want to do. Was there any reason to follow her? No, not a one. And at any other moment in her life, Mrs. Plansky would not have followed. But this moment was special, Mrs. Plansky feeling for the first time mysterious. Staying on her side and keeping her distance, she followed Annika down the street, the wind cold, but at her back.

TWENTY-EIGHT

An undercover op would surely have many tricks for following without being seen but Mrs. Plansky knew only one: don't get too close. That seemed to be good enough and in any case Annika never looked back, just kept clipping along in that stiff posture, perhaps moving even faster than before. Yes, faster for sure, and increasing the distance between them. Mrs. Plansky, losing sight of Annika as she came to the end of a long block and turned down a side street, realized the don't-get-too-close trick came with a drawback. She picked up the pace, but suddenly found herself huffing and puffing. How could that be? She played tennis three or four times a week, almost always doubles, true, but was never out of breath, also had never before felt this strange tightness in her chest, nothing she would call pain. But still. A short, round woman dressed all in black and carrying two shopping bags in each hand passed her with no sign of any effort at all.

Mrs. Plansky reached the end of the block, turned, and failed to spot Annika among the pedestrians, of which there seemed to be dozens, maybe more. Then, at least a hundred yards ahead, she caught a red-and-white flash: Annika crossing the street. Mrs. Plansky—who had once broken twenty-four minutes in a 5K—tried to walk faster but could not, not without provoking the tightness in her chest. Tighter and tighter. She lost sight of Annika, although she couldn't be sure because her vision had gone a bit blurry. Mrs.

Plansky stopped, her back to a lamppost, and tried to catch her breath. That took some time.

Meanwhile, the wind was dying down and the light was fading. She checked her phone: 16:00 on the nose, no calls, no texts. Feeling better, although strangely detached, she walked on, in the faint hope of picking up Annika's trail, but at the leisurely speed her body seemed to prefer right now. She became aware that she was leaving the old town, the architecture changing from faded grandeur mixed with a sort of medieval hipness to something more dismal that she thought of as Stalinist, four-and five-story apartment blocks separated from each other by bleak empty plots, with lots of litter scattered here and there. She knew almost nothing of Romanian history but felt she was somehow absorbing it by osmosis on this walk. Mrs. Plansky was lost in thoughts like that when she saw Annika, standing at the entrance to an apartment block across the street, not twenty yards away. Mrs. Plansky stepped behind a skinny leafless tree, planted in a tiny dirt plot cut into the sidewalk and reeking of pee.

Annika had her phone to her ear and was gazing up at the bleak façade of the building. No balconies? That was rather grim, in Mrs. Plansky's opinion. A face appeared in a window on the third floor, the face of a man, possibly young. He withdrew. Annika pocketed her phone. She appeared to take a long, deep breath.

The entry door to the apartment block—a plain, steel door with no pizzazz whatsoever—opened and a man came out. A youngish man in sweats and a T-shirt with what might have been the image of a skier on the front. One of his hands, the left, was wrapped in some sort of bandage or splint. The wind blew a forelock of his hair over one eye. Oh, and also he was wearing cowboy boots. Mrs. Plansky took a closer look at his face. Hard to be sure at this distance but he looked a lot like one of the motorcycle kids, not Romeo, but . . . but the other one, his name once again elusive. So frustrating! But in her moment of frustration Mrs. Plansky had an inspiration. She took out her phone and snapped a photo of the scene! How brilliant was that! Seconds later, using her thumb and index finger on the screen in a motion the designers probably considered instinctive—getting it wrong in her case—she expanded the image. Yes, the other boy, for sure. And then came his name: Dinu! She was on a roll.

In tennis you don't change a winning game. Applying that rule to the here and now, Mrs. Plansky kept watching the scene across the street through the screen of her phone, taking photos from time to time. A discussion was going on, Annika pointing to Dinu's bandaged hand and Dinu holding it behind his hip, like he was trying to hide it from sight. She reached out and touched his shoulder, kind of tentatively. He turned away, now had his back to the street and Mrs. Plansky. There were tears on Annika's face, silver in the fading light. She reached into her pocket, withdrew something Mrs. Plansky couldn't quite make out, just a tiny flash of blue and gold, and tried to give it to Dinu. He backed away, didn't want it. Annika took his good hand, which he'd folded into a fist, gently opened it, pressed the blue and gold object on his palm, folded his hand back up. Then she turned and ran off down the street. Dinu watched until she was out of sight. He went back inside the building, the steel door closing behind him.

Mrs. Plansky stood behind the skinny, leafless tree in its mephitic little patch of dirt. She was stunned, amazed, bewildered. Where to begin? Dinu knew Annika? Well, perhaps not actually a surprise. His uncle, Dragomir Tiriac, owned the hotel, and Annika filled in there from time to time, on breaks from the casino development job. Mrs. Plansky slowed down her mind, laying down all the little details as she would have before a presentation to a prospective client. Slow thinking, she'd learned, was best for planning, fast thinking for emergencies. But stop! Her undisciplined old mind was wandering. This was not the time. She turned to her phone and went through the pictures she'd just taken.

First, the flash of blue and gold. Yes, the sapphire necklace. She had clear images of it in Annika's hand and on Dinu's palm. Also, before going back inside the building, he'd opened his hand to give it a look. Somehow she'd missed that in real time, but here it was. And the expression on his face at that moment? So complicated, such an odd combination of very grown up and not grown up at all. Mrs. Plansky, who hardly knew the boy and had no clue about what was going on, felt bad for him. She zoomed in on his injured hand, bandaged and with the last three fingers splinted together.

She went over the facts she knew. Someone bought the sapphire necklace at Bijoux Parisien, paying $3195 U.S., not peanuts anywhere, and certainly not here. Dragomir Tiriac tried to give the necklace to Annika, an idea that seemed to have appalled her. Now Annika had given it to Dinu, who hadn't wanted it, either. The necklace was like some talisman in a fairy tale, a new one for Mrs. Plansky, in a language she didn't know.

She expanded another photo, this one of Annika with tears on her face. They both—Dinu and Annika—had expressive faces, almost like actors. Somewhere she'd read that actors, or maybe just movie actors, had faces that were big in proportion to their heads, which didn't seem to be the case with Dinu or Annika. But there went her mind again, off the leash. What did she see on Annika's face? That was the point. What she saw was grief, as though someone had died.

In this same photo of tear-faced Annika, Dinu had his back to the camera. There was something written on his T-shirt. Mrs. Plansky enlarged the image some more and read the words: BOGDAN PLUMBING AND HEATING, NUMBER 1 IN THE GRANITE STATE. Mrs. Plansky studied that little inscription, as though it held a hidden meaning. It was often strange and even funny to see how foreigners glommed on to bits of American culture, but what was their angle? Satiric? Ironic? Mocking? Mystified? Or maybe sometimes a T-shirt was just a T-shirt. Still, Mrs. Plansky couldn't quite completely let go of Bogdan Plumbing and Heating. Something about it bothered her, but she couldn't think what. Was it the Granite State part? Once, when she was a kid, she'd been stuck alone on a chair lift on a class ski trip in the White Mountains, hovering high over a gnarly slope for over an hour with the wind blowing and the temperature in single digits. But she hadn't thought of that episode in years, decades. Could whatever was bothering her be that far back? Mrs. Plansky doubted it, and in any case had no desire to roam around her life in search of unresolved traumas.

She checked the time: 16:22. No call from Max, no texts. She considered entering the apartment building and looking for Dinu. But why? Yes, she seemed to have stumbled on a little mystery, but it had nothing to do with her mystery. Even so, she scanned the building until she found the number of its street address: 971. She took a picture of it. Then she walked to the nearest corner and took a picture of the street sign: Strada Izvor. There! A tangible fact, almost certainly irrelevant yet it made her feel good anyway, like she'd accomplished something. Dinu lived at 971 Strada Izvor. And then she realized she knew the address of someone else in Alba Gemina, namely Max Leonte. Wasn't it written on his card? She dug through her purse and found it.

Max's card was written in Romanian and English and had a little line drawing of his face at the top left, not a bad rendering at all, catching his intelligence, which she'd seen in person, and perhaps something judgmental, which she had not. MAX LEONTE, JOURNALIST, AUTHOR, SEEKER OF TRUTH, it read. Then came his phone number, already captured by her own phone, and the address he'd added with the New Sunshine pen—56 Strada Vulcan, Alba Gemina. She checked the map, found Strada Vulcan, a minor street that backed onto the river, not far from the bridge she'd crossed when she'd first entered the town. Aha! The geography of the town began to make sense to her: the Soviet-style part where she was now, on the eastern side, and then moving west the old town, the main shopping district, the river. She texted Max—**haven't heard from you**—and started walking, steadily but not fast at all.

Fifty-six Strada Vulcan turned out to be near the top of a steep hill, which wasn't apparent from the map. Mrs. Plansky found she—or rather her lungs or heart or some other internal traitor—

wanted to stop for a rest on the way up. Nothing like this had ever happened before. What was going on? Then it hit her: delayed jet lag. She'd read about that in *AARP* magazine, which she didn't subscribe to but came anyway, like the AARP folks wanted to make sure she was under no illusions. So, now that she'd figured it out, no reason to extend this little break for one more second. Mrs. Plansky treaded up the hill, keeping the huffing and puffing under wraps, or at least their sound.

Strada Vulcan was lined with new-looking one-and two-story townhouses, all of them simple and quite similar although their colors were different, even numbers on the river side, odd on the east side where Mrs. Plansky was walking. Through the gaps between the townhouses she caught glimpses of the river, deep red in the dying light. The sky was almost fully dark, a few stars already visible. Fifty-six came into view, one story and painted pink. The windows were dark but a car was parked outside. Mrs. Plansky paused to send another text: **Max? I'm about to knock on your door.**

The very next moment that door opened. Mrs. Plansky had just enough time to think now we're getting somewhere when a man came outside, not Max but a much bigger fellow. He went quickly to the car—a bunch of papers and what might have been a notebook in his hand—squeezed in, being so big, and drove away, not looking once in her direction. She knew this enormous man, those shoulder muscles unmissable even at a distance and in poor light. It was Marius, who'd carried her suitcase up to the presidential suite, discussing Nixon and refusing a tip. Reluctantly carried her suitcase, as though it wasn't in his job description. So what was?

Mrs. Plansky stood watching number 56 from across the street, waiting for something to happen. Nothing did. After a while, she slung her purse over one shoulder, dusted off her hands, and got down to business, crossing Strada Vulcan and knocking on Max's door.

No answer. She knocked again. "Max? You there? It's me, Loretta." Perhaps she'd whispered that. She tried again, in a normal tone. Why not? Was anything abnormal going on? Not that she could define. She knocked again, harder. He'd promised a call by four. Was this the kind of country where you expected unpunctuality? Not to her knowledge. "Max? Max!"

No answer. Mrs. Plansky tried turning the knob, a move she'd seen in lots of noirish movies. Norm had a thing for noirish movies. If there was a shot of a rainy street on a dark night, he was in. But Max's door, unlike the doors in all those movies, was locked.

Mrs. Plansky glanced around, like someone up to no good. Which she was not. No need to be furtive! Especially since no one was around. She circled to the back of the townhouse like she had every right.

Max had a nice little patio behind his place, not unlike hers on Little Pine Lake with a similar wrought-iron glass-topped table. An empty beer bottle stood on the table, beside a paperback book. She checked the label on the bottle. The maker's name was long and full of diacritics but from the small print, all in Romanian, she gathered that the beer itself was a pilsner from Transylvania. The book, in English, was a guide to Florida. Mrs. Plansky picked it up and leafed through, stopping at a page with the corner turned down, a page devoted to her town, Punta D'Oro. There was a photo of the library, the oldest building in the county. Standing on the front step was Eleanor Fuentes, the librarian, who Mrs. Plansky knew to say hi to. She got a strange feeling out there on Max's patio, kind of lonely.

Mrs. Plansky turned to the back of the house. Max had glass sliders, also not unlike hers, with closed curtains behind them. Maybe for that reason she'd missed what she should have seen right away, a perfectly shaped round hole in the glass, the size of a dessert plate, near the frame and about halfway up. She went closer. Yes, perfectly shaped, like it had been cut by some tool designed for the task. She remembered a home-security commercial where she'd seen it done by an actor portraying a bad guy. He'd used a round stick-on hockey puck–like tool and something like an X-Acto knife.

Loud alarms sounded right away. Out here on the patio it was quiet. Mrs. Plansky could hear the river rippling and gurgling. She didn't know what to do.

What would she do at home in a situation like this? Well, at home she wouldn't be in a situation like this. At least not before these recent events—the Will masquerader, Safemo, !NorManConQuest!, all the rest. But wasn't that the point, the new square one of her life? All those recent events had happened! Did that change everything? At home and in the last square of her previous life, she would call the police. Was that a good idea here in Alba Gemina, where Captain Romulu might end up on the call? That was point one. Point two was that even back home she wouldn't have been able to resist a peek behind that curtain. You had to know yourself at least a little bit after all this time. So, being true to herself even in strange circumstances, Mrs. Plansky carefully stuck her hand in the dessert plate–size hole.

She got hold of a small handful of curtain and tugged. Nothing doing. She tugged harder. The curtain was stuck. Maybe little annoyances like flawed curtain track design were the same the world over, an unexploited human unifier. Mrs. Plansky reached around to the inside of the frame, where the locking mechanism would be, and finally realized that the slider would be unlocked. Which was the whole raison d'être for the hole in the glass! She blushed from embarrassment, then withdrew her hand and slid the damn thing open.

Mrs. Plansky stepped in and flung the curtain open as well. She was in a small living room, lit by a single table lamp. That lamp was not on a table, but lay sideways on the floor. The whole room was that way in some form or other, trashed: couch and chairs overturned, bookcase knocked sideways with books—many, many books—scattered all over the floor. The only undisturbed object was a framed photo of Max with a younger woman who looked a lot like him, especially the eyes, both of them laughing.

Mrs. Plansky went down the hall, switching on a light or two. She looked into a bedroom where the mattress was slashed, the kitchen, where all the cabinets were open and all the pots and pans had been knocked off their wall hooks, the bathroom, where the medicine cabinet door hung on its hinges, and a tiny office, where all the desk drawers had been torn loose and their contents dumped out. What she did not see was any sign of a fight, such as blood, for example. But she was no expert. She thought of Marius hurrying away with his armful of papers.

Mrs. Plansky left the way she'd come, closing the curtain and the slider. On the way she righted the table lamp in the living room, mindful of the risk of fire. Don't give fire a place to start was one of Miss Terrance's most important rules, and Mrs. Plansky never forgot.

TWENTY-NINE

Mrs. Plansky walked and walked, trying to find some benign explanation for what had happened at Max's place, and failing completely. She held up her hand and saw how unsteady it looked in the moonlight. Mrs. Plansky tried to subdue the unsteadiness—not just in her hand but all through her, mind and body—with rational thought, and maybe that, or all the walking, or something else, deep in her nature—maybe even something screwed up, such as optimism with blinders on, calmed her, at least to the point of realizing she was hungry.

Mrs. Plansky had never been one for skipping meals. On the way back to the hotel she made a slight detour to the Café des Artistes, mostly because she knew how to find it, but also in the hope that Max would be there, a forgetful and tardy foreigner after all. He was not. She ordered lamb chops and a glass of something red and Romanian. The first bite, the first sip: what power they had sometimes, especially, she now realized, when you'd left the beaten track of your life. She gazed into the wineglass, not seeing anything but thinking of all the times Norm—not a big eater, even fussy—said, "I love watching you eat." Her reply, often with her mouth full, was always the same: "Gotta keep my strength up."

A text came in from Lucrecia, back home: Hope you're having a good trip. Quick question—three cases of Krug champagne got delivered today from Al's A1 Liquors. Your dad says you have an account.

I checked and you do—you opened it yesterday? Just checking this is OK?

Mrs. Plansky's finger hovered uncertainly over the screen, waiting for a signal from her brain. Her brain was confused. No matter what, this latest shenanigan—if the word could be singular—of her dad's was not okay. But in her former life she would have just said what the hell, made some private arrangement with Al's A1 Liquors governing future orders, and moved on. Now, just weeks or even days away from a rapid and permanent descent down the financial ladder unless she came up with something close to a miracle, those three cases of Krug were not okay. Mrs. Plansky downed the rest of her Romanian red, the taste earthy, rough, foreign. She plunked down her glass with a firm thunk and decided to bet on herself. **OK**, she texted. **Cheers**. Al, if there was an Al, was depending on her, too. She had a grandiose thought: she was performing a duty to society. She quashed it at once.

Back at the hotel she was crossing the lobby when Annika came hurrying over from the desk.

"Ah, Mrs. Plansky. I've been looking for you."

"Oh?" She hoped that Annika wasn't about to offer thanks for giving her a shoulder to cry on that morning. That would feel uncomfortable given that later in the day Mrs. Plansky had been spying on her. This was probably a routine situation in the life of an undercover op, even a good sign. She needed to toughen up and get smarter. Starting this very moment.

But that wasn't where Annika was going. "My boss would like to buy you a welcome drink."

"Your boss—meaning the gentleman from the breakfast room?"

Annika's eyes showed nothing. "Exactly. Mr. Tiriac. He happens to be in the bar right now."

The brand-new toughened-up and smarter Mrs. Plansky lined up the facts. Mr. Tiriac was Annika's boss, but also Marius's boss, and drinking buddy of Captain Romulu, the iffy cop, according to

Max, who was now hours late making contact, and whose house had been ransacked, almost certainly by Marius. What would any self-respecting undercover op say at a moment like this?

"Why, certainly. Very nice of him."

Mrs. Plansky climbed the stairs to her room, freshened up, changed from the mules to the ballet flats, and came back down. Annika escorted her to the bar, a small dark room with more potted plants, framed prints of French music hall posters, and no one there except for the bartender and two men at a round corner table, one of whom was Dragomir Tiriac. She made a mental note to look up the derivation of Dragomir.

"I present Mrs. Plansky," Annika said. "Mrs. Plansky, Dragomir Tiriac, the patron, and Professor Bogdan."

Professor Bogdan rose. He had a small upside-down crescent bruise under one eye, purple and yellow, the color of healing after a black eye.

"Nice to meet you both," Mrs. Plansky said, shaking hands. Professor Bogdan's hand was thin and damp, Dragomir's immense and dry.

"The professor will translate," Annika said. "He is a teacher of English."

The professor bowed his head and sat down. Annika turned and left the room. Mrs. Plansky pulled up a chair.

"Drink?" said Dragomir in English.

"Yes, thank you," said Mrs. Plansky.

"Champagne is good?" Dragomir said.

"Very," Mrs. Plansky said.

Dragomir snapped his fingers. The bartender hurried over. Dragomir spoke to him in Romanian. The bartender clicked his heels—the first time in her life Mrs. Plansky had actually seen that—and headed back to the bar.

"You American?" Dragomir said in English. Everything about him seemed oversize and formidable, excepting his eyes, small, round, glinting—but also formidable.

"I am," said Mrs. Plansky.

He spoke to Professor Bogdan in Romanian, something that was more of a command than a request.

"Where in America?" said the professor.

"Florida."

The professor's tone changed, became more natural, like he wasn't translating but speaking for himself. "Have you ever been to New Hampshire?"

"Oh, yes." The question didn't surprise her. She'd been thinking of New Hampshire—and Dinu's T-shirt—from the moment she'd heard the professor's surname. "Why do you ask?"

Professor Bogdan looked like he was about to reply, but Dragomir interrupted with something in Romanian.

"Welcome to Romania," the professor said.

"Thank you."

Dragomir spoke to the professor.

"Mr. Tiriac asks if this is your first visit to our country," Bogdan said. His look was not formidable—a thin old guy—well, quite possibly younger than Mrs. Plansky, but an indoorsy type with nicotine-stained fingers and a neck too small for the buttoned-up collar of his shirt. He also wore a wool tie and an ancient-looking tweed jacket with a pack of cigarettes in the chest pocket.

"It is."

"And he would like to know your impressions."

Mrs. Plansky decided—based on nothing—that Dragomir understood English fairly well and so spoke directly to him. "It's too soon to have any opinion at all, but so far the country looks beautiful and the people are friendly."

Dragomir nodded. Professor Bogdan translated. Dragomir nodded again and spoke to the professor for a minute or two.

"Mr. Tiriac is glad you like the country so far," the professor said. "He notes that it's somewhat unusual to see tourists here in Alba Gemina at this time of year. Is there any special reason for your visit? Or maybe more American to say, what brought you here?"

Whatever this nice little welcoming get-together was about, Mrs.

Plansky—old version and new—knew one thing for sure: the truth was not the answer. But which untruth was best? "No special reason," she said. "I was in the mood for a quick getaway and saw some cheap flights to Bucharest."

The professor relayed that to Dragomir. He gazed at her for a moment, a sizing-up gaze, in Mrs. Plansky's interpretation, that found her on the shallow side. That had to be a good thing. She had every confidence that she could pull off the shallow persona without breaking a sweat.

"Is cold," Dragomir said. He crossed his arms and shivered. The sight, to her surprise, was kind of charming. "Cold winter."

Mrs. Plansky flashed him a smile she hoped was a little too bright. "When you live in Florida you don't travel for the weather."

Dragomir turned to the professor. "Ce?"

Bogdan started in on an explanation. Dragomir made a dismissive gesture, his hand so big Mrs. Plansky felt a tiny breeze from across the table.

"For what reason Alba Gemina?" he said in English.

"Oh, that," Mrs. Plansky said, hoping that whatever was coming next came soon. And then it did, just perfect, as though the goddess of ditziness was watching over her. "I'm interested in equestrian statues and happened across yours in a guidebook. I wanted to see it in person."

"Ce?" said Dragomir. But the professor looked baffled.

"Ours?" he said.

"Right outside—*Michael the Brave.*"

"But no one here pays the slightest attention. It's nothing but a copy—and a bad one, if I may say so. The original was blown up by the Nazis or possibly the Russians. The facts are forever in dispute."

This seemed like a handy cue for the too-bright smile. "That makes it all the more interesting!"

"Ce?" said Dragomir.

The professor began an explanation, soon interrupted by Dragomir who asked what sounded like an impatient question. Mrs. Plansky understood nothing except for one word. It sounded like *E.D. Ought,* and didn't come together at first. As for the context: possibly good if he was asking Bogdan if he thought she was an E.D. Ought; or bad, if he was saying only an E.D. Ought would believe her.

At that moment the waiter arrived. Professor Bogdan, Dragomir, and Mrs. Plansky watched the popping of the cork and the pouring of the champagne—except for Dragomir, who mostly watched her watching, as Mrs. Plansky was aware of without looking.

They clinked glasses. "Sănătate," the professor said, which Mrs. Plansky took to mean health.

"Si bogatie," said Dragomir.

"What's that?" Mrs. Plansky said.

"Wealth," said the professor.

"They rhyme in English," she said. "Health and wealth."

"Health and wealth?" Dragomir said, not getting the *th* sound right. "Hey! I like you!" If so, his eyes hadn't gotten the message. He drained his glass of champagne in one go and set it down. "Si acum Leonte," he said.

"Excuse me?" Mrs. Plansky's heart started racing, reacting before her brain.

"Mr. Tiriac would like to know your relationship with Max Leonte," Bogdan said.

"Well, my goodness," said Mrs. Plansky. "Are you talking about the writer?"

Bogdan nodded.

"How strange." The word in her frightened little heart was not *strange,* but *terrifying.* Here Mrs. Plansky took a chance. "I have nothing you would call a relationship with him. I came across his work and emailed a couple of questions through his publisher. Why are you asking?"

That led to a long back-and-forth between Bogdan and Dragomir. Mrs. Plansky had plenty of time to think of the holes and minefields in her little bit of improv. For example, did Dragomir somehow know she and Max had been in the bar of the Royale the night before? If he did, what would be the sign? If he didn't, how had he put them together? Right now all she heard in his voice was annoyance.

They both turned to her, catching her in the middle of a nonchalant sip of champagne, a lucky break, Mrs. Plansky's timing perhaps not usually one of her strengths, if she had to rate them.

"Why we ask," Bogdan said, "is that this man, Leonte, is not a good type. It is better—"

Dragomir interrupted, saying something that sounded like "moolt."

"Much better," Bogdan went on, "much better not to know him, certainly for you, such a respectable lady tourist."

"I'm a bit surprised," Mrs. Plansky said. "Not a good type in what way?"

"The man is not a patriot," Bogdan said. Dragomir nodded. "In fact, he is in league with a foreign power to harm the Romanian people."

"Really? How so? I'm curious."

That led to another exchange between Dragomir and Bogdan.

"By meddling in our internal affairs," Bogdan said. "Spreading false information. Raising doubts. Romania has a long history of which we are proud, but much of it is troubled. This explains our strong desire for stability. Do you understand?"

"I do."

Dragomir tapped the table twice with his middle finger. Bogdan leaned forward.

"So that is why," he said, "as good citizens we must ask you—are you yourself an agent of a foreign country?"

Mrs. Plansky was still for a moment. Then she burst out laughing, hand to her chest. "Me? Do I look like . . . like a spy? Good grief! You're joking, right?" For the first time, the expression in Dragomir's eyes, a changing combination of impatience and intelligence, with something violent a constant under the surface, grew a little murky, possibly confused.

"Therefore your answer is no?" Bogdan said.

"Do you want me to sign an affidavit? Watch out I don't use invisible ink!"

"What is an affidavit?" Bogdan said.

"Pardon me, just a joke," Mrs. Plansky said. "I am not an agent of a foreign power. In fact I have no job at all. I'm retired."

While Bogdan relayed that to Dragomir, Mrs. Plansky wondered whether to ask where they got the notion she knew Max, or to say nothing and let them conclude she was too dumb to think of the question. The answer seemed obvious. Meanwhile Dragomir was making another of his dismissive hand gestures.

The professor turned to her. "It's been a pleasure to meet you," he said. "Mr. Tiriac wishes you a pleasant stay." Dragomir took an envelope from his pocket and handed it to Mrs. Plansky. "And here is a gift card to Club Presto, which he owns also."

"Well that's very nice." Mrs. Plansky rose. "And thank you for the lovely champagne, gentlemen. Good night."

Mrs. Plansky walked out of the bar. In the lobby, she encountered Marius, just coming in from the street, a sheaf of papers in his hand.

THIRTY

Mrs. Plansky heard noises in the night. At first, still mostly in dreamland, she thought the noises were coming from the square, even had the crazy idea that the Nazis or the Russians had come again, this time to destroy the replica. But then she realized she was wrong. Yes, the sounds were real, but they weren't coming from the square. They were much closer than that. She sat up in bed and reached for the lamp on the bedside table, her hand encountering nothing. That was because she'd reached for where the lamp would have been at home. Here in the presidential suite, it was on the other side. She was shifting over in that direction, somewhat tangled in the sheets, when it struck her that the sounds were coming from inside the room. She went still.

Scratch, scratch, scratch scratch. Was there something metallic about that scratching, like a key was having trouble getting into a lock?

Scratch, scratch. No, not from inside the room, but close, behind the wall, maybe from an adjoining room. Or . . . or her own bathroom. Very quietly she got out of bed, the tile floor cold under her feet. How could she have forgotten to pack her slippers? She moved toward the bathroom, that enormous bathroom, and heard the scratching sounds more clearly, although they weren't coming from inside the bathroom. They seemed to be on the move, getting softer, fading away, perhaps on a staircase, descending. What sort of adjoining room had a staircase? A royal suite? That was her only thought, totally unhelpful.

Meanwhile her eyes—not so fast these days when it came to adjustments—were getting used to the darkness, not a total darkness, moonlight entering through a tiny gap in the curtains. She saw she was standing next to the shower stall, right in front of the old, heavy wooden door with no knob, no keyhole. Once again, Mrs. Plansky gave that door a push. Once again it didn't budge. She put her ear to it and heard nothing. She had the weird feeling that she'd traveled back to the time of Michael the Brave, whenever that was, exactly.

Mrs. Plansky went back to bed. But it was hopeless. Never mind sleep. Her eyes wouldn't even close. To pass the time—or even soothe herself to sleep—she decided to think about Norm and things they'd done together, something she did now and then, and in fact quite often, floating along on reveries. But now, for the very first time, her mind wouldn't go there. It refused to dwell on some memory of Norm, would not even begin, wouldn't try. No matter what she did, her mind could not be steered in the direction of Norm, like a sailboat that would not come up into the wind. Mrs. Plansky sat up and put her hands to her face. She was alone.

Self-pity? Oh, dear. "What is wrong with you?" She said that aloud, loud and clear, no question. Lowering her voice she went on a bit. "Think of what some people go through. You've had it way too easy. Spoiled! Spoiled frickin' rotten."

She got out of bed and marched to the bathroom, no moonlight now, the suite darker than before, but without thinking she knew the way. She turned on the tap, splashed cold water on her face. Had she really, for the first time in her life, said "frickin'"? She was falling apart. "Don't be a punching bag. Punch!"

Mrs. Plansky threw a punch in the darkness.

"Ow!"

Her punch, meant to hit nothing but air, instead struck something hard and unyielding. Well, perhaps not totally unyielding. She heard a splintering sound, not loud, very minor. Mrs. Plansky felt along the wall, found the switch, turned on the light, and looked around, blinking into the brightness. What she'd punched was the heavy old knobless door. Now it was open about an inch, like she was Mike Tyson. Mrs. Plansky rubbed her hand, sore already. Did boxers have to just live with sore hands? She'd always felt bad for them. She gave the heavy old door a little push. It creaked open another inch or two.

Mrs. Plansky stepped forward and peered into the little gap. In the narrow beam of light escaping from the bathroom, she could make out a cobweb forest, and through the cobwebs what seemed to be a stone wall a few feet away, old and rough-hewn. She felt a slight, cool breeze. It carried the faint scent of cigars. She stuck out her finger and tried another push. Now, without a sound, the door swung open some more, just enough for a person of her size to step through. Brushing cobwebs aside, Mrs. Plansky stepped through.

She stood in the little pool of light from the bathroom and looked both ways, the light on either side quickly swallowed up in darkness, but she could see this was some sort of stone-floored passageway, a stone wall on one side and a wooden one on the other. Mrs. Plansky crouched down, looking for footprints. She saw none. But hadn't someone been out here? Perhaps going somewhere? It was a passageway, after all. Room service, maybe? Or could there be rooms along the passageway, servants' rooms dating back to the Middle Ages, perhaps now used for the staff? But then why all the cobwebs? Mrs. Plansky had no other ideas. She took a few steps to her right and entered total darkness.

Some travelers, much savvier than her, took lots of gadgets on their trips, Swiss Army knives, for example, or mini-flashlights. A mini-flashlight right now would have been very useful. Instead, Mrs. Plansky just stood there in her nightie, bare feet getting cold on the stone floor, the faint, cool breeze in her face, and again feeling she'd gone back to the time of Michael the Brave. Wasn't that part of the lure of travel to some places, that you also traveled in time? Mrs. Plansky was wandering around in thoughts like that when it suddenly hit her that her phone was also a flashlight.

She went back into her room, found her phone, slipped into her flats, returned to the passageway. She got the phone light working and shone it to the left. The passageway petered out only a few yards away, ending in a narrow bricked-over wall. But in the other direction, to the right, it continued beyond the range of her light. Mrs. Plansky was about to set off that way when she remembered she was in her nightie, a rather short nightie but very comfortable, and of course no one ever saw her in it.

And no one ever would. Mrs. Plansky went back into her room and changed into her black woolen slacks—the wool thin but nice and warm—and gray cashmere mock turtle. Then she returned to the passageway, pushed the door closed, and began following her light beam through the darkness.

After not very long there was a change in the passageway, the flat flagstones of the floor replaced by bumpy cobbles, as in the square. The passageway narrowed and soon after that her beam seemed to be probing emptiness. Mrs. Plansky moved on, slow and cautious, until she came to a descending staircase. She followed it down, actually counting the steps, which struck her as a rather clever idea. There were fifteen. At the bottom she panned the light around, found she was in a sort of cellar, dirt-floored and dank. Huge wooden casks, very old and worn, lined one wall. She went closer, fixed her beam on something branded on the side of one of the casks: MDCLXXXIV. Ah, Roman numerals. M was a thousand, D had to be five hundred, C one hundred, L fifty, making what so far? Mrs. Plansky got lost in the Roman numerals—as the Romans, if they were being honest with themselves, probably did, too. Bottom line, the meaningful one: the feeling of long ago came close to being real in this place, like some historical character—Dracula being an obvious candidate— might step out from behind the casks at any moment. Here was just one reason why wandering around in too-short nighties was a bad idea. She sniffed the air, searching for some ancient boozy smell, but picked up only that faint cigar scent. When she tapped the cask the sound was hollow and empty.

Beyond the last cask a rectangular space was cut in the stone wall, leading to what looked like another staircase, this one wooden. Mrs. Plansky had to duck down to get through the space but once through she could stand upright. She shone the light up the stairs, very steep and roughly-made, but not old. The walls were made of plywood. She started up, once again counting the stairs. There turned out to be thirty-one and Mrs. Plansky, huffing and puffing, had to pause for breath at the top. She shone the light back down the stairs. Standing on the cellar floor, front paws on the first step, and staring up at her, was an enormous, very long-whiskered rat, its claws also enormous and glinting in the light. Mrs. Plansky's heart jumped in her chest. "Shoo!" she said, in a sort of furious whisper that had no effect on the rat. She brandished her phone at it, the beam of light streaking back and forth in a way that must have struck the rat as violent. It darted away, out of sight. *Scratch, scratch,* went those enormous claws, *scratch, scratch.*

Mrs. Plansky turned around, but with the phone still at her side and pointed down, so its strong beam didn't drown out the faint light that lay ahead. She switched off the phone light. Her eyes again took their time to catch up, but eventually she saw she was at the end of a long corridor, the floor linoleum and the walls plaster. The faint glow began about twenty feet farther ahead, flowing in from the right. She walked toward it.

Mrs. Plansky came to a window on the right hand side, a fairly narrow window, maybe only two-and-a-half-feet high, but very long horizontally, going on as far as she could see. She leaned forward and took a quick peek through the strangely dark glass.

Mrs. Plansky didn't understand what she was seeing at first. Down below was a huge room, the ceiling hung with unlit chandeliers and also some mirror balls, not rotating, a highly polished red-and-black-squared marble floor, glass-topped gilt tables, a stage with music stands, and a long translucent bar, all of this lit only by a couple of wall sconces. The last thing she noticed was what she should have noticed first, a neon sign behind the bar reading CLUB PRESTO. She was gazing at that sign and feeling some re-arrangements going on in her mind when she became aware of movement down below. A woman in a head scarf had entered from the other end of the room, carrying a mop and pail. She set them down and began lifting all the gilt chairs onto the glass-topped tables. A woman perhaps of Mrs. Plansky's age? She moved stiffly and—

And all at once, without the slightest warning, the woman in the head scarf turned her head and looked right at her. Mrs. Plansky froze, learning in that instant an important lesson: in total panic, that's what humans did. In partial panic they ran about wildly. She began preparing a little story involving her gift card. The woman— too thin and much younger than Mrs. Plansky had thought— turned away and went back to work.

Meaning? Meaning she hadn't seen Mrs. Plansky, although of course Mrs. Plansky had seen her. And therefore? The woman was blind—a complete nonstarter given her job, the way she moved, the look in her eyes—or this window was in fact the one-way kind, a window on Mrs. Plansky's side, a mirror on the Club Presto side.

Aha! She moved on and after twenty feet or so reached the end of the window, as well as the corridor itself. Ahead stood an unfinished wooden door with a spray-painted sign: CAMBIO. Cambio was a word you saw on signs all over Europe, meaning a place to exchange currency. In Mrs. Plansky's experience, this was not the usual type of location. She stood before the door and listened, hearing nothing. Cambios would be closed in the middle of the night, and of course locked as well. She tried the door knob. It turned. She gave a little push. The door opened easily and soundlessly. On the other side was a small room with a bit of light coming in from another dark window, not big, about the size of the window by her kitchen sink at home, with its nice view of her sunny little plot of black-eyed Susans, doing so well.

There was nothing cambio-like about this small room. It had no furniture at all except a single card table chair by the window. Along the back wall was a lot of musical equipment—mic stands, amplifiers, a few keyboards, a stand-up bass leaning against a bass drum. A broad shelf stood at the bottom of the window, and on that shelf were an ashtray containing cigar butts and a half-full bottle of Johnnie Walker Blue. She went closer, noticing a mesh grill, postcard size, built into the shelf, with a red button beside it. Mrs. Plansky looked through the glass.

Down below lay a room that looked like some combination of a radio studio and a mission control setup for sending astronauts into space. Mrs. Plansky tried to make sense of it all—the many screens, the stacks of blinking modular boxes connected by coiling cables, the mics, headphones, and so much other digital-type equipment she had no names for. Was there such a thing as bitcoin mining? So maybe this was some sort of cambio after all? She was trying to remember something about bitcoin mining, or bitcoins in general—anything at all, really, just one measly solid fact—when a door along the far wall of mission control opened and people started filing in. Mrs. Plansky knew them all except for the man who entered first, a wiry little dark-eyed guy with a waxed handlebar mustache. The others were Marius, Romeo, Dinu, and Dragomir, in that order. The way they came in, the way each one took his place, like the home side trotting onto the diamond at the top of the first inning—they were a team.

And taking a closer look, Mrs. Plansky saw there was something of the locker room about the setup—a few crushed soda cans on the floor, someone's hoodie rolled up in a corner—and even of a teenage boy's basement in a home lacking supervision. She thought she could make out a grimy sheen on the keyboards. It was actually kind of dirty down in that room.

Dragomir sat on a lumpy chair in one corner. Beside it stood a side table with a bottle and a glass. He took a cigar from his pocket. Marius sat on a stool in the corner diagonally across from him. He

drew the knife from his ankle sheath and began cleaning his fingernails with the tip of the blade. The wiry guy with the mustache stood
with his back to the far wall. He looked all around, his gaze passing
without a pause right over Mrs. Plansky. Her heart, already beating
too fast, speeded up a little more, even though she knew he couldn't
see her. Something or other—possibly the human geometry—gave
her the idea that the three of them, these tough, and yes, dangerous
men—didn't even like each other. She knew—from stories Norm
had told her—that could be a team thing. Hadn't two famous Yan-
kees hated each other? She thought so, but the names wouldn't come.

As for the boys—and the presence of the three men brought out
the boy in them and blotted out the man—she could see they were
friends just from how they walked together. Neither looked good
at the moment. Dinu's face was pale. His hand was still splinted.
Perhaps it was hurting. As for Romeo, poor Romeo, he wore a thick
bandage over his nose, taped to his cheeks, and his upper lip was
horribly swollen and purple. Had they been in a motorcycle wreck?
That was the only explanation that came to mind.

They sat beside each other at the radio studio–type table. Romeo
produced a printout. The boys went over it together, their heads almost touching, Romeo pointing things out, the two of them talking
from time to time, although Mrs. Plansky couldn't hear through the
glass. After a couple of minutes or so, Dinu nodded and Romeo set
the printout aside and got busy with the stack of modular compo-
nents, disconnecting and reconnecting cables, switching switches,
dialing dials, gazing at screens, all of them full of what might have
been numbers, some flashing. Dinu pulled the table mic a little closer.
Meanwhile, leaning against the wall at their backs, the wiry man
with the handlebar mustache never took his eyes off them.

Mrs. Plansky found she was sitting in the card table chair by the
window, her head inches from the glass. Dragomir's lips moved.
Romeo hunched forward, seemed to be trying to do whatever he
was doing faster. At last he sat up and nodded to Dinu. The boys
put on headphones. Dragomir lit his cigar. Marius stopped cleaning

his fingernails and sheathed his knife. The wiry guy leaned against the wall and watched the backs of the boys' heads. Romeo pressed a big button on one of the modules. Mrs. Plansky really wished she could hear what was going on. Then, perhaps a little later than most people would have done, she realized she had a button of her own, this red one by the mesh grill on the shelf by the window.

She pressed it. Nothing happened. Her hand, maybe getting impatient with her brain, took over and gave that button a twist. Ah, a dial. The sound of static came through the mesh grill. But that only lasted a few seconds. Then came a sort of unmarred and somehow vast silence, followed by something like a dial tone.

Yes, a dial tone for sure, followed by the sound of a phone ringing on the other end. It rang four times and Dinu and Romeo were just exchanging a possibly nervous glance when there was a little click, followed by the voice of a woman.

"Hello?" she said in English.

THIRTY-ONE

"Hello?" said the woman again, an American woman, not young. And from somewhere down South—Mrs. Plansky knew that from just those two syllables. "Hello?"

Dinu leaned closer to his mic. "Hey, Gram." He glanced at the printout. "It's me, Andy."

"Andy?"

"Yeah, Gram, your grandson, Andy. Have you forgotten me?"

Romeo's eyebrows rose. He gave Dinu a thumbs-up.

"Oh, no, honey, what a thing to say! But I haven't heard from you—gosh, in ages—and you sound so far away."

Romeo turned a dial.

"Well, jeez, Gram, the Beaver State is far away."

"Beaver State?"

"The Beaver State—Oregon. I'm at college in Oregon, Gram."

"Of course, of course. I knew that. It's just been so long. But that's not important. It's so good to hear from you, Andy. It can get a bit lonesome here, time to time. How's college life treating you?"

"Pretty good, Gram. I'm learning so much! Real things! Although there's a problem right now."

"Oh, dear. What kind of problem? Is there anything I can do to help?"

No, no, no, don't say that! Mrs. Plansky could hardly breathe. Anything but that! Or nothing, nothing at all. Gram! Hang up!

"Well, that's why I'm calling, Gram. You're the only one I can count on."

Yes, mission control, or something like that. They were landing a plane and now it was just touching down. How horrible! That poor grandchild-loving grandmother! This was so wrong. Mrs. Plansky wanted to bang on the glass and shout: Stop this instant! She's a human being just like you! Think what you're doing! Of course she was too cowardly to protest out loud, or lift a finger to—

But suddenly Dragomir was looking up, right in her direction, as though seeing her even though she was invisible. Mrs. Plansky couldn't turn away, like his eyes had taken her gaze prisoner. Was it possible she'd actually spoken those thoughts, her protest? No, no, she couldn't be that far gone. But maybe she had let out some sound? She didn't remember making a sound, but how to explain the fact that Dragomir now said something to the wiry man, quiet, in Romanian, and drowned out by the goings-on between Dinu and Gram, Mrs. Plansky picking up only the first word, which was "Timbo?" Possibly a name? And now Timbo, if that was his name, was headed toward a door on his side of the room. He opened it and went through—all his movements compact and swift—kicking the door closed with his heel in a quick movement Mrs. Plansky might have called elegant in another situation.

But not this one. She rose, so slowly, like one of those animals easily hypnotized by a predator, and glanced around. There was only one door to the Cambio, leading back to the corridor overlooking Club Presto. She moved—like through molasses—in that direction, but had taken no more than a couple of steps before she heard a door closing somewhere nearby, followed by the sound of soft and rapid footsteps in the corridor. Mrs. Plansky froze, again undone by total panic. She came close to hating herself at that moment, and in her anger came alive. There was only one thing to do. She hurried over to the stacks of musical equipment lining the back wall, got down on her hands and knees—not so easy—and crawled between the stand-up bass and the big bass drum. Then she made herself very small.

Mrs. Plansky heard the Cambio door open. Then came footsteps. The man himself appeared, at least partially. Mrs. Plansky, on her hands and knees, had a slight view from around the lower curve of the bass drum, a dim shadowy space where she was exposed, but only from the eyes up, all the rest of her completely concealed. Should she try to wriggle her way a little farther behind the drum? Drums could be loud, if you knocked them over, for example. She stayed where she was.

Meanwhile her eyes were fixed on what she could see of Timbo—at first just his lower half. He wore sneakers, form-fitting jeans, and a belt with a heavy gold buckle. His legs and his stance were those of a champion in some sort of sport.

Meanwhile, down in mission control, Dinu was working his way toward the climax, his dialogue with Gram coming through the speaker on the shelf by the glass.

"The password?" Gram was saying.

"For the account, Gram. It will encrypt and vanish faster than . . . than you can say Jack Robinson!"

Timbo turned toward the speaker. "Hei!" he said, and continued on with what sounded almost like baby talk. He headed toward the window, and that was when Mrs. Plansky noticed something new in the room. Standing next to the red button on the shelf—actually a dial—was a rat. A huge, long-whiskered rat, with enormous, curving claws—yes, her rat. Had it followed her the whole way, right at her heels? Or had it found another route? Now here it was, and it had Timbo's full attention.

"Hei," he said again, moving toward the rat, Timbo's top half coming into Mrs. Plansky's line of sight. His waxed handlebar mustache, such an extreme grooming statement, diverted her gaze from the rest of his face, but now she took it in. There was nothing unusual about any of his features and in his eyes she even thought she saw a gentle expression. Somehow it made his presence even more disturbing.

Timbo approached the rat and he was speaking to it for sure, in Romanian baby talk. The rat, which had been standing on all fours, now rose into a sitting position, its tail, very long and rather reptilian-looking for a mammal, curled around the red knob. Timbo laughed softly and kept moving. Mrs. Plansky had no idea what was going on and didn't want to find out, but she couldn't look away. In midstride, Timbo reached out, not especially speedily, took hold of the end of the rat's tail and—

But oh, the nastiness. Mrs. Plansky, too late, turned away. He'd—he'd dashed the animal headfirst against the edge of the shelf. Now he held it dangling, the animal lifeless, blood—not much—dripping from its head.

Through the speaker came Dinu's voice. "All done, Gram. Thank you so much!"

"You just take care of yourself. Bye now, Andy."

"I will. Bye-bye!"

Timbo walked out of the Cambio room, the rat still dangling from his hand, and closed the door behind him with that same slick flick of the heel.

Mrs. Plansky didn't move. Well, that wasn't quite true. She didn't change her position, but if shaking was movement then she was moving. But not puking. Mrs. Plansky had always had a strong stomach.

A click came over the speaker and then there was silence. She rose and walked toward the window, stepping carefully over the trail of blood drops. Down below in mission control Timbo was holding up the rat, as for a show-and-tell, explaining how he'd found the culprit in the observation room. Marius laughed, Dragomir showed no reaction, the boys looked a little sick, and in Romeo's case also afraid. Then Dragomir stubbed out his cigar in an ashtray, rose, and dropped a few brightly colored bills in front of the boys. The men left the room, the boys staying behind. Dinu gathered up their paperwork. Romeo started switching off the machines. There were tears on his cheeks. Mrs. Plansky had a brain wave. She took out her phone and snapped a picture, capturing the next moment, when Dinu laid a hand—his splinted hand—on Romeo's shoulder, comforting him. Romeo wiped his cheeks on his sleeve. At that moment she abandoned the motorcycle wreck explanation. Romeo gathered the money, divided it up. The boys headed out of mission control, shutting off the lights.

That left Mrs. Plansky in total darkness. She didn't dare turn on her phone light, trusting herself to find her way to the Cambio door without it, which she did, expecting that on the other side she'd again have the light from the wall sconces in Club Presto, but they, too, had been switched off. Well, no matter. She remembered how this went. First would come this long narrow gallery, followed by the thirty-one stairs down to the ancient cellar, where it would surely be safe to use the phone light. Voilà! So nice to have a plan. Although Mike Tyson—again, and so soon?—said everyone has a plan until they get punched in the mouth. She realized something important. I already got punched in the mouth, Mike. But I'm still here, planning away. She made a mental note to keep the braggadocio strictly to herself.

Mrs. Plansky moved slowly along the narrow corridor, sometimes running her hand along the plaster wall to her right. This went on longer than she'd expected and she was starting to wonder if she'd made some sort of mistake, when her hand touched what felt like a doorknob. Mrs. Plansky came to a halt. A door off to the side in the corridor? She had no memory of that, but could easily have missed it. Not that it made any difference. Her job now was just to get to the thirty-one stairs. And she was taking the first step when she heard a sound from behind the door, a human sound, the sound of a muffled groan.

Mrs. Plansky stood still, although her body was already weighted toward movement. There was such a thing as pushing your luck, according to gamblers, and she'd been very lucky so far on this little excursion. Therefore, Loretta, get on the stick! Maybe you imagined the groan, and if it was real what were the chances that the groaner was a bad guy, or whatever was going on behind that door was something beyond your understanding and best left alone? There! Her analysis was impregnable. Her toes rose to take that first step. And then came the groan again.

Damn, thought Mrs. Plansky. She turned the knob and gave the door a little push. On the other side was a small room with an earthen floor, a crude wooden table and chairs, the only light coming from a low-wattage lamp in one corner. A man—she was assuming that from the sound of the groan—his face hooded, was duct-taped to one of the chairs. So much duct tape, winding from his ankles all the way up his neck. Mrs. Plansky could sense that he was aware of her presence, or at least that the door had opened. She steeled herself, marched forward, and pulled off the hood.

It was Max.

Their eyes met. They'd duct-taped his mouth so he couldn't speak but in his eyes she saw amazement, and also pain.

Mrs. Plansky took hold of a corner of the duct tape strip over his mouth to gently peel it off. It wouldn't be gently pulled off.

"This will have to be like a Band-Aid," she said, and ripped off the tape.

Max didn't cry out, or make any sound at all. He closed his eyes for a second or two, then opened them. "Thank you." He kept his voice very low.

"Certainly." Mrs. Plansky glanced around, looking for something sharp. There was nothing like that in the room. She got to work on the duct tape with her bare hands.

"What are you doing here?" Max said. "And, please, a little more quietly."

"You first," said Mrs. Plansky, lowering her voice.

"I behaved like an American. I should have been devious, like a European."

"We're not devious?"

"You're clumsy when you try, at least from our perspective. I approached Dragomir directly—Clint Eastwood–style." Max's shoulders were now free. He shrugged, wincing at the motion.

"Are you hurt?"

"Nothing to speak of. My own fault. I told him I'm writing a book on cybercrime and wanted to get some quotes, anonymous, of course."

Max seemed rather talkative given the goings-on. But he was a writer, so it was probably to be expected. Mrs. Plansky, trying to move things along a little faster with the duct tape, had trouble taking it all in.

"For example," he was saying, "I asked if he kept records of the identities of the victims. He blew up. There are no victims, he shouted, only happy customers. I hardly had time to argue with that before Marius, the big one, was on me. They blindfolded me and brought me here." Max glanced around. "Wherever here is. And questioned me—mostly about who my book contract was with, who else I'd spoken to, nothing I couldn't dodge fairly easily. They also asked about you."

"Oh?"

"No worries. I gave the impression you were one of those readers."

"What readers are you talking about?" By now Mrs. Plansky was on her knees, having trouble with the duct tape that bound his arms to his sides.

"The kind who develop obsessions."

"What sort of obsessions?"

"Like . . . like a groupie."

"You told him I was a groupie?" A long strip of duct tape finally split down the middle, tearing the top off one of her fingernails in the process.

Max nodded, kind of sheepishly. "We have borrowed your word in Romanian."

She stared up at him. His gaze slid away. "That's one of the stupidest things I've ever heard," she said.

"But he believed it without question. So we know for sure they don't retain the names of the victims. They probably destroy all the records. It would make sense."

Suddenly much stronger—groupies being young, among all the rest of it—Mrs. Plansky ripped off the remaining duct tape in seconds, then rose, her knees cracking loudly but without pain.

"Can you get up?" she said.

"Yes."

But it turned out he couldn't, not without help from her.

"Maybe we should let you rest here for a bit," she said, getting his arm across her shoulders and taking a lot of his weight.

"Oh, no, no," said Max. "I will be okay. They'll be back, next time with an associate named Timbo."

That couldn't happen. Mrs. Plansky stepped forward, pretty much dragging Max along. She felt him gathering his strength. He leaned on her, but not as much. Together they walked out of the earthen-floored room.

"Where are we going?" he said.

"You'll see."

"I can't see a thing."

"Trust me."

What an odd thing to say! It had just popped out, like from the mouth of someone who knew what she was doing. The real Mrs. Plansky wasn't even sure she was back in the corridor, or had wandered off somewhere else, into a dungeon, for example. She felt her way along the wall with her right hand, her left arm around Max's waist. Trusting her or not, he kept his mouth shut. After a while, Mrs. Plansky felt a faint and slightly damp breeze in her face. She stopped, fished the phone from her pocket, turned on the light. And there, a half step away, was the void. Trust me—ha! A scary second or two, but it was the right void. She aimed the beam a little lower, illuminating the thirty-one steps.

"What's this?" he said.

"Concentrate," she said. "No rails."

"They took my phone."

"Of course. They're crafty."

Mrs. Plansky went first, but also took his hand, guiding him down step by step. In the beginning his hand felt awkward in hers, but by the time they got to the bottom it was perfectly normal.

Mrs. Plansky shone the light around the cellar, pausing over the enormous casks.

"My God," he said, still holding her hand. "I had no idea."

"And the end of all our exploring," Mrs. Plansky said, *"will be to arrive where we started and know the place for the first time."* She'd always loved that one. And now, to have a chance to actually say it? Things were looking up. Meanwhile Max's gaze was on her. She didn't have to see, just felt it.

"And here we are," said Mrs. Plansky, her voice low, just above a whisper, as she got a fingertip between the edge of the knobless door and the jamb, and pulled the door open. They entered her bathroom. "Welcome to the presidential suite," she said, switching on the light. Max's face was very pale, the blue of his light blue eyes faded almost to nothing. But he smiled.

"The one with Nixon's photo on the door?" he said.

"Correct."

He limped to the sink, turned on the tap, lowered his head to the flowing water, drank, and drank. When he finally raised his head he looked a little better.

"What are we going to do?" he said. "The truth is—and I'm not complaining—I'm still in something of a trap. Any ideas?"

"Sleep," said Mrs. Plansky. "We'll have ideas in the morning."

As things played out, ideas began arriving sooner than that. There was nowhere for Max to sleep but the love seat, much too small, but Mrs. Plansky removed the cushions and arranged them in a bed-

like form on the floor. Then she added one of the pillows from her
bed, covered him with an extra blanket, got him settled. While all
that was going on she tried to give him a concise recap of what she'd
witnessed in Club Presto and what it meant, but she wasn't sure he
was taking it in. After that, she hung the NU DERANJA sign on the
front door and went to bed herself.

It was very quiet, the hotel, the town, what remained of the night.
The only sounds were those Max made, trying to be comfortable,
trying, she could tell, in ways that wouldn't disturb her. After quite
enough of that, she made a pragmatic decision.

"You'll sleep better up here."

"Oh, I don't really think I—"

"Are you arguing?"

She could hear him rising, crossing the floor with some diffi-
culty, climbing into the bed. Of course there was no touching or
anything like that. For goodness sake. Just think of all the reasons.

So, no touching or anything like that. Not at first. But hadn't
something like this happened in *For Whom the Bell Tolls*? When
Mrs. Plansky first encountered that scene way back in English 101
she hadn't bought it. Now was different.

The Scottish scarf hung discreetly in the closet. Norm had always been—and seemed to be still—a very tactful man.

THIRTY-TWO

"What are we going to do?" Romeo said.

"About what?" said Dinu.

"Everything." Romeo took out his share of last night's pay—400 lei—and laid it on the kitchen table. They were at Dinu's place, an overcast, gray dawn just breaking and Dinu's mom still asleep. The walls were thin. They could hear her snores. "I mean look at this. Now we're serfs."

Dinu had boiled up instant coffee. He filled their cups and sat down. "It's just for now. He'll get over it and we'll be back to normal."

Romeo sipped the coffee and put down his cup. Dinu could tell the heat hurt his puffy lip. His own hand, which hadn't been bothering him, or at least not much, now started throbbing.

"Maybe we'll go back to what we were getting paid before," Romeo said, "but we'll always be on a leash. How is that fair? We're the talent."

"You are," Dinu said.

Romeo shook his head. "Your English is so good now."

"How would you know?"

"Bogdan was telling him."

In truth, Dinu knew his English was getting good, like he'd crossed some sort of language bridge and there was no going back. He would thank the professor the next time he saw him. Even if he could no longer turn English into big money, he'd come to like it for itself. Putting lipstick on a pig, for example, or shooting the breeze.

"You knew Marius tuned Bogdan up?" Romeo said.

"Yeah. But why?"

"Because Bogdan forgot he was a serf, that's why. It was for reminding him."

"How much does he get paid?" Dinu said.

"Shit, like us."

"What was the take last night?"

"From the old lady? Fourteen thousand dollars and a bit. We emptied the account. Not too bad but it didn't lead to anything else. Like with that other old lady—when was it? They all get mixed together. What was her name?"

Dinu shrugged.

"The people, not the numbers. The numbers I don't mix up. It was three million eight hundred thousand. Highest in almost three months. But I've been having this idea."

"For what?"

"For using AI to narrow down the field to just those that will lead to something else. I've even roughed out some of the code. But I'm putting it aside."

"Why?"

"Because." Romeo tapped the 400 lei with his finger. Gazing at the money, he said, "There are lots of Romanians in Hungary."

"So?"

"Not just in the border towns. In Budapest, too. I have cousins in Budapest. Ever been?"

"No."

"It's nice. More western."

"What are you saying?"

Romeo looked up. His swollen eye seemed to be on the verge of tears but his other eye was dry.

"You know what I'm saying."

"You're thinking of going to Hungary?"

"Not exactly. I'm thinking of both. The two of us go to Hungary."

"And do what?"

"What we do but for ourselves. We already know it works. You've forgotten? Thirty-eight thousand dollars in one go, Dinu! Just multiply!"

"What about school?"

"Hungary has schools."

"We don't speak Hungarian."

"So? We'll learn. We'll hire tutors. Pretty ones."

At that moment, Dinu's mom appeared in the doorway to the hall, wearing a frayed old tiger-stripe robe, and still in her hairnet.

"Pretty tutors?" she said. "What are you boys talking about?"

"Nothing," Dinu said.

She took a closer look at Romeo. "Oh my Jesus. What happened to you?"

"He was on the motorcycle when I had the accident," Dinu said, raising his splinted hand.

"You didn't tell me that."

"I'm telling you now."

Romeo rose. "Thanks for the coffee," he said. He turned to Dinu's mom. "Nice to see you, doamna."

"Be more careful," Dinu's mom said.

She sat down at the table. Dinu rinsed out Romeo's cup, poured in fresh coffee for her. She spooned in lots of sugar.

"What's going on?"

"Nothing."

"Everything's all right with Dragomir?"

"Why wouldn't it be?"

"Don't be rude."

Dinu didn't have the patience for her this morning. There seemed to be new lines on her face every day. So he felt sorry for her as well as impatient. Did he have to go on feeling sorry for her forever? He reached into his pocket and gave her half of his miserable take from the old lady in whatever state it was.

"What's this?" said his mom.

"What does it look like?"

His mother stuffed the money in the pocket of her robe. "You're sure about Dragomir? I mean no problems, and all?"

Dinu raised his voice. "Stop asking!"

"Don't you dare talk to me like that!"

They glared at each other across the table. That had grown less common lately, but only because he hadn't been around much. He took a gulp of coffee.

"We're going to Hungary."

"What?"

"You heard me."

"To Hungary? When? For how long? Who is we?"

Dinu, about to go into the details, changed his mind. The less she knew the better. "Not for long, but soon. We'll make money. I'll send you some." He nodded toward the pocket of her robe. "More than that, much more."

With no warning she burst into tears, sobbing, snot, the whole performance. He hated thinking about it in those terms but how often did he have to see this? "If only your poor dad hadn't died in that horrible fire! They should never have gone to Hungary. Don't you go, either. It's bad luck."

So she really didn't know the truth about how her husband died? "But it was Moldova, not Hungary," he said.

"Who told you that? Dragomir? But of course he doesn't like the mention of Hungary. He can't go back there."

"Why not?"

"They will arrest him for what he did that night. Here he is safe." She made the little money-talks gesture, rubbing thumb and index finger.

"What did he do that night?"

"All the bad things that got blamed on your poor dad. But in Hungary, not Moldova. There's no money for stealing in Moldova. In Hungary, yes, money." She buried her face in her hands.

Dinu didn't know what to believe. He went into the bathroom and took a shower. There was no hot water. By the time he was dressed, teeth brushed, hair combed, she'd gone back to bed. He gave in to an urge he'd been having but not given in to and called Tassa. She didn't pick up.

When he went outside he found that the wind had risen and snow was falling, not much snow but at a sharp angle, the flakes stinging his face. No one was around. The whole street looked so shabby. He texted Tassa: **Can I come over to your place?** The answer came back right away. **No.**

Dinu crossed the street. A woman he hadn't noticed was standing by a twisted little sidewalk tree. An older woman, wearing a navy-blue coat too nice for the neighborhood, and a scarf around her neck, the kind of scarf with one of those Scottish patterns, like in *Braveheart*. She was watching him. Was there something familiar about her? Why, yes. The American woman from the lookout, whom he and Romeo had guided into town. A very nice lady—she'd tried to tip them. And the name, like the coal miner's daughter. A career idea came to him: spinning country music records for a European audience! Out of some little studio in Budapest! Radio Free Dinu! He hurried over to her.

"Hey, Loretta! It's me, Dinu!"

She slapped him across the face.

Had that really happened? Mrs. Plansky would never have believed it, but there was all the proof anyone needed—the left side of Dinu's face bright red, her right hand hot and tingly, and the look in his eyes. The silo had opened at last and the heavy artillery had come rolling out.

Dinu reeled back, blinking. "Loretta? Dinu, remember?"

"There's nothing wrong with my memory." Well, not precisely true, but the only route forward in this conversation.

He put his hand to his cheek. "Then why did you do that?"

"Because you deserved it! What you did to that poor woman—disgraceful!"

"Poor woman?" Dinu looked baffled. That made it even more callous.

"Really?" said Mrs. Plansky. "You've forgotten already? It was only last night."

Dinu's mouth opened and closed, no sound coming out. It was easy to see him as a ten-year-old kid at that moment. Mrs. Plansky overrode that part of her nature.

"Gram, Andy? Think back. Gram, down in Alabama maybe—the Cotton State as you're no doubt aware? Gram, who gets lonesome from time to time and was so cheered up to hear from her loving grandson, unaware he was ruining the rest of her life? Is this how you live with yourself? By erasing the . . . the deeds right out of your mind?"

The deeds? That sounded so melodramatic, like from a Victorian potboiler. She was shaking—not from fear but with rage, a first in her life, terrifying in a way but also a strange kind of high—and should have been calling him out in the most vulgar language possible. Mrs. Plansky knew all the right words, of course, but even now she couldn't quite make herself voice them.

Meanwhile Dinu had turned white, except for the mark of her slap. "How do you—where—I don't understand."

"Same here." Mrs. Plansky lowered her voice, but it now sounded—at least to her—all the more dreadful, like something on the boil in a tightly-lidded container. "I don't understand lots of things. Start with you not calling Gram back. How come no second call?"

"Second call?" Dinu said.

"Stop sounding so stupid. I know perfectly well you're not stupid. That's not your problem. I'm talking about when you call back after the first call, after you've stolen all you can get your hot little hands on."

"But why would I—what sense would that be? Even, uh, suppose—supposing all that other what you say is true? What's going on? Was it all recorded? Did you see a tape?"

Mrs. Plansky laughed. She just couldn't keep it in. "One thing for sure—don't you ever testify in court. It won't go well."

Dinu glanced around, as though the paddy wagon might come careening around the corner any second. "Are—are you from the police?"

"The honest police," Mrs. Plansky said. "In spirit. Are you saying you never make a second call?"

Dinu gazed at her. He, too, was shaking, but in a little boy sort of way, like he was about to be sent to the principal's office, which probably didn't even happen anymore. He gave a tiny little nod.

"But Dinu, you called me back. You made a second call to me. Why?"

"Loretta? Is it . . . ? Are you—are you one of the people?"

"Loretta Plansky, one of the people. That name—Plansky—doesn't ring a bell?"

He shook his head.

"You've forgotten the night you were my grandson Will, locked up in some little Colorado town, desperate for bail money? Your research is good, by the way. Who does it, you or Romeo?"

Dinu's eyes shifted one way, then the other. "Romeo," he said in a small voice.

"So you remember?"

He nodded.

"Say it! Say I remember!"

"I remember."

Mrs. Plansky took a breath, composed herself. "Very well, then, let's get to that second call. Why?"

"I don't know."

"Think."

He closed his eyes tight, a ten-year-old thinking his pathetic hardest. "Did you tell me to get a lawyer, for representing in court?" He opened his eyes. In them now was a new look, a look she interpreted as asking for help.

"Yes, but obviously you weren't calling about that. What was the point? You had the money, three million, eight hundred thousand and whatever the hell else it was. Why, Dinu? You owe me an answer."

"Is that why you've come? You came all this way just to find out the reason for calling back?"

"Don't be dense," said Mrs. Plansky. "I came for my money. Mine, not yours. I want it back. So give."

What Dinu gave her was an unusual look. The longer it went on the older he seemed, even aging beyond where he was now. "No matter what was the subject of conversation—in the first place and everything—I . . . I liked talking to you. Like, you know, I really was . . ."

"Was what?"

He shrugged. "The grandson. Yours. There. That must be it. You can believe or not."

Dinu waited for a response. She said nothing.

"And now can I ask a question?" he said. "How do you know about last night?"

"The answer to that will depend on how things go between you and me." How menacing was that! Mrs. Plansky had amazed herself. "Here we are in person," she went on. "All we need now is the money and then we can start talking again, this time on even ground. Where's the money?"

"Gone. I'm sorry, Loretta."

"Sorry is not what I want from you. Gone where?"

"But I am sorry. Seeing you here. You came all this way?"

She nodded.

"To get your money back?"

"I already made that clear."

"No one does this."

"It's upsetting, isn't it?"

"Upsetting is . . . ?"

"It disturbs you."

He looked down, his gaze on his cowboy boots, or maybe right through them.

"Why?" she said. "What's so disturbing?"

Dinu looked up. His face seemed slightly disarranged, like tears were on the way, but his eyes were dry. "I would give you back the money if I could. I promise you that."

"Would you give Gram back her money, down in Alabama? And what about all the others? Would you give them back their money, too?"

"No," Dinu said. "Just you."

Mrs. Plansky, on this cold and windy day on a dilapidated Soviet-era street, hard little snowflakes stinging any exposed skin, laughed. "What are we going to do with you, Dinu?"

He thought for a bit, treating it as a real question. "I would like to live in America."

And just maybe it had been a real question. In any case, wasn't there a real vision in his answer? A potential deal began to take shape in Mrs. Plansky's mind.

"Let's put that in a box for now," she said.

"What box?"

"A box in our minds, that we can open when the time is right. But the time won't be right until we find out where the money is. Matter can neither be created nor destroyed—did they teach you that in school yet?"

"I don't think so."

"Never mind. It means the money must be somewhere."

Dinu gave that some thought, too. He did some more glancing up and down the street. There were a few pedestrians around, hunched against the wind, paying them no attention. "We could go see Romeo," he said. "He likes you, too."

Good grief. What was with the men of this country, or at least some of them? They seemed to have—but it couldn't be!—something of a thing for her. She thought of the look in the eyes of Max—her captive lover or whatever he was, she almost blushed to think—when she'd left that morning, the Nu Deranja sign firmly in place on the door to the presidential suite. What if she'd grown up here? She tried to imagine an alternate life, growing up as a glamorous figure. And failed.

Romeo turned out to have a dank and rank sort of office somewhere beneath the apartment block where he lived. Getting there involved a trial by ordeal—cobwebs across the face not once but many times, stepping on squishy things, never escaping the smell of pee, well-aged and brand-new. At last the three of them were sitting around a card table, the only light coming from Romeo's many screens. A long back-and-forth got going in Romanian between Dinu and Romeo. Romeo had a face made for dramatic reaction. Mrs. Plansky thought she could follow things pretty well just from his changes in expression. In the beginning there was lots of shock, amazement, fear. At the end his eyes were bright.

He leaned toward Mrs. Plansky. "Money you no make or destroy, only move around. I am loving that."

"I told him what you said," Dinu explained.

"I gathered that," said Mrs. Plansky.

Romeo laughed and pointed to a screen showing columns and columns of numbers. "There!" he said.

"What's there?" Mrs. Plansky said.

"Your money," said Dinu.

Mrs. Plansky peered at the screen and was no wiser, but what a nice moment anyway! She followed it by bringing up finder's fees, a notion the boys were unfamiliar with but grasped immediately. The three of them joined hands across the table, one of those hand stacks you see in the locker rooms of big-time teams. That was another nice moment. Then the subject of Hungary came up. After that, Romeo rummaged around and found a coil of nylon rope, thin but strong— and also black, which couldn't have been better. That led to a round of high-fiving. The boys were getting excited. Mrs. Plansky knew that too much excitement on the eve of big plans was not good.

"How am I going to rein you two in?" she said.

"Rain?" said Romeo, holding out his hands under an imaginary sky. "Is no rain!"

Dinu thought that was hilarious and started laughing. The laughter spread to Romeo and even to Mrs. Plansky herself. What was happening to her?

"Oh, and account," Romeo said.

"Account?"

"Bank," said Dinu, "plus password."

"We're doing it now?" she said.

"Not now," Dinu said. "The very last thing. But we must be all set."

For the second time but under different circumstances, Mrs. Plansky gave Dinu her banking information. She enjoyed a full-circle moment of accomplishment.

"Norman Conquest with exclamations?" Dinu said. "I remember that one."

"She keeps same password?" Romeo said.

The boys started laughing again, popping her accomplishment bubble. This time Mrs. Plansky did not join in. She half-remembered Allison Suarez calling to tell her to change the password immediately.

THIRTY-THREE

"Lazybones," said Mrs. Plansky, entering the presidential suite and finding Max still in bed, leafing through a glossy hotel magazine.

He looked up and smiled. A very handsome man for sure, and that one crooked tooth was just the kind of thing that caught her attention and wouldn't let go.

"Lazybones?" he said. "I love it. Yours?"

"You mean did I make it up? Good grief, no. It's a common expression."

"But there's nothing common about you." He patted the empty side of the bed.

Mrs. Plansky ignored that completely. "I've brought sandwiches from Café des Artistes," she said, taking a paper bag from her purse. "Smoked brisket or zacusca, I think it's called—roasted eggplant, onions, red peppers. Smells delicious. You pick." She set the bag on the empty side of the bed and took off her navy-blue woolen coat. Wound over one shoulder was the coil of black nylon rope.

Max's smile faded at once. "What's that?"

"The reason for the sandwiches," said Mrs. Plansky. "You need to keep your strength up."

"Oh?" he said, the smile returning. "I wasn't aware you had a problem with the upness—if that's a word—of my—"

"Stop right there," said Mrs. Plansky.

She went to the window. Outside lay the square with *Michael the*

Brave still on the warpath, snowflakes swirling around his head. It was a very public place, but there was no avoiding it. The problem was on the anchor end. There were no potential anchors. Mrs. Plansky went into the bathroom.

"What are you doing?" Max said.

"Just eat."

Mrs. Plansky checked the view from the bathroom window. Pretty much the same as from the bedroom, but an old-fashioned radiator stood right below the sill. She unwound the rope, tied one end to the thick pipe entering the radiator from the floor. Mrs. Plansky knew knots from Miss Terrance's class. *"A half hitch for a temporary hold, girls, but a rolling hitch for something that lasts."* She tied a rolling hitch, coiled the rope, and tucked it neatly under the radiator.

When she returned to the bedroom, she found that Max had polished off the smoked brisket sandwich and was patting the corners of his mouth with a paper napkin.

"Now I feel absurdly strong," he said.

"Store it up for tonight."

"What happens tonight?"

Mrs. Plansky sat on the edge of the bed. "There have been some developments."

Max sat up. "Should I put on clothes?"

Not just yet. That was Mrs. Plansky's first—and unruly—thought, a thought she kept strictly to herself. She said, "That's always best."

He raised an eyebrow—for some reason Mrs. Plansky's interest in him grew a lot at that moment—and lay back down. "What developments?"

"Do you remember last night?" she said.

"I'll never forget."

"Stop. I'm talking about what I saw in Club Presto."

"The scam in action?"

"Exactly. Do you recall the part about the boys?"

"Dinu and Romeo."

"Correct. I met with them a couple of hours ago."

"How did that happen?"

"Blind luck. Well, with a nudge or two."

"A nudge from you?"

"Yes."

"You're a good nudger. World-class if I might—"

"Zip it. The point is we have a plan. Have you ever been to Hungary?"

"Certainly. And you?"

"Tonight will be my first time. The hinge point of this whole thing is a kind of karma, if it all works out. Recently the boys decided it would be a good thing to set up on their own."

"Jesus."

"Dragomir found out, of course, and now, after actual physical punishment, they're back working for him, with the pay reduced— much reduced, I gather. Dragomir also made them give him all they'd gotten on their own, upward of thirty thousand dollars. But he had Romeo do the actual moving of the money to an account on something called the dark web. Is there really a dark web?"

"I'm working on a chapter about it right now."

"Oh, good, then this is all real," Mrs. Plansky said.

"Not real like you," Max said.

Their eyes met. "Why are you looking at me like that?" she said.

"You know."

"Well put a lid on it."

"Ha!"

"And stop acting like an adolescent. You have to concentrate."

"I am concentrating. The point is Romeo now knows how to get into the dark web account and Dragomir's too impressed by how frightening he is to have any concerns about Romeo. You're going to get your money back. Maybe you're paying a finder's fee. Maybe they plan to set up again across the border and make so much money they don't need a finder's fee. Maybe it's simply that they're still kids. Maybe it was just the way you are. But the transfer will happen at the very last minute, right before the four of us take off for Hungary. Is that it?"

"Pretty much."

"What I don't understand is why Hungary."

"Because Dragomir can't go there. He's wanted for some crime years ago."

"I'm getting so much material from you."

Mrs. Plansky gave him a severe look. "Not everything is printable."

"What about your photo?"

"Forget it."

"You didn't say that before."

"I'm saying it now."

Max nodded. "A deal. But in return for your help."

"What sort of help?"

"With the book. How to organize the story. The world of cybercrime, but personal."

"You don't need me for that."

"Oh, I do. Let's think."

"Just like that? Think and the book happens?"

"You can help it along."

"How?"

"For example, it's well known that humans think better lying down."

Mrs. Plansky laughed. Then she lay down. "But my clothes stay on."

A knock on the door. Mrs. Plansky opened her eyes. Perhaps she'd dreamed it. She felt odd, possibly because she never slept during the day. Odd, but actually quite good in a way. She glanced over and there was Max, fast asleep, the last dim fading daylight coming through a gap in the curtains and lending a reddish glow to his close-cropped white beard. What would he look like with it shaved off? Hmm. That raised a potential—

Knock knock knock.

Mrs. Plansky sat up.

A voice called through the door. "Mrs. Plansky? Mrs. Plansky?" It was Annika.

Max began to stir. Mrs. Plansky placed her hand over his mouth. His eyes popped open. She let her other hand do the talking, first making the quiet sign over her lips, then pointing toward the door. He gave her a slight nod.

"Coming," Mrs. Plansky called. By now she had a plan. "Just a minute."

She got out of bed, discovering that not all her clothes had come off, although what remained was in disarray. She quickly made herself presentable, at the same time signaling Max to get up. He was naked, articles of his clothing here and there on the floor. She made get-those-picked-up-for-God's-sake gestures. He started gathering the clothes. She gave him the hurry-up sign, followed almost immediately by the quiet sign again, then grabbed his hand and led him into the bathroom. His eyes were full of questions. She dismissed them all with a wave of her hand—perhaps a little on the impatient side—and moved to the knobless old wooden door. She gave it the quietest push she could. It opened.

"Mrs. Plansky? Mrs. Plansky?"

"Coming! Coming!"

Now she gave another quiet push, this one propelling Max through the doorway and into the passageway. She closed the door and pulled the towel rack in front of it. Patting her hair into place, she went into the bedroom, and, on the point of opening the front door, wheeled around in a swift detour and straightened the bed covers. Then, kicking the love seat cushions in the direction of the love seat on the way, she returned to the front door and opened it.

Annika stood in the hallway, but not alone. Timbo was behind her, his eyes not on Mrs. Plansky, but trained, in a questing way, on the room.

"Sorry to bother you, Mrs. Plansky," Annika said.

"Oh, no bother, no bother at all."

"Thank you. It seems that a previous guest may have left a thing of value behind. He has sent Mr. Timbo here to perhaps do a quick search."

"Why, of course," said Mrs. Plansky, stepping aside.

"You may leave the room if you like," Annika said. "I can send champagne for you into the bar, compliments of the hotel."

"More champagne? Goodness, no. But thank you. I'm happy to stay. What was the object of value, if I may ask?"

Annika turned to Timbo and spoke to him in Romanian. His eyes shifted. Really? Mrs. Plansky thought. Not prepared for such an obvious question? Finally he said something to Annika. She relayed it to Mrs. Plansky. "Mr. Timbo says it was a box of cigars."

"They must be Cuban," said Mrs. Plansky.

That led to another brief exchange in Romanian.

"Mr. Timbo says the box is platinum."

"Ah," said Mrs. Plansky. "Naturally, if I'd seen something like that I'd have brought it down to the front desk."

"For sure, for sure," Annika said. She made a little motion and Timbo entered the room. Mrs. Plansky gave him a smile, like she was the hostess. He didn't look at her, but went immediately to the closet, which he opened and saw all there was to see, namely the neat shelving of Mrs. Plansky's clothes. While he gazed into the closet, Mrs. Plansky's own gaze wandered around the room and came upon Max's underwear, lying in plain sight halfway between the door and the bed. She strolled over there and stood on it, looking as nonchalant as possible.

"Is it still snowing?" she said to Annika.

"A little, but more to come."

"Well, well, there's always the weather."

Annika looked at her like she was an idiot, and rightly so. Meanwhile Mrs. Plansky made a few foot movements—please, God, let them be subtle—to render Max's undies completely invisible. Norm always wore boxers of the loose-fitting kind. Max, it turned out, wore briefs, a rather brief form of brief that ordinarily would have given her pause, but were ideal in this situation. On the other hand, he'd left them right out there when his orders—well, not orders, more like a suggestion—had been to collect all his clothes. Mrs. Plansky had never been the type to generalize about men, and for that reason only, let this subject go.

Meanwhile, Timbo was on his hands and knees, peering under the bed. Under the bed had actually been Mrs. Plansky's first idea, which gave the lie to the old rule about the first thought being the best. She glanced over at Annika, who was scrolling through her phone.

Timbo went into the bathroom. Mrs. Plansky's mood, which had been rather breezy, like she was a character in a farce, a stupid character who had forgotten what Timbo was capable of, changed completely, her heart beating way too fast and a trembling starting up in her fingertips. She listened for the sounds of Timbo moving around and heard nothing. But he was so quiet on his feet, could have been doing anything in there. Was it possible he knew about the secret door? Not a secret, actually, known and obvious to anyone who saw it, but just as obviously not a working door, lacking knob and keyhole, so clearly—please clearly—a vestige, a remnant, made obsolete in some long-ago remodel, even centuries ago. And don't forget, Loretta, those cobwebs, so dense, the first time you entered the passageway. So Timbo! Enough! There's nothing to see!

Timbo came out of the bathroom. He walked right by Mrs. Plansky, again without a glance, and out the front door, also without a glance at Annika. She looked up from her phone.

"Well, then," Annika said, "I guess no cigar."

Mrs. Plansky laughed. She caught a look in Annika's eyes, a sort of yearning. But Mrs. Plansky couldn't help her. "I'll be leaving tomorrow, Annika," she said, her voice soft, even gentle. "Please prepare my bill."

"Certainly. I'll text it to you. You can pay by phone. I hope we'll see you again."

"Thank you," said Mrs. Plansky.

Annika closed the door and went away. Mrs. Plansky took a deep breath. She could never skip out on a bill. That went without saying. But it was also a clever—well, not all that clever— misdirection, because the real checkout time was going to be much sooner. Yes, clever, damn it, all that clever! She scooped up the too-brief briefs and marched into the bathroom.

"I've never had any actual mountaineering experience," Max said. "Have you?"

"No," said Mrs. Plansky. "What's your point?"

They were in the bathroom of the presidential suite, lights off, Max fully clothed, standing by the window, Mrs. Plansky tugging on the free end of the black nylon rope to make sure the knot around the radiator pipe was good and tight, and Max gazing into the night.

"Isn't this called rappelling?" he said. "That's a mountaineering term."

"Let's not overthink," said Mrs. Plansky.

"What do you mean?"

"The alternative is waltzing out through the lobby. That's what I mean."

"You don't have to get angry."

"I'm not angry."

How quickly they'd advanced to the bickering stage! But bickering was part of life. Mrs. Plansky felt full of life at the moment. She tied the free end of the rope with a half hitch to the handle of her suitcase, now fully packed.

"Ready?" she said.

"Yes, Commandant."

She gave him a little punch on the shoulder and then opened the window—the casement type—nice and wide. The square was dark and deserted, the wind still blowing, no snow falling but a light coating on the cobbles and the few cars parked in front of the hotel, the most distant being her rental. Mrs. Plansky checked the time, now exactly thirty minutes since Dinu had sent his text: **Blast Off!!!** She took hold of the suitcase and raised it up to the sill.

"Allow me," Max said.

He really was polite. Mrs. Plansky stepped back. Max swung the suitcase outside, then began lowering it, the rope sliding slowly through his hands—hands that were quite beautiful, strong, and finely shaped. She moved closer, watched her suitcase touch silently onto the cobbles.

"Now you," she said.

"But don't you think—"

"I do not."

"At times you can be a slight bit controlling."

"Think what you like."

Not a bad joke, in her opinion, a joke Max got at once. He laughed and swung one leg up over the sill, twisted around so he was straddling it. After that he took the rope in both hands, raised his other leg up and over, all his movements very smooth, like he was used to exits of this sort. And just like that he was facing her, hanging outside by the rope.

"À bientôt," he said, and began lowering himself, not bothering to walk his way down, feet against the façade of the hotel, but simply using his hands, hand under hand. Mrs. Plansky knew one thing for sure: she couldn't do that, not that way. Maybe Max realized that, too, because when he reached the bottom he changed the plan, quickly freeing the suitcase and making a gesture for her to haul up the rope.

What was à bientôt? French, and familiar, but the meaning wouldn't come. Meanwhile, down in the square, Max was pantomiming the new plan, much more involved than doing it his way, a plan that began with tying the rope around her waist. Mrs. Plansky found she was already doing that. She tied it nice and tight, secured with a half hitch, then got one leg over the sill, as Max had done. Well, not with the ease or speed, or grace, no fooling herself about that. Not too much later she was sitting astride the sill, her body with absolutely no idea of how to get fully outside and turned around. Meanwhile her new hip was not liking this position at all, fast on the way to finding it intolerable. With the rope around her waist what was the worst that could happen? It would be different, of course, if she'd tied the rope around her neck, but she'd been too savvy for that. Mrs. Plansky realized for the first time in her life that there was a strand of goofiness in her makeup, had been there from the start. Her mind was still occupied with this revelation as she got her inside leg over to the outside somehow or other and started down, a somewhat controlled fall partly broken by her hands trying to squeeze the rope as it slipped rapidly through them, by her low-heeled booties scrabbling for traction against the façade, and finally by Max, catching her in his arms. He was too much of a gentleman even to grunt.

"Nice work," he whispered. He pointed. "But you should have dropped that down first."

Mrs. Plansky found she'd done the whole thing with her purse slung over one shoulder. She needed her purse, of course. Dropping it out of windows could never be good.

She untied the rope. It swung back and hung straight down from the bathroom window, almost invisible. With any luck no one would notice until daybreak, and by that time she'd be having a nice breakfast, goulash waffles, or whatever was served in Hungary. They walked over to her car. Mrs. Plansky opened the trunk. Max loaded the suitcase inside. They glanced around. The boys should have been here by now. She checked her phone. Nothing from Dinu.

Max spoke softly in her ear. "They'll be coming up Strada Piata." He took her hand, leading her to a street off the square. After only a few steps Mrs. Plansky heard strange noises, squeaky and rumbling, in the distance. Then out of the night came the boys, pushing and pulling some sort of cart. They passed under a streetlamp. Not a cart but a small flatbed trailer, and on the trailer the two motorcycles. The motorcycles? Had anything been said about the motorcycles? Not a word.

Max ran forward.

"Hei!" Romeo called, oh, so loud.

"Shh!" said Max, also loudly.

By the time Mrs. Plansky arrived they were in the middle of a sort of hissing conversation. Max turned to her. "They want to bring the motorcycles."

"I see that."

"Romeo made a connector. He says it will work with any car."

"Okay. Let's go."

They headed back toward the square, Max and Mrs. Plansky in front, the boys following with the trailer. But when they reached the end of Strada Piata and started to turn the corner, Mrs. Plansky saw there had been one big change. Another car, engine running, was parked right behind her rental. This car had a light on the roof, not shining at the moment. The front door opened and a uniformed man got out. It was Captain Romulu. He switched on a flashlight and began circling the rental.

Mrs. Plansky shrank back. So did Max, giving the boys the stop sign as he did. They gathered together by the trailer.

"What are we going to do?" Dinu said.

"Are the bikes gassed up?" Mrs. Plansky said.

Romeo nodded.

"I don't know how to drive a motorcycle," Max said.

"That's all right," said Mrs. Plansky. "You get on the back with Romeo, I'll ride with Dinu."

Dinu raised his splinted hand. "I can't drive."

Then came a long moment, in which they heard Captain Romulu speaking, perhaps on a phone or that police car device, the name not coming to Mrs. Plansky.

"I can," she said, and there was plenty of truth, or at least some, in that. You could argue that she'd learned on a Harley Super Glide on that ranch in Montana when she was nineteen years old and now she was what she was and the bike was a Yamaha, but that was the half-empty-glass response. She looked in the eyes of the three and saw no doubt at all. Was that because of some image they had of American womanhood? Or—oh, for God's sake: it must be that strange effect she had on these guys! One thing for sure. She'd fallen in love with this country.

In the event, there turned out to be big differences between the bikes and between nineteen and seventy-one. But not insurmountable! After one or two false and noisy starts, they were off—Romeo with Max on the back in the lead, and Mrs. Plansky following with Dinu—and rolling away from the square, leaving all the big pieces of luggage behind, including her suitcase containing, among other things, the Italian ballet flats. By the time the river bridge appeared, she knew that this bike was easier to handle than the Super Glide. The thumb throttle for one thing—a nice innovation. Crossing the bridge she moved into the lead. Dinu, his hands lightly at her waist, leaned forward and spoke in her ear.

"You're a good biker chick."

"Where's your helmet?" said Mrs. Plansky.

"Must have forgot. But there were only two. And with you I have no worries."

"God in heaven." She checked for her purse, found it was snugly over her shoulder.

"Second right after the bridge," Dinu said.

"How far to the border?"

"One hundred and fifty kilometers. An hour and a half if you stay one hundred all the way. Oh, and by the by. Or is it by the way?"

"Depends."

"Such a smart lady. In any case, you have your money back. Romeo made all the arrangements. It's in your account at the Palm Coast Bank and Trust, three million eight hundred thousand and a little more, I forget the exact number."

She inhaled a deep, deep breath. His **Blast Off** text had meant the same thing but hearing him say it was so much more real. A thrill passed through her from head to toe, so profound she felt embarrassed. Strangely enough, and hard to explain, it had nothing to do with the money.

Mrs. Plansky took the second right after the bridge and they were soon out of Alba Gemina, riding up and up into the mountains and with no traffic except for Romeo, lagging behind. But she wasn't hitting one hundred kilometers or anything close, first because the road—a two-laner—was so winding, and also because the snow was falling again, although not hard, tiny flakes as before. These were big and fat and thick. Things were getting slippery under her tires and it was harder and harder to see. Sometime later, rounding a curve and topping a crest, she caught the flash of a faraway light in the side mirror. At first she thought it was Romeo's headlight, but how could he be so far back? Then his light popped into view as he came around the curve. The distant light was much farther away than Romeo, although perhaps not quite as distant as she'd thought.

They wound down the side of one mountain, started up another. The snowfall thickened and the pavement got slipperier. Mrs. Plansky leaned forward, geared down, throttled back, peered ahead, the snowflakes black in her headlight beam. Once or twice she caught light reflected in her mirror: Romeo falling farther and farther back now, and the other light, a double, not a single, getting closer and closer.

"That's the F-350," Dinu said.

"What F-350?"

"My uncle's. It's good in the snow." He patted her side. "But we are close. One last mountain and then a flat part and then the border."

Please, thought Mrs. Plansky, a please directed to no one in particular. She started down a series of switchbacks, leaning into every one, going as fast as she dared, Dinu leaning with her, moving together. Romeo fell farther behind. The F-350—Dinu had to be right about that—was getting closer and closer. The road leveled

out and entered a small village, stone walls on either side, not a light
showing. Mrs. Plansky hit 140 on the dial and kept it there all the
way through the village and on the lower, easier part of the mountain on the other side. Then came a series of long curves, up and
up, forcing her to throttle down. Down down down, all the way
to forty. My God! Forty? She checked the mirror. Several curves
below the double headlights had caught up to the single, and yes, a
pickup, she could see that clearly now. Eyes back on the road, Loretta! She found she'd drifted left, almost off the road and into the
rocky embankment. She turned the wheel, in fact over-turned it,
and they went skidding sideways. Mrs. Plansky knew anything she
did now would only make it worse. She just let it happen. The bike
skidded back across the road—Dinu sucking in his breath—and
then the tires found their grip and straightened things out on their
own. A few hundred yards farther on was a short straightaway. Mrs.
Plansky took a chance and checked the mirror. Now the F-350 was
only one curve back. Much farther behind she spotted the single
headlight. They'd gone right past Romeo and Max, hadn't even
bothered. There'd be plenty of time later for mopping up.

That angered Mrs. Plansky, perhaps unreasonably, but the feeling
was very real. She throttled back up, the bike roaring as it climbed
and climbed, the road now covered in snow. All at once they were
caught in a much mightier roar, and the powerful beams of the F-350
lit them up. Mrs. Plansky throttled up some more, far more than
she dared, through one last switchback, the wind howling, her bike
howling, the F-350 howling. And right at the crest, before the start
of the first descending turn, nothing but the void in view, the F-350
came up beside her. She could see their faces, Dragomir at the wheel,
Marius beside him, Timbo in back. Dragomir looked right at her, the
fury inside him distorting his face.

Someone else, not her, took over at the controls. Someone comfortable enough at a time like this to thumb that throttle way way up
and then at the last second or later, take the thumb right off the handle and gently, oh so gently, touch the brake pedal. The F-350 stayed

right beside her—until that touch of the brake pedal. Then it shot ahead, Dragomir now, too late, hitting his own brakes. The F-350 went airborne, off the crest of the mountain and into the void. Oh, what a terrible sight, although it barely registered with Mrs. Plansky in real time. She and Dinu went into another skid, so far over that her throttle hand touched the snow, and kept skidding and skidding right to the edge, where they bumped, not hard, into an old stone mile marker, Mrs. Plansky the merest of passengers at that point.

The motor conked out. There was nothing to hear but the wind. Mrs. Plansky lay half buried under the bike and snow, depleted, utterly spent, undone. She would have burst into tears but she didn't have the strength.

Dinu crawled out from underneath and pulled the bike off her.

"Loretta? Loretta? Are you all right?"

"We should know pretty soon," said Mrs. Plansky.

THIRTY-FOUR

The weather changed very quickly.

"That's how it is in these mountains," Dinu said. "Transylvanian mountains, in case you didn't know."

"I feel like I know them very well."

They stood side by side near the old stone milepost, whatever had been written on it now eroded away. The wind died down, the snow stopped falling, the clouds thinned out, and the moon appeared, spreading silvery light into the void that had been so dark. A heavily forested canyon opened up before them, the sides steep, the trees snow-covered. The F-350 had cut a road through those trees, shearing off branches and splitting whole trunks, and now lay upside down wedged between a massive tree trunk cut off at human head height, and two huge boulders. A very big and muscular body, Marius-size, lay facedown and motionless at the base of one of the boulders, the snow all around him dark red. Timbo was close by. He'd been—oh, no—impaled by a spear-shaped branch. Just recently Mrs. Plansky had been horrified by reading the mere definition of the word. Now the real thing would be the stuff of nightmares.

"I don't see him," Dinu said.

She knew who he meant. "Me, either."

He turned to her. "You're shivering."

"Not really."

"Where is your coat?"

She glanced down at herself, surprised to see she wasn't wearing her coat. Yet somehow her purse was still hanging off her shoulder? How was that possible? And she was still wearing the Scottish scarf? Wasn't it dangerous to wear scarves on motorcycles? She really could be clueless at times.

"Here is my jacket."

"Very kind of you, but no."

She set off in search of her coat, Dinu trailing after her.

"Loretta? Your purse—it's open."

She glanced at the purse, indeed open and twisted around almost behind her in an awkward position. Her fingers, too, were awkward, somehow unable to get the thing closed. Dinu came closer and fumbled around for a bit with the purse. "There we go."

"Thank you, Dinu."

"Do not mention it."

They were still looking for the coat when Romeo drove up with Max on the back of the bike, the faces of both of them stone-colored like the moon. A lot of excited talk started up, mostly in Romanian and mostly between Dinu and Romeo. Mrs. Plansky was aware of Max's gaze on her from time to time, but mostly she just felt detached. She couldn't even summon much interest when Max went down in the canyon, searching for Dragomir. There was no sign of him, not a surprise to Mrs. Plansky. Her mind was on a pair of fox-lined mittens that had belonged to her mother. Those mittens would be handy. What had become of them? They all climbed back on the bikes.

Mrs. Plansky didn't start feeling more like herself until a few hours later in a small town in Hungary, the dawn breaking and the four of them in a little café, Max, who turned out to be fluent in Hungarian, ordering her toast and jam and a bowl of hot chocolate. She stretched out her legs.

A little later Max rented a car and arranged for the bikes to be trucked to Romeo's cousins in Budapest. Then they drove there themselves, Max behind the wheel, Mrs. Plansky beside him, and the boys in back.

"Before you guys fall asleep," Mrs. Plansky said, "we better final-ize this matter of the finder's fee."

"Oh, no, not necessary," Dinu said.

"Maybe only a little bit?" said Romeo.

Dinu elbowed him, quite hard.

"Huh?" said Romeo.

"I understand about Tassa," Dinu hissed at him, an inexplicable reaction from Mrs. Plansky's point of view.

And perhaps from Romeo's as well. "Huh?" he said again.

"Who is Tassa?" Max said.

No answer from the backseat.

"First, Dinu," Mrs. Plansky went on, "this doesn't take the place of my promise. I will get you into the U.S. one way or an-other, at the very least on a visitor's visa. Second, a normal finder's fee is ten percent. In this case, ten percent for each of you. Any thoughts?"

The boys seemed to have no thoughts, but Max did.

"I beg your pardon? You propose to give them in excess of three hundred thousand dollars? Each?"

"I do."

"But think what will happen! They are children."

Mrs. Plansky considered that for a while. "Good point," she said at last. "I will give each ten percent of the ten percent now, and the rest when they turn twenty-one. I'll have my lawyer make the ar-rangements first thing when I get back. Deal?"

"Deal," said the boys.

She handed her phone to Romeo. "Do it now, the ten percent of the ten percent." She felt Max's gaze—perhaps an incredulous gaze—on her face. "Eyes on the road," she told him.

Romeo worked out the numbers and transferred the finder's fees into an account for him and an account for Dinu, all in what seemed like seconds. He handed back the phone, at the same time having a quick conversation in Romanian with Dinu.

"Romeo wants you to change your password."

"Now, please," Romeo said.

"The cursor is at the correct place," Dinu said. "Just type it in and save."

"Really? I don't see—"

"Now, please," Romeo repeated.

Mrs. Plansky caught a break. A password came to her, out of the blue. She made a slight revision, then typed it in and saved. Presi-DentialSweeT! Notice the pun? And the capitals mixed in? Plus that exclamation mark, giving the whole thing actual meaning? Pretty damn clever. Mrs. Plansky felt quite pleased with herself.

The boys fell asleep. There was a nice feeling in the car, like this was a family trip, one of those families that got along.

"What now?" Max said.

"Well, drop off the boys at Romeo's cousins, and then me at the airport, if you don't mind. After that I assume you'll head back to Alba Gemina."

"Not until I know it's safe," Max said. "And what if I do mind dropping you at the airport?"

She turned to him. His eyes were on the road. He really was a handsome man, and that soulful look in his eyes was no illusion. She knew that for a fact.

"How old are you, Max?"

"I don't see what difference it makes."

"Max?" She was prepared for something young, even as low as sixty-one, or God help her, fifty-nine.

"I will be forty-seven in November."

"Oh, Max," she said. She leaned across the console, wrapped her arm around his neck, and kissed his face. And kissed it again. "I'm seventy-one."

"But I knew that."

She disengaged, returned to her own side. "You didn't and you still don't."

There was silence after that, all the way to the first appearance of a distant spire in the west.

"What if I happened to come on vacation to Florida?" he said.

Mrs. Plansky thought about that. Vacationing in Florida? Millions of people did that every year. What heart could be so shrunken as to forbid it in his case? "That would be very nice," she said. At that moment she remembered the meaning of à bientôt—soon, as in see you soon. She came close to saying it out loud.

On the drive home from the off-site airport parking lot, Mrs. Plansky stopped at the first branch of Palm Coast Bank and Trust she saw. She went in, produced her driver's license, and asked to see her balance.

"Could you write it out by hand, please?" she said.

"By hand?"

Mrs. Plansky made a little writing motion. The teller wrote out her balance and gave her the slip. It was all there, less the two 10 percents of the percents. She stuck the slip in her purse. That was when she discovered—hidden in a fold way down at the bottom—the sapphire necklace. How had it gotten there? When? Ah.

"Have a nice day," the teller said.

"I'm home!" she called, entering her condo on Little Pine Lake. She found her dad at the kitchen table, enjoying a rather large Cuban sandwich.

"Oh, hi," he said.

His feet were bare. So were the feet of the woman sitting opposite him, a woman of her dad's age or even older. She, too, was eating a Cuban sandwich. One of his bare feet was resting on one of her bare feet.

Lucrecia came in, carrying two open beer bottles.

"Loretta! Welcome back! Did you have a nice trip?"

"Yes, thank you."

"I want you to meet my mom, Clara." Lucrecia set the beer bottles on the table. "Mama, this is Loretta I was telling you about."

"Hola!" said Clara, raising a bottle.

"She and your dad seem to be hitting it off," Lucrecia said. "Can I bring in your suitcase?"

"That won't be necessary," Mrs. Plansky said. Or even possible. She kept that to herself.

But amazingly, her suitcase turned up a couple of weeks later. Agent Rains brought it.

"I've had some extremely interesting conversations with Jamal Perryman," she said. "He heads our Secret Service post in Bucharest. You're familiar with him?"

"Slightly."

"First, he wishes me to pass on the message that Dragomir Tiriac has not reappeared. He may be in Russia and we're trying to substantiate that. But more important, what we'd very much like to do is debrief you, Mrs. Plansky, just have you run through the whole story in your own words. Mr. Perryman believes, and I strongly agree, that your experience will be most helpful in our battle against cybercrime."

"Meaning the others will get their money back?"

"Wouldn't that be nice?" said Agent Rains. "But no. Mr. Perryman actually sat down with the boys in our Budapest embassy and they went searching for the money but there wasn't a trace. We'd still appreciate your thoughts."

"Certainly," Mrs. Plansky said. "As soon as we nail down visa arrangements for Dinu. Something permanent would be best."

Mrs. Plansky's family was dynamic, meaning changes never stopped. First, it appeared that Nina and Matt, Matty, or Matthew had broken up. There were several stories, one with him meeting someone else, another with her meeting someone else, and a third with both of them meeting someone elses. But the upshot was that the $250K for the Love and the Caribbean start-up was no longer needed.

As for Jack, his cold chain partners out in Tempe, Ray and Rudy, had been indicted by the federal government on a number of charges—wire fraud, tax evasion, money laundering, and another category or two she couldn't remember. So the $750K was also not needed. Jack did send her a brand-new tennis racket model to try. Waving it around in the kitchen, she began feeling hopeful about him.

Nina and Jack were happy that her trip had gone well, which was their takeaway, but were both too preoccupied to press her for details. The grandkids, Emma and Will, showed much more interest. Will had whooped loudly on the phone, actually deafening Mrs. Plansky in one ear for a day or two, and Emma had called her the bravest grandma in the whole U.S. of A. Mrs. Plansky made a mental note to send her the sapphire necklace on her birthday. Then she had a selfish thought: but I want it. "Get a grip," she told herself. The necklace was Emma's, full stop.

Meanwhile, she took to wandering around her place a lot, like she was missing something. One morning she stopped in front of a photo of Norm she had, a lovely photo of him, head thrown back and laughing.

"Any advice?" she said.

And yes, he had plenty, all good. She read the message in the pixels of his eyes.

Later that same morning, even within the hour, Kev Dinardo called.

"I hear you've been away."

"I'm back."

"Great. I know this is a little late but friends of mine, a married couple, good tennis players, are going to be in town tomorrow and I thought you and I could show them how the game is played. Say, four o'clock at the club? And after if you like I could take you to dinner. That new sushi place by the marina is supposed to be good."

Well, why not? Good grief. She loved tennis, had a new racket to try, and Kev was a fine player with excellent manners on the court. "Thank you, it sounds like fun," Mrs. Plansky said. Despite all that rationalization, she felt like the whore of Babylon. Oddly enough, it wasn't all bad.

ACKNOWLEDGMENTS

Many thanks to my agents, Molly Friedrich and Lucy Carson, for their enthusiasm for Mrs. P when she was just an idea; to first readers nonpareil Diana, Meggy, and Alan; and to Kristin Sevick and the whole Tor Publishing Group team. No writing man is an island.